A Change of Fortunes

The 1ˢᵗ Book in the 'Change of' Series

A Pride & Prejudice Combination Variation

By Shana Granderson, A Lady

D&E PUBLISHING

CONTENTS

DEDICATION

This book, like all that I write, is dedicated to the love of my life, the holder of my heart. You are my one and only and you complete me. You make it all worthwhile and my world revolves around you. Until we reconnected, I had stopped believing in miracles, but now I most certainly do, you are my miracle.

Acknowledgement

First and foremost, thank you E.C.S. for standing by me while I dedicate many hours to my craft. You are my shining light and my one and only.

I want to thank my Alpha, Will Jamison and my Betas Caroline Piediscalzi Lippert and Kimbelle Pease. To Gayle Surrette and Carol M for taking on the role of proof-reader and additional editing, a huge thank you to you. All of you who have assisted me please know that your assistance is most appreciated.

I must include my heartfelt thanks to those of you who had read the story as a WIP on my website and through your comments and catches helped improve the book.

My undying love and appreciation to Jane Austen for her incredible literary masterpieces is more than can be expressed adequately here. I also thank all of the JAFF readers who make writing these stories a pleasure.

INTRODUCTION

What if, unlike canon, the Bennets had sons? Could it be, if both father and mother prayed to God and begged for a son that their prayers would be answered? If the prayers were granted how would the parents be different and what kind of life would the family have?

What will the consequences of their decisions be? In many Pride and Prejudice variations the Bennet parents are portrayed as borderline neglectful with Mr. Bennet caring only about making fun of others, reading, and drinking his port while shutting himself away in his study.

Mrs. Bennet is often shown as flighty, unintelligent and a character to make sport of. The Bennet parent's marriage is often shown as a mistake where there is no love; could there be love there that has been stifled due to circumstances?

In this book, some of those traits are present, but we see what a different set of circumstances and decisions do to the parents and the family as a whole. Most of the characters from canon are here along with some new characters to help broaden the story.

The normal villains are present with one added who is not normally a villain per se and I trust that you, my dear reader, will like the way that they are all 'rewarded' in my story. We find a much stronger and more resolute Bingley. Jane Bennet is serene, but not without a steely resolve. I feel that both need to be portrayed with more strength of character for the purposes of this book.

PROLOGUE

Fifteen Plus Years Ago...

M rs. Fanny Bennet was doing something that she had not done for many years, if ever. She was being introspective.

Her mind wandered back to seven years ago, when she met Thomas Bennet and fell deeply in love. Thomas had just come out of mourning for his father and his older brother, Oliver, both of whom had been killed in a carriage accident, making him the master of Longbourn.

They were close in those heady days of new love—inseparable. Thomas had cared not a whit that Fanny had not been born a gentlewoman. That her father was Meryton's solicitor had not been an issue for him. Fanny fell in love with him for his wit and kindness, not because he was a gentleman landowner. No other man had ever touched her heart.

What had gone wrong? How had their marriage devolved into a shadow of its former self?

She hated to admit it, even to herself, but the greater fault was hers. Although Thomas had withdrawn into his study with his books and his port, she was the one who had driven him there. He had told her of Longbourn's entailment before they married and explained once they had a son who survived past his tenth year the entail could be broken.

Thomas's great-grandfather created the entail to protect Longbourn's lands from his son, who had given himself over to gambling and dissipation. None of

1

Longbourn's lands could be sold due to the entail; it could be broken only in their own son's generation. If she did not bear a son, Thomas's ignorant cousin, Clem Collins—or his son, William Collins—would inherit when Thomas passed to his final reward.

Fanny fell with child three months after they married. Her first confinement resulted in a beautiful daughter, Jane Bennet. Jane grew into the very image of her mother at the same age. Fanny remained close to Thomas after Jane's birth. They both loved their daughter and were sure their next child would be a son. Two years after their first child was born, Fanny entered her second lying in, certain she would present Thomas with his heir. She had not.

The second child was also a daughter, who had been named Elizabeth. She favoured her father in colouring. Fanny remembered how disheartened she had been after another daughter's birth.

After the disappointment of failing to provide an heir, her now-famous *nerves* made their first appearance. Initially, she blamed little Lizzy for being a girl instead of a boy. Eventually, she realised the babe's sex was God's choice and not Lizzy's fault.

She survived two more confinements before her current pregnancy, both producing girls—Mary and Katherine. After each additional daughter was born, she made life even more unpleasant for her husband by constantly complaining of her nerves and by her oft-repeated calls of "Hill! My salts!" She treated Thomas to daily laments about being tossed into the hedgerows before he was cold in his grave.

That Clem Collins already had a son added to her worries. William Collins would be the end of the entail when he or his father inherited Longbourn. The fact the Collinses had an heir, while so far, she had been unable to produce one drove and increased her anxiety and her attacks of *nerves*.

The result had been to drive Thomas into his study to become a recluse from the world, including avoiding his friend from university, Reggie Fitzwilliam. Thomas had changed into an indolent landowner, resulting in the reduction in Longbourn's income from four thousand a year to less than two thousand.

The happy times they once shared were no more. Although—deep down—they still loved each other, anyone observing them now would not believe it. Fanny despised what her nerves and complaints had caused.

Thomas could have reacted differently; it was his own choice to withdraw into his study with his books and his port —but Fanny admitted her behaviour had driven him to it. She realised she continued to push her beloved Thomas away, although he did leave his study to spend time with their daughters, especially Lizzy, who displayed the intelligence and wit of a much older child.

She acknowledged thoughts of the infernal entail consumed her every waking hour. She did not like the sword of Damocles hanging over her and her daughters' futures. Her worries about being turned out *into the hedgerows* by the Collinses had made her into a woman she did not like, someone she never thought she could become when she married her love, her Thomas, seven years ago.

Although most in the neighbourhood believed Fanny was mean of understanding, that was not true. Fanny merely did not know how to control the anxiety and fear that gripped her; they had taken over her every waking moment.

After another moment of rumination, Fanny became resolved. She *had* to give Thomas a son *this* time! She would do what she felt she had to. She would prostrate herself before Him in the hope He would forgive her whatever transgressions had caused Him to deny her a son.

Fanny knew her labour had begun, and she soon

would enter her fifth lying in. Her pains had commenced that morning and she felt a dull ache in her back, but she had not mentioned a word about it to her husband or any of their servants.

She could not bear to see the disappointment on his face if she bore him another daughter. She loved her four daughters dearly, even though she often could not understand the intelligence and wit of her second daughter.

She wavered for a moment as she thought: *Should I speak to* Him *here, or should I go to* His *House? I am having pains, the walk there—although not a long one—will not be easy, but will* He *not hear me better in* His *House?'*

She **would** walk to Longbourn's church; she **would** endure what she must—no matter how much pain or mortification it cost her and no matter how difficult it might be. Fanny was determined to ask for help from the only one who could grant her wish—God himself. She knew there was nothing *she* could do to control whether she was about to birth a son or a daughter, but God Almighty could.

Cracking open her chamber door and peeking out, Fanny saw no one in the hallway. She made her way stealthily to the stairs, as best she could in her gravid state. She held onto the banister for dear life as she slowly descended, since she was far larger than her previous confinements.

Fanny took her pelisse and gloves from where they hung near the front door and donned them. With a conviction stronger than any she had ever felt, she set out on her mission to reach Longbourn's church which abutted the estate's park just past the drive. Fanny waddled rather than walked, due to her prodigious size.

She thought: *Oh, how undignified I look! I am not walking like the Mistress of Longbourn but like a duck. How mortified I would be if someone spied me crossing the park!*

Due to the size of this baby, she knew she was facing

her most perilous lying-in yet. The baby kicked far more than any of her previous children had, even Lizzy—and that was saying something! The Lord above knew Lizzy had been in a constant state of motion from quickening until birth—or at least, it had felt that way to Fanny.

The comparison between her pregnancy with Jane and her pregnancy with Lizzy had convinced her Lizzy would be a boy. Her disappointment when she birthed yet another daughter had tested her faith; she wondered if that was why God continued to punish her.

She had almost rejected the baby and sent it to be cared for by a tenant for the sin of being born female, but as she held her tiny daughter for the first time and looked into her expressive eyes Fanny fell in love with her, deciding not to take her maternal frustrations out on an innocent babe who, after all, had no say in the matter.

All of these thoughts were irrelevant to her purpose now. She was sure she was about to birth a fifth daughter. She had decided as soon as she knew she had fallen with child again that before her lying-in she would beg help from the only one who could do something about her babe's gender.

Fanny Bennet was a woman on a mission. This felt like the longest walk—waddle—she had ever undertaken, even though the church was but a five minute stroll from the manor house. On this day Fanny's walk took fifteen minutes before she reached her destination.

She threw open the inner vestibule doors with the last of her strength, causing a booming noise when they slammed against the wall and reverberated throughout the church. Fanny knew the pastor was visiting parishioners, so at least she would not be mortified by having to explain herself to him.

Fanny shuffled her way down the aisle and gingerly climbed to the altar, where she prostrated herself in supplication to the Lord God as well as she could in her condition. She began to offer her fervent prayer aloud in her bid to beg for divine intervention.

"Please God, grant me a son. Please protect me and this babe as it struggles to be born. If I do not provide a boy, my girls and I will be turned out by the Collinses, and thrown into the hedgerows to starve as soon as You call my husband home to You. They will do it before my poor Thomas is cold in his grave.

"Please Lord, grant me Thy grace and grant my wish, not for myself alone, but for my husband and daughters. I swear if you grant my prayer, I will never again complain of my nerves. I will become the best wife and mother possible. Please, Lord our God, in Jesus your only son's name, I pray for your forgiveness of all my transgressions."

Once Fanny had beseeched God to help her, she rose to a standing position with great effort, and then made her way back to the house. It was far more difficult a journey than her walk to the church, but she had to reach her chambers as soon as possible!

Her progress was so much slower it was frustrating, her pains were increasing in intensity and frequency and the ache in her back was more severe now. Her trek to and from Longbourn Church worsened her labour pains.

She was forced to stop many times to catch her breath and to wait until a contraction was over. Her pains kept intensifying during her odyssey back to the house. Her focus had shifted from beseeching to birthing and she feared for both the life of the babe she was carrying and for her own life.

She made her way into the foyer, throwing her pelisse and gloves unceremoniously to the floor. She saw the nursemaid for her four daughters, Miss Anita Jones, as she stepped from the drawing room.

"Miss Jones, please have Hill, the midwife, and Mr. Jones called," she gasped with her remaining breath.

For an instant, Miss Jones froze like a doe in a hunter's gunsight as her mouth dropped open in surprise after her mistress spoke to her. She recovered her equanimity when she realised Mrs. Bennet's state and moved quickly to call Longbourn's housekeeper, Mrs. Jenny Hill. Hill had held her position since before Mr. and Mrs. Bennet married, and would know what to do.

Hill took one of Mrs. Bennet's arms and a maid took the other to assist her upstairs. While doing so, Hill barked orders to the maids not assisting her with the mistress to ready towels and hot water. They scurried to comply with her orders. Mrs. Hill did not understand why Mrs. Bennet had not informed her that her labours had begun earlier, or why on earth she had been walking outside.

Mrs. Hill told her husband, Longbourn's butler, to send a groom to fetch Mrs. Abigail Richardson, the local midwife. Miss Jones was dispatched to fetch her uncle, the apothecary, who was in Longbourn's servants' quarters, seeing to an unwell servant.

Mrs. Richardson arrived within a half hour. Mr. Jones, the only physician and apothecary in the area, arrived as soon as his niece summoned him; he was waiting for the midwife in Mrs. Bennet's chambers.

Normally she did not need a physician to assist her with the birthing process, but Mrs. Richardson decided, due to the lady's size, she wished Mr. Jones to be nearby just in case. She made for the birthing chamber, glad to see Mrs. Hill had the foresight to have hot water and towels ready for her. The midwife shooed a visibly nervous Mr. Bennet out of his wife's chambers. To ease his worries, Bennet headed to the nursery to comfort and be comforted by his daughters.

Two hours later, after an early dinner and bath, Miss

Jones had settled the four Bennet daughters, who had fallen asleep for the night, with their father looking on indulgently.

The ever-present pain in Fanny's back grew nearly unbearable after her waters broke. Her pains were coming so frequently she knew the enormous babe within her was about to enter the world.

She prayed silently one more time, just in case it might help: *Oh Lord God and your son Jesus, please grant me a son. If you see fit to call me home to you after this birth, please save my babe.*

After that, Fanny finally let out the scream she had been holding in and kept on screaming. Mrs. Richardson knew the birth was approaching fast. She too prayed that Mrs. Bennet would survive this birth.

~~~~~~~/~~~~~~~

No one in the house slept through Fanny's screams. In the nursery, Miss Jones was pacifying the girls, who had been awakened by the sounds emanating from the floor below theirs. Whilst his wife was getting ready to birth what he was sure would be another daughter, Bennet sat in an armchair in the nursery with his daughters, wincing each time his wife screamed in pain.

All four girls were concerned for their mama, even though Mary and Kitty were too young to understand exactly what was happening. The noises made them cry; they were frightened, believing something was hurting their mama to make her scream so.

The two older girls knew Mama was going to give them a baby sister, but they did not understand why she was screaming. To calm and comfort Kitty and Mary, they were given hot chocolate with a drop of brandy in it and their favourite biscuits, followed by a warm hug from their father, who assured them their mother would be well.

Miss Jones soon settled them, and they returned to

the arms of Morpheus. The oldest Bennet daughter, Jane, had lived through her mother's three previous confinements.

Her innate serenity caused her to lie in her bed, showing no outward sign of her fear for her mother's life.

At this young age, she already excelled at hiding her feelings, which was remarkable for a girl of six years. She understood a bit more about what was going on below the nursery than her sisters.

Even though the sounds coming from her mother's chambers did not concern her quite as much as her sisters, since she was accustomed to Mama's nerves and high-pitched voice, it nevertheless caused her to worry, all the while hiding her concerns behind a mask of calmness.

Jane had been there to see Mama return to full health after each of her prior lying ins that she remembered, so she hoped it would be the same this time. She was looking forward to teaching her new baby sister how to be a proper little lady. After all, it *must* be a sister because Mama and Papa had decreed that it would be. She was not Lizzy to gainsay her parents.

Lizzy was intelligent and had a quick mind. She possessed and unquenchable thirst for knowledge greater than any of her sisters. She wished to know what was going on around her and was worried about Mama's wellbeing. That worry engendered an interminable string of questions for her father, because she wanted to know if Mama would be well.

Normally, Bennet indulged his sharp-as-a-pin daughter, who at four years of age was fast becoming his favourite. He had indulged her whenever she wanted to expand her knowledge, but not on this night. He was exhausted and frightened for his Fanny. She had never screamed, certainly not at this volume, or for so long, during a preceding birth.

He was shorter and more irritable than was his wont when replying to Lizzy, trying to get her to go back to sleep and stop asking questions. Lizzy was a bit put out and pouted; Papa had never dismissed her in this fashion before.

Bennet felt guilty; he knew his behaviour towards his wife, his daughters, and his estate was not as it should be. Although he had difficulties dealing with Fanny's so-called *nerves*, her constant complaining about the entail, and what would happen to her and the girls if he died without a son and heir—he loved her.

He realised he had become the worst kind of estate manager, doing little more than the minimum required of him. How many times had Fanny Bennet's brother, Edward Gardiner, begged him to invest with Gardiner and Associates? It had seemed too much like work for Bennet to bother with it—so he had not.

He felt guilty he had not saved for his family's future with Gardiner, who always achieved excellent returns on investments. He still loved his wife, but embittered and disappointed after the birth of each new daughter, he had withdrawn from her and from the world.

Why should he make Longbourn more profitable if someone else would reap the benefits of it after he passed to his eternal reward? He had—conveniently—forgotten funds earned before his passing would be his and his family's; they would not become part of the entailment.

He was ashamed because he had jested about Fanny's *nerves*. Her nerves were nothing more than an expression of her worries for their family's future. Instead of addressing her fears, even sans an heir, he had chosen to do nothing. He should have saved to provide for his wife and daughters so they would never have to worry.

What had he done instead? He had made sport of her! Rather than assuage her fears he turned to sarcastic, sardonic, and caustic comments about her Then he had hidden in his study. How could he do such things to the only woman he had ever loved? He blamed himself.

Bennet was convinced God was punishing him for his transgressions, and this guilt was the main reason he had withdrawn. To add to his sins, he used sarcasm to cover up the guilt and shame he felt. He was wracked with regret he had led his beloved Fanny to believe she was the only one who suffered fear and guilt because there was no heir to break the entail on Longbourn.

~~~~~~~/~~~~~~~

He recalled when he first met the bright, vivacious, beautiful Fanny Gardiner. *She was an intelligent woman, not just a pretty face, which was more of an attraction for him than it was for most men. She was a good person.*

Fanny cared about the wellbeing of others, and Bennet knew should he offer for her even though her father was but a solicitor, she would be a caring mistress for his estate and his tenants. A month after meeting her at one of the monthly assemblies in Meryton, Bennet had asked Miss Gardiner for a courtship. She had agreed, and that same night her father had granted his permission.

The young couple courted for six weeks. Thomas Bennet had been convinced he loved Fanny Gardiner and was as sure as he could be she returned his affections. They shared many interests, and she had a sharp wit when she chose to display it. Although she could be as silly as any girl of seventeen years and became nervous under stress, Thomas could see beyond that to the real Fanny Gardiner.

He had gone to the Gardiners' home, a house attached to Gardiner Law Practice in Meryton, and requested a private audience with Miss Gardiner. Her father had granted his request and led him to the study, where he fell on one knee before Fanny and had professed his deep and ardent love.

He had asked her to join him on life's journey by becoming his wife. She had said yes with tears of happiness in her eyes, then told him of her love for him. Her father had given his consent and blessing with an admonition to make his girl happy, which Bennet had vowed to do. Remembering his promise to Fanny's father, he was ashamed and embarrassed by what he had become and admitted to himself that he had broken his word.

As he snapped himself out of his remembrances of the past and Bennet's thoughts returned to the present, he surveyed his children sleeping in the nursery. He had not made Fanny happy by teasing her about her legitimate concerns.

He had made things worse with his indolence. Even though Fanny's *nerves* drove him away, he knew if he had chosen to address her concerns, he could have provided a secure future for his wife and daughters. He was ashamed of how he had used Fanny's worries as an excuse for his bad behaviour.

He resolved to do better, but he did not know if he could keep to his resolve after the birth of a fifth daughter. He did something he had not done for a long time; he lifted his eyes to the heavens in fervent prayer: *God of all creation, who created us and this world, please protect my Fanny. If you bless us with a son, I will be forever grateful, Lord. I promise to change my ways; I will become a better father and husband. In Jesus's name, I pledge to do this.* With no hope his prayer would be answered, Thomas drifted into a restless sleep.

~~~~~~~/~~~~~~~~

It was still pitch-black night outside when Thomas Bennet's valet woke him and told him Mrs. Hill wished him to come to the mistress's chambers. Bennet looked at his fob watch and saw that it was just after two o'clock.

He had fallen asleep in the nursery armchair and was stiff and sore. Bennet cocked his ear and heard only silence.

There was no more screaming coming from the birthing chamber on the floor below, and his girls were sleeping peacefully. Had Fanny survived? Was their new daughter well?

Once he blinked the sleep from his eyes, he rose gingerly and, as silently as he could, made his way to his wife's chambers. Bennet was surprised to see Mrs. Hill waiting for him outside the door, beaming like the rising sun. He was reasonably sure it portended his Fanny had survived the birthing of their newest daughter.

"Is Mrs. Bennet well?" Thomas asked with no little trepidation. Mrs. Hill simply nodded. He noted an unreadable expression on her countenance, one he had never seen before. She was smiling in a manner that reached all the way to her eyes.

He followed her into his beloved Fanny's bedchamber, which was bathed in the light of many candles and the blazing fire in the hearth. He was reticent because he did not wish to see Fanny's disappointment and shame at not birthing a son—something he had seen with each birth after Jane's. He and Fanny had been sure this babe would be another girl. In fact, they were so sure they had even settled on the name Lydia, after his wife's late Great Aunt Lydia Gardiner.

He hesitated before approaching. Despite the way he behaved to her, Bennet still loved her to distraction; he did not wish her to see his disappointment. Bennet turned to look at Mrs. Hill with a resigned look.

That unreadable expression was evident again; her mouth was still upturned in a smile. "You had best go in and meet the *newest members* of your family, Master," she stated, as her smile seemed to glow like the rays of the sun as she inclined her head towards the bed where his wife was propped up by pillows, then the housekeeper left the mistress's chambers.

His disappointment about being unable to father an heir to save Longbourn, home to Bennets since the signing of the Magna Carta, welled up in his chest.

Shame burned within him. He imagined how disappointed his forefathers must be with him. The despair he felt to be the last Bennet at Longbourn overwhelmed him. He almost fled back to his study.

He was positive it was another girl. He did not need confirmation; he knew it. It would be the same this time as it always had been.

Preparing himself for the disappointment of meeting another new daughter, he forced himself to approach the bed. Fanny greeted him, showing no trace of disappointment on her countenance.

His wife was reclining on a great mound of pillows the look of a cat that had gotten into the cream. She appeared as serene as Jane, and he was confused by it.

As Fanny Bennet noticed her husband's approach, she beamed happily at him. "My love, my Thomas, God heard me! I went to His house this afternoon and I prayed. I did not just pray, I begged Him for a son. He has granted my prayers. He has been so very good to our family!" Fanny cried out.

He was still confused as he had not really listened to what Fanny said. He noted his wife was holding two babes, one on each side.

Now he recalled that Hill had said *members*. Twin girls —what had he done for God to punish him so? How could Fanny say *God has been good to our family?* How could she say that? Six daughters and Fanny's nerves would drive him to distraction.

Before he could open his mouth to make a sarcastic comment at Fanny's expense, his wife looked up at him, the excitement in her eyes staying his words: "It is a miracle from God, Thomas! I knew how it would be if I prayed to God. He heard me and answered my prayers. I have told Mrs. Hill to tell Mr. Hill to share the wonderful news with the rest of the servants so everyone can participate in our joy.

"I instructed her to give all of the staff punch and cake. What a great happening! We have four daughters, and now we have two strong, healthy sons to go with our sweet girls," Fanny gushed. Bennet thought perhaps his wife had become addlepated after giving birth to twins until he heard the midwife speak.

"Your sons are fine, Sir. What a thing! It is not every day I deliver healthy twin boys, all pink and crying their little lungs out. Such strong little lads! This is such a blessing for you and your wife, and for all of Longbourn," the midwife said, offering her congratulations.

"Master, I know it is the middle of the night, but would you like some refreshment?" Mrs. Hill said as she walked back into the chamber.

Thomas Bennet was struck mute when the truth permeated his consciousness as to why Fanny was beaming up at him as she was, and why she said God had been good to them. Suddenly, he understood Hill's joy.

He grasped the meaning behind what his wife and the midwife had said to him. This was not another daughter but a son. No, *two* sons! God had answered his prayer. Perhaps he was not being punished for some offence. *It seems I am not the only one who prayed to God; he answered our combined prayers,* he thought just before he was consumed by elation.

Bennet turned to Mrs. Hill, who was patiently waiting for his response. "Thank you, Hill. This miracle calls for port! Please ask Mr. Hill to bring me a large glass. I will break my fast later this morning. No matter the time, I need fortification now. It is not every day my wife gifts me with twin sons. I want to stay here and meet my boys, and make sure my wife is healthy," he replied with a joy he had not experienced since the day he married his Fanny.

Curtsying and withdrawing from the chambers and closing the door as she departed, Mrs. Hill left to convey the master's request to her husband.

As he looked at his wife's beaming, happy face and both precious babes in her arms, it occurred to him the dreaded entail could be ended when his sons reached the age of ten. *I have two sons and Fanny is safe. Thank you, God of the universe, for hearing and answering my prayer, our prayers. That miserly...* Bennet paused and stopped himself from thinking of Collins; one did not insult others when giving thanks to God. *Cousin Collins will not be happy when my boys reach the age of ten.*

As he silently thanked his creator his smile grew larger. Yes, he had most definitely heard and understood correctly! This was not a dream; Longbourn had its long-awaited heir—an heir and a spare!

Full of joy after becoming the father of sons, he looked at his wife lovingly. "My dearest Fanny, I love you so very much. You have done us proud and saved Longbourn for the Bennets for generations to come." He was now a father of sons *and* daughters. Perhaps he should pray more often.

"I love you too, Thomas! Stop staring at me with that befuddled look on your countenance and let me introduce you to your heir and his brother. Had I not just given birth to them, I would not believe that we have twin boys myself! I am so proud and happy. I have done my duty to you and Longbourn at last. God has answered all my prayers! Thank you, God, for there will be no more infernal entail," Fanny stated, all the while beaming up at her husband.

Agreeing wholeheartedly with his ecstatic wife, he pulled a chair next to the bed and seated himself as close to Fanny as possible. "This is your firstborn son," Fanny revealed as she handed him one of the sleeping babes. "When you open his swaddling, you will notice the blue ribbon that Mrs. Richardson tied on his ankle so that there will be no confusion about the order of the births." He was passed his heir gently. This tiny, swaddled bundle which held his firstborn son had just changed their lives.

After he held him for a few minutes and had his fill of looking at his oldest son, he handed the sleeping babe back to his mother, who then passed their younger son to him. He moved the blanket aside to gaze on him as well. He counted ten tiny fingers and ten tiny toes on each of his newborn sons.

"What should we name them, Thomas?" asked the beaming, albeit very sore, mother.

"If you are in agreement, Fanny, I suggest that we name the older twin Thomas Edward. My father was named Thomas. Edward is for our brother Gardiner. We should call him Tom, so he and I do not both respond when someone calls *Thomas*. For the younger son, I suggest James Oliver. James for your late father and Oliver for my late younger brother."

"Oh Thomas, I think those are fine names for our sons. Tom sounds well, and I am sure Edward will be overjoyed as well." Fanny nodded with a radiant smile as she looked from him down at their sons.

"Who should we ask to be their godparents?" Bennet looked at each son to make sure they were still there, then again met the eyes of his Fanny.

"I think we should ask Reggie, Elaine, and Edward to be Tom's godparents; for James's how about Frank, Hattie, and Maddie?" She offered.

"You could not have suggested better people, my love; I agree with you completely," Bennet stated, marvelling at how they were again in perfect harmony.

Now the important decisions had been made, he was

transfixed, staring at one of his sons as he was being fed by his mother. It was his heir, Tom; once he was sated, his mother began feeding his brother. Bennet held his heir proudly.

He held Tom over his shoulder and patted his back until he gave a soft burp. Then Bennet moved him to the crook of his arm; the baby squirmed and cooed as Bennet rubbed his tiny belly.

Once Fanny had fed his brother, Bennet replaced Tom in his cradle and picked up his second son, James, and did the same as he had with Tom. This time, the babe merely regarded his father with his bright blue eyes.

The older twin had Lizzy's colouring—a darker complexion, a full head of dark hair, and blue eyes, although his eye colour might change. Like his older sister, he seemed to be very active.

The younger babe had Jane's colouring. He had a tuft of blonde hair, not that there was much of it, and deep blue eyes. Even now as a newly born babe, Bennet imagined he seemed to possess her serenity as well, something that many of the Gardiners had.

Bennet's heart swelled as he looked adoringly on his sons. He envisioned all he would have to do to secure their futures and those of the rest of his family. Longbourn was safe now. Due to the birth of an heir, his family had a future at his estate. The timely answer to both of their prayers meant—in ten short years—the end of the dreaded entail. The Bennet line at Longbourn would not *end* with him!

As he continued to lovingly look at his newborn sons, Thomas Bennet had an epiphany. That he *must* change hit him like a bolt of lightning. Not just a few changes would do; he would have to change many things, some small and some greater, equating to major changes in how he led his life.

He vowed to himself and to God Almighty, he would

do everything in his power to improve his family's fortunes and change his ways. He would live up to the promises he made when he prayed for a son. He would also live up to the vow he made to his late father-in-law when he was granted his wife's hand.

He would no longer be indolent; he would no longer hide from Fanny in his study. His responsibilities and his duties as husband, father, and the head of the family would be paramount. He would work hard every day and do everything in his power to ensure a good life for his family.

On the morrow, he would contact his brother Edward about investing with him, as he had been begged to do years ago. Edward would help him to build wealth for his sons and to become the means of securing good men for his beloved daughters by ensuring they had reasonable dowries.

He would not squander the gift God had bestowed on them in answer to his prayers. He would again make the name Bennet an example to the neighbourhood, as it had been in the past. He would restore Longbourn to its former glory and realise the dreams he had once hoped to achieve.

Bennet turned to his wife, who was looking at him with all the love he had thought he had lost due to his treatment of her. He beamed at her and returned a look of pure adoration and love.

"My dear Fanny, *look* at what you have done. You have saved us from the entail and completed our family," Bennet said with the deepest reverence and love. He then reached over and began to drop kisses over her face. "Fanny, how I love my beautiful, vivacious wife! You have done very well indeed. I am ashamed of the way I have treated you these last years, and I swear to you that I will become the man you deserve again, the one you married. I am so proud of you, my love, and I will endeavour to be a husband and father both you and my family will be proud of."

"Thomas, I should apologise as well. Instead of using reason and trying to assist you, I chased you into your study with my *nerves* and nonsensical complaints. I am no longer that woman; I vow to be the best wife and mother in the future." Both agreed each of them was at fault, then sealed their new understanding with kisses, vowing to look to the future, and not to the past.

~~~~~~~/~~~~~~~

The ever-present worry about the entail which had changed Fanny Bennet's persona in many ways was gone in an instant. Her nightmare of being thrown out into the hedgerows by the Collinses and her concerns for the future had dissipated after the hours of intense labour that proved worth the pain.

The subject often spoken of in Sunday sermons, that many of life's greatest trials bring the greatest rewards, proved true. She would no longer be ashamed of failing in her duty to her husband and to Longbourn—the duty of providing an heir. She felt a weight akin to a millstone tied around her neck lift, at long last, from her.

Fanny Bennet intended to keep the promises she made to God before He gifted her with the strength to birth her sons. Her attacks of *nerves* would be a thing of the past, and the shouts of "Hill! My salts!" would never again be heard in the halls of Longbourn, unless a peer of the realm proposed to one of her girls, that is—but in that she would not be acting differently from any other woman.

Her gossiping days, her boastful ways, and her attempts to outdo her friends would set aside. She would convince her older sister Hattie, now Mrs. Phillips, to stop gossiping as well. She knew beyond a shadow of a doubt the new understanding between herself and her husband would not be a fleeting fancy.

Their family and home were safe, and their future was

bright. She was finally free to be the wife and mother she always wished to be, the one she knew she should be.

Fanny felt contentment that she had not experienced since her wedding day when all was new and possible. She smiled warmly, knowing her family would be taking a new path, a path where they would all be happy. She would no longer question her future. She once again felt like the Fanny Gardiner who married her beloved Thomas Bennet.

Thomas Bennet grew even firmer in his resolve to become the best father, the best husband, and the best provider. He repeated his oath that he would do whatever he must to solve the problems caused by his indolence and self-imposed exile.

He vowed to make sure each and every day his Fanny would know he loved, respected, and appreciated her. He would cease making jokes at her expense; if they were to laugh, they would laugh together. Bennet's bearing was stronger and more evident; there was no mistaking the resolve in his mien.

~~~~~~~/~~~~~~~

With the passage of time subsequent to the birth of the twins, the Bennets' friends and acquaintances living in and near Meryton were amazed by the obvious changes taking place in Longbourn's family.

The most notable changes were in Thomas and Fanny Bennet. Ever since they had been blessed with the twin boys, the most striking change was the glow of love and mutual respect emanating from them. Many found themselves blushing when they were in the couple's presence, as they were always whispering together and laughing. Gone were Fanny's gossiping and boastful ways—and no one ever heard her complain about her nerves again.

Thomas Bennet stopped making sport of his wife, as he had vowed he would. He ceased the sarcastic and sardonic comments made at the expense of his wife and his neighbours. He was no longer indolent or indifferent to the needs of his tenants.

Rather than burying himself in his study with his books and port, Bennet took an active role in managing his estate. He was often seen out and about in his fields, more so than many of the masters considered the best in Hertfordshire. Unbeknownst to Bennet, he soon became known as one of them.

To their very welcome surprise and comfort, he saw to his tenants' needs. He offered immediate responses and aid to them when requested, as expected of an attentive estate owner.

Bennet worked assiduously to provide for his family. He interacted with his girls, assigning and helping them with small tasks appropriate for their age. Even in their early years, the boys were brought along with him when he rode out to check that the tenants' concerns were being addressed.

His friends and neighbours were most surprised he began to accompany his wife and his family to social events, including assemblies. To the amazement of all, he danced with his wife multiple times, something he had not done in the years before the birth of his sons. Unlike most other husbands at these gatherings, he seemed to enjoy his time with his wife; he did not avoid her as he had done in the past.

At the same time Bennet was doing everything he could to increase Longbourn's income, Fanny economised as much as she could while still maintaining their lifestyle as gently bred folk.

~~~~~~~/~~~~~~~

For many years, Reggie and Elaine Fitzwilliam had invited the Bennets to visit their estate, Snowhaven near Matlock, or their townhouse on Grosvenor Square in London,

Matlock House. The invitations were, without fail, declined by Bennet; his friends were always disappointed to receive his latest excuse.

In the past, Bennet would not make the effort to travel with his family, even to London, and certainly not all the way to Snowhaven in Derbyshire.

To maintain the connection, on rare occasions, the Fitzwilliams would stop at Longbourn when going to or returning from Town. No matter how much he liked Reggie Fitzwilliam, his oldest friend, Bennet always politely refused the invitations to visit his homes.

This changed after the birth of the Bennets' sons. Reggie and Elaine Fitzwilliam were asked to accept the role of godparents to young Tom Bennet, and were happy to agree. When the babes were old enough to travel, the Bennets accepted an invitation from the Fitzwilliams and travelled to Snowhaven to visit them.

No invitations were ever refused again without good reason and many reciprocal invitations were issued by the Bennets and accepted by the Fitzwilliams. Their families grew close over the years—their connection and relationships grew to the point they felt as close as family, although they were not connected by ties of blood. They felt closer ties than many families who were indeed related.

~~~~~~~/~~~~~~~

Once he decided to change, to his brother-in-law's relief, Bennet sent the express he had said he would the day after the boys were delivered. In it, and as he had vowed to himself and to God, he finally did something Edward Gardiner had begged him to do since his marriage to Fanny— he started to invest all that he could afford with his brother.

Thomas knew Edward had one of the best business minds in the country and often berated himself that he had not invested with Gardiner and Associates sooner. He should have done so beginning the day he married Fanny, as Gardiner had suggested after he congratulated him and welcomed him to the family.

His best friend Reggie, and others in the *Ton*, invested with Gardiner and did very well with those investments. He remembered Reggie had dubbed Gardiner '*King Midas*' and had often advised Bennet to invest as well.

On Reggie's recommendation, his brother-in-law, George Darcy, who was married to Lady Anne, Reggie Fitzwilliam's younger sister, had also invested heavily. Until Bennet had had his epiphany, he lacked the will and motivation to trouble himself to invest; he was not interested in anything that involved effort, concentration, and time away from his port and his books. That was in the past now.

Planning for and providing comfort and a future for his family was everything to him. Bennet had vows to keep, ones he had made to God above, to himself, and to his Fanny. He intended to do his best to keep them faithfully until his final breath left his body.

Thanks to the investments Edward Gardiner made on his behalf, to cutting unnecessary costs, and to the increase in Longbourn's income—which now exceeded the level before he had let things go—Bennet acquired enough capital to expand the estate.

In the end, he more than doubled the estate's farmland by purchasing the neighbouring Bennington Fields estate, which he renamed Bennet Fields. The previous owners, the Benningtons, sold their estate after deciding to seek their fortune in the New World; they had no intention of returning to the area.

With this purchase, he also secured a safe future for James Bennet, who would not have to seek a profession as did most second sons. Bennet, with the help of Frank Phillips, the solicitor who married Fanny's sister, Hattie, made James the heir to the newly acquired and renamed estate, Bennet Fields. Tom Bennet, his firstborn son, would inherit Longbourn, of course.

As the family's wealth grew, Bennet started to acquire all of the Longbourn lands an ancestor had once been forced to sell off to satisfy the debts of honour incurred by his dissolute son and heir. In addition to these lands, Bennet quietly purchased as much land close to Longbourn as he could. As parcels became available, Bennet worked with Gardiner and Phillips to secure them. Utilizing the shrewd negotiating skills of his brother Phillips as his agent, he was able to acquire tracts of land before they were offered for sale to the public.

With two estates and added acreage, Longbourn was about four times the size it had been before the twins were born. Due to the expansion, the estate now had more than triple the number of tenants.

Bennet rebuilt and substantially increased the size of Longbourn's stables. After a number of visits to Tattersalls with Reggie and his sons, Andrew and Richard, Bennet had acquired brood mares from some of the best bloodlines available, which he would use in a breeding programme he had been planning. Through the connections he had with the Fitzwilliams, he purchased stallions to further strengthen his programme. An agent was able to acquire bloodstock from Spain for crossbreeding.

Longbourn's income had more than quadrupled from the two thousand pound income before Bennet's epiphany. Bennet had started to build wealth, still primarily from the investments his brother Edward was making on his behalf.

His horse breeding programme became renowned for the quality of the horses it produced. It was not long before Longbourn's programme became known for the quality of the horseflesh it produced, especially those produced by crossbreeding with Andalusians and Arabians. These horses were in demand by some of the leading members of the peerage and the ton in general.

The line of horses bred with Arabians was often acquired by the army, as their stamina made them perfect cavalry mounts. The breeding programme added a substantial amount to the family's ever-expanding income, and as their horses travelled with their new owners, so did the news of them. There was a long waiting list to acquire horses from Longbourn's stables.

Concurrently with the land purchases and investment of profits, the Bennets' wealth continued to grow. With his vows to God and his wife well on their way, Bennet turned his focus to his beloved daughters. He began to set aside as much as he could to build good dowries for each of them in funds controlled by his brother Gardiner.

As with the rest of his investments, the income generated by the girls' dowries was reinvested and compounded with the wise investments made on the Bennets' behalf by Edward Gardiner. As all of his investments and income continued to grow substantially, Bennet was able to increase the dowries whenever he earned funds for which he had no marked plans.

After three years, the amounts of each dowry had reached over ten thousand pounds, and the funds were expected to double every five years or so. This made his precious daughters heiresses in their own right, although they were unaware of it.

His hope was each of his daughters would find men they could love and respect and who would make them happy. However, so there would be no pressure on them to marry if they did not have the inclination, he had requested Phillips to draft documents stating each daughter would be granted their dowry if they did not marry before they turned five and twenty.

He also had Phillips add language to ensure they could not be forced to marry if they were compromised. Bennet wanted to make sure his daughters would never be forced into loveless marriages, or marriages of convenience. Gardiner, Phillips, and Matlock were named guardians of his daughters if he passed before they reached their majority.

Additionally, Bennet stipulated that a portion of interest earned on their dowries was to be provided to each daughter quarterly, with which she could do as she pleased. He already knew, because he knew them, that Jane would give a portion, if not all, to families experiencing hardship. Elizabeth's interest in seeing servants and tenants educated would be funded from her money. Mary would give most, if not all, to the parish to assist those in need. The orphans of the county would be Kitty's crusade.

Bennet would only spend time in his study with a glass of port long after his duties for the day were done and all other concerns had been managed. Only then did he allow himself the pleasure of reading one of his beloved tomes.

His aim had been to provide security for his family, but thanks to his brother Gardiner, his wealth was not merely growing apace; it was increasing exponentially. Gardiner's investments kept earning dividends, so the returns for all of his partners were substantial.

Bennet added all of the clear profits from both expanded estates to his investment portfolio and reinvested the profits made by the investments each year. This meant that even in a lean year, or years of lower than expected productivity, would not have a negative impact on his family. His friend Reggie had not dubbed Gardiner 'King Midas' without good reason; what he touched really did turn to gold.

~~~~~~~/~~~~~~~

Mr. and Mrs. Bennet had become a team in every respect. Bennet apprised and consulted with his wife about everything he was doing, and anything significant he planned to do.

They had a true partnership, and when a man looked at him in confusion on an occasion when Bennet said he would first consult his wife, he looked back at him with pity for not understanding the immense treasure a true meeting of the minds was.

With his Fanny's blessing and wholehearted support, and a glowing recommendation from Elaine Fitzwilliam, they employed a governess, Mrs. Henrietta Chandler. She was charged with teaching his daughters what they needed to know to become proper gentlewomen, including educating them and assisting each to hone her natural gifts—turning them into true accomplishments. Masters were hired to expand on those accomplishments as soon as they were required.

Later, as the Bennet sons reached the appropriate age, tutors and more masters were employed. It came as no surprise to anyone when Lizzy took in as much additional education as she could. She could never learn enough to satisfy her thirst for knowledge.

Her brain soaked up lessons and enjoyed a challenge, as all good education evokes. She was like a sponge soaking up water; she even asked to join the other girls in their individual lessons, with that sister's approval, of course.

The Bennets' other three daughters, while not quite as witty or intelligent as Lizzy, each took full advantage of the educational opportunities made available at Longbourn. Thanks to the guiding hand of their mama, Mrs. Chandler, and their masters, they all became proficient in music, languages, dancing, their preferred talent in the arts, and all the other accomplishments gently bred ladies were expected to have.

However, they were not satisfied to become

accomplished in ladies' pursuits only; with Lizzy blazing the path, they persuaded their parents to allow a much broader education, though not quite as broad as the scope of Lizzy's learning.

Initially, their parents worried about teaching them subjects considered to be the sole province of men. One day the Earl of Matlock listened to Lizzy's reasoning for why a particular plant could not grow in his conservatory.

Matlock had grinned at both Fanny and Bennet, and told them it was no surprise to him their girls were so knowledgeable and were growing into the kind of women only the best of men would earn one day.

That statement helped Fanny accept the girls could learn all they chose, because the more they knew the less they might fall for one of the scoundrels she knew hunted in society.

~~~~~~~/~~~~~~~

The Bennets eventually became wealthier than the wealthiest five families in Hertfordshire combined. They never flaunted their wealth or boasted about it, although they were generous to those around them—especially in times of genuine need or tragedy. They never wasted their wealth, nor did they spend it frivolously.

Others in the area suspected they were well off, based on Bennet's land purchases they were aware of. The general suspicion was merely that the Bennets were somewhat wealthier than their neighbours, who were, thankfully, unaware the Bennets' wealth rivalled that of some of the wealthier families of the *Ton*.

Once the Bennet sons reached the age of thirteen, Bennet planned to send them to Eton. After Eton, they would be enrolled at Cambridge to complete their gentleman's education.

He often joked with them he would disinherit one or

both should they apply at that *other* school, Oxford. Tom and James Bennet would be sorely missed at Longbourn, but schooling was a necessary part of their journey to manhood, and imperative if they were to take their rightful places as the heirs of thriving estates.

Fanny Bennet's new outlook on life and the sense of peace and accomplishment she had attained after the birth of her sons was not transitory; that outlook would remain with her for the rest of her long and happy life.

While in the guise of her motherly duty, she watched them as they attended all their lessons. She saw all that was being taught and learnt, and sometimes was afraid for their Lizzy, who had an intelligence greater than most boys. She was careful to ensure both her sons and her daughters were taught the rules of propriety.

After the compliment from their good friend Reggie, rather than suppress the girls' lessons that might be considered unladylike, she encouraged and supported their quest for an education, especially her Lizzy. This included teaching all four of her daughters how to be effective mistresses of an estate, and how to respect and care for its tenants.

Respect for servants was also part of the credo she emphasised to her daughters. Her main goal in life was all her children were to be happy, even if it meant some of them chose to never marry. When she thanked God every night for all the wonders her life had been blessed with, she added the gift of her Thomas and the stipulation which meant her daughters could find their true happiness, no matter the course it took.

The boys were her pride and joy, but she never showed favouritism to any of her children. Bennet, who before the twins had started to favour Lizzy, now showed no favouritism to any of his sons or daughters. Fanny loved her daughters, but openly acknowledged the changes the birth of her darling boys had wrought on her relationship with Thomas, her girls, and her outlook on life.

Further, the Thomas she married was back, a change that made Fanny glow with happiness. She was more in love with her husband now than the day she married him all those years ago.

As time and the years rolled by, Longbourn's manor house was enlarged substantially. Two wings were added to it, one containing a library fast growing into an enviable collection of books, including many rare first editions. It was the one indulgence Bennet allowed himself, but it was well-regulated.

Thanks to all the additional lands Bennet purchased, he was also able to enlarge Longbourn's park. He and Fanny deepened their friendships with those they were close to, Including Reggie and Elaine Fitzwilliam and their family. Visits to Snowhaven or Matlock House became commonplace, as were the Fitzwilliams' reciprocal visits to Longbourn.

What had once been merely friendship had grown so the bond between the two families became unbreakable. If one injured a member of one family, the affront was felt by the other.

Visitors were forever coming and going, as Fanny kept an excellent table, but she still economised no matter how wealthy they became—she did not overindulge just because she could. She had discarded her former pastimes of boasting and gossiping and replaced them with charitable works in the parish—an orphanage, a school, and a clinic.

She spent time with her husband each morning, planning their day, discussing plans for investments, and dealing with personal and estate correspondence.

The change in Fanny caused a great deal of head-scratching among her neighbours, who would have died from shock and envy had they known the change in the family's wealth. They found it difficult to fathom the changes they *did* know about.

When husband and wife had quiet time, they would spend it together or with their children, not apart from them. They displayed parental pride for their children. Bennet would often lean over to his Fanny and whisper in her ear: "I love you so very much, my beloved Fanny. Look at what we have done together."

"Thomas, I love you more and more each day." Fanny would say, squeezing Thomas's hand and whispering back to him whenever she heard this particular statement.

The Bennet family, quietly and unassumingly, became the principal family in the area once again, if not the principal family in all of Hertfordshire.

CHAPTER 1

Present Day, 1810...

It had been more than sixteen years since their sons' birth and the years had been good to the Bennets. On the boys' tenth birthday, in spite of many vociferous protests from Bennet's illiterate and miserly cousin Clem Collins, the entail was broken irrevocably.

Bennet's buffoon of a cousin had tried to challenge the breaking of the entail, first with letters and later in court. In accordance with the stipulations in the entail documents —which required when the entail was broken all heirs presumptive were to be notified in writing—Bennet notified his cousin.

After someone read the notice to him, Collins retained a solicitor, who wrote letters of demand claiming the twins were not Bennet's sons. Bennet's barrister, Sir Randolph Norman, head of one of the most feared firms of solicitors and barristers in the Kingdom, responded in writing categorically stating either Mr. Collins must present his evidence to the courts or Sir Randolph would sue for slander on behalf of the Bennets.

Collins's solicitors then advised him to drop the matter and apologise, but their advice was ignored. The man made a claim in court, *pro se*, as no solicitor would agree to represent him. Collins was assisted by his teenage son, William, who could read, but unfortunately had no more sense, common or otherwise, than his father.

Sir Randolph presented proof of birth to the court in the form of affidavits from both Mr. Jones and Mrs. Richardson, the physician and midwife assisting Fanny at the births. If needed, both stated they were willing to testify in person. He also pointed out, by presenting portraits, that Tom resembled his father at the same age, while James looked like a younger version of his late grandfather Gardiner.

When His Honour asked Collins what proof he had to support his assertions, he presented none, instead ranting Longbourn was his and he knew the twins were foundlings the Bennets were using to steal his rightful property.

It took His Honour less than five minutes to throw out Mr. Collins's case and certify the breaking of the entail. Bennet remembered how outraged both Collins and his son were after they were summarily ejected from the court.

To make sure no Collins could ever own Longbourn, Bennet instituted a new entail, which stated none of the Bennets' land holdings could be sold off piece by piece under any circumstances, and only if there was no by-blood Bennet heir, either male or female, could the estates be sold.

The new entail ensured the Bennet holdings would remain in Bennet hands, until there were no by-blood Bennets of either gender living—something not likely to happen. The Bennets celebrated the breaking of the original entail and the boys' tenth birthday with a massive party that included the Phillipses, the Gardiners, and the Fitzwilliams.

~~~~~~~/~~~~~~~

With the future of his family secure, Bennet, with Gardiner's guidance, decided to make both conservative investments and a some in the high-risk - high-reward range. The result was, by the time the twins turned fifteen, each of the Bennet daughters had a dowry of forty thousand pounds and Bennet had purchased a townhouse on Grosvenor

Square in London which a peer had gambled away after a life of debauchery and dissipation.

Although it was empty now save for a skeleton staff, his plan was to refurbish it and lease it out, as his family rarely spent time in London. When they did, they either stayed with the Gardiners at Gardiner House on Portman Square, or the Fitzwilliams at Matlock House on Grosvenor Square. Matlock House was on the same side of the square and but a few doors from the townhouse Bennet had acquired.

Five years previously, Netherfield Park, the largest estate near Meryton before Longbourn was expanded, had come on the market. The owner, Mr. Timmons, was deeply in debt due to senseless, risky investments which failed, depleting his funds to the extent he was no longer able to repay his debts, including the mortgage he had taken out on Netherfield Park to fund his investments.

He needed a speedy sale to obtain funds to satisfy his creditors—otherwise, he was in danger of being sent to either Marshalsea or Kings Bench debtor's prison. For that reason, the purchase price was far below market and Bennet realised it would be a sound investment. The plan was to purchase the estate and lease out the manor house; at the same time, Bennet would increase his agricultural acreage, thanks to the extensive tract of prime farmland which was annexed from Netherfield Park to Longbourn.

This of course added more tenants to the number that rented farms from the Bennets. After the addition of the Netherfield Park lands, Bennet's income rose again.

Netherfield's tenants were overjoyed to find the Bennets were now their landlords; they knew from the tenants living on Bennet lands the family would be attentive to their needs, unlike the neglect they had suffered under Mr. Timmons.

After the purchase of Netherfield Park, Bennet still had about four hundred thousand pounds invested, which was growing exponentially. He also had two hundred thousand pounds of funds and jewels held in reserve. In addition, there was an account with a healthy balance which was used to pay the daily expenses of Longbourn.

This additional estate would eventually clear a little over four thousand pounds a year—not including the projected revenue from leasing out the manor house and home farm—although it only brought in about two thousand a year at the time Bennet purchased it, due to the former owner's mismanagement. This would make Bennet's total income from his three estates about fifteen thousand pounds a year.

Under Bennet's management, and after the installation of a good steward, Mr. Cedric Heaton, Netherfield Park achieved and exceeded its prior level of income once all of the issues had been corrected—the neglect of the land, the house, and the tenants.

Bennet's income from his investment income was substantially larger than the income from his three estates. Bennets' total combined annual income, not including the money generated by the funds that held the girl's dowries, grew to be in excess of thirty thousand pounds.

~~~~~~~/~~~~~~~

Thomas and Fanny Bennet remained deeply in love and revelled in each other's company. They had built a true equal partnership. If one asked them, they would have admitted they were now far more in love than they had been when they married. They had not been blessed with additional children after the twins, but they were more than content with the family they had been granted.

The twin boys were at Eton, in their final year before they moved on to Cambridge.

Lizzy, in addition to the education her sisters received, spent time with her father, the boys' tutors, and the many masters that came to Longbourn for both her sisters and her brothers. She used her intelligence and wit to achieve a level of education that one would have after completing a stringent course of study at university.

Now the girls no longer needed a governess, Mrs. Chandler stayed on as their companion. The Bennets did not see the need for more than a single companion for all the girls because they spent little time in Town.

Because Kitty was not yet out, she was Mrs. Chandler's primary charge unless one or more of the older girls went to stay in Town. The three eldest had been sponsored by Elaine Fitzwilliam, Countess of Matlock, when they took their curtsies before Queen Charlotte.

The Bennet daughters, while accomplished and beautiful, were not vain, conceited, or proud. They did not hold themselves above the friends they had known all their lives just because they were now wealthy.

None of the Bennet children felt they needed to make others feel bad so that they would feel superior. They were beautiful inside and out, Jane always being a shining example for them to follow.

~~~~~~~/~~~~~~~

One afternoon, as Bennet revelled in knowing how happy his family was and how close they were to the Fitzwilliams, his thoughts drifted back to the first time he met Lord Reginald Fitzwilliam, Viscount Hilldale, then the heir to the Earldom of Matlock.

Bennet was three months into his first year of Trinity College. He was sitting in the college library one afternoon, lost in concentration, with a chess board in front of him. He played against his brother Oliver via post.

Not being a sociable person, Bennet had not put himself

forward to meet any of the gentleman students unless required. As he was contemplating the next move to send to his younger brother, he felt a presence over his shoulder and heard, "king to rook seven."

After that simple piece of strategic advice, he met his first acquaintance at Cambridge. Lord Hilldale introduced himself and seemed to care not a whit that Bennet was not of his social circle.

They began to play chess once a week, and soon Bennet was helping Lord Hilldale—Reggie—with Latin, Greek, and mathematics.

Bennet found these subjects easy. He had a deep intellect, and as such, he was able to help his friend to understand subjects Hilldale was struggling with. For his side, the Viscount introduced Thomas Bennet to his small but preferred group of friends.

The Viscount was a year ahead of Bennet and had shared with him that he was very much in love with Miss Elaine Worthington. She was from an untitled family with a medium-sized estate, and his father had suggested his son seek an heiress from among the ton instead.

Reggie saw how unhappy his older sister, Lady Catherine de Bourgh, was in her marriage of convenience to a baronet chosen only for his status and wealth after her fourth unsuccessful season.

He was determined to marry for love, and as his father's only male child, there was no option for his father but to accept his choice. His sister Catherine railed against Elaine for her lack of breeding, wealth, or connections she considered inappropriate for the wife of a future Earl of Matlock. As did most people with sense, Reggie ignored the pompous pronouncements of his older sister.

Bennet and Fitzwilliam's friendship grew strong. At the end of his first year, Bennet was invited to join his now best *friend at Snowhaven, the Matlock estate, and at Hilldale, the Viscount's estate, for a month complete.*

At Snowhaven he met the Viscount's younger and affable sister, Lady Anne Fitzwilliam, who was being courted by Mr. George Darcy. Mr. Darcy had inherited his estate, Pemberley, just over a year ago at the age of two and thirty, after his father was killed in a hunting accident.

It was well known Lady Anne Fitzwilliam's older sister, Lady Catherine, was envious of her sister due to one fact—the Darcy estate was far larger and more prosperous than Rosings Park, her husband's estate in Kent.

Two years later, when the Viscount graduated, he and Bennet had become inseparable. They complemented each other nicely, Bennet being more studious and stoic, and his friend Reggie more social and affable.

As Bennet sat at his desk thinking of his friendship with Reginald Fitzwilliam, he was snapped out of his reverie by thoughts of how he might do everything in his power to protect his family.

Due to his concerns about fortune hunters, he had concealed the real value of the girls' dowries from the neighbourhood, and the extent of the Bennets' wealth. The neighbours only knew the Bennet girls had five thousand pounds each, more than anyone else in the area, but not an amount sufficient to tempt a fortune hunter.

Along with his brothers Gardiner and Phillips, Bennet had arranged for a safety mechanism—without consent from all three of them, no dowry could be released. That would prevent any unscrupulous rakes from attempting to compromise one of his girls!

Bennet did one more thing to protect his girls— something known only to his closest confidants. Using the best firm of investigators money could buy, he had any potential suitor thoroughly investigated, as he did any potential lessees of his properties.

Jane was soon to turn two and twenty, Elizabeth—Lizzy—was twenty. Mary was now almost nineteen and had only been out in society for one year. Catherine—Kitty—was seventeen and not yet out.

Tom and James Bennet, the catalysts of so much good, they could be called nothing else but gifts from God, were almost sixteen. Although the three eldest had taken their curtsies before the Queen, the Bennets did not host coming out balls for any of the girls. They would have given a ball if any of their girls had wanted one, but each of them declined the offer. This meant the Bennets remained relatively unknown among the *Ton*, except for a few of the Fitzwilliams' closest friends.

~~~~~~~/~~~~~~~

One fine Hertfordshire morning Bennet sat in his study with his brother Phillips reviewing a potential new lessee for Netherfield Park, Mr. Charles Bingley. The man had applied for a one-year lease of the estate. Mr. Bingley's only contact was with Mr. Phillips because Bennet preferred to remain anonymous to the lessees of his properties.

Phillips recommended that at some point Bennet reveal his ownership of Netherfield Park to Mr. Bingley at some point because they would have a great deal of social contact. Bennet agreed to lease the property—but only after his investigator had returned a favourable report on both Bingley's character and his finances.

The fact he was a tradesman's son did not concern Bennet; both of his brothers were in trade, after all. Mr. Bingley was to take up residence at Netherfield Park just before Michaelmas. His sisters, a Mrs. Louisa Hurst and a Miss Caroline Bingley, the latter of whom would act as his hostess, would be arriving with him. His brother-in-law, Mr. Harold Hurst, would also be one of the party.

His investigator's report was less favourable with respect to the Bingley sisters, especially the younger sister, Caroline. She was characterised as a grasping, social climbing fortune hunter in the report before him. Bennet groaned at the tediousness of these types of women, almost dropping to his knees to again give thanks to God for his Fanny.

He exhaled slowly and read on. It was not she who was the lessee and so should not sway his decision, though he would warn Lizzy to keep an eye out for any bad behaviour during the times a father could not politely intrude on the ladies.

The investigator also noted Miss Bingley had set her cap for one Mr. Fitzwilliam Darcy, who reportedly had no interest in the lady. It was hinted he tolerated her only for the sake of his friendship with her brother.

Bennet knew the Darcy name well; Mr. Darcy was the nephew of Reggie and Elaine Fitzwilliam, the one they had always missed meeting during their trips to Snowhaven and Matlock House. From the information in the report, the older sister apparently followed the lead of the younger one, placating her to keep the peace.

After Phillips departed Longbourn once their discussion about the Bingleys was completed, Bennet joined his family. He told them about their new tenants and warned his family about the two sisters.

He chastised Lizzy mildly, all the while amused when she dubbed them *the superior sisters* before meeting them. Lizzy had gleaned from the report that Mr. Bingley's sisters believed themselves above almost everyone except the very top of the first circles, even though the sisters were naught but a tradesman's daughters.

CHAPTER 2

Resplendent in the blue regimentals of the Household Cavalry, Colonel Richard Fitzwilliam strutted into Whites Gentleman's Club and handed his great coat, hat, and gloves to the attendant on duty. His mind was pleasantly engaged, thinking about the young woman he had been courting—unofficially—for more than two years.

It was his intention to request a formal courtship on her nineteenth birthday, now only a few short weeks hence. Richard Fitzwilliam was hopelessly and irrevocably in love with Miss Mary Bennet. Her father, Thomas Bennet, was the best friend of his father, the Earl of Matlock. The families were so close they counted each other more as family than friends.

Mr. and Mrs. Bennet had told him as much as they would love for him to become their son, they wanted him to wait until Mary was nineteen before he declared himself. That way, Mary would have a year after her coming-out before he requested a courtship.

The wait was so they could be sure Mary would find her happiness where she currently believed it lay if her intent remained constant. Further, they had told the Colonel the courtship, and the subsequent engagement if they both decided on it, would be a minimum of six months each. Not normally a patient man, the Colonel had accepted those restrictions as his love for his raven-haired beauty, Mary Bennet, was deep. He would wait as long as her parents required to be able to ask for her hand.

Other than his parents, his brother, and his sister-in-law, no one in his family, not even his cousin Darcy—with whom he shared guardianship of Darcy's young sister, Georgiana—knew Richard Fitzwilliam was in love with Mary Bennet.

He was snapped out of his reverie when he saw his cousin's best friend, Charles Bingley, sitting and staring into space as he nursed a drink. Charles Bingley was the best natured of his cousin Darcy's small group of friends. Bingley always tried to see the best in everyone and every situation, which frequently reminded him of Jane Bennet, as she shared that trait.

The Colonel enjoyed Bingley's company and outlook on life; it was similar to his own. Bingley had an ebullient and affable character, the opposite of his sometimes dour and occasionally taciturn cousin Darcy.

The Colonel, who usually liked or tolerated everyone, had no time for Bingley's sisters, especially the younger one. He suspected the older sister was not as bad, and she only went along with the younger one to keep the peace.

They were daughters of a tradesman, which in and of itself was not an issue. The problem was the two sisters acted as if they believed themselves above almost everyone they encountered, when, in fact, their station was near the bottom of the social ladder, regardless of their wealth.

His dislike for the younger sister, Caroline, was deep. In his mind she lacked even physical beauty, her perfume was cloying and too generously applied. Her personality was the embodiment of those characteristics which most men detested; she was shrewish, a social climber, and an obvious fortune hunter. In addition, she had made the mistake of setting her cap at his cousin Darcy after she saw Pemberley for the first time; she was the only one who did not realise her desire would never be realised.

He could not hold the sister's behaviour against Bingley, as he did not choose who his relations were. How could he judge Bingley for his sisters when he had the dubious honour of having Lady Catherine de Bourgh as an aunt?

The Colonel walked over to Bingley, who rose to shake his hand and invited the Colonel to sit and have a drink with him. Once they had ordered, Richard noticed Bingley was not his normal affable self; he seemed worried.

Bingley greeted him with as much warmth as he could muster, saying, "Colonel, it has been a long time. How are you? I have not seen you since you returned from the continent. Congratulations on your promotion to full Colonel." He prattled on as he looked the Colonel up and down, seeking to find evidence of his injuries from the Battles of Badajoz during the Peninsular Campaign.

"Thank you, Bingley. It is gratifying to earn one's rank, not purchase it. As you can see, I am as well as can be expected. I have no visible wounds from my foray on the continent fighting the little tyrant's troops. I trust you are doing well. Have you seen Darcy lately, and is my cousin still in a dark mood?" Richard asked with concern for a cousin who was as much a brother to him as his brother Andrew, Viscount Hilldale.

Bingley's smile did not reach his eyes. Richard surmised that was because of his concern for Darcy. "His mood is as bad as I have ever seen it. He seems to carry the weight of the world on his shoulders. When I ask what is troubling him, all he says is it is a private family matter," Bingley related, then continued in a lighter vein, "other than worrying about Darce, I am well, thank you.

"I have just signed the lease for an estate in Hertfordshire. I was going to buy, but I was advised to lease first to get my feet wet. It is just more than twenty miles from

Town; proximity to Town was one of my requirements. The landlord's agent is a solicitor named Mr. Philips, who tells me the area is a pleasant one. We are to move in next week. When I went to sign the lease, I also heard tell there are some uncommonly pretty young ladies in the neighbourhood," he stated with a dreamy look, so much so Richard could practically see his visions of his next angel dancing in his mind's eye. The name Philips should have stirred the Colonel's memory, but his active mind skipped over it.

"Darcy is correct; it is a family matter. I hope he snaps out of his mood soon. As to your second piece of news, Bingley, I have never met anyone who falls in and out of love with an angel as fast as you do. I suggest, since you will be living in the area, that you be a little more circumspect before displaying the outward signs of falling in love only to find out again that it is not real love," Richard gently chastised him.

"That has only happened three—well, four—times. After the last time, when I was almost compromised by one of the harpies Caroline tried to foist on me, I have learnt my lesson. I will be on my guard and a great deal more careful in the future." After he thought about Darcy's reluctance for a moment, Bingley decided to extend an invitation to the Colonel. "If you have leave available, you should join us when we take possession of the house next week. It would be my supreme pleasure to host you since I have never been able to do so before. If you join us, perhaps Darcy will as well. He told me when I acquired an estate, he would help me, but just now he is not sure he will be able to join me.

"I told him if he does come, he should use his own carriage so he will not be forced into my sister's company for a four-hour carriage ride in cramped quarters. I extended the invitation to include Miss Darcy, although he said he doubted she could accompany him. Given how my sister fawns over both of the Darcys, I cannot say I blame Miss Darcy if she chooses to remain at Darcy House with Mrs. Annesley, even if her brother relents." He added as an afterthought, "I suspect Caroline is also the reason for Darcy's hesitancy. However, I move to the estate in less than a sennight and would appreciate his assistance," Bingley admitted.

"I am not sure I can get away by the time you plan to leave. I may be able to join you the following week, duty to King and country, you know," Richard drawled in an affected manner, full of put on self-importance and sporting a grin; then he sobered. "I am sorry if this is an impertinent or indecorous thing to ask, but do you realise the reason Darcy is hesitant is he cannot tolerate your sisters' behaviour anymore, and most especially Miss Bingley's?" Richard asked Bingley as delicately as he could. "As you yourself just hinted, that may be the principal reason he is thinking about not joining you, as I assume they are part of your family party."

He suspected Bingley was aware of his cousin's feelings on the subject, but he needed to know for sure. Richard knew his parent's best friends lived near Meryton in Hertfordshire, and he had been to their estate many times, but because the knowledge was so innate to him, he neglected to mention this nugget of information to Bingley or ask him for the name of the estate he was leasing.

"Yes," Bingley said, chagrined, "you are correct in your assumption; both my sisters and Hurst are coming with me. I also suspect what you pointed out about Caroline is the reason why Darcy is hedging about joining me. I need a hostess in order to entertain, and my sisters are my only options. Caroline has condescended to fill that office and take on the duties of mistress of the estate. My aim is to meet and entertain the surrounding neighbours. Without a hostess I cannot do that. So, as long as Caroline behaves and does not manage to alienate the neighbourhood, she will act as my hostess," Bingley sighed in resignation.

"If I am able to join you, I suspect my presence may

deflect attention from Darcy and make it easier for him to accept your invitation. My military mind can help us devise schemes to keep him away from your sisters. I am sorry, Bingley." Richard's unrepentant grin took the sting out of his words even as it showed he was not sorry in the slightest.

"You have no need to apologise. I am aware of Darcy's feelings and would appreciate your help. You are correct, it may make it easier for him to accept my invitation. I would like you to know you are welcome to come whether or not he accepts. I am loath to admit it, but your help in protecting him was one of my initial reasons for inviting you.

"When you are free from your duties and if you choose to come, send me a note, or just arrive. I will have a bedchamber waiting for you since it is my fervent hope you will be able to join us." Bingley noticed the time on the longcase clock against the wall and he used it as an excuse to end the uncomfortable conversation about his sisters. "I am sorry; I must away. I have business to attend to before I depart from London."

"Before you go, I have decided I will come and visit you, Bingley. I am sure General Atherton will spare me after my pressing duties have been completed. I will see Darcy later today and inform him as soon as I know the date the General can release me," Richard said as he settled into his chair with the ease of a man who knew his path forward.

"Thank you, Colonel. I look forward to hosting you and I hope Darcy will choose to come now as well," Bingley stated as he prepared to stand.

Bingley had not missed the moue of distaste on the Colonel's face when he mentioned his sisters. He knew their social-climbing ways, especially pronounced in his younger, unmarried sister Caroline, were only tolerated because of his friendship with Darcy and the Colonel.

He never understood where their pretentions and

high opinion of themselves came from. His older sister, Louisa, had never acted so until she began to capitulate to Caroline for the sake of peace. Bingley was sure, separated from Caroline's bad influence, Louisa would revert to her pleasant self. Like him, they were the progeny of a tradesman, and no matter how high they held their noses in the air and tried to ignore that fact; it would not change reality.

He was aware members of the *Ton* sneered at and mocked his sisters, and knew one day they would push Darcy beyond the limit of his patience, causing him to deliver a much-deserved set-down to Caroline.

Bingley was positive no matter what Caroline did, Darcy would never offer for her, nor would Bingley want him to settle for so unhappy a union for the rest of his life. Even if she engineered a compromise—and he knew she was scheming enough to attempt it—he would not force Darcy to marry her. Much to Caroline's dismay, should she attempt it, he would withhold his permission if Darcy's ideas of honour and duty overrode his good sense.

"I understand the situation clearly, Bingley. I thank you for your kind invitation." The words of the Colonel snapped him out of his wool-gathering, "I will inform you of the day I hope to arrive as soon as I know when I will have leave," the Colonel said.

Then Bingley stood, bowed to the Colonel, and went to the cloak room to retrieve his outerwear from the attendant. Bingley donned his hat and greatcoat, and with a flourish and a good-natured grin he was on his way.

~~~~~~~/~~~~~~~

The servants employed at Darcy House, from Mr. and Mrs. Killion, the housekeeper and butler, down to the maids and under-gardeners, were concerned. Their master, although sometimes reserved and taciturn, was now dour and melancholy. He had been so for the last four months, ever since he had accompanied Miss Georgiana Darcy back from Ramsgate without her companion, Mrs. Younge. He had always been the best master and landlord, so his behaviour and sudden fits of temper were entirely out of character.

They knew something had happened to significantly change the mood of both the master and his much younger sister. However, Darcy servants never gossiped; they went about their duties as unobtrusively as possible, and without asking questions.

As it had been for the last few months, Darcy House was as quiet as a mausoleum, the silence broken only occasionally by the shuffling feet of servants performing their duties as quietly as they were able to. The atmosphere was depressed and dark in the Darcy household, reflecting the mood of its master, Fitzwilliam Darcy. That mood, however, did not hide the fact Darcy House was grand. It was located in Mayfair, on the most exclusive Grosvenor Square, opposite Matlock House.

Mr. Killion and his wife made sure the servants knew there would be consequences if any of them made noise that disturbed the master and raised his ire; his temper now seemed to explode after the slightest provocation. The mood of Darcy House had not just become dark; it was as though an aura of depression had settled over the entire house. This master was no longer the one they had known and respected since his father passed.

The servants also noticed Miss Georgiana Darcy, who had always been shy, had now completely withdrawn and was willing to speak only with her brother or her new companion, Mrs. Annesley. On the few occasions she said something to anyone else, it was no more than a barely-heard monosyllable, spoken without lifting her eyes from her feet. Often, she would burst into tears spontaneously and bolt for her chambers for no reason they could detect.

~~~~~~~/~~~~~~~

Darcy, who had averted a near-disaster in Ramsgate by pure luck, saw only the negative after that event. He wore his blame like a cloak of shame rather than celebrating the fact he had saved his beloved sister.

He sat in his study reliving the event once again— as he did almost every hour of the day. Since his return, he not only replayed what happened, he imagined what almost happened. His mind attempted to pinpoint his faults. Darcy forced himself to accept the blame for all of his real and imagined failures, convinced he had done nothing correctly for years. As he had a hundred times before, he sat in his chair and allowed himself to wallow in these dark memories once again.

His business took far less time than he thought it would, he travelled to Ramsgate to visit Georgie and her companion, Mrs. Younge, two days earlier than expected. It was only by the grace of God disaster had been averted when he decided to surprise his young sister with an early arrival.

When he reached the rented house in Ramsgate, he noticed there was no footman on duty at the entrance. Unhappy with this lapse of duty, he was already annoyed when he rapped on the door.

Mrs. Younge, not the butler, opened the door. She went as white as a sheet when she saw him. Her shock and mortification at seeing her employer made him suspicious—and, thankfully, caused him to be in a greatly heightened state of alert. What he saw when he entered the drawing room had curdled his blood. He saw George Wickham—the dissolute debaucher, profligate, and wastrel—sitting far too close for propriety and holding the hand of his innocent young sister.

With a sneer on his face, Wickham informed Darcy that he and Georgiana were in love and engaged to be married. Darcy, knowing the libertine was only after his sister's fortune, explained the restrictions placed on her dowry to him. Not a penny would be released unless both he and her co-guardian, Colonel Richard Fitzwilliam, consented to the match.

After hearing her dowry of thirty thousand pounds—his object—would never be his, he made disparaging remarks about Georgiana, stating how distasteful it had been to pretend to love her. His words were intended to hurt, and they had the effect he desired on Georgiana. She burst into tears with huge racking sobs that did nothing but amuse the blackguard.

Darcy bit his tongue until it bled to keep the descriptive adjective about his former friend from escaping, then he continued his train of thought, allowing the memories to replay yet again.

Before Wickham left the house, Darcy warned him—in no uncertain terms—his debts would be called in and he would be sent to Marshalsea for the rest of his miserable, and probably short, life if he ever breathed a word about his sister to a living soul, or if he ever approached any member of the Darcy family again.

He also warned the dastard he should pray fervently that no word of what had happened in Ramsgate would ever be heard anywhere. In his fury and rage at having his revenge against Darcy thwarted, and because this latest get-rich scheme had been foiled, Wickham had quit the house, slammed the front door on his way out, mounted his horse, and had ridden away.

Darcy had talked to Georgie once her heart-rending sobs had ceased. It became clear to him, and to her, that she had been lied to and manipulated into believing herself in love.

He discovered Mrs. Younge was in league with Wickham. When Georgiana had been unsure about the propriety of spending time alone with Wickham, Mrs. Younge had assured her—more than that, encouraged her—telling her it was normal when one was planning on a life together, then she had helped plan the elopement with Georgiana's suitor—all without informing her charge's guardians.

It became crystal clear Georgie's companion had promoted Wickham's suit while discouraging Georgie from informing her brother about it. Georgiana's missives were being intercepted by Mrs. Younge; despite her companion's advice, Georgie had written to her guardians because she refused to lie to them, even by omission.

Mrs. Younge told her since George Wickham was an old family friend and her late father's godson, there was no breach of propriety. She told her charge her brother's lack of response indicated he agreed with her actions and would be happy for her.

Darcy threatened the malevolent Mrs. Younge with ruin and possible arrest for her part in the conspiracy, and dismissed her immediately—without pay or a character.

Later, he and Colonel Fitzwilliam discovered all of Mrs. Younge's references were forged; she was sent to them by Wickham to assist him in carrying out his planned revenge for the perceived, if unfounded, offences he felt Darcy had perpetrated against him.

Fitzwilliam Darcy—William to his family and close friends—sat alone in his study as the remembrance of that fateful day spun in his head. His time was spent berating himself for what he felt were his failures as a brother and a guardian.

His mood was as dark as it had been after the passing of his beloved parents. First his mother had passed, and then his father seven years later. Orphaned at two and twenty, he became master of a vast estate, a house in Town, and three smaller estates; he managed these holdings and all of the Darcy investments. Together with his co-guardian, Richard Fitzwilliam, he had been given the responsibility for raising his then ten-year-old sister.

Darcy knew he was unfit for company now, which was why he had been keeping to himself. He sat at his desk with his elbows resting on the surface and his head in his hands, massaging his temples in an attempt to minimize the constant deafening drumbeat in his head.

The fire had burned low in the grate and his study had cooled, but he did not notice or care. Bingley had visited that morning with the news he had at last found an estate close to Town to lease. He had asked Darcy to join him, which Darcy had previously assured him he would. Although he wanted to honour his word to Bingley, he could not manage residing in the same house with Caroline Bingley.

Georgiana had retired to her bedchamber after dinner, as she had every evening since their return. Persuading her to eat with him had been a victory of sorts. She no longer played her pianoforte; before his failure, it had been one of her favourite pastimes. She remained depressed and burst into tears at the slightest provocation.

~~~~~~~/~~~~~~~

Upstairs in her bedchamber, Georgiana Darcy, now almost sixteen, was crying herself to sleep—as she had every night since returning from Ramsgate. Her mortification and shame felt as heavy as if a mountain had fallen on her.

Her brother and Colonel Fitzwilliam had both told her the bulk of the blame was to be laid at George Wickham's feet, and the rest at Mrs. Younge's. However, no matter how many times William or Richard told her she was not at fault, she knew she was.

Georgiana wondered if they were contemplating returning her to the nursery, if so, she could not blame them. She could see the look of despair in her brother's eyes, and she knew it was disgust at her actions. It was no less than she deserved, after all she was disgusted by what she had done; how could William and Richard not be?

She was not aware William was blaming himself, not her. That she had not recovered was causing his feelings of guilt and despair, not what she interpreted as his disgust for her actions.

Uncle Reggie, Aunt Elaine, and her cousins Andrew and Marie had also told her it was not her fault, but Georgie did not believe them; she knew it was her fault.

She had willingly broken the rules of propriety. She had known what Mrs. Younge told her was not true. She should have waited for a reply from her brother before agreeing to any sort of courtship. She had been caught up in what she believed was romance and had ignored all the warning signs she now realised were there. Yes, she knew better now; hindsight was always clear, but at the time she had willingly let the two of them lie to her and manipulate her. She had, knowingly and wilfully, ignored many of the rules of propriety she had been taught.

She was aware of the sad truth now. All the lying, manipulating tormentor had wanted from her was to harm her honourable brother. Wickham desired to gain his revenge for perceived slights, and in the process gain her fortune of thirty thousand pounds. He would have gambled her dowry away, just as he had the funds her brother had given him already. He would probably have treated her worse than he did his horse.

Even had they eloped, Wickham would have gotten nothing, since her dowry would only be released if both of her guardians approved of the match. She was sure he would then have abandoned her out of spite, or tried to ransom her to her brother.

She remembered how, after hearing about the restrictions on her dowry, her loving suitor had denigrated her and walked out of the house with a sneer on his face, slamming the door in his anger.

Georgiana was filled with guilt and more sadness than she had known anyone could feel. She had almost brought infamy and dishonour to the Darcy and Fitzwilliam names. If not for her wonderful brother arriving when he did, she would have been utterly ruined.

Georgiana Darcy did not know how she could ever face anyone in her family again, never mind people outside of her family circle. She was sure they would see her guilt as plainly as if she were wearing a scarlet letter. They would all see through her; they would judge her; then, they would despise her.

She was now more shy than she had ever been. She heard one of the maids whisper to her new companion that she had gone from a shy young woman to a girl with no confidence at all. How had she made such a mess of her life at just fifteen?

CHAPTER 3

In his study, a brooding Fitzwilliam Darcy was second guessing his decisions yet again, as he did almost hourly.

'I should have called him out, not let him go with an admonition. Richard was correct, he should pay for what he did. Why did I intercede when Richard wanted to hunt him down and make him disappear? If I were not so worried about Georgiana's reputation—I hold over three thousand pounds of his debts purchased over the years; why did I let that damned wastrel go? Why did not I send him to a debtor's prison immediately?' He knew the answer even as he questioned himself again and again; he had made a snap decision, one he thought would be the best way to protect his sister's reputation.

His thoughts turned to his good friend Charles Bingley, who had visited him with a request earlier in the day. Were it Bingley alone, he would go without question. Under normal circumstances, Bingley would cheer him up, but today he had not been successful.

Although Bingley asked him what was troubling him, he had dismissed his friend's query. *'I dislike going back on my word, but how can I reside at his estate, where I will have to deal with the unwanted advances of Miss Caroline Bingley?'* At the best of times she was a trial, but now...

Darcy hated times when he had no occupation to take his mind from his failures. All his business had been completed for the day, and that of tomorrow and perhaps the day after. The only occupations he now had were dark thoughts and his liquor cabinet.

Although it was not in his character to over-imbibe, he had done so on a number of occasions during these last four months. He reached for the snifter of brandy on his desk and took a long swallow. He hated not being in control, but the drink dulled his mind and almost made him stop caring about his failures, if only for a short while.

He was aware he was not eating as he should, but his appetite was gone. He detested how Georgie had lost her hard-won confidence and constantly burst into tears, often before he so much as asked her how she was feeling.

No matter how many times he tried to convince her she was not to blame; the blame fell on a blackguard seducer almost twice her age—a man who had taken advantage of her tender heart, she refused to believe she was not the one at fault. He failed to realise the irony; she blamed herself for things she should not, just as he did.

He knew she still suffered, and he could not help her out of the melancholy into which she had sunk. He was at fault for not being a better guardian to her. He had not yet accepted he could have done no more; he had pushed that knowledge to the recesses of his consciousness.

Darcy had been proud when Georgiana had admitted some culpability in the scheme. She told him she had known better but had been caught up in what she believed was love. Before she knew what Wickham was, she had believed William would be happy for her. So deep was her belief in his approval, she had written to him—letters he never received.

He had tried to protect his sister by withholding information about George Wickham from her. In his mind, this was his worst failure; in trying to protect her sensibility and innocence, he had left her vulnerable because she did not have the knowledge which would have enabled her to withstand the lies, manipulation, and false charm employed against her.

In his misguided attempts to protect her, Darcy believed he had robbed his sister of the ability to recognise the signs of falsehood. In the depths of his despair, he failed to consider had Georgiana resisted, Wickham would have ruined her by force, kidnapped her, or both. The bastard might have done even worse to her.

Uncle Reggie and Aunt Elaine, the Earl and Countess of Matlock; cousins Andrew and Marie Fitzwilliam, Viscount and Viscountess Hilldale; and his cousin Colonel Richard Fitzwilliam had tried to tell him he was taking too much on himself. They attempted to convince him the fault lay squarely at the feet of Mrs. Younge and Wickham, and only on them.

They acknowledged Georgie had exercised poor judgement but given her age and the skill of the manipulator, they understood why she reacted as she had. Although he appreciated their kindness and attempted to see things as they did, he could not agree with them; neither could his sister.

Thank goodness everyone had agreed Lady Catherine de Bourgh was not to be told anything of the matter, under any circumstances. They knew she would attempt to use the information to bolster the myth she perpetuated that Darcy's mother, Lady Anne, had agreed Darcy was to marry his cousin Anne De Bourgh in order to unite the great estates of Pemberly in Derbyshire and Rosings Park in Kent.

Such an agreement had never been mentioned before his mother's death. Everyone in the family knew this was a lie, a fantasy created by Lady Catherine to control Rosings Park and to access Pemberley's coffers.

Darcy feared, should Lady Catherine learn what had happened, she would attempt to bring his sister under her control. However, his parents had made sure that would never happen. George Darcy not only vociferously refused

Lady Catherine; he had ordered her out of his house.

Both of William's parents had placed stipulations in their wills refuting Lady Catherine's claims. Further, Lady Anne had expressed her wishes in a letter to her brother Reggie, the Earl of Matlock and head of the family. In it, she made it clear neither she nor her husband had ever agreed to a match between their son and Catherine's daughter, and no one could claim they had.

They would never force their children to marry without love or against their inclination; neither favoured arranged marriages. Both their son and their daughter would have the freedom to find life partners they would respect and love. Lady Anne had told Darcy before she died that he was to marry for love, and only for love. Her only restriction was his choice should be, at least, the daughter of a gentleman. This was re-stated by his late father before he passed.

Although Rosings Park had belonged to Anne since her five and twentieth birthday, in order to justify retaining control of Anne's estate, Lady Catherine convinced the family Anne was too ill to manage her inheritance. When Anne reached the age when she might consider marriage, she insisted she had no interest whatsoever in marrying Darcy— but that never deterred Lady Catherine.

After her numerous requests to George and Lady Anne Darcy for a marriage contract had been rejected out of hand, Lady Catherine was displeased. She had always coveted Pemberley's vast wealth and believe the match she proposed would give her access to the Darcy fortune she lusted after. Her wish for Darcy to marry her daughter grew into an obsession, fuelled only by her greed.

The family was aware she was jealous of her sister, who had made a love match with George Darcy—and thereby gained a husband with one of the largest fortunes in the Kingdom. Lady Catherine's avarice now knew no bounds; however, she learned to remain silent about the match she desired while Fitzwilliam Darcy's parents were alive.

After her sister's untimely passing, she once again had the temerity to demand a marriage contract from her grieving husband, claiming Lady Anne had agreed to it—dismissing the fact both parents had rejected all of her previous requests.

Only days after George Darcy's funeral, Lady Catherine arrived at Pemberley for the purpose of assuming control of the house she wanted her daughter Anne to be mistress of. She was again seriously displeased when she was unceremoniously shown out and told everyone knew her claims of an agreement were false. She returned to Rosings Park forthwith.

After her return, she began parroting her delusion to anyone who would listen, thinking to force the issue. However, all who knew her were aware Lady Catherine was a fortune hunter disguised as an overbearing mother. Her current interest was in maintaining control over the fortune that now belonged to her daughter, not herself.

Everyone knew one day there would be a war of wills when the time came to remove Lady Catherine from her throne. Any who had seen her guilt-edged raised chair, the one she sat in when company was present, the one from which she dispensed unwanted advice, had dubbed it the throne.

She claimed absolute knowledge of any subject. She would have been horrified had she known nearly everyone knew she was usually wrong. Lady Catherine had little education and even fewer accomplishments. Her family never confided in her.

~~~~~~~/~~~~~~~

In lucid moments, Fitzwilliam Darcy knew he was unhappy with the trajectory his life had taken, but he did not know how to change course. Ever since Ramsgate he needed more and more liquor to relax, to dull his senses, and to quiet his mind. He had begun to hate himself for it.

Darcy was haunted continually by the realisation of his failures. He was unable to sleep; when he tried, there were nightmares. He had difficulty eating; food tasted like dirt in his mouth. He no longer took pleasure in the things that had previously given him enjoyment, not even in performing his duties.

Although he had failed to ensure his sister's wellbeing, he had kept the promise he had sworn to his parents—to remain celibate until marriage. This meant he did not have the physical outlets most men in his social circle did. He never smiled—unless he occasionally forced a smile for his sister—he was too angry with himself.

One bright hope in his life was that, after many interviews and an exacting confirmation of her characters, he and his co-guardian had hired a new companion for Georgiana, a Mrs. Helena Annesley. She, they had found, had genuine, impeccable references, and was born a gentlewoman.

Mrs Annesley had married at the age of sixteen and was widowed when her husband drowned after falling into a river while fishing. He had not been a good manager of their money; he had lost most of it in risky investments. His widow was left destitute, with no choice but to go into service.

Her previous employers were the Duke and Duchess of Bedford, both of whom had given her a glowing character. Their newly-married younger daughter told them she was only sorry she could not keep her companion with her after her marriage.

They related the entire story of what Georgiana had been through to Mrs. Annesley; it did not daunt her. Darcy and the Colonel were sure she would, eventually, be able to reach Georgiana—something they had both failed to do.

No matter what anyone said, including the voice in his head he ignored, Darcy knew it to be his fault alone. He had failed his father, his family, and his name by failing in his most basic duties.

He acknowledged God must have been with him that day. By pure chance he had reached Ramsgate before the elopement was to take place. Georgiana was now safe in her bedchamber at Darcy House.

Wickham had slunk away to lick his wounds after his latest scheme failed. The investigators Darcy had hired to locate the wastrel reported he had hidden in the bowels of London, in Seven Dials, where only the lowest of the low went to skulk in the shadows. There would be no help for Georgiana's manipulator if his cousin Richard ever got his hands on him.

Sitting in his study, he reminded himself, were his excellent father still living, he would never have allowed this to happen. It struck Darcy for the first time, that his father may have had some modicum of blame in this as well.

Blind to any of Wickham's faults, had not his father educated George as a gentleman? Had not his father ignored what he was told about him, saying he was but sowing his wild oats? Wickham had grown up expecting and demanding more and more from his father—and receiving it. For the first time since Ramsgate, seeds of doubt regarding his own culpability were sown.

~~~~~~~/~~~~~~~

After finishing his drink at White's the Colonel recovered his outerwear from an attendant, returned to his barracks, and asked to meet with his commanding officer, General Grant Atherton. He requested, and was granted, a leave of absence that would start the following Sunday. Armed with this knowledge, he headed to Darcy House after the completion of his duties.

Killion opened the door, took his outerwear, and confirmed the master was ensconced in his study. The Colonel did not have to ask about his cousin's mood; he could tell by the sombre feeling in the house.

The Colonel gave a perfunctory knock on the study door and entered, which he intended to do whether or not his cousin bade him enter. The study, much like everything else in Darcy's life, was neat and tidy, a reflection of his cousin's fastidious nature. Everything had its place. There were neat piles of documents on Darcy's desk, which the Colonel knew were organised by subject.

Darcy was sitting at his desk, deep in concentration and chewing on the end of his quill as he contemplated what to write next. Richard knew his cousin always carefully considered his words before he put pen to paper. His attention was fully captured by the words on the page before him.

The study was cold. The fire in the grate had been allowed to burn low. The Colonel was sure Darcy was oblivious to everything but his work and his dark thoughts and had not summoned a servant to make up the fire.

There were books shelved in the room; a few were neatly stacked on Darcy's desk, one lay open near his right hand. There was a spacious library next to the study, and although large and well stocked, it was nothing to the one at Pemberley.

Knowing Darcy would ignore him until he had completed his current task, the Colonel helped himself to a glass of Darcy's best port from a decanter on the sideboard, then spread himself out on a settee below the window, propping his feet up on the armrest—knowing it would bother his ever-proper cousin once he noticed it. He lounged patiently there, allowing himself the luxury of wool-gathering while Darcy finished his correspondence.

Little more than fifteen minutes later, Darcy acknowledged him gruffly, stood, and poured himself a glass of port as well. The Colonel noticed but did not comment on the almost empty snifter on the desk that still had traces of brandy in it. He also took note of the level of liquid in the bottles on the sideboard; they were much lower than normal.

As Darcy sat back down in his oversized desk chair, the Colonel looked at and assessed his younger cousin. He did not berate the man, but he had to check himself before he did; Darcy should not have allowed himself to descend into the condition he saw before him. The man sitting opposite him was a far cry from the fastidious cousin he was used to seeing.

He had never seen Darcy so unkempt, and he was positively gaunt! Darcy's appearance was much altered; his clothes hung loosely on him. The Colonel surmised Darcy had lost weight by failing to eat properly.

The Colonel noticed the dark rings under his eyes. Darcy also appeared not to have slept well. He could understand why—his cousin probably had nightmares about what might have happened at Ramsgate. He seemed a shadow of his former self. What worried Richard Fitzwilliam most were the emotions of despair and defeat that radiated from his cousin.

Darcy's proud and noble mien had been replaced by slumped shoulders. Normally impeccably dressed, his cousin was dishevelled. He seemed like a man ready to give up.

Richard recognised the look; he had seen the same hopeless look on his own soldiers and enemy soldiers when all appeared lost and defeat on the battlefield seemed imminent. He had never before seen his cousin so lost in despair, not even after the deaths of each of his parents. His cousin was not living; he was just going through the motions.

The Colonel knew if he asked directly his cousin would not be forthcoming, so he talked of business first. "William, have you checked on your investments with Gardiner lately? I know father is overjoyed at the returns he has been receiving, as am I."

It seemed to distract his cousin momentarily as he focused and answered, "I could not be happier with my returns. I know you invest as much as you can with Gardiner as well, and I suspect you are not the poor second son we often hear tales of woe about."

"Very true, William," Richard said. He could not help noticing that although his cousin answered he was still far away, so he tried another subject. "William, did you notice Lord Blake sold his townhouse across the square from you? Do you know who purchased it? What a waste to lose his family's fortune in games of chance."

"No, Richard; I have no idea who purchased it," Darcy replied, his tone still distracted and distant.

"William, what is going on with you?" the Colonel demanded, deciding it was high time to be direct.

"Nothing..." Darcy began to reply.

The Colonel would have nothing to do with his lies and said, "I am not blind, William. I have known you all your life. You are like a brother to me, and I can see you are not yourself."

"I said nothing, Fitzwilliam!" Darcy spat out as he pounded the arms of his chair in obvious pain and frustration, his fists so clenched that his knuckles were white.

Darcy only called him by his last name when he was perturbed or angry. "Deny it all you like, but I know you are still blaming yourself over what almost happened in Ramsgate. You are not her sole guardian, and I was duped by

Mrs. Younge as well. Imagine what would have happened to poor Georgie if you had not arrived when you did?"

"Enough Richard! I do not want to discuss this now," Darcy growled.

Richard knew when not to push his cousin, so he backed off. He drained his port and got up to refill it. "I met Bingley at White's earlier today. He informed me you are debating whether or not to assist him when he settles at the estate he leased. It is close to London, he says. I thought you promised to assist him when he made a foray into estate management. Are you going to go with him to make sure he does not burn it down, or something equally negligent?" Richard said, attempting to lighten his cousin's mood with humour.

Darcy relaxed somewhat, his hands returning to a normal colour as he opened the fists he had not realised he made. *'The tease must have helped some,'* Richard thought, relieved he had lowered his cousin's stress level even slightly.

"Bingley has never managed an estate before. It was his parents' wish he purchase an estate and allow his family to leave their roots in trade behind. Bingley's parents were never able to make their dream a reality due to their untimely death. In his father's will, he directed that on his passing if there was not yet a Bingley estate, his son was to be charged with making it a reality.

"Most of Bingley's father's estate was tied up in his majority stake in Bingley Coach Works. Bingley sold his stake in the business for a handsome profit. Now that the sale has been finalised and the funds transferred, the major portion of Bingley's inheritance is unfettered and liquid, so Bingley has decided to try his hand at estate management."

Darcy did not mention the name of the estate being leased, and the Colonel did not bother to ask. If the Colonel had been aware of that information, he would have known exactly where the estate was located, and who the landlord was.

Darcy continued on, "I am sure you know why I hesitate to assist him, even though I had told him I would help him after he took a lease. Normally, I would not fail to keep my word. However, as you know, I cannot bear to torture myself further by being in close company with Caroline Bingley."

"I know that, Cousin. When I spoke with him I could tell he knows why you are hesitant. He is aware of the nightmare that is Miss Bingley. I may have devised a solution that will make it possible for you to keep your word. By the way, I almost forgot when Bingley told me that he is leasing, He did not tell me his landlord's name. I thought his father's will charged him with purchasing an estate."

"He wanted to jump right in and buy an estate sight unseen, but he may have been advised to lease before taking the irrevocable step of purchasing an estate. This will get his feet wet; he can learn about estate management before he takes on the responsibility of ownership.

"I understand the landlord of the estate he is leasing has no interest in selling. Bingley does not know who the landlord is, so he could not ask him about purchasing if he wished to. He is only able to deal with the owner's solicitor."

"Were you the one who advised him to lease first, William?" Richard said, attempting not to smirk. While both he and Bingley appreciated Darcy's advice, he sometimes dispensed it without being asked.

"I was," Darcy said, nodding solemnly.

"I think it was good advice; we both know how impulsive he can be. I am glad you care about him enough to advise him, for I sometimes think of him as a little puppy." Richard said.

"It was my pleasure to advise him. I have experience in

this area, and he asked for my advice!" Darcy snapped.

Richard could see his cousin's mood was growing dark again. "William, I hope it will not be long before Bingley has the self-confidence to make his own decisions."

As his cousin had not been in a good mood since Ramsgate, the Colonel knew he could not push Darcy too hard on that subject; it might cause an explosion of anger.

Although he had tried to share the blame for hiring Mrs. Younge's, attempting to shoulder some of the responsibility for what had almost occurred, his cousin still refused to see the truth of the matter; he blamed only himself.

Regardless of how many times Richard reminded Darcy that they shared guardianship of Georgie, and blame should be apportioned equally between them, William refused to allow Richard any share of the blame. Knowing William was not ready for that discussion once again, he decided to distract him instead.

"Bingley informed me when he extended the invitation to you and Georgie to join him at his new estate, you replied in the negative for Georgie and doubtful for yourself. He explained why he has no choice but to bring his sisters, and his reasoning is sound. I wonder if that social-climbing harpy will ever understand she will never be the mistress of Pemberley, no matter what tactics she employs. Bingley understands your hesitation to accept his invitation but, as I said earlier, I have an offer for you."

"What offer could you have, Richard?" Darcy asked wearily. As he asked, he remembered the harridan's first visit to his beloved home.

From the moment the shrew alighted in front of Pemberley, overdressed and reeking of perfume applied too liberally, he had seen her beady eyes grow large as she calculated the worth of his estate.

What avarice! This tradesman's daughter seemed to think she would be the next mistress of Pemberley. Even his servants soon learned she thought of herself as inhabiting the first circles. Anyone with eyes could see she had her cap firmly set at the master of the estate.

At first Hannah Reynolds, his long-time and respected housekeeper, was as worried as Pemberley's servants that her master would be caught in the clutches of the deceitful woman, but they all soon saw the disdain he felt for the harridan. Then she, and all of his servants, had breathed easier.

He would never make her mistress of his homes, not under any circumstances. The only one who did not realise Mr. Darcy had no interest in her was the woman herself—perhaps she merely did not wish to see it.

Darcy had almost thrown her out of Pemberley then. He had made sure she would never be invited there again.

"William, where did you go?" Richard broke into his reverie. "Never mind! This afternoon Bingley also invited me to visit his estate. I have spoken to General Atherton, and he has granted me leave, starting the Sunday after the date Bingley wants you to join him. That would mean you would be there without me only five days. Both you and Georgie can go safely now since I will arrive to help you less than a sennight later. I am sure you are capable of fending off the harpy yourself for five days."

"That will make it easier for me to go, but I still do not believe it would be good for Georgie to come with me, Richard. Since Ramsgate she has withdrawn into herself. The presence of that harpy would be detrimental to her recovery; she still hasn't recovered much at all. It has nothing to do with my not wanting her with me," he said with a pained expression, knowing Georgie would assume that to be the reason. "You know she detests the attention Miss Bingley pays her. She also hates watching the shrew stalk me, staking a claim on my time and attention—because Georgie knows how much I hate it myself. Right now, having to tolerate Miss Bingley would be more damaging than ever to Georgie.

"She would be unable to support me as she might wish, because she has lost what little self-confidence she had." Darcy grimaced, thinking of Georgie's suffering, then said, "I have to admit that the one time she did—before Ramsgate—she made me the proudest of brothers.

"She was calm when she told Bingley's sister, who had made one of her uninvited visits, she was sorry she could not visit with her because it was time for me to take her walking in the park. I had promised to walk with her after I completed my business for the day. When Miss Bingley insisted she would join us, Georgie told her that we had matters to discuss between brother and sister. The harridan had no option but to depart with a sour look on her countenance. My little sister did not lie; we discussed purchasing new gloves for her to match her pelisse." Darcy almost forgot himself and smiled at the memory.

"You know, William, part of our error, and I mean ours, not yours, was treating Georgie like a delicate flower and not trusting her with information we thought her sensibilities could not handle—like the truth about Wickham." He saw William was about to object, but he stayed him with his hand and continued. "I have a suggestion so Georgie would not have to be there without both of us. If you agree, I will bring Georgie with me when I travel to Bingley's estate. That would mean she would not have to endure Bingley's sisters on her own before I arrive to reinforce you.

"Besides, we know you will don your mask and avoid the shrew as much as possible. I will be there to keep Georgie company. I pledge if you cannot be with her, I will. That way she will never be alone with the Bingley sisters." Richard smirked, not missing the scowl on Darcy's face at the mention of the superior sisters. "I have not spent much time with Georgie these past few years; I was away fighting for King and Country. I often feel like an absentee co-guardian, so let me bring her and have the pleasure of spending time with both of you, which is as it should be. By the way, Hertfordshire makes me think of Mr. Thomas Bennet, my father's best friend. I wonder if he lives in the area?"

"You cannot be blamed for being away doing your duty to King and Country, Richard, and it is not like you begged the little tyrant to invade the continent with no justification but to satisfy his ego by building an empire in Europe, risking the lives of many. We are all so relieved you returned to us with naught but minor injuries," Darcy reminded him with a smile that was, for the first time today, not forced. Darcy had missed, however, what Richard had said about his uncle's best friend.

Darcy had heard many good things about the Bennets from the Fitzwilliams over the years but had never had the pleasure of meeting them. He and the Bennets never seemed to be at Snowhaven or in Town at the same time. He was unaware of the connection between Edward Gardiner and the Bennets. Neither did he know his cousin was in love with one of the Bennet girls.

"So, what do you say? I am going to come anyway, so let me bring Georgie with me. I may have to overrule you as a guardian if you say no without good cause. This ensures neither you nor Georgie will be defenceless in the forthcoming battle for survival against the feared Bingley sisters. I just remembered something Bingley said to me. He told me my help in diverting his sister away from you was part of his reason for wanting me to join him in Hertfordshire," Richard said, grinning.

Darcy smiled again, and this time it almost reached his eyes. "Good for Bingley! He sees the reality that is his sister. To be honest, I would love to see you use your impressive skills to help me, and I know Georgie would relish more time with you. It is a pity there are no young women her age in the area; that would give us additional excuses to keep her away from the Bingley sisters." The last was said softly, almost wistfully, so Richard did not catch what his cousin had said.

If he had, he would have told Darcy that he was acquainted with genteel and accomplished young women in Hertfordshire, and one who had held his heart for years now. Just how close they lived to Bingley's leased estate he did not know yet, but would soon find out.

"I have so much saved up from my time on the continent, I have been allowed six weeks leave. However, I am sure if I need it, my general will not deny my request for extended leave.

"I must see Edward Gardiner to go over my investment portfolio, but other than that and my duties, I do not currently have much to do. As you will not be here, I will look in on Georgie and Mrs. Annesley often. Georgie, Mrs. Annesley, and I will join you a week after you arrive, on Monday morning."

"Please pass on my warmest regards to Mr. and Mrs. Gardiner and their children." Darcy offered sincerely; it was the warmest speech Fitzwilliam had heard from his cousin in weeks.

"I will pass on your regards when I see Gardiner on the morrow, William. Do try to buck up." The Colonel felt this was a good resolution. Mayhap concentrating on helping Bingley and being in the country would help Darcy to regain his equanimity. Then his cousin might throw off the crushing weight of guilt he was carrying, all caused by the actions of others he could not have foreseen. He was happy to finally see a little of the old Darcy emerge as they discussed their plans.

When they were in the vicinity, he would not be averse to visiting a certain young lady again. He hoped the Bennets were close by, although no distance was too great to ride to see his Mary. Hertfordshire was not such a large shire that it would be a hardship to visit her, no matter the distance. She was to turn nineteen soon, and he would then request a courtship from her and permission from her parents.

Darcy sent a message via courier to Bingley, who was staying at the Hurst townhouse, to inform him that he was accepting the invitation and would arrive later in the same day that Bingley was to arrive. He also informed Bingley the Colonel and his sister would be joining them a few days later.

Bingley's younger sister loudly lamented the fact Mr. Darcy was not travelling with them to the backwater county where her brother was taking them. Bingley, rather than inform her Darcy had almost declined the invitation due to her presence, went into Hurst's study, leaving a pinch-faced Miss Bingley to her own devices.

~~~~~~~/~~~~~~~

On the appointed day, a Darcy coach left Darcy House and journeyed to Bingley's newly-leased estate in Hertfordshire, carrying both Darcy and his valet, Carstens.

Bingley had not bothered to pass on his sister's entreaty for Darcy to travel with them in their coach, no matter how many times Caroline beseeched him to do so.

He was aware Darcy would never countenance travelling in the same carriage as his sister. Considering Darcy's current surliness, however, he might have delivered the set-down his sister desperately needed. The Bingley coach departed early that morning, but Darcy had business to attend to before his departure, and so began his journey after midday.

Before he departed, Darcy left a note for his cousin with direction to Netherfield Park, the estate Bingley had leased. Colonel Richard Fitzwilliam, after reading the note some hours later, was ecstatic. He would be but three miles from his beloved and her well-loved family, and would be staying in a house they owned.

Darcy appreciated that Bingley understood his reason to avoid being trapped in a coach with Caroline Bingley, even though the journey would be for a little more than twenty miles on good road.

Darcy was overjoyed his sister was excited about this trip. Georgie was looking forward to something for the first time since Ramsgate. She prayed this change of scenery would lighten her brother's spirits. She was also delighted that Richard would be there to help shield her from the Bingley sisters, especially the disingenuous Caroline Bingley.

CHAPTER 4

Mr. Thomas Bennet, the largest landholder in the area, rode to Netherfield Park mounted on a fine piece of horseflesh, his stallion Apollo. He intended to be there to welcome the Bingleys and Hursts to the neighbourhood when they arrived this afternoon.

The Bingleys were not aware Netherfield Park belonged to the Bennets, although Thomas Bennet intended to disclose that fact to him soon.

After he was welcomed into the drawing room by Mr. Bingley, he saw Bingley's brother-in-law, Harold Hurst, snoring on a chaise, and his sisters with their noses in the air. Bennet smiled to himself, realising Lizzy had aptly named them the superior sisters, even though they were anything but superior.

After waking his brother-in-law, Bingley shook Bennet's hand. "My friend, Mr. Darcy, will arrive later today. His sister, Miss Georgiana Darcy, and his cousin, the Honourable Colonel Richard Fitzwilliam, will join us on Monday." Bingley offered a genuine, easy smile. "Richard is a Colonel in the regulars and the son of Lord Matlock," he disclosed affably.

"Yes, I know Richard, the Earl, Reginald Fitzwilliam, and the rest of his family well. Reggie and I were at school together. He is one of my best friends, as is his family to mine. My wife and Elaine Fitzwilliam correspond regularly," Bennet related as he inclined his head.

Miss Bingley had never learnt, and likely never would, given her age, that when angered she was not wise. She often lacked any sense or decorum and never understood the only person she injured with her rude and cutting comments was herself.

She was already in a bad mood because her brother had refused to persuade Mr. Darcy to ride with them to Netherfield Park. She spoke snidely to their guest, not bothering to offer him the courtesy due a gentleman, regardless of what she thought of his means.

"How dare you refer to an earl and his countess so familiarly? We are close to the family and know he would never allow an insignificant country nobody of no fortune or standing to address him so," Miss Bingley stated in her grating voice.

She conveniently ignored the fact Lord Matlock and his family had steadfastly refused to be in her company or to be introduced to her. She believed they were merely waiting for Mr. Darcy to propose to her before they did so.

"The pretentions you have, claiming a connection with Lord and Lady Matlock and their family!" Miss Bingley added in a derisive and mocking tone, "What grasping, insignificant people you are. I cannot believe your temerity or your blatant attempt at social climbing. You should be aware you are in company with your betters," Miss Bingley sneered.

"Caroline," Bingley chastised her in a slightly elevated tone due to company in the room. He was about to say more when Mr. Bennet raised his hand to stop him.

Bingley and Mr. and Mrs. Hurst were mortified, but after Mr. Bennet's sign for them to be silent for now, they did not say anything to the shrew.

"So, Miss Bingley," Bennet stood and faced her calmly, "you, a tradesman's daughter, thinks she knows who my friends are and how I am allowed to address them? Just when did the spawn of a tradesman become higher than a landed gentleman?" he asked as easily as he would ask his daughters for a cup of coffee. He enjoyed watching the shrew change colours, in a pallet of reds and purples. Without guilt, he continued his line of conversation.

"Mayhap you can tell me, with your *superior* knowledge, how many times you have been hosted at one of the Earl and Countess's residences? How many times they have stayed at your estate? You did not grow up on an estate, did you? Your reputation as a social-climbing shrew has preceded you, Miss Bingley. I see that, in the flesh, you do not disappoint." Bennet then waited calmly.

"How dare you speak to your betters in such a way you..." she screeched, not only ignoring the fact Bennet was above her as a landed gentleman but was her brother's guest. "You, you, worthless nobody! I myself have twenty thousand pounds, which is more than an insignificant owner of an unheard-of estate will see in his lifetime!" The enraged women spat out.

As she finished her diatribe, Miss Bingley, whose face had turned almost purple with rage, looked for support in the room. She found none, not even from her sister who was looking on in mortification. She spat some expletives that would be harsh even to the ears of sailors and sashayed from the room.

"Mr. Bingley, I beseech you to accept my apology. I should have held my tongue, but having someone denigrate me and mine without knowing anything about me and my family, and assuming they know better than I about the oldest friendship I have, did not allow me to remain silent." Bennet looked at Bingley contritely.

"Mr. Bennet, if there is an apology to be made it is on behalf of my sister's unfounded comments, and it will come from me. Please do not judge the rest of us based on her actions. If she had any sense, she would know a guest should never have been treated so. I am ashamed for her most unladylike outburst." Bingley winced visibly as he faced the elder gentleman.

"I will not hold it against you, Mr. Bingley, but I suggest you make sure both of your sisters understand," he stated while looking directly at Louisa, "that if there is a repeat of this kind of behaviour, it will not be good for their future in society. One word from me to Elaine—Lady Matlock to you—and her daughter Marie—Lady Hilldale to you—and anyone who dares to behave in this manner will be irrevocably ruined in society.

"This is not a threat I make lightly. I will not abide your sisters harming any of my children or my neighbours, either physically or emotionally. Based on what I have seen here, Miss Bingley needs serious counselling, not to mention a reminder of her duties as a hostess and what her own roots are," Bennet stated with the ease of a gentleman with an understanding of life, with all its disappointments and joys.

After Mr. Bennet admonished Bingley about his sister Caroline, Bingley's mind drifted back to when she was a sweet, considerate girl.

Their father began as a modest tradesman but built a substantial fortune with his carriage works. As their fortune grew, Bingley saw his formerly-amiable sisters take on airs and graces, thinking themselves above the people in their circle.

Their parents did not encourage this behaviour, but neither did they discourage it. They indulged and spoilt their daughters, especially Caroline. Louisa was the first to be sent to an exclusive seminary in London, followed a year later by Caroline.

There the sisters were snubbed for being a tradesman's daughters. Being snubbed by daughters of the gentry, who made up the majority of the school's students, changed both sisters—

especially Caroline. They began to emulate the haughty attitudes displayed by those students; somehow, Caroline had convinced herself they should be considered as members of the Ton, not merely a tradesman's daughters. Louisa went along with her to keep the peace.

When Louisa was nineteen, their father arranged her marriage to Harold Hurst, whose family had a small estate in Yorkshire and was willing to allow their son and heir to marry a girl with roots in trade. They had needed the infusion of funds that Louisa's dowry of twenty thousand pounds would bring to them.

After a short courtship and engagement, Louisa married Mr. Hurst, a gentlemen, even though his family was not from the first circles. Caroline was disgusted Louisa had settled for a gentleman from such a low circle, ignoring the fact the match had been arranged by their father.

Miss Bingley vowed to marry a gentleman from the first circles, the wealthier the better. If he had a title, so much the better. By now, she had deluded herself into believing a man of that circle would lower himself to marry the daughter of a tradesman.

Some men might, but only if they were in dire financial straits. Even then, they would be able to find better options than a woman with the stench of trade still so fresh.

Bingley became friends with Darcy after he protected Bingley from a group of bullies attacking him for being a tradesman's son during his first year at Cambridge. He was two years behind Darcy, and they were opposites in status and outlooks on life.

Darcy was serious, stoic, and taciturn; Bingley was ebullient and outgoing. Despite that, or mayhap because of it, they became fast friends. The scion of many generations of landed gentlemen and the son of a tradesman had become best friends almost instantly. Bingley was invited to Pemberley for the summer break one year; the invitation had been extended to his family as well, so to Pemberley the Hursts and Bingleys went.

After seeing Pemberley and meeting his friend Darcy, Caroline immediately set her cap for his friend, or more accurately for his wealth and social position. Her behaviour on that first visit had almost caused her to be sent away from the estate after two days.

Darcy had endured her behaviour out of politeness, but Bingley knew his friend hated the excessive praise of his estate, his sister, and himself. After that, there were no more invitations to Pemberley that included his family; all subsequent invitations expressly stated they were for himself alone.

As Bingley's consciousness returned to the present, he looked at his new neighbour and nodded. "You have my promise, Mr. Bennet, that my sister will behave, or she will be sent to Scarborough for a long—or permanent—sojourn with our spinster aunt," he vowed.

Louisa Hurst winced but tried not to react. She knew she would be having a contentious discussion with her headstrong younger sister. If Caroline refused to heed her, she would be on her own. Louisa would not sacrifice her place in society for Caroline.

She had always indulged Caroline to keep the peace, even to the detriment of her relationship with her husband. The price would be too high to pay this time. She could see in this instance; Caroline had finally gone too far. She noticed Mr. Bennet's clothes were very fine, and were form-fitting and tailored just as those worn by members of the *Ton*.

There was no way he was a man of little standing and no fortune as Caroline had believed and expounded during her tirade. Reasoning no one would claim a non-existent connection other than her sister, who regularly lied about hers, she decided that were Caroline to cause any more trouble, she would no longer support her. Louisa determined it was high time she grew a backbone and stood up to Caroline rather than continuously placating the youngest Bingley.

After Mr. Bennet left, Bingley called a footman and had him escort Caroline back to the drawing room. As soon as she entered, he gestured for her to sit on the settee. "Caroline, how could you?" he demanded.

"Me!" She shrieked, never sounding more like a harridan. Me? I did not do anything wrong. That country lowlife insulted me, and no one defended me! You should all be ashamed of yourselves!" she shrieked in her high-pitched voice.

Before her brother could answer, Mrs. Hurst spoke up, to the surprise of both her brother and her husband. "Shut up, Caroline," she spat out, secretly gloating when her sister looked shocked. "For too long I have sat by and allowed you to persist in this delusion that you are higher in society than those that are, in fact, far higher than ourselves.

"Besides being intimate with the Matlocks and the rest of the Fitzwilliams, Mr. Bennet is a land-owning gentleman. As such, he is far above you, me, and Charles. He did not seem to judge us for being so far below him. He even wished to be in our company—except for you. Did you not notice his clothes? Are you so blind you think our fortune and our seminary education is what counts?"

Before Caroline could spew her vitriol, Louisa continued as if she had not known Caroline wanted to respond. "It is birth that counts. None of your airs or graces will ever change the fact you are naught but a tradesman's daughter, just as I am, and Charles is the son of one. In this you are on your own. If you ruin yourself, you will ruin yourself alone. Mr. Bennet told us if there is one more problem from you he will inform Lady Matlock and you will be ruined in society forever."

"Lady Matlock indeed! She would never deign to associate with country bumpkins like the Bennets. He is nothing but a name-dropping nobody and he is a liar!" Caroline retorted, then lifted her nose in the air before she rose and left, convinced as she always was that she was correct.

Her brother and sister looked on as she stormed out, knowing the only way she would learn would be the hard way. "No, Caroline, the only name-dropping, social-climbing liar we know is you," Bingley said quietly to himself.

"I am proud of you, my dear." Mr. Hurst smiled at his wife as he patted her hand.

"I appreciate you saying so, Mr. Hurst, but what do you mean?" She frowned, thinking she had just made an embarrassing scene.

"Louisa, when I married you, I loved spending time with you, but the more your sister was around, the more distance opened between us. I have been disappointed by the way you placate her rather than following your own good sense, which I know you possess.

"She is a shrew, and if you knew how men speak about her, you would be more ashamed of her than you are now. My dear, I am not asleep when you see me reclining in drawing rooms, and I do not drink the amount people think I do. I pretend to drink and sleep to avoid interacting with Caroline! It has gotten to the point I was about to give you a choice, her or me. Luckily, you seem to have made the correct choice on your own." He chuckled at her surprise.

"You would have left me if I chose Caroline?" She stared at him in fear and surprise.

"Yes, Louisa, although it would have pained me. I long have hoped you would come to your senses; if you had not done so soon, I would have separated from you permanently," Mr. Hurst said, edging closer to his wife as she grew upset.

"B-B-But I thought you loved me, Harold," she whispered as big tears rolled down her cheeks, realising what her sister almost cost her.

"It is not a question of love, Louisa. I do love you, but I did not like the person you had transformed into, always deferring to Caroline. Even though ours was an arranged marriage, I came to love the woman I married, the same one I saw again just now when she finally took her sister to task. Better late than never." He looked at her with a smile and a twinkle she had not seen in his eyes for too long, realising just how much she had missed it. Louisa Hurst thanked God for the strength He granted her, enabling her to stand up to her younger sister, finally.

"Sister, I always knew you were intelligent and knew your own mind, so I never understood why you bowed to Caroline's wishes and fed her delusion she would become Mrs. Darcy." Bingley smiled at the sister he, too, had missed.

"Charles, I know it was not the right thing to do, but I found it more peaceful. You know how she is when she does not get what she wants. I do know it was wrong, and I am so sorry. Will you both forgive me, please? I did not see the harm in her chasing Mr. Darcy, but I admit she has gone too far in her obsession." Louisa looked from her husband to her brother.

"Darcy does not just find her annoying, he dislikes her intensely. He will never offer for her, even if she is ill advised enough to try and compromise him. I would absolutely support him if she tried to do so. He hates that both of you use his name to gain entry to society events. You may have noticed any invitations that include my sisters are now few and far between, have you not?" Charles pressed, needing Louisa to understand how much damage had been done to their standing, and that some could yet be avoided.

"I had noticed, Charles; why is that?" Mrs. Hurst asked softly, then nodded in resignation. "Is it because of her constant pursuit of Mr. Darcy?"

"No, but it is simple. Darcy has let it be known although he is my friend, he has never given leave for anyone to use his name to gain entry to the ton and any rumour circulating about the possibility of his marrying Caroline is false." Bingley frowned, realising the damage his younger sister had wrought had almost ruined them in society. There was still time to repair the damage she had done, but she could not be allowed to continue to act as she had. He intended to make sure she did not.

Louisa's lips made a perfect "O" after she understood how close she had come to committing social suicide. She decided she would never again defer to Caroline and looked forward to rebuilding the relationship with the husband she had come to love.

~~~~~~~/~~~~~~~

When Bennet returned home, there were five expectant female faces waiting for him in the drawing room. "What are you and your daughters waiting for, Fanny?" he asked with a smile, knowing full well what they wanted to know.

"Papa!" Kitty whined.

"Miss Catherine, ladies do not whine," Mrs. Chandler rebuked her gently with a smile on her face as she sat in a corner doing needlework.

"I will not keep you in suspense," Bennet chuckled. "Mr. Bingley is a very affable young man. His brother Mr. Hurst was asleep when I arrived and had to be woken and never said a word, so I have no idea what he is like. But the sisters! I can attest one sister thinks herself superior but has the manners and vocabulary of a sailor. I did not wish to do so, but I was forced to give her a set-down. The older sister had the good sense to refrain from speaking and seemed ashamed of the younger's behaviour, so there is hope for her yet."

"Papa, what did she do?" Lizzy asked with an inquisitive look on her face.

"Bingley mentioned his friend Mr. Darcy would be joining him and that Mr. Darcy's sister and his cousin Colonel Fitzwilliam will be arriving on Monday." He winked at Fanny as Mary jolted and looked up at him with wide, hopeful eyes he pretended not to see.

"Richard is coming?" the girls chorused. Mary's eyes quickly changed to a dreamy look as she thought about the man she loved.

"Correct," affirmed Bennet "When he mentioned this, I told them that Reggie was one of my best friends and Miss Caroline Bingley thought it was her duty to take me to task on the manner in which I addressed my friend." Bennet smirked playfully.

"She did not!" was the chorus of incredulous female voices.

"She most certainly did. I took it upon myself to point out our societal differences from the daughter of a tradesman, and I told the rest after she exited from the room that I would speak with Elaine and Marie about her if she did not behave herself. I am of the opinion she will be unable to amend her behaviour. It probably will be necessary to put her in her place," Bennet stated with resignation.

"Mayhap I was wrong in naming them the superior sisters;" Lizzy said slyly, "it should be the self-proclaimed superior sister!" This started giggles and laughter in the room; once they died down, the Bennet matriarch grew serious and addressed her family.

"Then she will pay the price and it will be on her head," Fanny Bennet pointed out. "Elaine and Marie will not stand for that kind of behaviour as they consider us family; neither would I stand for any slight to the Fitzwilliams."

Fanny tensed in resolve and Bennet grinned, a small part of him hoping that the next time Miss Bingley slighted them his Fanny would be within hearing of it so he would be able to witness his wife taking the harridan to task.

~~~~~~~/~~~~~~~

Darcy arrived at Netherfield Park just as the sun was setting. Bingley and his hostess, Miss Bingley, were waiting on the front steps to welcome him. A footman took his trunk off the carriage and to his room so his valet, Carstens, could unpack for him.

Darcy was unsurprised when Miss Bingley flew down the stairs and attached her talons to his arm. She appeared surprised when Darcy physically removed her hand and stepped away from her. She did not understand why he pushed her away, she, the perfect candidate for Pemberley's mistress.

'*Mayhap he is tired from the trip and has been upset by being forced to travel to this backwater country,*' she told herself, conveniently forgetting two salient facts: first, she had been told more times than memory would serve that Darcy did not like her and only tolerated her to be polite and second, Darcy himself spent the bulk of his time at Pemberley, in the country near the town of Lambton, an area much like the one where they were now. '*If he does not offer for me soon, then I will affect a compromise and he will have to marry me. He will thank me for helping him get to the point!*'

Seeing how uncomfortable Darcy was with Caroline's behaviour, her brother requested she go inside to make sure everything was in order for dinner, as he was sure their guest was hungry after journeying from Town.

She believed she could display her skills as a hostess by doing so, so she made her excuses and went into the house.

She intended to make an entrance at dinner that would dazzle her Mr. Darcy.

"Bingley, so there will be no misunderstanding, I repeat what I have previously told you; no matter how much your sister desires it, I will never offer for her, even if she attempts to compromise me," Darcy stated in a tone that brooked no opposition as soon as Miss Bingley was gone, and the gentlemen were alone.

"Darcy, you have no idea how many times I have told her exactly that," Bingley said despondently. "I know what she is like. As it now stands, she is but one faux pax away from someone setting Lady Matlock and her daughter-in-law on my sister." Bingley grinned.

At Darcy's inquisitive look, Bingley relayed all of the drama from earlier in the afternoon. It need not be said that Darcy was anything less than astonished. "I wonder why Richard did not mention my uncle's friend, Thomas Bennet, lives here. Maybe he did and I forgot," Darcy mused aloud.

"I owe him a call in return. Would you like to come with me in the morning and meet him?" Bingley offered hopefully.

"Yes, thank you, Bingley; I would very much like to meet Mr. Thomas Bennet. By the way, he is a very good, if not the best, friend of my uncle's family; they have stayed at each other's estates many times. Unfortunately, those visits never coincided with a visit of mine, so I never met his family," Darcy informed Bingley. "However, I have heard Richard's family talk very warmly about the Bennets. Mr. Bennet was correct; one word from him to my Aunt Elaine and Cousin Marie and your sister would be done in society forever.

"As an aside, from what Richard and Andrew both told me, the Bennet daughters are all beautiful and highly accomplished. The eldest three were sponsored for their curtsey before the Queen by Aunt Elaine. They consider the

Bennets' offspring as nieces and nephews."

"Darce, I have a favour to ask of you: If Caroline is stupid enough not to heed the warnings she is been given, do not say anything. She has to learn, and the hard way may be the only way she ever will," Bingley requested with a pained look. "All I can hope is the whole family will not be ruined by association. This afternoon I had to apologise to Mr. Bennet. He was gracious and told us he did not hold the rest of us responsible for Caroline's despicable behaviour. I was shamed by the foul language she spewed. Even Louisa took her to task after her embarrassing performance. If Caroline refuses to listen, she will feel the repercussions."

Darcy made for his chambers to change for dinner and wash the dust of the road from his person. He descended to the drawing room a little while before the meal. As soon as he entered, Caroline Bingley latched onto his arm again, conveniently forgetting his reaction when he arrived and ignoring the look of disgust on his countenance as he tensed at her touch. Even through his clothing, she made his skin crawl.

"My dear Mr. Darcy," she cooed, "you will not believe the lies a pretentious country nobody told today. He claimed a connection with your esteemed uncle and aunt, the Earl and Countess of Matlock. How preposterous!" she continued, not noticing the look of disgust on the faces of everyone, especially Darcy's. "As if your noble relations would ever suffer the degradation of connecting themselves to a mere country bumpkin without fortune." She simpered, thinking that she had his ear and believing she was showing her superior knowledge of all he held dear.

Darcy was having a hard time keeping his word to Bingley already. He practically threw Caroline's hand from his arm and glowered at her when she tried to reclaim it. "I have never given you leave to be so familiar with me, Madame. You are the sister of my friend, naught more!"

Darcy said through clenched teeth.

Miss Bingley gaped at him as if she could not comprehend what Mr. Darcy was saying. More than that, she did not understand how he was saying it. "But, Mr. Darcy," she stammered, "we have always been best of friends. We do not associate with those below our circle..."

She got no further. "Our circle?" Darcy cut her off. "What circle is that, or is it you believe you belong to mine?" He turned to Bingley and said, "I am sorry, Bingley." Bingley gave him a nod, granting permission for him to continue. "Do you, Miss Bingley, think that, like you, I am the offspring of a tradesman?" She paled but did not reply. "Miss Bingley, let me speak plainly. I have only tolerated your presence for the sake of my friendship with your brother, no more than that. You have never been my friend, nor will you ever be more than my friend's sister—an acquaintance tolerated at best!"

Caroline Bingley felt her dream crashing down around her as everyone in the room looked at her with scorn, even her brother-in-law, Harold Hurst, who normally showed no interest in anything but food and drink. Even more shocking was the look of disgust, and rejection that she saw on Louisa's face!

She could always manipulate Louisa, could she not? For the first time since she had begun, at twelve, to take on the airs and graces of those at the seminary, Miss Bingley suspected she would not get what she wanted this time. With this insight, for the second time this day, Caroline left the drawing room red as a beet, but unfortunately for those in her family, no wiser.

After reaching her room and slamming her door so it sounded like a clap of thunder, she let out a screech a harpy would envy. What followed thereafter was a tantrum of epic proportions. She hurled every piece of bric-a-brac in her room into the fireplace; the sounds of breaking porcelain reverberated throughout the house.

Had she known the landlord was the very Mr. Bennet she had so soundly denigrated, she might have destroyed even more in her fit of pique. When her anger lessened, she rationalised her brother would pay for the breakages. She could always manipulate him into doing so in the past.

Once she calmed down, she filtered what Mr. Darcy had said through her delusional mind, and discarded whatever did not fit with the narrative she continued to tell herself; it was as if he had never said it.

In the world she had created for herself, there was only one reality, one where she would be given whatever she wanted. She wanted Pemberley and the status that went along with being the mistress of one of the largest estates in the country.

Dinner at Netherfield Park that night was pleasant because it lacked the company of the hostess.

CHAPTER 5

The next morning, as soon as it was an acceptable hour for making calls, both Darcy and Bingley mounted their horses and rode toward Longbourn, only three miles distant.

As they approached the house, which was larger than Netherfield Park's manor house, Darcy knew it housed a family of considerable means.

The house was in excellent repair, and he could see there had been extensive, well-built additions to the original house. The park was well-maintained, and nothing seemed to counteract nature or be ostentatious, unlike the estate of a certain aunt of his from Kent and its gaudy and vulgar displays of wealth.

Darcy noticed an extensive stable on one side of the house, at least as large as his stables at Pemberley. Beyond that stood a number of very fine horses sunning themselves or grazing in paddocks. As he looked, he recalled his uncle and cousins had spoken about the famed Longbourn stables and the quality of the horses bred there. They told him the demand for Longbourn's horses were so great among the ton there was a waiting list for them.

Darcy could not have known that Bennet had more than tripled the size of Longbourn by adding two wings to it. He also had no idea that Bennet had recovered land gambled away in the past by dissolute members of his family, quadrupling the size of the park. He could see many signs of wealth but, like most in the area, had no idea of just how wealthy the Bennets were.

They were met in front of the house by two smartly-dressed grooms. Once the gentlemen dismounted, the grooms led their horses toward the stables. One nodded to the gentlemen, vowing to care for their horses as they did the Bennets'. Darcy noticed their gentle touch with his mount and was impressed.

When the two friends offered coins to them in thanks, their astonishment deepened when both grooms politely refused them, saying they were merely just doing their duty and they were more than well compensated by the master.

Just as they reached the oak front door it was opened by the butler, Mr. Hill. Both men handed him their cards and requested to meet with the master of the house. Hill took their outerwear and left them standing in the entrance hall, admiring the quality of what they saw.

Hill walked down a hall and they heard him knocking on a door. When bade enter, he complied with an easy manner, one Darcy knew only occurred when the master and mistress of a household respected their servants and treated them with fairness. "The master will see you now. Follow me, please," Hill stated as he returned to the visitors after but a moment's delay.

As they walked toward the study, they could hear the dulcet tones of female voices in one of the drawing rooms. Normally, Darcy would be far less eager to pay his respects to the ladies of the house than Bingley. However, having heard of the Bennet ladies almost all of their lives, he was even more eager than Bingley to be introduced.

They followed Hill into Bennet's study. As they entered, he announced them to his master, who was standing in front of his desk. The gentlemen bowed to each other. A moment later, they heard the door click behind them as it closed almost silently.

Darcy surveyed the room. It was a well-used study

with a substantial number of books, many of which he knew he had in Pemberley's library. Mr. Bennet looked to be an intelligent man in his late forties or early fifties.

"Welcome, gentlemen," Bennet offered with an affable smile, "I have long wanted to meet Reggie's nephew. Please be seated."

"And I have wished to meet you, Sir. I am sorry we have not met before now," Darcy said, inclining his head.

Once they were seated, Bennet asked if they would like refreshments. The two visitors declined gracefully, having broken their fasts before leaving Netherfield Park.

"Mr. Bennet, please allow me to apologise again for the behaviour of my sister Caroline when you called on me yesterday," Bingley addressed the topic which was causing him unease directly. It caught him by surprise that Darcy had relaxed; apparently, the closeness of the Fitzwilliams and the Bennets had not been exaggerated if Darcy was this comfortable meeting someone for the first time.

Bennet assured Bingley that he did not hold him accountable for his sister's actions. After this welcome statement, Bingley breathed a sigh of relief. Bennet asked Darcy if all was well with his best friend, his wife, and his family. Darcy assured him the family was all well when he saw them in town the day before he travelled into Hertfordshire.

"My family was excited to hear Richard will join you at Netherfield Park soon. He is a favourite of ours, especially with my fifteen-year-old sons who love to listen to his battle tales from when he was serving King and Country in the army on the Peninsula. They will listen to those, and his other yarns, for as long as he is willing to tell them. He is careful to not share too many details with them, although Tom and James would not object if he did," Bennet chuckled.

"Now that I think back, Richard did say something

about knowing people in Hertfordshire, but I was not paying attention," Darcy said. "There was a near disaster that affected my sister this summer past and I was distracted by thoughts of that when we spoke last.

"My sister Georgiana is almost sixteen and Richard is her co-guardian with me." Darcy had a faraway look as he continued. "I blame myself for what happened, even though by the grace of God I arrived in time to stop the disaster from happening. Uncle Reggie says I take too much on myself."

Bingley's jaw dropped at this most unexpected turn of events. Fitzwilliam Darcy was sharing personal details of his life with someone he had never before met. Not only that, he was sharing details he had not yet related to himself, his best friend.

Darcy settled in the chair across from Bennet, a huge exhale of emotion finally escaping. For some reason he felt comfortable talking to Bennet, a closeness he never had with someone not an intimate acquaintance or close family like the Fitzwilliams.

"Reggie was correct," Bennet opined with conviction, "He has shared his worries with me that you take too much on yourself and you think you can control things that are beyond anyone's control. Only God can control all, Son, not mortals." Bennet offered quietly. His eyes locked on Darcy so Darcy could see the truth a man can find only when addressed by another man. Bennet had to check his chuckle when Darcy looked chagrined.

'He has my measure and we have only just met!' he thought, but aloud he offered words he had thus far been unable to say. "Maybe you have the right of it, but I would never have forgiven myself if something had happened to Georgie."

Darcy had never shared any of what had been troubling him for so long with Bingley, and the latter could see his friend was sinking into a dark mood again, so he intervened to change the subject, telling Bennet that Caroline had not learned her lesson and the things she had said before dinner.

"As I told Darcy, I am afraid the only way she will learn is the hard way. I love my sister, but I no longer like her, and I abhor her behaviour as it reflects badly on all of us. Even after Darce here told her as clearly as he could that she is nothing to him, her delusions persist, and she tells all she will soon be Mistress of Pemberley.

"She also had a monstrous tantrum last night and broke all the bric-a-brac in her chambers. She does not know it yet, but the money for the replacement will come from her allowance. I will no longer foot the bill for her bad behaviour." Bingley understood Darcy's sceptical look he was not hiding. "Just you wait and see, I am resolved that she will have to live with the consequences of her appalling behaviour."

"I was going to acquaint you with some facts before her outburst, but now, especially after what you just told me Mr. Bingley, I feel I should tell you all." Bennet settled back in his chair, also at ease with the company as he imagined he would one day talk as such with his sons. Bennet proceeded to tell them everything, from the birth of the twins onward. By the end of the tale, Darcy and Bingley were equally dumbfounded. *'I could see they had wealth,'* Darcy thought to himself, *'but this is far beyond anything I imagined. Their wealth rivals my own.'*

"You are my landlord?" Bingley blurted out once he had regained his equanimity. "I must apologise once again; Caroline disrespected you in your own house." Bennet nodded. "My sister is in for a much bigger shock than she expects."

"As I told you a few minutes ago, there is nothing for you to apologise for, so please do not make yourself uneasy.

You do not control the words or actions of your sister." Bennet's reply helped Bingley to relax knowing for sure he was not being held accountable for the actions of his ill-bred sister.

After Bennet's disclosure and knowing at some point he would have shared the whole sordid story with Bingley anyway, Darcy swore both men to secrecy and proceeded to tell Bennet and Bingley his story. He started with the early facts regarding his nemesis George Wickham, then when after his father died how he had refused the living, stating he would never take orders, been compensated for it, and then wasted four thousand pounds.

How after signing away any claim to the living, he came back and asked for more and for the living that he had resigned all claim to. He explained how when refused Wickham had sworn revenge. He then relayed to them how the blackguard seducer had left a string of ruined girls and natural children in his wake across the country, and many debts to unsuspecting tradesmen who had allowed him credit.

Darcy added that he held Wickham's vowels for debts worth well over three thousand pounds. Bingley was aghast now he finally understood why his friend had been in such a dark mood. Darcy finished the outpouring with a full recounting of what had happened, and what had almost happened in Ramsgate.

The two men in the study with him were the first people outside of the Fitzwilliams that he had been so open with about his private matters. His doing so here, was truly unlike him. From the moment he had been admonished by this man, Darcy had known sharing his burdens would be good for him, a catharsis. It was rare he found someone who so obviously took the same level of care in his estate, stables, and those who were dependent on him.

At the end of the recitation, Bennet ruminated and

then again met that anguished stare. "Son, I understand why you blame yourself, but you have no true share in the blame. Both you and Richard were fooled by the dishonest Mrs. Younge, and if you had not arrived earlier than you planned, think of the disaster that would have ensued," Bennet pointed out with much empathy. "This Wickham is a despoiler of maidens, a debaucher, a profligate, a blackguard and by the sounds of things an accomplished manipulator and liar. Your father, unadvisedly, gave him every advantage, and he chose to waste every one of his chances then blamed his misdeeds on everyone except himself."

"You have his measure, Sir!" Darcy exclaimed with a slight upturn of his mouth. It felt good to discuss this with an objective party for the first time since the near disaster in Ramsgate.

Darcy felt he was ready to accept that this was not all his fault. A man who Darcy knew loved his family, was reminding him what that meant, and it was time to forgive himself and start living again. He felt the catharsis he had sorely needed begin to lift the self-imposed weight he had placed on his shoulders.

After a moment Darcy looked at the two gentlemen and for the first time in too long, smiled at his own thoughts. "I have an idea which will put Miss Bingley in her place once and for all, if Bingley agrees," Darcy stated as he looked to his friend.

"Whatever needs to be done to finally show Caroline her own insignificance is something I will hear," Bingley allowed.

"When I last saw them, the Fitzwilliams were getting ready to leave Town. They planned to depart by this coming weekend. Bingley told me Tuesday next there is an assembly in Meryton. I suggest you invite my aunt and uncle to arrive on Friday and to come to the assembly with you and your family.

"As much as Miss Bingley has always desired it, and lies about meeting them, she has never been introduced to any of them other than Richard. With them in attendance, she will either behave or be the author of her own demise in society." He settled back into the comfortable chair he was sitting in and then looked at Bingley. "Bingley, if you truly want her to learn, I suggest you do not inform anyone at Netherfield Park about what we learned today, and let things play out as they will."

Bingley agreed to the scheme and so did Bennet, who rang for Hill and asked if he would call his wife. On her entry, Mrs. Bennet was introduced to the young men. When meeting Mr. Darcy, she walked up to him and hugged him quickly as she captured his face in her hands.

"We have been hoping to meet you all your life, young man." She kissed the top of his head and pulled back, asking about Georgiana. Darcy, initially caught off guard, had to wonder how much more happiness in his and Georgiana's life there could have been had he met the Bennets sooner.

"She is well, Mrs. Bennet, thank you for asking." Darcy bowed his head in her direction. "And as much as I would be happy to continue talking about Georgie, we have a more immediate matter to address, if that is acceptable," he asked, smiling at the silent communication between her and Bennet that ended with Mrs. Bennet nodding.

Fanny was apprised of the plan, agreed, and returned to the drawing room. After the door closed once his wife exited, Bennet wrote the express inviting the Fitzwilliams to join them at Longbourn.

Darcy was, for the first time in too long, looking forward to something with the expectation of pleasure, not only seeing his closest relations himself, but his knowledge of how much his family loved the Bennets and the way acceptance was extended to him made him very grateful to now be included in the warmth he felt at Longbourn.

Once the missive was completed, Bennet rang for Hill and asked him to send one of his grooms to Matlock house in Town, then to await any reply. After the door closed, Bennet told the friends he was going to collect his sons from Eton on Thursday as the school year was ending.

He would be departing that afternoon and returning on Friday morning. He knew his boys would be overjoyed if the Fitzwilliams responded in the affirmative, especially with Richard in residence at Netherfield Park.

It was hard to believe in the next school year come August that his little boys, both already taller than him, would then begin their studies at Cambridge. Bennet suggested that they adjourn to the drawing room to meet the rest of the family that was in residence.

The two men agreed, and they all made for the drawing room. Bennet grinned to himself when he noted the same look on the faces of the two gentlemen, he had seen many times before when others beheld the sight of his daughters.

The two friends were frozen before they had fully stepped in. Darcy knew he, and he was certain he could speak for Bingley, had never before seen so much beauty and genuine gentility before. They had heard from the other callers the Bennet daughters were beauties, but the vision before them was far and away above what they had expected.

Bingley saw a blonde, blue-eyed beauty who was standing and waiting for the introductions and was transfixed by her. She appeared as if she was serene, but he could see a steely resolve in her countenance as she assessed him, and Darcy suspected anyone trifling with her or any of her sisters would do so at their peril.

Darcy was struck dumb by a raven-haired beauty with sparkling hazel eyes that even from this distance he could spy flecks of gold and green; her amused smile exuding wit and intelligence. He, who had on many occasions derided those talking of love at first sight, was mesmerised and shocked to understand it would not take very long before he would be well on his way to his heart being irrevocably lost.

Lizzy, who until now had never been seriously attracted to any particular man, was frozen when the most handsome man she had ever before seen was now in front of her in her own home. A quick appraisal meant she could surmise he had recently lost too much weight too fast, and instinctively felt he had been, or was now, troubled and knew she wanted to help him ease his cares away, was in fact, determined to.

Jolted back to reality, she rebuked herself for getting carried away until she again met his eyes and saw his perfect deep blue eyes looking at her with what could only be described as esteem. *'He is so much more than tolerable, and more than handsome enough to tempt me,'* she admitted, if only to herself.

The ladies had all risen from their seats, so Bennet took pity on the thunderstruck men, and equally amusing two awed daughters and made the introductions. "My wife Fanny Bennet, who you just saw in the study, my eldest daughter, Miss Jane Bennet, followed by Elizabeth, Mary, and last but not at all least, Catherine Bennet, who we call Kitty and is not yet out."

As he named them, each lady gave a curtsey and the gentlemen bowed. "The lady you see standing behind Kitty is her companion, Mrs. Henrietta Chandler." The lady stood and curtsied as she was introduced. "Ladies, it is my pleasure to introduce you to Mr. Charles Bingley of Scarborough, who is our tenant at Netherfield, and Mr. Fitzwilliam Darcy of Pemberley in Derbyshire."

On seeing the looks from his daughters, he chuckled and nodded. "Yes, he is Reggie and Elaine's nephew, the one we always miss seeing by a day or even hours. Kitty, you especially will be happy to hear his sister will arrive on Monday. She is almost the same age as you and also not yet out."

Kitty's brilliant smile brightened her face and she looked truly delighted. "Oh, how nice it will be to have another in the area besides myself and Maria Lucas that is close to our age," she professed with affection and Darcy was taken aback, wondering if this band of beauties was the answer to almost all of his prayers.

Darcy knew, just as he had with Bennet earlier, that his sister's cares would lighten when she met the friends, who had been part of their family for far too long to consider new. He was positive the Bennets would be very good for her and assist Georgie to recover her confidence.

He knew she would love to have a friend her own age, the elder sisters to guide her and help her with questions she probably would never ask him, and if it had the added benefit of keeping her away from the cloying and fake Caroline Bingley, so much the better.

Bennet informed his daughters he had extended an invitation to the Fitzwilliams to join them, surprising Darcy when he looked pointedly at his third daughter Mary as he revealed Richard would be arriving with Miss Georgiana and her companion to stay at Netherfield Park.

Mary, with heightened colour on her cheeks, seemed more than passingly pleased when she heard Richard would be one of the arriving individuals on Monday. On noting this, Darcy felt it was time to interrogate his playful cousin rather than the other way around, as was usually the case. That is, if he could stay away from the Bennet ladies long enough to allow for it.

With that thought, he was struck by what he hoped was a brilliant idea that would not only help Georgie recover but save her from having to hide from Caroline Bingley. "If I may, Georgiana, we call her Georgie, is very shy and I know she would love to be among other ladies close to her age and away from a certain lady at Netherfield Park," he looked apologetically at Bingley who waved away his concern. "If I can impose on you after just being introduced, and if it is agreeable to you and she acquiesces, would you object to her staying here? Being among other genteel young ladies would do Georgie a world of good, and she too has heard our cousins speak of you often. She laments never having had the chance to meet you as have I over the years."

"She would be most welcome, as any member of Reggie and Elaine's family would be without question," said Fanny. "I would love to have another girl here around the same age as Kitty, what could be better? What is the issue at Netherfield Park is there a problem with the house?" She looked to her husband, reading that there was much more to this.

Bennet and Darcy looked to Bingley, who glanced at Miss Bennet. On seeing her nod that she too was concerned, he in turn looked at Bennet and gave his approval, also having the grace to blush when he finally saw Bennet's amused look. At his approval, Bennet, Darcy, and Bingley explained the Caroline Bingley problem and what steps were being taken to put her in her place, which included the invitation to the Fitzwilliams.

"Georgiana is shy, but around Miss Bingley she is ever more so and more withdrawn than normal. She knows that Miss Bingley offers her false friendship with the intent to induce me to offer for her, something that will *never* happen!" He met Elizabeth's eyes and shook his head once. "She set her cap for me after seeing Pemberley, but I never considered her for the role of my wife for a moment. Not once, and Bingley supports me in this."

After hearing Miss Bingley was continuing her

ridiculous behaviour, even after Bennet's warnings, Georgiana's stay was reaffirmed by all the ladies individually and Darcy chuckled, wondering what would happen should someone even attempt to gainsay this decision now.

He would be most amused to watch someone try but was not himself so stupid as to go against the wishes of the collective Bennet ladies. With that settled, everyone agreed it was best to allow Miss Bingley to dig her own societal grave. If, as they expected, the invitation to the Fitzwilliams was accepted, the choice of what her future in society would be was to be hers, and hers alone.

"The audacity of the woman!" Lizzy spat out; her hands balled into fists. "She will experience my wrath if she tries to make trouble for Georgiana or any of my other sisters, or anyone else I love," Elizabeth vowed as she looked at Darcy, the flashing of her eyes gave him an insight to the fire and passion within.

Then the words she had said struck him and he was lost to her. While amazed at how her eyes sparkled when angry, the love and protection of all he held most dear was more than he had ever before been gifted in his life by another save for Richard.

"Now Lizzy," Bennet said with a look of pride on his face, "Miss Bingley will be the author of her own downfall. We will make sure we are not in her company before the assembly, then it is strictly her behaviour that will dictate what happens."

This seemed to mollify Elizabeth to some extent. Darcy glanced at Bennet, wondering if he would remind his daughter Georgiana was not her sister and Bennet arched a brow, silently asking if he dared.

Darcy chuckled as he shook his head because he did not, and more than that, he wanted nothing more than for Georgiana to experience the love and compassion he had since he had entered the house.

"Would you gentlemen like to see the estate and the environs?" Bennet offered. Upon getting an affirmative nod from both, he turned to his daughters and asked who would like to lead the gentlemen on a horseback tour, unsurprised when all four of his daughters chorused that they would go. They excused themselves to go change into their riding habits, proclaiming they would meet the gentlemen at the stables in half an hour.

~~~~~~~/~~~~~~~

Entering the stables complex, Darcy could see the structure was even more impressive than he first had thought, and it was not speculation to surmise it was quite possibly more extensive than his own now that he could see all.

The ladies arrived, accompanied by the companion and an additional chaperone, as well as the two grooms who had taken the gentlemen's horses on their arrival.

It was an extremely enjoyable three hours, and the more time Darcy and Bingley spent in the oldest two Bennet daughters' company, and spoke with them, the more their hearts were lost to them.

Unbeknownst to Darcy, as Lizzy was collecting the pieces of his, she was losing her heart to him. The more they talked, the more she was able to sketch his character. And the more she discovered, the more she liked him.

Luckily for them, without yet knowing they were admired in return, Jane and Lizzy were very impressed by the gentlemen and felt at last they had met men they may be able to love and respect, not knowing the men were already well on their way to losing their hearts to them. For each couple it would prove happiness was possible and often revealed at the most unexpected of times.

Once it was explained to the gentlemen that they

had seen but a small fraction of the estate, Darcy realised with the addition of Bennet Fields and Netherfield Park, as well as the other ex-Longbourn land Bennet had purchased back, and the additional tracts that he had added besides, Longbourn rivalled the size of the land that Pemberley claimed.

Darcy, who was a natural born horseman, was impressed beyond words at the riding ability of all four Bennet daughters. They had no problem keeping up with the men, and in the playful way he always presumed sisters would behave, sometimes raced one another for small distances or surged ahead of the men in a gallop.

Darcy knew horseflesh and was initially concerned when the eldest two Bennet sisters had mounted stallions, noting the younger two rode mares. Throughout the tour, he watched most closely, and was taken aback at the ease of which the two eldest Bennet daughters handled their stallions.

Truth was, they rode better than a lot of men that he had seen. Once his concern proved unnecessary, he watched the two in wonder, especially Miss Elizabeth on her mount Mercury, aptly named for his speed. He suddenly had a vision of her racing him at breakneck speed on their stallions across the hills and dales of Pemberley and was overcome by the warmth of the very pleasant sensation that such thoughts evoked.

When they returned to the house, the gentlemen were invited for dinner which they accepted with much alacrity as with relief of not having to part from their chosen ladies so soon. A groom was dispatched to Netherfield Park to inform the party there that the two men would not return for dinner.

~~~~~~~/~~~~~~~

When the groom re-entered the drawing room to

inform Bennet his task was complete, his frown made all uneasy.

"Tell us what happened. Is my house still standing?" Bennet asked drolly, making even the groom chuckle despite being well used to his master's ways.

"Sir," he nodded at Bennet then turned to Mr. Bingley, "your sister, Miss Bingley, was not happy to hear you had forced Darcy to dine out with..." he hesitated until he saw Bennet nod for him to continue, "a group of country nobodies." He stated, himself angry on the Bennet's behalf. "She threw a vase at the door as I was closing it, Sir." He looked at Bennet alone.

On hearing this, everyone present realised the sad truth, the assembly would more than likely be the end in society for Miss Bingley as she had not displayed the ability to keep herself in check, and likely had not learned to hold her tongue through the course of the day.

~~~~~~~/~~~~~~~

After the most pleasurable dinner Darcy had had in months, maybe even years excepting those with his Aunt, Uncle, and cousins, he was exceptionally pleased, as was Bingley. It may have been simply because Mrs. Bennet had allowed them to sit next to their preferred Bennet daughter, after which there was a brief separation of the sexes.

Fanny had noticed the attention from the gentlemen to her two oldest and was surprised she was so soon required to issue a warning to Jane and Elizabeth just after the drawing room door was closed and the ladies took their seats.

"Girls do be careful with your hearts," Fanny admonished gently. "I know both gentlemen seem very nice and good, and especially Mr. Darcy with his connection to the Fitzwilliams. But please, make sure that you know you can love them if they ever ask for a courtship which may eventually lead to a proposal. We want you only to accept your future husbands for the deepest love, respect, and esteem you deserve. The kind of love you know helps you become the best version of yourself as it has for me."

"Mama you should know with the example of you and Papa before us every day, add to that Aunt and Uncle Gardiner's respectful and loving marriage, and Aunt and Uncle Fitzwilliam's marriage which proves love surpasses societal obligations, that none of us would ever settle for less!" Lizzy stated emphatically while Jane nodded agreement, her serene smile hiding a heart thudding with the hope Papa would not keep the gentlemen with him for too long.

Bennet chuckled at the astonishment on Darcy's face as he led them into the drawing room where his ladies were. He felt they had stayed away long enough to give the impression they had not overheard Fanny's speech to her daughters, unsurprised it raised his family to an even higher estimation in the eyes of the friends.

To hear and see such a family care nothing for position, fortune, or connections was so refreshing after years of dealing with the connivance of the *Ton*. There was no avarice here, just the best of motives by parents wanting only true happiness for their children.

How many matchmaking mothers of the *Ton* would ever impart advice like that to their daughters? None! The friends were well aware mothers in polite society were too intent to matchmake rather than take their children's preferences and personal needs into consideration.

A few minutes before the guests were about to depart, the groom who had ridden to town returned with an affirmative response from the Fitzwilliams. The party would include Andrew and Marie Fitzwilliam, and of course their two-year-old son and the heir to the Earldom of Matlock after his father, David, would be with his parents.

The house became even livelier when it was learned the Fitzwilliams were arriving on Saturday. The Bennet offspring all loved their Uncle Reggie and Aunt Elaine, as well as the rest of the family. It was agreed there would be a family dinner on Monday, once Richard Fitzwilliam and Georgiana Darcy arrived.

To complete the party Darcy and Bingley would join them, but without his sisters, though Bingley's description of Mrs. Hursts reactions as she distanced herself from, and stood up to, the harpy that morning helped them see her in a more amiable light.

CHAPTER 6

After Darcy's family arrived on Saturday, he had visited them at Longbourn a number of times. He had been impressed with both Tom and James Bennet, who he met soon after they arrived home with their father on Friday afternoon.

The twins were well-behaved, respectful, and obviously paid attention to their studies. They were well-informed conversationalists. Based on the way the ladies of the house behaved, Darcy would have been surprised to find them otherwise. What pleased him most was they had been allowed to be normal, lively, sixteen-year-old young men, who clearly enjoyed being home with their sisters and parents.

They were both to inherit substantial estates, and Darcy had already had informed conversations about estate management and equine husbandry with them. The two Bennet sons loved horses as much as Darcy did.

James informed Darcy there would be four birthdays at Longbourn during the next two or three weeks: Kitty would turn seventeen, the twins would turn sixteen, then Mary would turn nineteen.

~~~~~~~/~~~~~~~

The carriage bearing Richard and Georgiana to Hertfordshire pulled up just short of the entrance of Netherfield Park's manor house. Before Miss Bingley could make his sister uncomfortable by imposing her unwanted company on her, Darcy opened the carriage door, entered the conveyance, and closed the door behind him—preventing Miss Bingley from following him.

Her expression turned sour, but no one paid her any mind. Bingley knew what was about to happen, so he was ready to restrain his sister if needs be. Both Hurst and Louisa stood poised to assist.

Miss Bingley, who had been waiting to welcome her *dearest friend*, was astounded Darcy asked her brother to join him in the carriage. She had reached for the carriage door, but the coach started to move before she could open it. She was unaware Darcy had asked the footman to ensure the coachmen moved the carriage before she could get her claws on the door handle. As soon as the door had closed the driver had flicked the reins and the conveyance lurched forward following the circular drive and left Netherfield in a cloud of dust that made Caroline Bingley cough amidst her complaints and demands for it to return.

"Well, I never!" Caroline Bingley screeched. She returned to the house, where her sister, her brother-in-law, and the Netherfield servants were treated to her third tantrum in two days. She did not understand why things were not going in accordance with her desires. Did she not always get her way?

~~~~~~~/~~~~~~~

Once he settled on one of the padded seat cushions, Darcy met Georgiana's eyes; she was surprised to see him smile. "Georgie, the Bennets have invited you to stay with them for the duration of your visit here."

Glancing at his cousin, he continued, "The Bennets are the family dearest to our aunt and uncle. We have often heard of their four daughters, one of whom is near your age. Not only did they wish you to stay with them, they refused to countenance your stay at Netherfield Park, where you would have to fend off you-know-who. After you meet Mrs. Bennet, you will understand why I did not dare gainsay her wishes, even to keep you close to me."

Georgiana stared at her brother, looked down towards the floor, and said, "Are you sure they want me to stay?"

"Not want, Georgie, expect." He chuckled when Richard laughed, and she was caught off guard when Richard took her hand, lifted her head, and nodded.

"I do not doubt what he is saying, Georgie. Mrs. Bennet has loved you by extension since you were born," Richard told his ward as he pulled her into a hug.

"This invitation has an added benefit; you will not have to stay in the same house as Miss Bingley, which I know you were concerned about," Darcy added.

After hearing what her brother had to say about the Bennet daughters, and with both her guardians' approval and approbation of the Bennet family, Georgiana smiled tentatively. Richard Fitzwilliam again heartily stated his approval of her staying with them, reminding Georgiana he had told her of the Bennets before he collected her and her companion to travel to Hertfordshire.

Miss Darcy's companion could not but approve of any plan that separated her charge from the younger Bingley sister.

Georgiana nodded, reminding Darcy that she had heard about the Bennets many times in the past. Knowing her aunt, uncle, and cousins also were in residence at Longbourn, helped to convince her she would enjoy staying there as long as she was no inconvenience to the Bennets.

For Darcy, a benefit to his sister would be that she would reside with young, genteel ladies near her age. It would lift her spirits. He knew the Bennet sisters would protect his sister as they would protect their own. Another benefit would be the shrewish and condescending Caroline Bingley would be unable to interfere with her recovery.

Perhaps the greatest benefit was it meant he would visit his sister daily—allowing him to be in the company of the beautiful and intelligent Miss Elizabeth Bennet.

After arriving at Longbourn, the occupants of the coach alighted as soon as the door was opened and the step placed. Colonel Richard Fitzwilliam descended first, then helped his young cousin down. Darcy and Bingley descended quickly, both joyful at the prospect of being in close quarters with the ladies of Longbourn. Mrs. Annesley, Miss Darcy's companion, was handed out last.

The twins saw Richard alight, ran to him, and embraced him; he returned their embrace with gusto. Then Richard greeted his parents, his brother and sister-in-law, and his nephew. After that, he greeted each of the Bennet daughters by their Christian names, then Mr. and Mrs. Bennet. Darcy and Bingley were astonished at his familiarity and breach of propriety. Darcy was a bit jealous of his cousin, although he knew he had no cause for it; Richard and the other Fitzwilliams had been acquainted with the Bennet offspring since their birth.

Darcy noted the greeting between Richard and Mary was more intimate in nature. Seeing the blush spreading across Mary's face, Darcy realised his supposition there might be something between Richard and the third Bennet daughter was correct.

'Rich and I may finally become brothers," he ruminated silently. 'That will happen if my dearest wish becomes reality.' A look of pleasure suffused his countenance and drew the eyes of all those who had worried about him. Everyone noticed he stared at Lizzy and Lizzy seemed equally captivated.

Hearing a cough, Darcy and Lizzy broke eye contact, not realising they had revealed their focus on one another to everyone. Darcy smiled at his cousins, his aunt, and his uncle. He was now more determined than ever to court Elizabeth if she returned his regard.

Georgiana walked with her head down, guided by her companion. She had made the appropriate curtsies when she was introduced but had not looked anyone in the eye. After the two had been shown to their chambers—which shared a sitting room—they washed off the dust of the road and changed their clothing. After that, they descended the stairs prepared to join everyone in the yellow drawing room.

Georgiana was surprised when Mrs. Bennet left the drawing room to meet them in the hallway, closing the door behind her to ensure privacy. Then she gently lifted Georgiana's chin, gave her a warm smile, and pulled her into a motherly hug.

"Georgiana, dear, you are here at last. I have loved you all your life after hearing about you from your aunt. Forgive me; I do not want to overwhelm you, but I have wanted to hug you since the day you were born. I almost demanded we travel to Pemberly to get both you and your brother after your father died."

Mrs. Bennet hugged Georgiana even tighter. "You are as stiff as your brother was," she said, sighing in frustration. Georgiana gasped. "Yes, I walked in and hugged your poor brother, he did not know if he should hide under Thomas —my husband's—desk or run for the hills." She winked at Georgiana, nodding when a small laugh escaped from the young girl. "Come, I am being selfish with you. My girls have been longing to meet you for many years as well." Fanny opened the door to the drawing room before Georgiana could reply.

~~~~~~~/~~~~~~~

After the subject of Caroline Bingley had been canvassed, Ladies Matlock and Hilldale agreed the social-climbing shrew seemed in danger of committing societal suicide if she failed to control herself. They agreed not to allow anyone to denigrate their friends.

Darcy heard his aunt and her daughter-in-law state they would ruin the harpy—depending on her actions, of course. Suddenly remembering Miss Bingley's brother was present, the group looked toward him apologetically.

"She made her bed; now she must lie in it. I have warned her for years that Darcy has no interest in her and she is not of the circle she believes herself in. She will have to live with the consequences of her actions," Bingley said, realising everything being said of his sister was just. "I now regret bringing her here; unfortunately, I had nowhere to leave her, and I needed a hostess. She has burnt every bridge with the *friends* she claims to have, and I had little choice. I hoped she would, finally, act as a hostess and mistress should, but I must acknowledge a leopard cannot change its spots!" Bingley assured the party he understood and was sanguine with what may have to happen to his sister.

It was decided only Frank and Hattie Philips would be informed the Fitzwilliams were visiting Longbourn before the assembly on Tuesday night, where a confrontation might reasonably be expected. The Fitzwilliams had met Hattie and Frank on many previous visits, so Fanny insisted such genial company should not be denied them merely because of Miss Caroline Bingley.

When Georgiana came to join them, Darcy intended to walk with her into the room, but Lizzy reached her first and escorted her to a seat between her and Jane. Darcy noticed Georgie seemed comfortable seated between the two Bennet ladies and was not displaying her usual extreme shyness. He saw her engage in conversation with all four Bennet daughters, most particularly with Kitty and Mary—the two closest to her in age. It was not long before they were all on a first-name basis.

Darcy's heart warmed as he saw the Bennet girls drawing Georgie out. She appeared to have dropped the protective mask she had donned—much like the mask he wore at times. He watched in awe as Elizabeth Bennet led the effort to make Georgie feel at home and accepted. Eventually, he would learn it was rare, very rare, for Jane and Lizzy to allow someone to sit between them. They only did so with those they loved dearly, or those they wished to protect. What he noticed immediately, however, was genuine fellowship without judgement; it was a balm to Georgie's soul—and by extension, his.

Darcy realised few were lucky enough to have such an enjoyable evening. He, and everyone else, agreed Fanny Bennet kept an excellent table and complimented her. Fanny blushed becomingly at each compliment, replying with her thanks after each.

The Earl and Bennet retired to the latter's library after dinner, which contained a very impressive collection, although not the equal of Pemberley's. To be sure, Pemberley's collection was the work of many generations. After entering, the long-time friends became engrossed in a game of chess while they sipped snifters of rare French cognac.

The Countess and Fanny Bennet sat together, the dear friends chatting for some time since they had been parted for over six months. The younger crowd sat around them in various groups.

The twins settled with Richard and Andrew; Marie sat with Lizzy, Jane, Bingley, and Darcy; and the last group was comprised of Mary, Kitty, and Georgie. The two companions spoke together off to the side and seemed to be getting along well. Darcy could not remember being so at ease in company since the Ramsgate incident.

Before the evening closed, Georgiana slid into the spot next to her brother and looked up at him with tears in her eyes. "Georgie, are you well? If you do not..." he started, surprised when Georgiana bade him stop.

"Mrs. Bennet told me she hugged you, William. Is that true?" Georgie asked softly, shocked when her brother nodded.

"I was in Mr. Bennet's study, and she was asked to come in to meet me. To be honest, I had just been more open and honest with Mr. Bennet than I had been with anyone, perhaps even myself. I was grateful for his acceptance. When Mrs. Bennet came in and hugged me, it was not unwanted," Darcy related quietly.

"It felt so good, brother. It is not that you..." she tried to explain and was again caught by surprise when her brother hugged her.

~~~~~~~/~~~~~~~

As Bingley readied himself for the assembly, he felt both foreboding and relief. Either Caroline would no longer be a problem after receiving a long-overdue comeuppance, or she would demonstrate she had learnt to behave with propriety.

He still loved his sister, even though he did not like who she had become, flaunting her airs and condescending behaviour. She was his sister, after all. He recalled her performance the previous night when she demanded Darcy bring her *dear friend* to reside at Netherfield Park rather than with the *wild savages*—the Bennets. He also recalled the tirade she unleashed the day Bennet came to call, and the tantrum she threw after learning Georgiana would not be returning to Netherfield Park.

Unfortunately, Caroline had demanded the maids replace the items in her chamber she smashed—so the sounds of bric-a-brac being broken had echoed throughout the house a second time. This caused Bingley to arrive at a sad conclusion: Caroline would not act with propriety at the assembly; hence the time of Caroline's reckoning was close at hand.

It was likely his younger sister would be unable to control her temper and might spew a stream of vitriol that would embarrass him and Louisa and would cause her to be forever banished from society.

He had spoken with Louisa, who assured him she would no longer cover for, or excuse, Caroline's behaviour. He had been pleased to see Louisa take Caroline to task the day Bennet visited them and was pleased to learn Louisa would not suffer the same consequences as their sister, if Caroline decided to hammer the nails into the coffin lid of her societal hopes.

Bingley met Darcy and his brother Hurst in the entryway of Netherfield Park. He and Darcy had secured the first, supper, and last dances with Jane and Lizzy respectively. Hence he did not intend to allow Caroline's penchant to be *fashionably late* in order to make a grand entrance to delay them.

Besides, the less attention she garnered at the assembly, the better. The shades of orange she wore had made her the laughingstock of their actual circle for many years. Further, the object of her machinations, Darcy, was nauseated by her presence, due in no small part to her liberal use of expensive—but cloyingly pungent—perfume. Certainly, others had been nauseated by it as well.

When Louisa descended the stairs, Bingley asked where Caroline was; Louisa merely shrugged her shoulders. The two friends decided to take Darcy's carriage, securing the Hursts' agreement to bring Caroline as soon as she deigned to join them.

Eventually, Miss Bingley descended the stairs in a hideous orange gown with a matching turban and oversized, dyed ostrich feathers, expecting to be admired by Darcy. She was furious when she learned he and her brother had already departed.

The two men's absence only ignited her fury. Every time she watched her brother force Darcy to accompany him somewhere else, usually starting with or ending with a visit to the lowly Bennets, she had begun to hate Charles with a passion. He had deprived her of the time she needed to spend with Darcy to convince him to make her the next mistress of Pemberley.

"Go upstairs and throw your tantrum or hold your tongue and come with us," Hurst demanded, winking at Louisa when she hid her laugh in a becoming cough.

Miss Bingley reined in her anger in order to prove she was dignified enough to become the mistress of Mr. Darcy's estate. The sooner they reached the so-called assembly, the sooner she could convince him how far above the Bennet sisters she was, in spite of their reputed beauty.

~~~~~~~/~~~~~~~

As they had planned, Darcy and Bingley arrived at the assembly on time. On entering the hall, Sir William Lucas, the Master of Ceremonies, introduced them to the principal families in the area.

When the music began, each gentleman went to claim his respective Bennet daughter for the first set. Darcy noticed Richard lined up with a happy, glowing Mary Bennet. Darcy could not but notice the contentment on Lizzy's face as he took her hand and led her to the line forming for the dance and was charmed by it.

After five minutes of silent dancing, Lizzy chose to speak. "Come now, Mr. Darcy, we must have some conversation; a very little will do. We cannot spend a half hour completely in silence."

"Do you hold conversations as a rule when you dance, madam? If so, what would you like to discuss?" he asked, his eyes soaking in her beauty as he waited for her reply.

"I suppose I could be unsociable and taciturn and

remain silent, but this evening I prefer otherwise," Elizabeth teased.

"I am happy to oblige you, Miss Bennet, please advise me what you would most like to hear," he returned her jest.

"I could mention the number of couples enjoying the dance and you could remark on the size of the room," she quipped. "Perhaps by and by I may observe that public balls are not as pleasant as private ones," she said, arching a brow.

Darcy laughed at her impertinence, enjoying it very much because her words were spoken without malice. "Tell me, do you and your sisters often ride, Miss Elizabeth? I was most impressed with your equestrian skills," Darcy said, wanting to prove he admired her abilities.

"Yes, Mr. Darcy we do. We ride as often as we can. I also like long rambles in the country. I love to walk as much as I love to ride my stallion, Mercury. Some have called me a great walker. I have been known to return from my walks with petticoats six inches deep in mud. It vexes my maid most exceedingly." She smiled playfully and he chuckled.

"Both Georgiana and I share your forms of exercise as well, Miss Elizabeth. Pemberley gives us the opportunity for both," he informed her, holding his breath as he waited for her reaction.

"I think I would like to see Pemberley one day. I have heard both you and Georgiana describing it in glowing terms. Aunt Elaine, Uncle Reggie, Andrew, and Richard have also admired your estate, and have spoken of it and you often through the years." She started to blush, knowing her speech could be construed as fishing for an invitation to Pemberley.

He noticed it, and his smile deepened. "Do not make yourself uneasy, Miss Elizabeth. Both Georgiana and I would love for you and your family to visit Pemberley. It is, after all, less than two hours by carriage from Snowhaven. I have been considering taking the Earl to task for not bringing you to see us. How pleased we would have been had he done so." He grinned, relief and pride filling him when she laughed.

They had no chance to continue their conversation because the explosion they all expected, but had hoped would not happen, took place.

After entering the assembly rooms and garnering none of the notice she thought her due, hearing persons of low standing daring to snicker after noticing her outfit, and then noticing the raven-haired beauty dancing with *her* Mr. Darcy—that last straw broke the camel's back—Caroline told herself, '*Pemberley is mine! No country chit will take what is mine from me! He has **never** danced the first set with me!*'

When the Master of Ceremonies came to offer his services to Miss Bingley and make introductions, she soon discovered the chit dancing the first set with *her* Mr. Darcy was none other than one of the Bennet daughters.

She now despised anyone named Bennet. The Mr. Bennet she had met displayed such pretensions! The rest of his family could be no different. It was, however, the smile on Darcy's face that made Caroline see red. Ignoring the rules of the floor, she strode directly to where the grasping Bennet father was standing with a group of other never-will-be's.

She had no idea who any of them were, but they were here—that was all she needed to know about their standing in society. She had her fill of those so low being amused at her expense. Louisa tried to rein her in, but Caroline slapped her hand away. As soon as she reached Mr. Bennet and the other persons of no consequence, she launched into her speech, which was naught more than another of her tirades.

"It is time to expose your lies once and for all!" she screeched at Mr. Bennet, not noticing—or caring—that everyone in the assembly rooms had gone silent—all dancing having halted. Getting no reaction from him, she pushed herself even closer to carry her point, which to all others in the room was merely an inappropriate tirade of a ridiculous woman.

"Just who do you think you are? You have lied about your connection to my friends the Fitzwilliams, who are Mr. Darcy's family. The Earl and Countess are far above you, as I am. Now you have presumed to push your grasping daughter to dance with my Mr. Darcy! I know your daughters have but five thousand pounds, which is nothing to my twenty thousand. You will gain nothing from your attempts. Your machinations will not go unpunished. I will be sure to ensure everyone learns of your pathetic attempts to raise your status," Miss Bingley shrieked in a high-pitched voice. "You are a nobody. No one in my circle would deign to recognise you, you insignificant cockroach!" She stopped to take a breath, nose in the air and pleased with the set-down she had delivered, then glanced around to see how much her words had been appreciated.

It was only then she noticed the disgust on every face —all directed at her. "What are you staring at? Do you not know your betters when you see them," she hissed.

"**Enough!**" A voice too near her for comfort exclaimed.

It was a lady unknown to Caroline standing next to Mr. Bennet. How dare she address her in such a manner!

While Miss Bingley paused to take a breath before responding, the woman did not wait for her to speak, asking with calm assurance, "Do you know who I am? I am confused, since you have used my name as if you are known to me. Since you appear ignorant of it, I am Lady Elaine Fitzwilliam, Countess of Matlock.

"When you were rude to our friend, Mr. Bennet, in his own home, mind you, did he not warn your family what he would do if your behaviour was repeated? I find it pitiable when someone naught but a tradesman's daughter makes the presumptions you have." Lady Matlock stopped herself from speaking before she could say anything that might stoop to the same level as the virago before her. Then she turned to the man on her right and asked, "Since when have tradesmen's daughters been included in our circle, Thomas?"

"Elaine, only the angels on high are in the same circle with you and my Fanny. As for the society in which we partake, few use their power with compassion and care. They do not emulate the best of their circle; it is always the worst they follow." Bennet bowed to her and winked at his Fanny, causing Lord Matlock to chuckle and approve, demonstrated by his clapping Thomas on the back.

Miss Bingley stood frozen in place, the haze of her anger receding only far enough for her to register the unknown lady had said *in his own house*, which meant that Mr. Bennet owned Netherfield Park. She had a sinking feeling, although she attempted to maintain an outward display of confidence.

Forcing herself to realise what else had been said, her world began to splinter when she finally realised who she had just denigrated. The woman was the Countess of Matlock, Mr. Darcy's aunt, the woman she had wanted to meet but had never succeeded in doing so.

'*What have I done?*' she thought, then she heard the Countess speak again.

"William, be a dear and introduce us to this...lady." The Countess' voice remained pleasant, but her tone dripped with disdain.

"With pleasure, Aunt Elaine." Darcy turned to his aunt and bowed. "Aunt Elaine, Uncle Reggie, Andrew, and Marie, this is Miss Caroline Bingley, daughter of a most respected tradesman and sister to my very good friend, Charles Bingley. Richard and I have often related tales of her social gaffes to you. Miss Bingley, my uncle and aunt, the Earl and Countess of Matlock; my cousins, the Viscount and Viscountess

Hilldale; and my cousin, the Honourable Colonel Richard Fitzwilliam."

After that introduction, the finality of what she had done hit Caroline. Before her, in an assembly far from the ton, in a shire she had never heard anyone speak of, stood the very persons she had wished to ingratiate herself with—but they looked at her as if she was below a speck of dirt on their shoes. Hearing the Countess inhale, she knew this nightmare was not yet over.

"I will make sure, as will my daughter, Lady Hilldale, that you will never be received in polite society again. Your transgressions are too numerous to name, but you have forgotten your place. You thought yourself above gently bred landowners and were not merely rude; you were as uncouth as a woman of the streets. You are far too high in the instep! Allow me to inform you, Miss Bingley, the Bennets have owned their land for many generations. They are members of the first circles, something you will *never* be. Insulting our friend in his own house was beyond the pale!"

Caroline now realised how wrong she had been, and wished her actions undone, but that horse had left the barn. The Bennets owned Netherfield Park; they were members of the first circles; everything Mr. Bennet had said was true.

As she looked at the Bennet ladies, Caroline finally noticed their dresses and jewellery were of the quality one might expect of those of the first circles. Her brother was merely a Bennet tenant. She felt she might cast up her accounts. She thought it could not grow worse when she heard her brother speak.

"You will return to Netherfield immediately. Your trunks have been packed already. You will be moved to the inn; your maid will act as your chaperone. At first light tomorrow, the footmen I will send to the inn to ensure you cause no further mischief will make sure you are on the post. One of them will accompany you to Scarborough. When you arrive, what is left of your dowry after I deduct funds to replace what you have broken in Mr. Bennet's house will be released to you, and you will be on your own thereafter.

"Lady Matlock warned you to never show your face in Town again; I suggest you heed her warning," Bingley stated with a look of cold fury on his face, then he looked towards Jane. He saw steely resolve and approval on Jane's face, then her barely contained anger for the way Caroline had treated her family. He knew then he had made the right decision.

"But Charles..." Miss Bingley beseeched, white as a ghost. Then she glanced up and saw distaste on Darcy's face; she could no longer deny he could not abide her presence.

Charles then said, "By the grace of God, those here will not hold the rest of our family responsible for your actions. You would have ruined us all! I am grateful everyone who matters to both Louisa and me knows you alone are the problem. You have done this to yourself even after ample warning; now you must live with the consequences. No matter your plan, no matter had it succeeded, I would never have forced Darcy to marry you. He deserves happiness and Miss Elizabeth is a better match for him than you could ever be."

After listening to her brother, Miss Bingley realised her plan to compromise Mr. Darcy had died along with her hopes of a life in society.

"By the way, Caroline, the Bennet daughters have more than forty thousand pounds each, so your twenty thousand is nothing to theirs. Their true value, however, is their compassion, love of family, and accomplishments."

There were audible gasps from Miss Bingley and the neighbours, who until then had believed the story of five-thousand-pound dowries. Bingley looked apologetically at Bennet for revealing the last, but it seemed Bennet would not hold the slip against him.

His speech completed, he turned his back on Caroline and walked toward Jane Bennet, giving his sister the cut direct. Everyone at the assembly followed his example, even Mrs. Hurst.

A footman escorted a chastised and dejected Caroline Bingley from the room. To her detriment, she had learnt nothing from the experience. She continued to blame her downfall on everyone except herself.

After she left, Sir William ask the musicians to resume playing and everyone went back to enjoying the assembly. Jane, Lizzy, and Mary each danced a total of three times with the gentlemen they had opened the assembly with. The faces of their family, friends, and neighbours sported knowing smiles. There was little doubt of the preferences of the gentlemen.

"I could not be happier for soon we will be more than friends; we will be family," the Countess whispered to Fanny Bennet.

"Elaine, I cannot wait to call Richard, son." Fanny held the hand of the sister of her heart.

"What about William?" The countess inclined her head in the direction of her nephew, who was dancing with Lizzy. Both could see their mutual attraction. "She is the first young woman to catch his attention. He never dances the first and never has danced more than once with any young lady. He has been careful about not raising expectations until he met our Lizzy."

"If he is who Lizzy wants and they love, respect, and esteem each other, I will be happy to welcome Mr. Darcy as a son as well." Fanny smiled sweetly at the couple few could take their eyes from.

"I have known him since birth, and I have never seen the boy besotted before. His entire countenance has brightened. After what almost happened, I never thought I would see him smile again. Oh, I have said too much..." Elaine looked at Darcy in fearful apology.

"Do not worry, Elaine; I know all. He unburdened himself to Thomas; there are no secrets between us. Thomas shared with me and that is as far as it will ever go. Since he spoke to Thomas and was set straight about things beyond his control, I have noticed he has displayed a brighter countenance. As my Lizzy says, he is handsome when he remembers to smile," Fanny said, beaming at her second eldest, who seemed lost in something Mr. Darcy said to her.

"It is a relief to know he has given over blaming himself for what happened. Your acceptance of Georgie even after you learnt of her folly warms my heart. Reggie and I will be grateful forever to both you and Thomas. Since both their parents passed, we have been more parents than aunt and uncle to the Darcys." Elaine pressed her hand to her chest, her heart swelling with love and affection.

"That is obvious to anyone who sees you together. It is a pity we only recently met the Darcys. I understand George and Lady Anne were wonderful people. How well Georgiana gets along with my girls! She seems to have formed a strong bond with Kitty, as they are so close in age," Fanny said. "Please hug them both more. They were stiff as boards when I hugged them the day they arrived." She winked at Elaine, whose rich laughter rang out and made those who heard it smile.

"I will make it my life's mission," the Countess promised. "At least, I will until Lizzy makes it hers," she teased. This time Fanny's laugh filled the air. They linked arms, waiting for the final dance to end, knowing that there was more happiness on the horizon for their families.

CHAPTER 7

A week after the assembly the combined Longbourn and Netherfield Park party was invited to dinner at Lucas Lodge, the home of Sir William and Lady Lucas.

Sir William had been knighted by George III after he gave a speech honouring the King during the Monarch's visit to Meryton. After his investiture at St. James, Sir William had sold his store, feeling his elevation to knighthood precluded him from being in trade.

He purchased a small estate just outside of Meryton that he renamed Lucas Lodge. Sir William was much enamoured by St James and would recount the tale of his investiture to anyone who would listen. Were they like many of the other self-important, sneering members of the *Ton*, the Darcys, and Fitzwilliams could have found Sir William ridiculous. As they were nothing like that, they listened to his oft told tale about receiving his knighthood with good natured patience.

On this night, Sir William was not his normal verbose self. He was awed by the fact he was entertaining an Earl, a Countess, a Viscount, and Viscountess, and their extended family, which were all of the upper first circles, as well as the Bennets, the Philipses, and a few of the other prominent families from around Meryton like the Longs and the Gouldings.

Sir William had been flabbergasted to learn his friend of many years, Thomas Bennet, was not only extremely wealthy, but he owned far more land than anyone in the area imagined and was also a member of the first circles!

Mr. Spencer Goulding tentatively approached Bennet. "Bennet, your girls have forty thousand each, and in addition to Longbourn you own Bennington Fields that you renamed Bennet Fields, and now I find out you own Netherfield! How did this happen? We all noticed you changed after Tom and James were born, but this is beyond even the scope of the most vivid of imaginings here in Meryton," Goulding asked in what he hoped was not too embarrassing an amount of awe.

"It is simple. After the birth of my boys, I looked at what I had become and was not at all proud of myself. The day Tom and James were born, I swore an oath before Almighty God that I would change. Based on that oath, I decided I had to do anything and everything I could to protect my family, and I could not do that hidden away in my study lost in a book and drinking port," Bennet admitted.

Goulding, who had known Bennet almost from birth, was astounded. "Bu-u-u-t the kind of wealth you now possess, how did you manage this Bennet?" he stammered.

"Firstly, we cut costs in any way Fanny and I could manage, and right away through being an attentive estate manager I almost doubled Longbourn's yields. I implemented some new farming methods, and I worked as many hours as were needed to see substantial increases in my tenant's yields. Any adjacent land that became available was purchased to increase Longbourn's acreage, and therefore its profits.

"All profit, anything which could be spared, was invested with my brother Edward Gardiner. After a few years, I had purchased back all the land my profligate ancestor had caused his father to sell off, and besides the two additional estates, I procured as much additional land that became available as I could. It was not long before my income from my estates increased a number of times more than what I had first achieved," Bennet explained. As he spoke, Darcy, who overheard part of the conversation, looked at Bennet in astonishment.

"Edward? Edward Gardiner? Married to Maddie Gardiner née Hamilton that grew up in Lambton where her father was the rector of the Lambton Church?" Darcy exclaimed.

"Yes, he is Fanny's brother. She was Fanny Gardiner before she married me. She, Hattie Philips, and Edward are siblings. That is where Tom's middle name comes from. How do you know Edward and Maddie, Darcy?" Bennet asked inquisitively.

"I am astounded at another connection, Bennet. Years ago, Uncle Reggie recommended my esteemed departed father invest with Gardiner and Associates, Uncle called your brother *King Midas* as he claimed everything Gardiner touches turns to gold.

"My father followed Uncle's advice and invested, and I have continued to since I became the Master of our estates. I had no idea he was your brother. Oh, but excuse me for disturbing your conversation, gentlemen. Please accept my most profound apologies." Darcy looked sheepishly at Bennet and nodded to Goulding.

"Nothing to forgive," both men stated simultaneously, impressed Darcy was not too proud to apologise, even for a perceived slight neither man took as one.

"Now, where were we?" Bennet ribbed Darcy. "Ah yes, recounting my former mistakes. I had not invested with Gardiner despite his urging me to after I married my Fanny. When the twins were born, I started to invest every available penny.

"Gardiner has always far exceeded projections of profits, so I think Reggie's moniker of *King Midas* is apropos. The important point is I never touched the money other than to buy the two estates and land added to Longbourn which has increased my profits. I left all of the money not marked for management of my estates and households with Gardiner to reinvest, so it gets compounded.

"Over the years, the funds have grown as the principal and profits were reinvested, as well as almost all profits from my estates. *That* is how I was able to do what I have done. I left the girl's dowries with Edward as well; they were forty thousand some two years ago, from the last statement Edward gave me they have grown substantially. Please keep this to yourself. It is bad enough that the forty thousand pounds number is out in the world now.

"If fortune hunters knew the real number, it would be so much worse. I have written the contract that only with my, Edward's, and Frank's consent will a dowry be released with Reggie as a stand-in as three signatures are required, so if some fortune hunter tried to compromise one of my girls, or kidnaps her and takes her to Scotland, he will see nothing. I would never force one of my girls to marry where she does not want to even if some blackguard compromises her," Bennet stated protectively.

"When I noted you were increasing Longbourn's lands, and especially when you acquired Bennet Fields, I should have asked you how, but I felt I would be prying into personal and private matters, so I said nothing. I will be contacting Gardiner to invest with him at his soonest convenience," Goulding stated with conviction.

"You are in luck. The Gardiners will arrive on the morrow to join us for a sennight, so you may speak to him directly if you choose," Bennet Informed his friend. Goulding thanked Bennet, stating he would contact Gardiner anon, and wandered off in the direction of his wife.

It was noted how pleasant the gathering was without Miss Bingley to cast a pall on the event. Bingley passingly wondered if it was wrong to not miss his sister, then reminded himself no one other than Caroline herself decided the fate she was now consigned to.

Besides, he had far more pleasant things to think about, the most pressing of which was in the form of his angel, as he had started to call Jane Bennet, when thoughts of her occupied, crossed, or leapt into his mind unbidden.

He had growing self-doubts though, now he knew about the connections and fortune of the Bennets, and that they were accepted into the first circles. He could not help but wonder if he would be considered good enough for one of the Bennet daughters, let alone the one he considered the most beautiful of them.

Caroline's machinations must surely have lowered him in the estimation of the Bennets and Fitzwilliams, regardless of what they said. He had been on the cusp of requesting a courtship with the ethereal and sweet Jane Bennet, but now he was not sure he should. He determined his next step would be to talk to Darcy and the Colonel when they got back to Netherfield Park later that night.

Sir William introduced residents of the neighbourhood to Colonel Forster, who was in command of the Derbyshire Militia that would be setting up camp in Meryton for about three months before heading to an encampment outside of Brighton.

Colonel Forster in turn introduced two of his officers, Captains Carter and Saunderson. As the introductions were being made, a booming *"Forster"* was heard from Colonel Fitzwilliam despite the volume of the discussions in the drawing room.

The Colonels acknowledged one another and moved to meet on one side of the room. The two men grasped each other's hand in obvious comradery that is often shared among military men.

"Fitzwilliam, what are you doing here amongst this

polite society? Should not you be outside with the riff-raff?" Colonel Forster responded with a large grin while the two Colonels were shaking hands vigorously and then slapped each other on the back. "We have known each other for many years," Colonel Forster clarified for those closest, "we trained together when we purchased our first commissions. Like my friend here, I have also risen through the ranks, not purchased my way to Colonel." He turned to Colonel Fitzwilliam. "Does the bet still stand as to who will make General first?" he winked at the group watching and again locked eyes with Richard Fitzwilliam.

"That is easy, I will as I am in the regulars. You know we advance faster than *lowly* militia officers," Colonel Fitzwilliam ribbed. "Where are the rest of your troops, Forster? Or do they only trust you with two Captains?" Richard razzed his friend.

Both Captains had to stop themselves from laughing at the good-natured bantering between the two Colonels, though they continued to watch in wide-eyed amazement because both, for a moment, seemed almost human.

"The main body is on the way from Hampshire and will arrive by the end of the week. I dispatched some officers under the command of Lieutenant Denny to London to recruit some more gentlemen for my unit. I am a little light in gentlemen officers. How would you like to join my unit as one of my lieutenants, Fitzwilliam, even if you are lacking as a gentleman?" Forster jested. At this, the group around the two Colonels, including the two militia officers, laughed heartily.

Richard introduced Colonel Forster and the two Captains to his parents, family, and the Bennets. Forster had met his parents many years before, so it was good to renew the acquaintance.

The Bennet twins were ecstatic at the prospect of more officers to pepper with questions. As noted, their favourite pastime, whenever Richard Fitzwilliam was present, was to ask about military life and exploits. Now they had two Colonels and two Captains to ask their questions of, and more officers to soon come!

"Please tell us more of your time on the peninsular, Richard?" Tom begged.

"Please do, Richard. You know how much we love hearing about your exploits in the army, and we would love to listen to Colonel Forster and Captains Carter and Saunderson tell us about their experiences in the militia as well," James added with a hopeful sparkle in his eye.

"Now boys," their mother interjected with a loving smile. "Please allow the officers to enjoy themselves with the adults. Next time Richard and any of the officers visit Longbourn, and they acquiesce, you may ask all your questions. Colonel Forster, you and your gentlemen officers are welcome to call on us at Longbourn. Thank you for being patient with my babies."

"Mama!" was Tom's indignant response for both his brother and himself. "We will soon be sixteen! *We are not babies!*"

"Calm down, my sweet boys. No matter how old you are or will be, you will always be my babies. Are you not the youngest of my children?" she teased her sons.

"Very well, Mama," the twins responded together, as they often did.

The Captains were very happy at the invitation after hearing about the massive dowries the Bennet sisters had, not knowing what was now public was less than the real number. The excitement was severely dampened when they heard whispers about the restrictions Bennet had put in place.

It was not long after that they realised these were not ladies who would have their heads turned by a man in regimentals wearing a scarlet coat. It was obvious to anyone with eyes in his head that the eldest three were no longer available in the so-called marriage mart.

"Thank you, ma'am," said Colonel Forster. "I will take you up on the offer when my wife arrives." With that acceptance, Mrs. Bennet returned to talk to her friends.

Charlotte Lucas, the oldest daughter, unmarried at the age of seven and twenty, and a long-time very good friend of the eldest two Bennet girls joined the group consisting of the Bennet sisters, Miss Darcy, Bingley, Darcy, and Colonel Fitzwilliam.

"Come now, Eliza, you know what follows. I have opened the pianoforte and the harp is ready for Jane." She looked upon Lizzy with a bright smile.

"Some friend you are, always asking us to play for company," Lizzy retorted good naturedly.

Lizzy liked Charlotte very well, even though she could not agree with her friend's views on matrimony. Lizzy, like her parents and the rest of the Bennets, would only be induced to marry for the deepest love. Charlotte only sought a good situation that would unburden her parents of her care.

She had often shared her belief with Lizzy that felicity in marriage was purely a matter of chance. That if a man showed any interest, the young lady had better show more feeling than she felt so the man would have no misunderstanding whether she was receptive to him or not. She had also opined she did not want to know too much about her future partner ahead of time as she would find out as much as she needed to know after the wedding.

None of the Bennets agreed with what they referred to as her strange beliefs on matrimony, but they were nevertheless very good friends to Charlotte Lucas.

"And I would have you sing as well. Why would I not

when there is none to match the Bennet sisters in singing and playing!" Charlotte enquired. Not prone to false modesty, the four Bennets nodded to Charlotte acknowledging her praise.

Lizzy looked at Jane who gave a slight nod, then she enlisted Mary and Kitty. "If Jane and I are to play then you two can sing," Lizzy requested with a look that rarely allowed for opposition from her younger sisters.

As soon as the assembled guests heard the Bennet sisters were to perform, a hush came over the assembled crowd. "Prepare yourself to be amazed, William," the Countess leaned over to Darcy and offered softly as Lizzy and Jane sat at their instruments.

The four Bennets started with a Mozart aria from the opera *Le nozze di Figaro*. Those who had not had the privilege of hearing the Bennets play and sing before thought they were at a professional concert at the height of the season in London. Lizzy and Jane played while Mary and Kitty raised their voices to the heavens, and just when Darcy thought he had never heard better, he heard the voice of an angel here on earth. Elizabeth Bennet joined the singing with her perfect mezzo-soprano voice.

Darcy was speechless. He had never heard anyone's voice come close to the quality of the tones and notes produced by his Elizabeth. '*When did she become my Elizabeth?*' he asked himself silently. It dawned on him it had been some days since he had fallen irrevocably in love with Elizabeth Bennet.

'*I must speak with her on the morrow,*' he instructed himself. He loved how they debated when they were in each other's company. Not only did Lizzy hold her own with well thought out and intelligent positions, but she sometimes beat him and proved her opinions superior to his. Darcy, who had been the captain of the debating club at Cambridge and undefeated in the debate competition, was amazed how this young woman could run verbal circles about him when she chose to.

In addition to her debating skills, Elizabeth Bennet was a masterful chess player and routinely beat him. Rather than be chagrined, it only increased his ardour for her. The first time she beat him in chess, Uncle Reggie had consoled him sharing it had been many years since he was able to beat her at the game.

He knew at times she would take a position contrary to her own beliefs just so they could have one of their friendly debates. Yes, he acknowledged to himself, he was in the deepest, most ardent of love with this phenomenal woman.

The assembled crowd exhorted them to continue to play and sing, and the sisters ended up performing three songs for the very appreciative audience. Charlotte Lucas leaned to Darcy and the officers, mentioning when the Regent and Queen Charlotte had heard of the musical prowess of the Bennet sisters, they had commanded them to perform for them at Buckingham House, and the Royals had been extremely impressed. Darcy was even more impressed, not by the honour the Royals had bestowed on the Bennets, but by the fact they never boasted about it or anything else.

Meanwhile, Bennet was explaining the same thing he had earlier said to Spencer Goulding about how he changed his family's fortunes to Mr. Jonathan Long and Sir William Lucas, who had asked similar questions.

Both were agog and requested Bennet ask his brother Edward Gardiner when a good time would be for them to come to meet with him on the morrow. Bennet said he would do so as he was already performing the office for Goulding so he would request Gardiner set times for all three of them.

Lady Lucas had always thought of herself in competition with Fanny Bennet, way back from the days before Fanny resigned the name Gardiner. The two had grown up in Meryton and were less than a year apart in age. As she sat ruminating, she understood why Fanny stopped gossiping and never could be bated into doing so after her twins.

There was no point competing when one was not playing on the same field, or in the Bennets' case, in the same universe. Lady Lucas realised she was in one of the lower circles of the gentry for those just out of trade while Fanny and the Bennets were in the first circles and had wealth rivalling that of a peer of the realm.

The Bennet girls had more than forty thousand pounds each as dowries and her two daughters had less than four thousand between them. She did not know their fortunes were about to rise significantly after her husband had his meeting with Edward Gardiner and started to invest everything he could with Gardiner and Associates.

Fanny had said something and Lady Lucas, Sarah to her friends, smiled ruefully. "I am so sorry Fanny, I was wool-gathering. Excuse me, but what did you just say?" she asked softly.

"Nothing of much import, Sarah. I just wondered where you were as you seemed very far from here," Fanny asked quietly, her eyes filled with kindness.

"I owe you an apology, Fanny," Sarah Lucas said with a contrite look on her face.

"What do you think you need to apologise for, Sarah? I cannot think of anything." Fanny had a confused look on her face.

"Fanny, as much as it chagrins me to admit to you, I have always held the belief I was better than you. Of the two of us, however, you changed for the better. So much so after the twins that I was envious and refused to allow myself to acknowledge all the ways you had bettered yourself.

You stopped boasting and gossiping; you had an air of contentment about you that I could not fathom or emulate, so I suppose I felt if I looked at how you changed then I would have to look at myself. Not being ready to do so, I was so jealous and petty..." she stopped when Fanny locked onto her arm.

"*Sarah Lucas*, let me stop you there! You have nothing to apologise for. You cannot be held accountable for your thoughts, and as far as I know, you have never slighted me or any in my family. The fact you recognise now that you may need to make changes only points to your inherent goodness and value as a friend.

"Heaven forbid, but you could be another Miss Bingley, and never see your faults, ignore anyone who tried to point you in the right direction, and become very bitter. Sarah, I have known you as far back as I can remember so if there is anything I can ever do to help you as you take steps to become the woman you want to be, I am here for you," Fanny told her friend lovingly.

"From the bottom of my heart, I thank you, Fanny, but you do not need me when your friends include peers of the realm." Sarah shook her head, trying to understand why Fanny was bothering with her when she had been so very unkind in her own thoughts.

"Do you think we have ever selected our friends by social standing? What is important to us is genuine friendship, character, and that we enjoy each other's company. Social standing has nothing to do with it, so please put such thoughts out of your mind now and forever. You have been my friend since I was a little girl holding onto my mama's apron strings, do you think so little of me that I would cast you off because of wealth or our other friends?" Fanny challenged.

"You became so calm, and you had no more attacks of nerves, they stopped from one day to the next, I could not fathom what had changed. I was so very confused," Lady Lucas stated with a smile.

At that, both friends giggled like they once had so many years ago when they were schoolgirls. When the comfort of laughing with her friend enveloped her, Sarah knew no matter how wealthy the Bennets were, or who their friends and connections were, the Bennets would never cut the connection to the Lucases as so many others in the same position who rose to higher social circles would have. The Bennets esteemed each person by the content of their character, and Sarah resolved she would always be worthy of Fanny's friendship.

As Kitty and Georgie were not out yet, they were requested to play some music the party could dance to. The girls acquiesced with alacrity. This was such a big change for Georgiana, as before she had come to stay with the Bennets, she never would have considered playing the pianoforte for anyone outside the immediate family circle, even before Ramsgate.

Now she could not wait to share the experience with her friends, and the joy she took in it made all those who loved her fill with love and gratitude for the Bennet girls who had helped her not only find herself but help her transcend the timid and shy girl she had once been.

Darcy was overjoyed at the transformation he saw in his sister, and almost as much at the changes he had noticed in himself. He knew it was all due to the Bennets and their warm, loving, familial, genteel, kind, and welcoming ways.

The Darcys had been made to feel like long-lost family and were valued for themselves, not their wealth, connections, or standing. It was a whole new experience for him, being amongst personages that not only matched his wealth and moral codes but had so much more in ways he had not considered because their world was more naturally inclusive of others due to so many in the household.

After Georgie had been at Longbourn but a few days, she had felt comfortable enough to share with the Bennet sisters her misadventure from the summer. Darcy remembered the happy tears she had cried when she told him none of the sisters had judged the Darcys generally, or her specifically, for the occurrences that culminated in what they helped her call *The Ramsgate Debacle*.

All of their rebukes were for the companion who lied and deceived the Darcys and the Colonel, and the dastardly wicked Wickham who manipulated, lied to, and tried to seduce a fifteen-year-old girl.

That unburdening was the final turning point for Georgie, and when combined with his own discussion sharing all with Bennet before Georgie arrived, he had been able to literally watch the dark fog that had weighted down their mood since Ramsgate lift and fade away.

As soon as Georgie and Kitty sat down at the pianoforte, Darcy approached Elizabeth and was granted a dance, as was Richard with Mary, and Bingley with Jane. Charlotte and Maria, Charlotte's seventeen-year-old sister who was out, each danced with one of the Captains who had accompanied Colonel Forster.

Unlike the Bennet girls, Maria thought a man in a red coat looked very fine indeed and had always dreamed about marrying an officer in regimentals and him whisking her off to far away and exotic places.

If she knew the reality of the poverty most militia officers under the rank of major suffered, and the fact they never left England's shores, she might have reconsidered her opinions of militia officers as marriage material.

CHAPTER 8

There were three very nervous suitors readying themselves to ride the three miles to Longbourn the next morning. Without Caroline Bingley there, the stay at Netherfield Park for both the Colonel and Darcy had become much more pleasant.

There was no more need for military strategy to keep them away from the termagant, nor the need to find things to do before and after visiting hours, not that any of them had actually paid attention to the proper hours of late.

The three single men staying at Netherfield Park had broken their fasts earlier than their wont and were pacing around the drawing room trying to burn off their nervous energy as they waited for an acceptable time to make a call. Richard knew he could have gone to break his fast at Longbourn like he had many times since his parents, brother, and sister had been in residence, but today was not a normal day. Not for him, his cousin, or Bingley.

Richard Fitzwilliam was sure of Mary's answer as they had long planned for this day. Darcy was not sure, but he felt his entreaty would be welcomed by the lovely Elizabeth Bennet, and Bingley had no idea whether the answer he would receive would be affirmative or negative. Even after the assurances he had received from his friends, he was still worried about his reception.

While they were waiting to leave Richard's mind drifted back to when he first took an interest in Mary beyond that of a cousin-like family friend, he remembered the exact day.

It was on her fifteenth birthday that I noticed her more than before. We were at Longbourn to celebrate her, and the twins as well as they were to become teenagers.

From thirteen until that birthday Mary had gone through a stage. She had found and diligently started to read that idiot Fordyce's sermons and had begun to spew inane quotes in her conversation from his tripe. She had worn her hair in a severe style and had worn unflattering dresses that hid her womanly assets.

Father and mother asked the Bennets why they did not correct her, and they said they knew she was intelligent enough to come to the realisation on her own without their interference. They knew what they were about!

When we arrived for that visit, I thought my eyes were deceiving me. Mary was dressed in a very becoming day dress and her hair was not in the severe bun she had taken to wearing; she wore it down, as was appropriate for a girl not out in society. Her green eyes were shining, and she had the same colour hair as Lizzy. There were no more quotes from Fordyce as she allowed her innate intelligence to shine through.

When I asked her what happened, she told me that some months prior she had a long conversation with Longbourn's rector as she was confused that no one seemed to appreciate her moralistic views. Mr. Hastings had taken the time to explain the difference between living as a Christian and talking as one. She had quickly understood what he was explaining to her, and just as her parents had predicted, she changed her ways on her own.

We started to talk that visit, and the more we talked the more I became fascinated with her and that is when the infatuation started. She was too young for me to do more than talk to, but over the next two years we got closer and closer and whenever the families were together, we found we spent most of our time together. There was never anything outside of the bounds of propriety, we talked, debated, and argued, but never with acrimony.

By the time that she turned seventeen, she was a beauty that matched her older sisters, inside and out. The Bennets were visiting Snowhaven, it was the year William and Georgie were at the Darcy estate in Scotland. Bennet called me in and asked my intentions as he could not help but observe my marked attention to Mary.

By then I knew she was not indifferent to me and that my infatuation was now full-blown and deep love. I informed him that I intended to ask for a courtship when she came out. Bennet told me he would be happy to entertain that request from me, but he wanted me to wait until she was nineteen, a year after her entry into society. I agreed, of course, she was worth the wait.

Not long after her come out I admitted my feelings to her, my relief was immense when she told me that she returned them in full measure. Now I am less than an hour away from making the request I have wanted to make for over two years.

Richard was snapped out of his reverie by Bingley's nervous pacing. Bingley was much relieved after reviewing his doubts with his two friends the previous evening when they had returned home, but still not sure. The Colonel, who had known the Bennets for many years, assured Bingley the only thing that would be important to them was the content of his character, and whether Jane loved him and he her.

Darcy agreed with his cousin, adding that everything he had observed about the Bennets agreed with Richard's conclusion. He reminded Bingley what they had heard Mrs. Bennet say to her girls that one day not long after they had made their acquaintance about only marrying for the deepest love. Bingley had felt much better after the discussion, the result of the relief meant he was one of now three getting ready for a mad dash to Longbourn.

The Hursts smiled knowingly at them as they observed the three anxiously watching the clock, paying attention to little else other than not walking into one another or any furniture as they roamed about the sitting room. At the first chime indicating it was at last nine o'clock in the morning, they took their leave with barely a word, and they sprang on their waiting horses.

Richard had requested the mounts be made ready as soon as he had descended the stairs that morning. The three men eagerly galloped off in the direction of Longbourn. Richard had waited years to claim his Mary but this ride, to him, seemed like the longest trial though in fact none of them had ever ridden to Longbourn so fast.

~~~~~~~/~~~~~~~

All three handed their coats and hats to Bennet's butler, then were shown in and announced to the group sitting in the blue drawing room where bows and curtsies were made.

"Welcome gentlemen," Bennet smirked as he looked at their faces brightened by the exercise. He had watched them galloping and then slow as they reached the gate and had little doubt what the morning would bring. He had determined it was best to make them squirm a little as he had for his Fanny, otherwise one might miss the opportunity to so keenly appreciate a positive response.

"You have arrived as we are being entertained with the most ridiculous letter I have ever read." He offered the three young men who had practically taken residence in his house leave to sit, amused they were waiting for the offer when of late they had acted as family because his Fanny had given them leeway to do so since the Fitzwilliams were, in fact, in residence.

Bennet provided some background to the amusement of the listeners, explaining that prior to the birth of his sons, Tom and James, the estate had been entailed to a very narrow-minded, illiterate, and otherwise uneducated, miserly cousin, a Mr. Ned Collins.

The cousin had felt it a personal affront Fanny had dared to produce not one, but two sons, and had in jealousy and disgust severed all contact while apoplectic over the usurping of what he deemed his God given right to inherit Longbourn. Bennet also explained the man had unsuccessfully tried to stop the breaking of the entail in front of a judge.

This same cousin had since passed away and now his son, who had taken orders and was the rector at Hunsford, which was the living gifted by Rosings Park, had written a letter inviting himself to come visit. In Collins's expressed words, he wanted to *heal the breach and offer an olive branch*, as instructed by his much-exalted patroness, none other than the *great* Lady Catherine de Bourgh.

As soon as William and Richard heard this, they knew this vicar would be as obsequious and sycophantic as all the others Lady Catherine appointed, never mind it was no longer her gift to appoint. The more of a sycophant the appointee was, the more she preferred it. She was the kind of person that needed her ego puffed up by senseless and unwarranted grovelling.

The Fitzwilliams in residence had already apprised Bennet of the type of man that the rector would be. From what Bennet described of Collins's letter, this inhabitant of Hunsford was the worst specimen yet, and that was really saying something.

Not only had he invited himself with no prior acquaintance or introduction, but he was a mixture of servile, praising, pomposity, and pandering obsequiousness rolled into one. Even worse, it was determined from his writing that he was no smarter than, as he called him, *his dear honourable departed father.*

Based on the manner in which he went on about

Lady Catherine and her condescension to him, one could rightly be confused whether he worshiped the Lord on High or Lady Catherine or both. Due to his lack of attention, or his inherent inability to handle details, the letter had been misdirected and he was due to arrive on the morrow at four o'clock.

Bennet decided not to send his express rider to Hunsford to deliver a response telling him that he was not welcome because he was certain the parson would ignore the express and come anyway.

The fact Collins had the gall to suggest his offering of an olive branch would be to marry one of the Bennet daughters, so when Mr. Bennet went to his eternal reward he would be there to lead and guide the family when he took over the estate, was the point that made him most unwilling to host this idiot.

"He does realise Longbourn will be mine one day hopefully many, many years from now, does he not? In addition, I have my brother James so there are two sons, and the entail was broken almost six years ago. Was he not in the court when the judge delivered his verdict?" Tom stated incredulously.

"Given the mean understanding he displays in his letter, Son, he more than likely believes with Lady Catherine's permission, and his being a member of the clergy, the rules do not apply to him. He seems to share a trait with Miss Bingley in that he considers no facts that do not fit with what he wants and makes up his own reality," Bennet opined.

"That would make him very compatible with Catherine. She has always believed the rules are what she decides they are, and the truth is whatever she wants it to be. She thinks she is above the law, the King, and even God, I dare say. I have no proof, but I strongly suspect she had a hand in my late brother Lewis de Bourgh's death these fifteen years past," Lord Matlock stated. "Why do you think that in the face of both written and oral proof contradicting her nonsense of an agreement for William to marry his cousin, Anne, she steadfastly repeats the lie she has told since my brother George passed?"

"Is she really that bad, that delusional?" asked Thomas.

"**YES**!!" All the Darcys and Fitzwilliams present simultaneously responded.

"And far worse! You thought Caroline Bingley lived in her own dream world? She has nothing on our Aunt Catherine," Richard added in not too *sotto voce*.

"Other than ride out to meet him on the road on the morrow, there is nothing we can do but wait for this interesting specimen of humanity to arrive. Once he arrives and we assess the situation, we will decide what to do with my uninvited, distant cousin." Bennet sighed in resignation.

If the three young men did not have a very specific purpose in mind for that day, they may have thought about volunteering for the office of riding out right away to send the wayward parson home. But this day their minds were much more pleasantly engaged.

The three besotted men asked the Bennet siblings and Georgie if they would like to take a turn in the park. Once the group of ten had their outerwear, they all exited the house for their walk.

It did not escape Fanny and Thomas, Reggie and Elaine, and Andrew and Marie that the three men who had shown up at the earliest possible moment a gentleman caller could come were paired with the very same ladies they had danced with thrice at the assembly.

~~~~~~~/~~~~~~~

Very soon the three couples created some separation from the group, leaving the twins, Georgie, and Kitty to act as ineffectual chaperones.

Having a long understanding with Mary, Richard was less hesitant so was the first to speak. "Mary, you know I have loved you for many years now, not as a friend or like a family member, but as a man loves a woman. I had agreed with your parents to not request a courtship of you until you turned nineteen.

"Yes, I know it is next week, but I cannot wait any longer. I love you more than anything and could not imagine living my life without you by my side." He watched her, elated his Mary was blushing becomingly, so he felt encouraged to continue. "Considering the length of time we have already waited, I would ask for an engagement now, but I know your parents desire a six-month courtship.

"As much as I love you, I would never ask you to go against your parents by offering you an engagement already, though know my intentions are what others call honourable, but I call inevitable. If I have any say they will end only when you let me marry you. Mary Anne Bennet, will you grant me the honour of a courtship?" Richard asked gently, tenderly, only with the barest hint of a tremor detectable in the rich timbre of his voice.

Mary, who had been longer in love with him than he with her, did not have to think before she answered in the affirmative. Richard and Mary turned back toward the house so that Richard could finally request consent from Mr. Bennet.

~~~~~~~/~~~~~~~

The next pair to pause and face one another were Jane and Bingley. Though he was still a little unsure if he would be accepted by the Bennets, he knew he would never forgive himself if he did not at least try to win the happiness he was just only starting to comprehend.

"I know I am a mere tradesman's son, and one who must claim a sister that leaves much to be desired. She has, in fact, insulted your estimable and genteel family at every turn, but I would never be able to forgive myself if I do not at the very least ask..."

The normally serene Jane cut him off with a loud inhaled breath which stopped Bingley's speech. There was a definite glint of anger in her eye that those that knew her best would have identified as her about to defend those she held dearest.

Bingley did not have that experience with her, so he feared he was sunk, and his shoulders hunched with dejection as he deflated.

"Mr. Charles Bingley do not dare to so denigrate yourself! Firstly, and we have *ALL* told you this, we do not hold you responsible in any way for the actions of your sister. You took resolute and immediate action to deal with her. Secondly, do you not see and realise that we Bennets judge people by the content of their characters, by how they behave and treat others, not by where they come from or the size of their bank account?

"My beloved Uncle Edward is in trade, as you well know. My Uncle Philips is the local solicitor in Meryton, and my own esteemed mother is the daughter of a solicitor. Would it not be hypocritical of us to reject one with roots in trade?

"It is time you come to terms with those facts and accept them as truths. If you do not, that means you do not trust those I love or me," Jane challenged, her eyebrows arched as she let him work through his astonishment at her speech. Jane could read the truth in his eyes, he believed her. "Now, Sir, if you were about to ask me what I suspect that you were, I suggest you start again without reference to your social position or the actions of your sister!" Jane instructed with a steely disposition.

Bingley let out a breath he had been holding for the

length of her speech as he felt a feeling of relief wash over him. "Miss Bennet, from the moment I met you, from when your father introduced us that fateful, perfect day I called on your family for the first time, I have been falling in love with you.

"Your kindness, charitable works, your accomplishments, and the love I see in your family all tell me you are a woman that for me personifies all goodness. I find it hard to believe I can deserve one as good as you, but I would like to try and see if we fit as well as I believe we will. Would you do me the greatest honour and grant me a courtship so the world will know you are the woman I hope to earn the love of as you already have mine," Bingley requested with ever-increasing confidence as Jane's serenity returned but for a light blush.

After a minute of silence, in which Bingley's insecurities made him think portended bad news, Jane offered her reply. "Mr. Bingley, although I may not love you today, I do esteem you above any man of my acquaintance and I too find you to be a very honourable man. I can easily see you are everything a young man should be. The fact you were able to stand up to your sister speaks very well of your resolve. However, I will not pretend an emotion I do not yet fully possess. So therefore, it is with pleasure I agree to your request for a courtship." Jane smiled a smile which to Bingley rivalled one he expected to see on the angels on High.

At hearing the response he had dreamed of but had not allowed himself to hope for, Bingley too lit up with a smile that stretched from ear to ear. Even if she did not love him yet, he would do everything in his power to be worthy of earning her love during the courtship, that is, if Mr. Bennet granted his permission.

He gently took her hands, after she nodded her permission, and bestowed kisses on her gloves right over her pulse. As he did Jane felt a warmth and a stirring she had never felt before. This set a second couple off toward the house to request an interview with Mr. Bennet.

~~~~~~~/~~~~~~~

And then there was one couple left. After being lost in each other's company and not seeing anyone but themselves, they looked around and saw the other two couples, as well as Kitty and Georgie, had all returned to the house and it was just them and the twins, who were out of earshot, in the park.

"It seems we have been all but deserted," offered Lizzy in a teasing fashion as she looked around the park for her missing sisters and their gentlemen.

"So it seems," Darcy agreed. He determined there was no better time than this as if it had been a request he had personally made of the Fates. "Miss Elizabeth, you are too intelligent to have not noted my marked attention toward yourself, and too good to trifle with my affections," he began, overjoyed when Miss Elizabeth nodded for him to continue.

"When I arrived in Hertfordshire, I was in a very dark place. Georgie has shared what almost happened to her this summer in Ramsgate, correct?" Lizzy nodded again. Darcy continued, "However, that all changed when I met your father, your family, and especially you."

Now Lizzy was blushing from her hairline to the top of her gown. This reaction told him she was not unaffected by or indifferent to him, so he continued on his path, feeling much encouraged. "I have always scoffed at the notion of love at first sight, or at least I had until that first time I saw your countenance and your very fine eyes assessing me as you sat in your drawing room." His colour heightened with the intense way she was looking into his eyes. Elizabeth worried her lip and blushed into an even deeper shade of crimson.

"From that moment on I could feel my melancholy lifting. The process had started when I had spoken to your father and felt comfortable enough to confide in him and telling him the tale lightened the load on my shoulders. However, when I saw you that first time it was like you had lightened the burden on my soul.

"I must inform you that I am usually a very private person who does not like to lay his actions bare for others to see. Your father helped me understand what others had tried to tell me, that I was taking blame for the actions of others, that I had taken on blame not mine to take." Darcy paused and looked introspective for a moment. "Now that I have been able to lay the blame where it truly belongs, I find I can live with a positive outlook again, but as I look forward, I know my life would be empty and incomplete without you in it.

"You make me feel whole. You complete me. It is as if I have been only surviving until I found you, and now I am anxious to live again. I have never wanted someone who would just defer to me, and you have demonstrated time and time again in our lively debates that you have a very sharp mind of your own. Nor do I want a mindless trophy wife who mindlessly clings to my arm.

"What I want, no, what I need like I need the air I breathe, is you. My life without you would be meaningless and empty, would be bleak, and having existed in that state, I know what it means and will do all in my power to avoid such a fate. Without you, my life will be empty and devoid of pleasure.

"With the intellect and vivacious wit that you have honed, you will challenge me and not back down when needed, I hope you will continue to debate with me even if sometimes you take opinions not your own, and you have said you too will be as happy with a good book in front of a fire rather than so-called polite society in London.

"My life will always be full and interesting with you in it. You are my soul mate. Everything I have seen here tells me that you would not hesitate to be my partner in every sense of the word.

"My parents' greatest desire for Georgie and me was for us to find our match; the one who would love and complete us. If they could have met you, they would have seen we were perfectly formed for each other, and you are the *only* one for me. Elizabeth Bennet, it may seem quick to some, but please believe me when I say I love you. Most ardently."

He did not know it yet, but he could not have declared himself with more convincing words which demonstrated his love and respect for Elizabeth. Further, his words helped her allow herself to be open to him in ways she was not sure she ever would be able to with any man.

"I had intended to only ask for a courtship today Elizabeth, but I find I have no questions for which a courtship would be needed to answer. I know I want you to share my life with me, the good and the bad. I know you have a large fortune, but I do not need it.

"I have more than enough for the two of us and any children we may have in the future. Of course, if you accept me. I have told you how much I love and respect you, but your thoughts and feelings are much more important to me than my own. I will live and die for you, Elizabeth, for only you, and will do all I can to make sure that in my care none of your days see you come to harm.

"If you, however, feel you are not in love with me yet and that you need to get to know me better, I will request a courtship for as long a period you feel you need. But if, as I truly hope that you do," Darcy dropped down onto one knee, "if your feelings match mine in any way, then my dearest, loveliest Elizabeth, again I confess my everlasting and most ardent love and would ask you make me the happiest of men should you consent to marry me, to be my helpmeet, to allow me the deepest of happiness by being my wife."

Tears started to roll down Lizzy's cheeks and at first,

Darcy thought she was upset. He was about to apologise and stood up when she rose onto her tiptoes and placed a chaste kiss on his lips. Darcy froze; not daring to hope that this meant what he thought it did.

"Yes, William, and yes again. I will marry you, yes, infinite times, yes. I love you so very much, I could burst with joy. Almost from our first meeting, I too have been falling in love with you. When I see how patient you are with my brothers and sisters, your sister, and all the rest of the family, how genuine you are, I am lost. You have demonstrated respect for me in our debates and discussions, you have treated me as an intellectual equal rather than some silly girl to be merely tolerated.

"When we play chess, you really play to win, and I have never detected any animus when I won." Elizabeth arched an eyebrow with an impertinent look that made him smile and display the dimples that she loved to see. "Another thing that convinced me how worthy and honourable a man you are was seeing your interaction with the servants. You treat them with respect, not disdain.

"With just these facts how could I not but love you? When you look at me, I see the love, respect, and esteem which I require my husband to regard me with within your eyes. So yes, William as previously stated, I will marry you. I too do not need a courtship to find out what I have known for a while, that you are the only man I could ever be prevailed upon to marry." Elizabeth's heart filled to almost bursting and she sniffled as any moment of great joy requires.

Darcy was overcome by her answer, so it took some moments for him too to regain his sensibilities. "Do you prefer Elizabeth or Lizzy?" he asked glowing with happiness.

"Either my love," she replied softly, and her response sounded like music to his ears.

Their lips met again in a longer, deeper, and more

passionate kiss heavy with the promise of more to come in the future, until a voice intruded and made them pull apart.

"Hey! Darcy and Lizzy, what do you think you are doing?" James demanded.

The newly declared engaged couple blushed with embarrassment for having forgotten the twins were not too far away in the park. They looked up and saw both boys glaring at them as they strode closer. "This better mean you are to be our brother!" Tom stated with authority as they reached the furiously blushing couple.

"I have just proposed, and Elizabeth has accepted my hand. Unless your father refuses my suit then yes, we will be brothers," Darcy replied with the widest of smiles, one that displayed his dimples again and made his fiancée's stomach flutter. His small Darcy family would expand exponentially.

"You should smile more often. You are so very handsome when you smile like that." Elizabeth leaned toward him speaking softly so only he would hear.

"After you speak to Papa, I expect you to come to James and me and get our approval as well!" Tom smirked as he ribbed William as the twins walked the newly declared lovers back toward the house.

~~~~~~~/~~~~~~~

Mr. Bennet entered the drawing room with a grinning Charles Bingley just as the four from outside arrived. "Bingley here has requested a courtship with Jane, and she has accepted him, which makes the second today although we all expected Richard's request this week." Bennet stood up proud and tall, glad his daughters were finding just the kind of men he hoped keeping their dowries secret would attract.

As everyone was congratulating the second newly courting couple, James went up to his father. "Papa, I think William wants to talk to you," he stated quietly.

Bennet glanced at his Lizzy and surmised he was

about to be asked for a third courtship, so he indicated for Darcy to follow him into his study. Once in the study with the door closed, Bennet sat behind the desk while Darcy sat stiffly in front of it, guessing correctly that Bennet expected another courtship request.

Darcy cleared his throat and then started to speak nervously. "Mr. Bennet, if you are expecting another request for a courtship, I must disabuse you of that notion." He noticed a questioning look on Bennet's face. "I am here to ask for Miss Elizabeth's hand in marriage," Darcy stated plainly so there could be no confusion about his intent or desires.

Bennet and his wife had both seen this was inevitable, that Lizzy and William suited each other like a hand in glove, but Bennet had not expected this exact request today. "Her hand in marriage?" Bennet asked with no little surprise.

"Yes sir, I asked Eliza...Miss Elizabeth for her hand and she has granted my fondest wish and my deepest desire. She has honoured me by accepting me as her fiancé," Darcy informed Bennet.

"I see," Bennet said noncommittedly as he rang a bell. Hill knocked once on the door and opened it. "Please request Mrs. Bennet and Miss Elizabeth join us, and thank you, Hill."

Hill silently closed the door and very soon it opened to admit Mrs. Bennet and Lizzy. Once everyone was comfortably seated, Bennet turned to address his partner in life, his beloved Fanny. "Darcy has not asked for a courtship like we speculated, my love. He asked for her hand in marriage and has told me that Lizzy accepted him," Bennet explained.

"That is correct Papa and Mama," Elizabeth confirmed as she looked at each of her beloved parents in turn. "We are deeply in love, so we do not need a courtship to find out if we fit. We already know that we do," she stated calmly as she slipped her hand into her William's, intertwining their fingers and squeezing his hand to help him relax and winning a private thank you and a smile that was hers alone.

"William is looking for a partner, not someone to defer to him. He needs someone to challenge him, to debate with him, to read books with, to play chess with, and to have the kind of partnership I see before me every day. For as long as I can remember, we have all gotten to watch the excellent example you have set for us, and you should not be surprised I would settle for none but the promise of the kind of marriage you share.

"You must have noticed how we love to debate all sorts of issues, and William always respects my point of view, even when he does not agree with it. And most importantly, when he sees the sense of my point, he has no problem adjusting his opinion to match mine and learn from me as I will learn from him. He has never dismissed anything I have said just because of my sex."

Both Bennet and Fanny cogitated for a minute or two, in which they watched the young couple offer calm assurances of knowing each other's desires. What they were asking for was surely as inevitable as the sun would rise in the east on the morrow. After a silent communication between the Bennet parents, Bennet cleared his throat.

"Do you know her dowry by now is over fifty thousand pounds?" Bennet asked Darcy, waiting for his reply.

"I, in fact, did not know the exact number other than the *more than forty thousand* which is publicly known, but it is immaterial to me," Darcy stated. "My reported income is ten thousand clear a year, but that is just from Pemberley and is less than the actual. The truth is that my income from all my estates and investments with your brother Edward is over five and thirty thousand a year. Money is not a motivating factor in my proposal, only my deep and abiding love for Elizabeth. You have my unreserved permission to ask Mr. Gardiner yourself, as he is here at Longbourn. I have increased Georgie's dowry to sixty thousand pounds, but as far as the *Ton* knows she still has thirty thousand. Whatever Elizabeth brings to the marriage will remain hers to use as she sees fit."

Bennet looked at Fanny and they again silently communicated, then he stood and extended his hand to Darcy. "Welcome to the family, Son," Bennet offered then he looked to his second daughter. "I could never have parted with you to anyone less worthy, my Lizzy. You will be very happy together." Bennet smiled sadly at his second daughter. He was happy she had found a man worthy of her, but sad she would be leaving his home.

Darcy, anxious to start the next phase of their lives, asked those present how long they would like the engagement to be, admitting for his own part the shorter the better. He wanted to never have to part from Lizzy again.

"I believe that six weeks would be sufficient," Fanny allowed.

The newly engaged man requested there would be no public announcement in the papers until he had conferred with the Fitzwilliams about how to deal with the Lady Catherine problem. Bennet and Fanny, long knowing the issue, gave their amused agreement, offering their unreserved support.

The four rose from their chairs, and after hugs and handshakes were given and received, they headed back to the drawing room to share the news with the soon-to-be shocked, albeit very happy, party within.

As they entered the drawing room, Fanny saw her housekeeper and quietly asked her to have the butler bring champagne for the party, which was unobtrusively and efficiently done. Once all the glasses were charged, Bennet again asked for everyone's attention.

"As you know, Richard and Charles have requested and

been granted courtships with Mary and Jane respectively. I thought William and Lizzy were going to be the third couple to make such a request of me today, but I erred. In fact, William requested and was granted Lizzy's hand, with both mine and Fanny's blessing." He smiled at the initial surprise on the faces of many in the room, and envy on more than just one, for skipping the courtship period.

Whatever else Bennet about to say was lost in a sea of congratulations. Georgie threw herself at Lizzy and fell into her arms, tears of happiness rolling down her cheeks as she hugged her tightly. "Oh Lizzy, I am to gain four sisters and two brothers! Thank you for making William so very happy," Georgiana gushed as her tears made streaks on her cheeks and her smile made them almost brighter than diamonds.

"Well well," boomed the Earl, "Andrew and Richard will finally have you and Georgie for siblings. Elaine and I could not be happier for you. I hope you know we have considered you more children than niece and nephew since Anne and then George died. We are very proud of you, William." The Earl's voice was gruff with emotion as his lady wife held and squeezed his hand.

"With us knowing Lizzy almost from birth," added Andrew with a mischievous glint in his eye, "I do not know if you are quite good enough for our Lizzy, Cousin." He winked at Lizzy and again turned a doleful stare on Darcy, making Marie smack his arm playfully.

"Do not tease poor William, Andrew. You know he will get you back when you least expect it." His wife reminded him, winking at William who barked out a laugh that turned all in the room toward him, his lack of reserve worthy of being noted. Already he was changed for the better because of Lizzy.

"Yes dear, sorry William." The Viscount cleared his throat and pretended to be serious.

"No slight taken, Andrew. But mark your wife's words well, you never know when to expect me to return the favour," Darcy jested in return.

"Now boys," the Countess looked between the two, "there will be none of that revenge or retaliation business."

"Yes mother, but you well know we were only teasing." Andrew chuckled, marvelling that no matter how old he got, his mother could always make him feel like a boy again.

"It is true, Aunt Elaine. I was well aware Andrew was only ribbing, so no harm done," William vowed solemnly. He felt his betrothed squeeze his large hand with her dainty and delicate one. His fiancée, how well that sounded.

Lizzy was hugged by her Aunt Maddie and Uncle Edward, then swarmed by her nieces and nephews. "Our little Lizzy will be Mistress of Pemberley, Edward. Lizzy, you have no idea how beautiful the estate is, and you know I think Derbyshire to be the best shire in all of England." Aunt Maddie smiled down at Lizzy.

"Have you been to Pemberley, Mrs. Gardiner?" Darcy asked in surprise.

"We are to be family in six weeks, so you must call me Aunt or Madeline, whichever you please. One harvest festival when I was but twelve, I had the pleasure of seeing Pemberley and meeting your esteemed, late parents, long before your late father started to invest with my Edward." Aunt Maddie smiled warmly as she met Darcy's eyes.

"Maddie has told me that she believes I would get lost fishing at Pemberley and forget to come back to the house," Gardiner chuckled.

"When you are in the area next, you must stay at Pemberley, Mr. Gardiner, from now on you and any of our extended family have an open invitation to visit Pemberley at any time. It would be my pleasure to provide you with rod, reel, and tackle, and to show you the best places to fish," Darcy invited with alacrity, already imagining more and more family around him and Georgiana than he ever fathomed before meeting the Bennets.

"I thank you for your offer, as I do so love to fish. Please call me Gardiner or Uncle Edward. Besides soon being family, we have known each other for years and we are now practically neighbours since Maddie and I moved the family to Portman Square." Gardiner chuckled as he nodded at Darcy's look of pleasure. "It surprises me that Maddie never mentioned seeing Pemberley to you before today, but as those times we saw each other were business meetings, that may explain it."

The long-time family by choice and soon-to-be family by marriage celebrated well into the night and all seemed right with the world.

CHAPTER 9

I t was right at four o'clock the next day when the threatened, unwanted visit of the hapless and dim-witted parson occurred. A gig pulled up in front of Longbourn at the exact time the letter had said he would arrive so the inhabitants thought the parson must have stopped and waited until the appointed time he had indicated.

The Bennets, who were outside to greet him, found him to be worse than any of them expected. He was greasy-haired, or at least what hair there was left was greasy, and the odour that wafted from him was definitely more than a day of travel's smell. The repugnant smell preceded him as he descended from the gig. He was of middling height, had a large belly, and was sweating profusely which could not but add to the rank smell of one who had obviously not bathed in far too long.

Bennet and Fanny had stepped out to meet him and they could not help but notice the covetous way he looked at the house and park. "William Collins, at your service...." the parson started to bow but only got to the initial stages of the gesture when he was brought up short.

"Do you always invite yourself to a home of one you have never been introduced to, or arrive without any confirmation your presence is either welcomed or wanted?" Bennet demanded.

"B-b-but I am a member of the clergy," he claimed as he tried to puff up his chest, "and my beneficent patroness, the honourable Lady Catherine de Bourgh, told me it was acceptable to condescend to visit my poor relations. She is never wrong." It was a most ridiculous statement. No one is never wrong.

Before Bennet could respond in anger, the Earl had come outside unnoticed. "You ignorant sycophant, she is, in fact, never *right!*" the Earl bit out; his anger controlled but awesome to behold.

"How dare you speak of that great lady in such a manner? Just who are you to slander my patroness so?" Collins demanded, obviously not recognizing the clues he was addressing a peer.

"As you do not have the sense to be introduced first, I will elucidate you. I am Reginald Henry Andrew Fitzwilliam, the Earl of Matlock and brother to your termagant of a patroness, and I am head of the Fitzwilliam family!" boomed the Earl.

At this, Collins bowed so low he almost kissed the ground. Everyone watching was amazed he did not actually topple over. "Y-y-your Lordship! I did not realise I was talking to an illustrious personage such as yourself. I would have never..." Collins stammered, not daring to look directly at the Earl.

"That is why sensible people wait to be introduced before they make fools of themselves." The Earl cut the parson off, who was, it was noted, sweating even more profusely than before.

The man had turned white with fear, but once he regained some of his colour he turned to Bennet and requested a room so he could rest from the road. Now it was Bennet's turn to let out a guffaw. "Are you really so dim as to think I would accommodate one who shows up at my door uninvited and so clearly unwanted?" he asked with little patience. "There is a perfectly good inn in Meryton." The kindness of his granting the information was all he was willing to offer.

"Please, Cousin. I did not bring money for an inn, and I can ill afford it as well as food on a lowly parson's income," Collins begged, almost as if he was on the verge of tears, though it was hard to tell with the beading of sweat that had begun to trickle down his face.

Bennet pinched the bridge of his nose and conferred quietly with Fanny. "We will allow you three days, Collins, but there are conditions." Bennet could see Collins was about to speak so he continued before the parson could utter a word. "Firstly, before you join us you will fully bathe, and you will do so every day you are here. Secondly, you will not importune any friends or family residing in this house or any of our guests, but most especially my daughters.

"I will never approve of you marrying anyone under my protection, and though the entail is a moot point now, I want you to know even were it not I would never have allowed such a union. These conditions are not open for discussion, so if you do not agree please leave now. If you stay and do not follow my conditions, you will be tossed out of the house forthwith."

Collins looked affronted, but at least had the good sense to nod his agreement. He would follow the rules, for now at least. Hill led him to a guest chamber in an unoccupied guest wing, as far from the rest of the family and their invited guests as possible.

He was amazed at the apparent wealth the Bennets had; he could not fail to notice the house was more than triple the size his honoured father had told him it was. The furnishings and artwork spoke of wealth, and the number of servants he saw in their neat liveries rivalled, even exceeded, what he saw at Rosings. This was all meant to be his! He would do whatever he had to in order to ensure that it would be.

Collins was trudging behind the housekeeper, fuming at the disrespect he, a member of the clergy under the patronage of Lady Catherine de Bourgh, had been accorded. The more he thought about it, the more resentment built up in his narrow-minded brain and filled it to capacity because while he was certain he was above all reproach and had proven to all his superiority, the truth was he could only handle so much information at a time.

'The nerve of my own relation! What disrespect he is showing to a man of the cloth and his heir no less! He would do well to please me, so I do not throw his spawn out as soon as he is dead. My beneficent patroness was correct, ladies as low born as his wife cannot bear sons, so just as my honoured father said the interlopers must be foundlings my cousin is using to steal what is mine.' He was, even more, affronted when he observed his chamber was as far away from where everyone was housed as could be.

As he sat in his chamber fuming, waiting for his bath to be drawn. He was scheming, as much as one with such mean understanding could. "I will show them," he said to the chamber walls, "this will all be mine, not bequeathed to some interloper who claims to be Bennet's son.

"Lady Catherine and my esteemed departed father were correct! I will not stand idly by and allow conveniently found orphans to be passed off as sons to take what is mine by right. I will put an end to this travesty!"

Collins, who had been introduced to Tom and James when he arrived, ignored the family resemblance the boys had to their parents as this did not fit the narrative in his head. Tom resembled his father very closely while James had more of the Gardiner looks about him.

The fact there was visual as well as documentary proof of the twins' parentage, verified and confirmed by the courts in the ill-fated attempt his father had made to challenge the breaking of the entail, would not deter someone like Collins. It was not often he let uncomfortable things like truth and facts get in his way. In this way, among many others, the sycophantic parson emulated his patroness.

~~~~~~~/~~~~~~~

After his distasteful bath, which he was still fuming about being forced to take, he believed bathing above once a week was an unhealthy practice, Collins dressed in as clean a set of clerical garb that he had and exited his bedchamber.

The bumbling parson was shown to the yellow drawing room where all of the family and friends were assembled. He was the only one who did not know yet that in six weeks the Darcys and the Fitzwilliams would be family to the Bennets as well.

As he stumbled in past the doorway of the drawing room, looking very surprised at seeing so many extremely fashionable people therein, the Earl asked Bennet to introduce his cousin to his family, as was his right to request being the highest ranked member present.

Under normal circumstances, there was no formality between all of those assembled but given Collins' seeming reverence for rank the Earl had decided to cow him some more. In turn, Collins was introduced to a Countess, a Viscount, and a Viscountess, the Darcys who were niece and nephew to his esteemed patroness, and then the rest of the Bennets.

He almost started to drool when he was introduced to the ladies, each one more lovely than the next. Lastly, he was introduced to the Gardiners, Bingley, and his sister Louisa and her husband, Harold Hurst.

As his small brain almost overloaded with so many highborn personages and so much beauty before him, he realised when Elizabeth Bennet was introduced, it was mentioned she was engaged to Mr. Fitzwilliam Darcy of Pemberley. This he knew could not be so. Had not his esteemed patroness informed him many times that her nephew Darcy was betrothed to her own magnificent daughter, the Rose of Kent?

He determined there must be a mistake, or he was alarmed at what feminine arts and allurements the hussy used to make Mr. Darcy forget his duty to his aunt. "Did you say that Cousin Elizabeth is engaged to my esteemed patroness's nephew, Mr. Darcy?" he asked indignantly.

"Yes, that is what I said," Bennet agreed with an amused smile as he and the rest of the assembled people had a good idea of what was coming next.

"That must be a mistake," he announced with more conviction than he had yet shown as he grovelled before Darcy. "My good sir, your most esteemed aunt and my beneficent patroness has told me many times you are, and have long been, engaged to her daughter, the Rose of Kent and the most magnificent jewel in the crown of the British Empire, Miss Anne de Bourgh."

Before anyone else could refute the dim-witted parson, the Earl took it upon himself to intervene. "Collins, when you arrived and told me your *esteemed* patroness is never wrong, what did I tell you?" the Earl demanded; his expression most stern.

"But surely, that was a jest, your Lordship?" Collins gushed, again profusely sweating as he genuflected.

"Why would I jest with you, when at that point we had not even been introduced?" The Earl scoffed at the idea, waving away the intimation as inconsequential. Collins was about to respond but the Earl cut him off. "My nephew Darcy is not now, nor has he ever been, engaged to my niece Anne. And I know for a fact it is not the match Anne desires, either," the Earl stated in what all present knew was a warning to accept, but Collins was never praised for his being able to understand the tone of a conversation.

"As much as it pains me to contradict a personage of your rank your Lordship, you must be in error. My patroness is never wrong, she knows all. Why she even told me to put shelves in my closets at my humble abode, the parsonage at Hunsford, which was nothing less than brilliance on her part," Collins related with pride.

As Collins spoke of his patroness, all watching noted he looked like he was in raptures. It was to his deep displeasure to discover everyone was laughing at him and he could not understand why. Unfortunately for those present, he was then even more determined to carry his point, but the Earl had heard enough of the idiotic pronouncements emanating from the very stupid parson.

"Mr. Collins, do you worship God or my sister?" The Earl asked with gravity that stopped the merriment in the room.

The parson was once again sweating profusely, undoing almost all of the good that was done by his bathing. "God, of course. What kind of question is that? I am not a heretic!" Collins replied with a look of the deepest offence.

"Is God always right?" the Earl pressed, and the parson allowed it was indeed so. "Is there any mere mortal, man or women, that like God, is always right?" the Earl asked, trapping Collins so obviously all others there, other than the dim-witted Collins, knew it was occurring.

"No, your Lordship. That distinction is for God on High and His Son Jesus alone," the stupid parson said smugly, not seeing the hole he had just dug for himself.

During this exchange, the rest of the party was doing whatever they could to stop from bursting out in laughter at the ridiculousness spewing from the man that had forced his company on them.

"So, you are saying no man is like God who is always right?" the Earl continued his lesson.

"I just said that, your Lordship." Collins replied with barely contained exasperation but allowing that the Earl must be hard of hearing.

"Well then, Collins, you must be a heretic. You have multiple times now put my *dear* sister on the same plain as our Lord God on High. Did you not say more than once that she is never wrong? And did you not say there is no man or a woman who is never wrong? Did you not just say that distinction is only for God Almighty and His Son?" The Earl tightened the figurative noose around the throat slightly obscured by Collins's flapping jowls.

It took the very dull parson some time to assimilate the Earl's words, then he almost had an apoplexy as he realised what he himself had said. He had, in fact, made Lady Catherine equal to God. He fell back into a chair and forced himself to calm down somewhat.

He was succeeding until Darcy addressed him. "The Archbishop of Canterbury is my cousin. I believe I should ask him how your theological leanings fit into the Church of England's doctrine," Darcy stated with absolute solemnity.

"Please Mr. Darcy, I pray you would not. I misspoke. No one other than God, my patroness included, is never wrong, although I do submit she is right most of the time," Collins offered in what he fervently hoped was deference to both.

"So now you, who have known Lady Catherine since she appointed you what, four months ago?" Darcy waited and Collins nodded, "you think you know her better than her brother who has known her all of her life, or those that make up the rest of her family here that have known her since their birth?"

Darcy was far from done with this excuse of a parson who had dared attempt to come between him and his Lizzy.

"As my uncle, the *Earl*, has already told you, my being engaged or promised to my cousin Anne in any way, shape, or form is a complete fabrication Lady Catherine started to pronounce after the death of my honourable father."

The parson was about to reply but Darcy kept on without giving him a chance to interrupt. "Your patroness is aught but a fortune hunter. Do you know Rosings Park actually belongs to my cousin Anne, not to my Aunt Catherine, and that my Aunt has always coveted Pemberley's fortune? Is not coveting that which belongs to someone else breaking one of the Ten Commandments?"

"You have been tricked into this engagement by my cousin. I am sure she used her arts and allurements to distract you and induce you to say these things that cannot be true since my patroness would never say something that was not true," the parson rationalised, looking like he was going to be ill at the desperation of separating Darcy from Miss Elizabeth Bennet. As the near head of the household, it was his duty to see it done.

"I am not now, nor have I *ever* been engaged to my Cousin Anne. If I hear you repeat this lie one more time or speak a word of disrespect about my betrothed, I will call you out! **DO I MAKE MYSELF VERY CLEAR?**" Darcy growled, his eyes narrowing in warning and anger as he looked down at this far from shining example of a human being, let alone the type of person who should lead a flock of God's children.

Unable to speak, the parson merely nodded. He was very close to soiling his pants, so he asked to be excused and lurched toward the door. As he reached it, Bennet told him a tray would be sent up with his dinner.

"I suggest you take the evening to think about things since you are to depart Longbourn on the morrow. If you want to stay in the area, you will have to take a room at the Inn," Bennet stated firmly, making it clear that once he departed right after he broke his fast, which too would be taken in his room alone, Collins would never be welcome back at Longbourn.

"I am very sorry Bennet; I know he is your cousin, but that man needs to be defrocked," the Earl said to Bennet after a very dejected Collins left the room.

"No apology needed, Reggie. I could not agree with you more." Bennet sighed, relieved this farce would soon be over.

"I will speak to my Cousin Archibald Darcy, who is, as I said, the Archbishop of Canterbury. Once he hears about this debacle of a rector, he will defrock him and remove the Hunsford gift for as long as Aunt Catherine tries to make appointments," Darcy started to calm down, taking Elizabeth's waiting hand and kissing it in thanks and appreciation.

"Do that, Darcy!" his uncle agreed.

Darcy asked Bennet if he could use the study to write an express to his cousin, which Bennet assented to with alacrity.

"How can anyone be so obtuse? He is obsequies, proud, and a sycophant all in one, and no intelligence at all," Tom asked after Darcy went to the study.

"He is terribly odoriferous, even after Papa sent him to bathe before dinner," James put his finger under his nose as if smelling a very bad odour.

"You are lucky you did not smell him before his bath," The Earl agreed with clear disgust on his face.

CHAPTER 10

Back in his bedchamber, the hapless parson sat with a dinner tray. '*Such disrespect!*' he fumed to himself. '*I will break that abomination of an engagement. When everyone is asleep tonight, I will creep into Cousin Elizabeth's room and compromise her. Mister high and mighty Darcy will not be able or willing to marry her after I have had my way with the wench.*

'*Her father will force us to marry then she will be mine to do with as I wish, and Lady Catherine's wish will come true. Her nephew will be freed from the hussy to fulfil his duty.*' Then another thought hit his overworked brain. '*Throw me out of the home that will be mine! I will show that cousin of mine; my excellent father was right. As he stole what is ours, I will help him meet his eternal reward and then I will own all of this.*' He told himself.

He wrote a letter to his patroness detailing all the verbal abuse and disrespect they had both received that day from the unworthy crowd at Longbourn. He told her in detail about the presumption of his cousin, the trollop who was even now trying to usurp her daughter's rightful place as Mr. Darcy's fiancée.

He informed her of his plan to destroy the supposed engagement between his wayward cousin and her nephew. He would even sacrifice himself and take her as a wife to further his patroness's aims.

He laid out, in great detail, with as much ingratiating praise for his deified patroness as he could use in his every sentence, all the news he believed she needed to know. He also told her as she had suggested, he would rid Longbourn of the foundling imposters trying to steal his birthright by ending their worthless lives.

As quietly as he was able, he descended the stairs and deposited the letter on the salver containing the outgoing mail then slunk back up to his bedchamber. Why should he pay for postage when he could have his cousin foot the bill? Yes, the parson was just as miserly as his late father.

On his return to his chamber, he started to plot his intended actions for that night. He would find the interlopers first and dispatch them back to hell where they belonged for daring to try and steal what was rightfully his. Next, he would compromise and despoil that hussy, Elizabeth.

What he was going to do was being done in service to his patroness. When he imagined what his cousin's breasts would feel like in his hands, how he would have his way with her, he felt a stirring as this was part of the night he most looked forward to; he became hard at the thought of taking her. The actual compromise may be deemed questionable were she to claim it so or to be examined by a doctor. He would declare it to be true and no one could gainsay his word as he was an ordained minister.

Collins determined after he was done despoiling his cousin, he would dispatch the current master of Longbourn to meet his maker. On the morrow he would not leave; he would assume his rightful place as the new master of Longbourn.

~~~~~~~/~~~~~~~

Without Collins to disturb them, an enjoyable evening was had by all. Richard shared that his friend, Colonel Forster, had told him his troops and his wife had arrived from Hampshire, and he expected his recruiting party and the new recruits from London to arrive in the next day or two.

An evening of music and cards was filled with excitement and laughter, which could not but delight all. Much later than was usual everyone started to retire to their bedchambers for the night. The Netherfield party said their goodbyes and prepared to leave.

After being allowed to say a private goodbye to his fiancée, where it can be said no words were needed, Darcy, along with the Colonel, Bingley, and the Hursts' returned to Netherfield Park.

'*Less than six weeks until I never need to be parted from my Elizabeth again,*' Darcy thought with a satisfied smile. '*I still cannot believe I have been granted the gift of her love. She is the only one for me. I will thank Bingley and Richard for the rest of my life: Bingley invited me to Netherfield Park and Richard came to assist me and have my back. I love my brother Richard and am grateful he formulated the solution that made it possible for me to come here where I have finally found a home for my heart.*'

He was shaken out of his reverie by Louisa Hurst. "I apologise profusely, Mr. Darcy, for ever indulging Caroline's fantasies that she would one day be Mistress of Pemberley. Also, I am sorry for any of my behaviour that has ever made you or your sister uncomfortable," she offered with her head up and her eyes open, looking at Darcy, so he could assess the truth of her words.

Darcy knew this admission from Mrs. Hurst could not have been easy, and he could see she was sincere and genuine. "All is forgiven, I think we should adopt some of my betrothed's philosophy, *think only of the past as the remembrance gives you pleasure.*

As a Christian, in time I will forgive Miss Bingley, as will the rest of us. But I will never forget, and I do not ever want to see your sister again, I am afraid. She will never be allowed into any of my houses or on any of my estates."

Louisa was happy to be forgiven and her husband squeezed her hand in support. Things were much better between them since Caroline had been removed from their company. Her husband no longer feigned sleep to avoid her sister. The five rode the rest of the way in companionable silence.

~~~~~~~/~~~~~~~

It was about one o'clock in the morning when the ill-intending parson put his ill-advised and ill-conceived plan into practice. The footmen had been asked to watch the parson carefully but to not take any action unless he crossed a line, and it became necessary to do so.

As silently as an overweight, puffing parson could, he made his way to the end of the corridor to the stairs where there was a landing. He descended to the level below where he had ascertained the family wing was. Once on that level, he slowly headed toward the first bedchamber doors he saw in the hall.

He stood looking around, and it suddenly hit him that he had no idea who was in which chamber. As the parson advanced, he stopped at the first door he reached. His ultimate goal was to despoil and compromise his cousin Elizabeth, however, his plan was to eliminate the fake son interlopers who stood between himself and inheriting first.

By some stroke of pure dumb luck, the first door he opened was the chamber of the so-called son they had named James. Once the parson, recognised this was one of the twins, he decided to proceed, making sure no supposed sons were alive so he would again be the rightful heir.

Now faced with opportunity, his avarice overrode all human decency. It even overrode God's commandment of *Thou shalt not murder*. While thinking of dispatching the one called James, he reminded himself he still had to eliminate the one they called Tom, and Bennet himself.

He had seen the clues demonstrating how much wealth the Bennets must have, and he wanted it all for himself, the bonus of which was being able to have his way with his delectable cousin Elizabeth and make her his own to do with as he pleased. He started drooling with lust and felt himself hardened again as he imagined the things he would force on his cousin Elizabeth, and the screams he would savour as he gave her all the attention she wanted.

Like all bullies, Collins loved the thought of wielding power over the weak. He looked around for an implement with which to achieve his murderous aim and noticed a pillow that had fallen on the floor.

He walked over and grabbed the pillow, lifting it above his head, and as he attempted to bring it down toward James's sleeping form to smother him, he felt someone, or something, grab him from behind and throw him backwards with great force.

The burly but nimble footman who had been following Collins had ejected the clergyman from the room hard enough that he landed back in the hallway with a tremendous thud. Collins landed awkwardly on the floor, breaking his arm, and started to howl like a tomcat having his tail pulled.

The caterwauling brought Bennet, Lord Matlock, Lord Hilldale, and the twins out of their chambers. Fanny, Lizzy, Mary, Kitty, Marie, Georgiana, and Jane's doors were cracked to watch the scene unfold. The Fitzwilliams always resided in the family wing when resident at Longbourn, and Bennet was never so grateful as he was now because Reggie might be the only thing between him and the murder of his cousin.

On seeing the parson lying prostrate on the floor holding his arm and wailing, Bennet looked to the footman, Biggs, who all agreed was aptly named, asking him what was going on.

"Master, this 'ere man you instruct'd us to watch start'd wonderin' the halls just after one this mornin. I seen 'im go in Master James's bedchamber and kept watchin, just like you instruct'd, though I admit it 'twas mighty hard once 'e opened the door. Then 'e picked up a pillow and was about to smother our Master James, so I made sure 'e left the room with great speed," Biggs stated, glowering as he stood over the caterwauling parson.

"Well done, Biggs. Please have someone get Sir William, and as you do, explain we need him to fulfil his magistrate duties as soon as he can. Ask someone else to go fetch Mr. Darcy and Colonel Fitzwilliam from Netherfield Park.

"And Biggs," Biggs looked at his master expectantly, "make sure this scum who attempted to murder my son is guarded under lock and key in the coal cellar. There is no need to be gentle with him," Bennet instructed vindictively. "For your service to me and my family this night, there will be a big bonus for you this month." Bennet nodded at his loyal footman who was loyal because he was treated with respect. No one was afraid of him due to his size which had often been the case as he had shuffled around from position to position before the Bennets employed him, but they had a healthy respect for his skills.

"I was only doin' me duty, Master," Biggs replied gruffly.

"I know you were, but you have our thanks, Biggs, and regardless you will get that bonus," Bennet stated firmly. Biggs knew better than to argue with his master. Bennet thought for a second and turned back towards Biggs. "Before you lock him in the coal cellar, stand him up so we can talk to this poor excuse of a man, who is as far from a man of the cloth one can be, as we have ample evidence." Bennet glared at Collins. Biggs and a second footman hauled the blubbering, snivelling Collins to his feet.

"If he does not stop his dramatics you may hit him, Biggs!" Bennet ordered, his anger simmering hotter as he continued to glare at the man that would soon swing from the hangman's noose, if he had a say in the matter. Biggs pulled his fist back with a purposeful pause, waiting for Collins to make his decision. As if by magic, the noise emanating from Collins ceased and was replaced by fear as he started to fully comprehend his situation, clutching his clearly broken arm in close.

"What in damnation did you think you were doing? You were a guest in my house and tried to murder one of my sons?" Bennet spat at the parson, leaning down and hovering his face inches above that of Collins whose smell was so disgusting he had to pull back three inches as he looked on the uninvited man with disgust. Bennet had been forced to draw back because Collins had also soiled his pants, and the stench was worse than one could imagine.

Knowing he had nothing to lose, Collins spewed his venomous anger. "I wanted to ruin that stuck-up hussy of a daughter of yours so she would not marry the man my patroness chose for *her* daughter. I decided to first rid the world of the imposters who had stolen what is rightly mine, and God in His wisdom guided me into one of the rooms of your so-called sons, which we all know are foundlings!" Collins spat out, a deranged look overtaking his countenance as he went on. "I am a member of the clergy, and as such I can do what I want if I decide it is the right thing to do!" he reminded all of his authority as ordained by God.

"Has your foul odour addled your brain?" Tom asked with no less than disgust. "Only a blind man would look at me and not see the likeness to my father. James is the spitting image of Grandfather Gardiner at the same age. You must be the most wilfully blind person I have ever had the displeasure of meeting in my almost sixteen years. Not to mention the most reviled and stupid one to boot. I had not known so much of God's worst for humanity could be stuffed into the same person," Tom scoffed. James's laughter made Tom crack a smile.

"How dare you address a member of the clergy in such a manner, you insolent imposter!" spat out Collins as he tried to raise himself to his full height to intimidate Tom. Once he had gained his goal, he again faced failure since Tom was taller than he.

"I am not sure what will end first, your tenure as a parson or your miserable life. This evening my soon to be son-in-law sent an express to His Excellency, the Archbishop of Canterbury, laying out your many deficiencies as a parson. Adding the attempted murder of one of my sons, your intent to murder the other, and your further intent to despoil my Lizzy makes your defrocking a certainty, not to mention your date with the hangman for the crimes you attempted here tonight," Bennet warned.

With attempted false bravado, Collins gathered himself and stood up straight as he looked up and met Bennet's eyes. "You are the ones that will answer to the law when my beneficent and all-knowing patroness hears about this. She will make sure you will pay for the crimes you have perpetrated against me. You are trying to fob off foundlings as your sons in order to steal what should be mine! I should have dispatched you first. I did nothing wrong since my patroness told me I could remove the interlopers any way I saw fit which would just be righting a wrong," Collins announced with growing confidence.

"You are utterly and completely delusional, Collins, just as your father before you. Besides the fact they bear a striking resemblance to me and their late grandfather, we have documented proof of and witnesses to, their birth.

"You were in the courtroom when the verdict was rendered, so please enlighten me on how you are able to wilfully ignore the facts? Attempted murder, no matter the imagined justification, is a hanging offence. Nothing you or your patroness can do or say will ever change that! Do you realise you just implicated your dear patroness in a conspiracy to commit murder?" he smirked. "I wonder how she will feel when she is arrested and placed in a gaol cell right next to you. That way you can pray to your false god until you are dispatched to be judged by our real God on High!" Bennet challenged.

Collins, who was now petrified he may have put his patroness in peril, was about to answer when Darcy and the Colonel came bounding up the stairs at breakneck speed. After hearing what the parson had tried to do, and also planned to do to his beloved Lizzy, Darcy spun around towards the snivelling man and with all of his considerable might planted his fist in Collins's face.

Everyone heard the sickening but satisfying sound of a nose shattering. Blood was streaming from Collins's nose, and he was howling loudly again. In fact, he was crying at a volume that would wake the dead, so Biggs sent his fist crashing into Collins's stomach to restore some quiet.

The parson was gasping for breath while blood streamed out of his nose as he attempted to hold onto his broken arm while covering his nose to stem the bleeding when Sir William came up the stairs with the constable and his men.

It did not take long for Bennet, Biggs, and the rest of the party to impart all that the conniving, criminal parson had attempted to Sir William, as well as what he further intended. Sir William, who was usually an affable and jolly man, was livid for the first time in his life, and it did not bode well for the parson that it was directed at him.

Collins did not even have the sense to deny the charges, so Sir William ordered Constable Paul Crossman to take the useless example of a man to the town gaol. At least then he would not bleed on the Bennet's stores of coal.

The soon-to-be ex-parson was now quaking in his shoes and relieved his bladder once again as the full folly of his actions started to come into focus. Once he realised all being levied against him, he knew then and there that in his need to be heard, he had effectively ended his own life.

Constable Crossman and his men clapped the now blubbering Collins in irons, regardless of his broken arm, and dragged him kicking and screaming out of Longbourn. It was to the relief of all that Collins would never darken their doorstep again.

The next day he was transported to the Old Bailey in Town and then onto Newgate Prison for holding until all the charges against him were determined and the trial date could be set. Two days after arriving at the gaol in London he was defrocked by the Archbishop of Canterbury after the great man received the express from Darcy and the follow-up express that detailed the attempted murder.

The Archbishop also stated no appointment to Hunsford would be allowed by Lady Catherine de Bourgh again. He sent a letter of apology on behalf of the church for the actions of the, at the time, representative of the Church of England. In the same letter, he sent his heartfelt congratulations on his cousin's engagement and offered his services to perform the wedding ceremony.

The day after his defrocking, the very short trial commenced for the ex-parson at the Old Bailey. He had no funds to retain a barrister for his defence, and in vain he waited for his exulted patroness to intercede and his behalf.

All notes begging for her to send him funds for a barrister were ignored, so in the end he had to defend himself. The trial was quick, with Bennet and Biggs as the key witnesses. The jury returned after but a moment's conference and remitted a verdict of guilty. Even after his verdict, Lady Catherine ignored all of his written entreaties for help.

Collins finally realised all of her relatives had been right about her, and he had been wrong. In the end, as he was sitting by himself locked away, he finally found the courage to wonder why he had ever listened to her and gone to Longbourn to offer his *olive branch* as he had been instructed to do by her.

Some days after his guilty verdict had been handed down, just after dawn on a blustery morning as the sun started to rise in the east, the snivelling ex-parson was led, actually dragged kicking and screaming, to the gallows and the hangman's noose was placed around his neck.

The hangman pulled the lever to open the trapdoor, and the last of the Collins line ended at the end of a short drop and a sudden stop. Collins had ended his life as he came into it, wailing like a baby.

CHAPTER 11

The day after the attempt on James's life, Lieutenant Denny returned from his recruiting trip to London. Among others, he had recruited one George Wickham. Denny had met him briefly in Lambton some years back and remembered him to be a charming man but did not know much else about him. He was blissfully unaware of the true character of the viper he had recruited.

Wickham had used almost all of his available funds to purchase the commission. Being recruited was very timely for him, he needed to hide away from the dangerous men looking for him to collect debts he owed and others who wanted to revenge themselves on him for despoiling sisters and daughters.

He was an equal opportunity taker of young ladies' virtues; Wickham cared not whether they were servants, tradesman's daughters, or gentlewomen. For the first number of days after joining the Derbyshire Militia quartered in Meryton for the summer, Wickham was kept very busy training, so he had no time for his normal dissolute pursuits.

~~~~~~~/~~~~~~~

Collins's letter had arrived at Rosings Park in Kent the day he was being transported to Newgate in order for him to stand trial at the Old Bailey in London. It was dropped and slipped under a sideboard, and only found three days later by Miss Anne de Bourgh. The day it was found happened to be the fateful day her mother's idiot parson had his date with the hangman's noose. After Anne found it under the

183

sideboard, she handed it to her controlling and imperious mother.

It was eventually read later that morning by Lady Catherine de Bourgh, though she had almost consigned it to the flames thinking Collins was beseeching her for help again; help that would, of course, never be given.

Curiosity got the best of her, so she condescended to read the missive from her former parson. On reading the letter, she was most seriously displeased, and the level of her displeasure resulted in an eruption of temper that was a near apoplexy.

She yelled for Smythe, her long-suffering butler, to have her barouche box readied for immediate travel. She would travel to Matlock House in Town and make sure her brother put an end to that farce of an engagement of Darcy's, since Collins did not seem to be able to handle this himself.

No one, especially some country hussy with no connections or fortune, was going to come between her and Pemberley's coffers. It would not be borne. She would end this pretence of an abomination of an engagement, and she was delusional enough to be sure that the Earl would support her as head of the family.

Once Lady Catherine was micromanaging the packing of her trunks, Anne picked up the letter her mother had discarded and read it:

Longbourn Estate

7th of July 1811

My dear beneficent, honourable patroness, Lady Catherine de Bourgh.

As directed by you, I arrived at my cousin's estate, the one you with your all-encompassing knowledge opined should be mine, at exactly four o'clock in the afternoon as you suggested. I know how your ladyship demands punctuality.

Imagine my surprise when rather than accept the olive branch that in your infinite wisdom you told me to bestow, I was met with derision and laughter. Worse still, the people present had the temerity to question your wisdom and to mock you. Mock you, the great lady that you are!

It was not only the Bennets, but some members of your family partook in the disrespect for one such as you who is due all deference possible. They dared opine your beneficent ladyship is not right all the time, and in fact made it a point to say you were often not right, if ever!

I had the honour of meeting your nephew, Mr. Fitzwilliam Darcy of Pemberley in Derbyshire, your daughter's esteemed betrothed. I was then told a scandalous falsehood, as he was introduced as the fiancé of my cousin Elizabeth.

I am positive she has trapped your nephew with her arts and allurements despite his proclamation otherwise. I can account for no other possibility that would make him forsake you, honour, and duty to align himself with such a woman.

When I pointed out it could not be true, as I had heard from yourself, my Ladyship, on many occasions that he was engaged to your daughter since they were in their cradles, I attempted to set my cousin to rights.

Rather than listen to me, I was rudely sent to my chamber like an errant schoolboy, not an honoured member of the clergy. My cousin told me I would be turned out of my future home on the morrow and was not to return.

I resolved this affront to you would not stand, so to that end, I will compromise my cousin Elizabeth and make sure your nephew will be released from the trap he has unwittingly fallen into.

I will also rid my future home of the two interlopers my cousin claims are his sons, and to speed up my inheritance I will dispatch my irreverent cousin. As you so generously advised me it would not be a crime to dispatch foundlings of no rank or consequence, I am also willing to permanently remove the temptation from your nephew by marrying the hussy myself.

For your honour, my beneficent and honourable patroness I will not fail.
Your most humble servant,

William Collins, Parson of the Parish at Hunsford

Miss de Bourgh now understood why her mother was to go to Town, the bumbling parson had not mentioned her Fitzwilliam family was the family visiting the Bennets. Disgusted with the sentiments the idiotic parson expressed in the missive she had just read, and with the machinations of her mother, she was very happy for her cousin William. However, she could only hope that the parson had not been successful.

What was written made her mother complicit in the murders the parson was planning to carry out. Anne could see her mother was far worse than she had imagined!

Then and there she decided it was time to assert her rights and knowing Uncle Reggie and Aunt Elaine were in Hertfordshire, news she had not shared with her mother, she wrote an express and had her personal and faithful courier make all haste to carry it directly to her uncle at the Longbourn Estate. She would learn whether Collins had succeeded or failed in his dastardly plan; hoping desperately that he had failed.

As soon as that was done, she prepared to travel just after her maniacal mother left in her barouche for Town.

~~~~~~~/~~~~~~~

The Longbourn and Netherfield inhabitants were all enjoying the peace and quiet after the drama created by the late Mr. Collins. They were too decent to be happy the hapless parson had been hanged, but they were relieved he could no longer harm anyone ever again.

They did not yet know a storm was heading their way

so when an express arrived for Lord Matlock, delivered by his niece Anne's personal courier, he was concerned that Anne needed urgent help. The missive did not indicate that she was in trouble, however, he was most surprised as he read it:

Rosings Park

July 7, 1811

Dear Uncle,

My mother received a letter from her ubiquitous ex-parson this morning telling her his cousin, Elizabeth Bennet is engaged to William. As you can imagine, she used her oft-repeated words: I am most seriously displeased.

No sooner had she read the missive and ranted, she called for her carriage and set off for Town to see you, then, of course, to see William. I have never seen her in such a fury as she was today.

While she was yelling at her maid to pack, I was able to tell the coachman to make the trip as slow as possible so I would be sure you would receive this warning before she arrives at either Matlock or Darcy Houses. She assumes William has returned to Town. Little does she know you are both still in Hertfordshire.

Uncle, it is time for me to assume my rightful place and claim my inheritance from the gross mismanagement of my mother. I request your help in this venture. I am past my five and twentieth birthday and I should have asserted my rights the day after I celebrated it, but I made the error we have all too often made in placating rather than confronting my mother.

I will leave Rosings Park for Hertfordshire as soon as I am packed now that Lady Catherine has departed. I hope I will not be an imposition on your friends. Please tell William I wish he and his betrothed all happiness.

Your niece,

Anne Catherine de Bourgh

"I knew it was too much to expect peace and quiet!"

The Earl sighed with disgust.

"What is it father?" asked Andrew, frowning at the look on his father's face even as he was passed the express from Anne which the courier had delivered. The man was drinking and eating in Longbourn's kitchen while his mount rested and was cared for. Richard read over his shoulder while Andrew digested the short missive.

"The dragon has taken flight," Richard snorted.

"What has our *dear* aunt done now?" William sighed as he sat next to his fiancée.

Once the whole party was assembled, Lord Matlock informed them his sister was on the warpath. "For too long we have tolerated her nonsense, but that stops now!" the Earl stated emphatically. Those in the party who were unfortunate to have an acquaintance with the *great lady*, as she liked to think of herself, nodded in agreement.

"She has all but run Rosings into the ground, it is a miracle there are any tenants left, given her dictatorial ways," Darcy explained. He and Richard, had the unfortunate duty of travelling to Rosings each Easter to look over the books and make recommendations for the running of the estate. While there they would attempt to correct some of his aunt's worst mistakes. "I put things to right and she undoes almost everything days after I leave."

"As Anne has requested our help, we will wait for my sister to arrive. I am sure Collins wrote from here, so when she does not find either William or me in town I believe we can expect another uninvited guest tomorrow." The Earl said the last apologetically, looking at Fanny and Bennet. "I just remembered, Anne said she would travel to us once her mother departed Rosings Park. Thomas and Fanny? Would you object if we send the courier back with an invitation for Anne to join us so she knows it is not an imposition?"

"Please do not give it a thought, Reggie. We have heard

of her from all of you for so many years we know what to expect. And unless you want her to, your sister will not be invited to stay here. Like Collins, she is welcome to visit the inn in Meryton if it is too late for her to return to London when she gets here.

"And of course, your niece Anne is more than welcome. If the horse the courier rode here is not rested, please feel free to tell him to take one of ours. Send an invitation from all of us that she is expected and most welcome," Fanny replied for all her family.

The Earl quickly penned the note to his niece with the confirmation she was welcome to join them, reassuring her that her coming would be no imposition to the Bennets of Hertfordshire. After being supplied with a fresh horse from the Longbourn stables, Anne's courier was on his way back toward Rosings knowing his mistress would be leaving, so he would watch for her along the road to deliver the Earl's missive.

Anne de Bourgh arrived in the evening and was most profuse in her thanks, as she had set off without an invitation. She was reassured she was most welcome and had retired soon after being introduced to all for a short rest.

At dinner that night, she was delighted to see how happy William was with his intended and was initially caught off guard when Fanny hugged her in welcome and asked her about her gardens. She was even more surprised when Mrs. Bennet's was followed by Elaine's and Georgiana's hugs.

"We have missed too many opportunities to show we love you, Anne. Fanny has taken me to task." Aunt Elaine winked at Fanny who laughed as she held Georgiana's and Kitty's hands while they showed her their drawings they had done that day.

Anne sat and watched, realising she had never been

with such an open and happy group. She was sure she would enjoy getting to know her soon-to-be cousins, and they would all be the best of friends.

~~~~~~~/~~~~~~~

'*This is a backward little town,*' George Wickham thought as he swaggered down the main street of Meryton. '*I see some nice little treats here; I wonder how many of them I will be able to bed before the shopkeepers expect me to pay my debts?*' he asked himself.

George Wickham liked his girls young. Young girls were easier for him to manipulate with his practised lies and required little true attention. A promise of a wedding and the old *if you love me, you will not make me wait for the wedding night...* hint and he was more often than not able to get what he wanted from girls in towns such as this.

Occasionally a little drama followed, and he shuddered as he thought about how close the brother of one of his conquests had got to him in London. That, and the debt collectors on his trail, was one of the reasons why he used most of the funds he had left to buy an ensign's commission in the infernal militia.

As he was walking past Captain Carter, he overheard a part of a conversation where Carter was telling Lieutenant Denny about four daughters, all beauties, who had more than forty thousand each for a dowry.

His attention was firmly engaged, forty thousand was much better than the thirty thousand he had tried to claim as his own before that prig Darcy had spoiled his plans. Wickham needed to know all he could about these heiresses.

He had let that insipid sister of his nemesis, Georgiana Darcy, slip through his fingers, but here was his chance to make an easy and far greater fortune. This time he would not fail, and there was no Darcy here to spoil his plans. Nor was there a Fitzwilliam to put the fear of God into him.

He heard the name Bennet of Longbourn, and that was enough for him. Unfortunately for Wickham, drooling at the thought of acquiring such a fortune, he left before he was able to hear about the restrictions the girl's father had put in place to protect them against one such as him. He decided he would make some, in his opinion, subtle enquiries about these Bennets.

~~~~~~~/~~~~~~~

Bennet was in his study with Darcy as they had just reviewed the marriage settlement that Darcy's solicitor had personally delivered an hour previously. It was as Darcy said it would be, Elizabeth's fortune would remain at her discretion, and he had settled a further one hundred thousand pounds on her with very generous pin money of five thousand per annum.

Each son, up to four, would inherit an estate, and the daughters would currently have fifty thousand for their dowries, with the expectation that these would increase as their holdings were well managed by the parents. Bennet asked for Lizzy to be called to join them since both men wanted her approval before signing. They knew her well enough to be sure she would not like things being decided for her without her input.

After she joined the men and sat down and read the document, she looked at William and voiced her protest. "William, this is far too much! I have my own fortune; I do not need all of this money," She stated emphatically.

"Your quarterly allowance and portion of the interest that your father releases to you is used for charity. He informed me you assist two causes alternately, the soldiers who come home wounded and need things like crutches or even a leg, and anonymous grants for scientific studies.

"Please do not stop either, and I will match your donation so we may do twice the good. I will leave you to determine which are the top three grants you would like to bestow, but would like to be there with you as you decide. I cannot wait to see how you pick." He winked at her, and Bennet laughed.

"With our Richard at war, I could not but help those returning who may have helped save his life, even unwittingly," Elizabeth said. "As to the grants; I just pick whatever sounds most important and deserving. You cannot expect a poor country nobody to understand the sciences," she teased both men.

"You are also free to use your fortune for whatever pleases you, my love. As Mrs. Darcy, I could not do less, so please do not ask it of me." He kissed her hand and held it, pretending not to notice Bennet's arched brow.

"In that case William, my fortune will be used for any sons we have beyond four, or to enhance the dowries of our daughters." Lizzy looked at both of the men in her life and smiled when they nodded, so she too nodded her agreement to the settlement.

Four copies were signed. One was given to Darcy's solicitor to keep on file in his law office, one would go to Philips, Bennet's local solicitor, one would be kept in Bennet's safe, and the last would be kept in the safe at Darcy house.

Just as Darcy's solicitor left, Hill knocked on the study door and informed Bennet that two messengers had arrived from two of the merchants in Meryton with urgent information for the Master. Bennet bade Hill show them in.

What Wickham had not been aware of was Bennet rewarded anyone who informed him when there were inquiries made about his family by a stranger and especially about their dowries.

The two boys each handed him a note. They were almost identical, and Bennet immediately passed them onto Darcy whose smiling face changed to a countenance that looked like a dark storm. His whole body tensed as he read the name of who was seeking information about the Bennet daughters, and bile rose in the back of his throat when he saw it was the last man he ever wanted to be around again.

Bennet rewarded each lad with half a crown and told them to have their employers quietly make it known no credit should be extended to any of the militia officers. He added the request to spread it through the community the man in question was not to be allowed near any of their daughters or servants, and should be watched at all times when he was around the village.

To one of the boys he gave a short note for Colonel Forster, requesting his and his wife's presence for dinner that night. He told Hill to reward any more messengers with a half crown each, as he expected more, and to thank them.

"I cannot believe that dissolute wastrel is here of all towns in the kingdom," Darcy growled, feeling tension build with every passing second.

"If you think about it calmly, Son, this may be most fortuitous," Bennet offered to calm Darcy, much like Richard and his Uncle would do.

"How so?" Darcy asked, bewildered.

"We have the advantage. We know he is here, but he does not know we are aware of his presence. In addition, I am sure he has no clue the Fitzwilliams are in the area, from what I have been told he is terrified of Richard.

"We have warned the merchants so they can protect themselves and their families. If you will help me write notes to all of the families in the area, we will warn them of his propensities. We can then plan to give him enough rope to hang himself, similar to how we handled Caroline Bingley. If by some miracle he is reformed and does not act as we expect he will, then we will leave him be.

"Given everything you and your family have imparted

about him, I expect as soon as he hears about the girl's dowries, he will be blind and deaf to all else and will put his own head in a noose of his own making." Bennet waited, relieved to see Darcy start to comprehend both his words and that he was not alone in this as he had always been in the past.

"I am sure you are correct; he will come up with many a scheme to try to get money without having to work for it. It has always been thus," Darcy agreed.

The two men sat in companionable silence and wrote notes to all of the families living on estates and in houses in the area that were not in the town itself. When completed, Bennet asked Hill to send five grooms out to deliver the missives and then requested everyone in the house assemble in the yellow drawing room.

By the time the gentlemen entered everyone was assembled, and Darcy went to sit next to Lizzy, needing her closeness to burn off the residual anger he felt at the libertine. He took her hand; grateful she offered it freely as Bennet addressed the group.

"As the head of a prominent family in the area that cares greatly about his family," he nodded at Fanny who smiled at him in a way that proved he was as loved as they were, "I have a standing request to be informed if any unknown people are making inquiries about me or any of my family, especially the girls and their fortunes.

"I have received and read two messages just this morning, and Hill informed me that three more lads bearing almost identical messages have since arrived." Bennet took a breath while the group looked at him expectantly. "A new recruit, an ensign, is asking about the Bennets, my daughters and their reported dowries, in particular, and his name is George Wickham." He paused.

There was but a moment of stunned silence then

Georgie made an audible gasp, and Mary and Kitty each took one of her hands to comfort her. For a few additional ticks of the clock silence reigned, and then there was an eruption of sound. Everyone started talking all at once, but one voice rose above the rest.

"*I will kill him!*" Colonel Fitzwilliam spat out furiously. "I will run that scoundrel through like I wanted to after Ramsgate," he growled.

"**No**, you will *not!*" A forceful voice interrupted from a very unexpected quarter and Mary looked at him square in the eye. "When our courtship is over, I fully intend to marry you so I will not allow you to do something that will end with you being hung at the gallows like that despicable cousin of ours."

"The ordering you around has started already, Son," the Earl chuckled with a wink to try to reduce the tension.

The Colonel's parents, his brother and sister, the Bennet sons and daughters, Darcy, and Georgie, along with everyone else also told him to calm down and they would find another way to deal with this particular issue.

"So far..." Bennet informed everyone about the steps to protect the merchants and their daughters. Then he let them know about the missives dispatched to all of the estates and dwellings not in Meryton, along with his request for Colonel and Mrs. Forster to join them for dinner. "Did we not allow both Miss Bingley and my late, wayward cousin to determine their own fates while always ensuring no one here would be physically harmed?" He scanned the crowd.

"Bennet is correct. We have the resources and manpower to make sure he does not hurt anyone while we wait to spring a trap when we are ready. Given what Bennet and Darcy have already set in motion, the profligate will be very frustrated when he attempts his normal ways in Meryton," the Earl gave his nephew a calculating look.

"William, do you not hold over three thousand in debt markers and vowels for this particular profligate man?"

"Yes, I do, Uncle Reggie. In fact, close to four thousand pounds now. I have them safely stored in Mr. Reed's safe in his office in London. I will send him an express to have the vowels delivered to me here by special messenger as soon as can be. And as Bennet has wisely invited Colonel Forster and his wife for dinner, we will be able to warn the Colonel and so his fellow officers will be warned that he never pays debts of honour and cheats at cards.

"By virtue of the fact Bennet asked the tradesmen to not extend credit to any officers, Wickham's suspicions will not be raised as they would be if he was the only one denied credit." Darcy inclined his head towards Bennet in appreciation.

Georgie moved to sit next to Lizzy who was holding William's hand tightly. "He will not be allowed to hurt anyone, will he William?" Lizzy asked worriedly as she looked between him and her father, her other hand holding Georgiana's and was just as unwilling to let her soon to be sister face this moment without her full support as she was her future husband. All in the room were surprised when they heard Georgiana's voice, and that it was not meek or merely a whisper when she finally relieved their worry by speaking.

"I thought I would be terrified when I heard his name or if I was ever so close to him again. I admit at first, it shocked me, but I find I am not. He holds no more power over me. All I care about is that he is not allowed to hurt anyone else. If he also gets his comeuppance for all of the misery he has visited on many more than just me, so much the better. Please let me help if I can. I will not let him come near any of my sisters or Anne." She looked at William, stilling his protest then looked at Richard so he too was forced to accept she was stronger now than she had ever been.

"No, we will not permit him to hurt anyone, Georgie," Darcy promised with a relieved smile. "My Lizzy and I are so proud of you, Georgie. I cannot believe you are the same girl, ehhmm, young lady that arrived in Hertfordshire mere weeks ago. It makes me happy, so very happy to see my confident sister back with us. I swear by all I hold dear that we will make sure he is never able to hurt anyone again." Darcy repeated his vow, proving his acceptance of her growth and making Elizabeth love him even more for his not disregarding Georgie's need to be part of this.

Soon after, an acceptance for dinner was received from Colonel Forster for himself and his wife, Harriet. As it was still about four hours before the Forsters would arrive, the group employed themselves with various activities to pass the time.

Edward Gardiner, in particular, used a smaller study Bennet had available for gentlemen visiting his estate to meet with local gentry that had particularly requested meetings with him regarding investment opportunities.

~~~~~~~/~~~~~~~

In town, Lady Catherine's barouche box had just pulled to a stop at Matlock House. She was more than a little frustrated because it had never taken so long to reach London before. It had been more than six hours since she had left Rosings Park when it normally took under four hours for this particular trip.

Her footman lowered the steps and opened the carriage door for her. Not waiting; the frustrated lady pushed the footman out of her way and marched up the steps to her brother's door. There was no knocker up, but that did not deter Lady Catherine as it would anyone of good breeding. She beat on the door with the head of her overly ornate walking stick until she heard movement. The door was cracked open by the Matlock House butler.

Before Jones was able to make a sound, Lady Catherine's yell echoed in the hall: *"Do you know who I am? I am your master's sister, and I will have you dismissed for being so slow to get to the door! Now, I demand you open the door and show me to my brother without further delay!"* she commanded imperiously.

"If you would have allowed me to explain, my Lady. Lord Matlock and his family are not in residence. Before you ask, I am not at liberty to tell you where he is," the butler stated evenly.

With that Jones pushed the door shut and locked it. Knowing the opinion the master and his family held of the virago, he was absolutely sure there would be no negative consequences to his shutting the door in her face.

"Why you, you, you..." For a moment she stared at the door, stunned. "I will have my brother dismiss you! I have never been thus treated in all of the years of my life," Lady Catherine hissed.

After some futile banging on the door that only achieved cracking the head on her walking stick, she returned to her conveyance. She was forced to realise the butler would not give her what she desired no matter how displeased she was, so she instructed the driver to go to Darcy House with all possible haste. The driver, as Miss Anne had instructed, took a much longer route than required for the short trip.

Instead of moving ahead a couple of doors across the square, he felt it imperative they start again from the outskirts of Mayfair. The result at Darcy House was almost identical to the reception she had received at Matlock House.

Killion would not tell her where his master was, and no she was not allowed entry for the night before she continued her trip. So far things were not going as she had intended and further more on picking up a copy of the times, she read her parson had been defrocked, then tried and convicted at the Old Bailey for a number of crimes including attempted murder, and had been hung at the gallows but the day before.

She reluctantly made her way to her own townhouse that only had a skeleton staff as she almost never used it anymore and was just maintained for appearances.

~~~~~~~/~~~~~~~

Colonel Forster and his relatively young wife, Harriet, who was but one and twenty yet impressively sensible, arrived on time, as would be expected of a military man. They were shown to the blue drawing room by the butler, and introductions between the Colonel's wife and the extensive Longbourn party were made.

Everyone chatted amiably and soon after Hill announced dinner was served, so the party made their way toward the dining room. The Earl took Fanny's arm and Bennet the Countess's, then the rest of the party formed in their natural pairings, next being Lord Hilldale and his wife, Colonel and Mrs. Forster, Darcy and Lizzy, Edward and Maddie Gardiner, Colonel Fitzwilliam and Mary, Bingley and Jane, and they were followed by Kitty, Georgiana, and the Bennet twins.

After dinner, which was also a goodbye dinner for the Gardiners who were to return with their delightful children to Town on the morrow, Fanny led the ladies to the blue drawing room, which was the largest of the drawing rooms and housed an elegant Broadwood Grand pianoforte.

The men sat around the table with cigars and the expected libations, Colonel Forster himself had not had brandy of this quality in many a year. None of the men had a propensity to overindulge, so they had one snifter each. Once the business of compliments and ribbing of the bachelors was finished, Colonel Fitzwilliam opened the discussion they needed to have with Forster.

"Forster, you had a new recruit purchase an Ensign's rank who arrived recently did you not? One from the London recruiting drive?" he asked in as even a tone as he could muster without Mary close by.

"I had several from Town that joined," Forster nodded, "is there one, in particular, you want to discuss or all of them?"

"Yes," Darcy cleared his throat in an attempt to temper his own frustration as he looked at the glowing tip of his cigar; "George Wickham," he spat out, proving even a name can be distasteful on the tongue.

"Yes, he is one of my new recruits," agreed Forster, his voice betraying he was questioning the intent of dinner as a whole, suspecting he was about to hear a lot more about this particular recruit.

The calmest of those in the family, Bennet glanced at Reggie and was given a nod of approval none of the others would gainsay, and so he imparted the facts without the anger they could see plainly might erupt from either of Georgiana's guardians.

"Wickham was just this morning brought to my notice because he was making what the ensign considers *discreet* enquiries about my daughters, and more particularly their dowries. The residents of Meryton are most loyal to me and my family, not only because my estates generate the bulk of their livelihoods, but because my daughters are known and loved in the town and beyond," Bennet started with the catalyst of why they were gathered.

"After just meeting them at Lucas Lodge where I got to watch them perform and mingle with those in attendance, I have no doubt they all inspire such," Forster nodded in agreement.

"The enquiries in and of themselves would have put

me on alert, but would not have necessitated this discussion, however, other misdeeds he has committed does." Bennet nodded at the look of concern, allowing those present to lay out the deeds they witnessed and messes he had left behind and they had cleaned up, not the least of which was children who now had no father and mothers with nowhere to turn after being taken advantage of and left behind.

Forster's look of concern changed to disbelief then melded to absolute disgust that deepened when Bennet and his family and friends laid out Wickham's long history of ruining maidens, seducing wives, debts with merchants, debts of honour from gambling, and his additional maligning of others characters, and assigning them the blame for his actions.

"It is mostly Darcy he blames for all of his supposed misfortunes, immoral, and sometimes illegal choices he alone is responsible for," Richard scowled, warning Darcy with a look to not make excuses for Wickham this time.

"What Richard says is true. And he is right to be frustrated with me. I have at last come to see the responsibility of Wickham and his actions is not mine to bear." He nodded his thanks to Bennet, a tight smile proffered to his uncle and cousins when they looked at him like he had grown two additional heads.

"It never was your responsibility, Son," Bennet agreed. "But your character and moral compass prove you are exactly the kind of man I am proud to soon have as my son-in-law. I think it a good idea for you to add the facts about the living so when Colonel Forster hears the practised lie, he does not presume it is truth," Bennet suggested.

"Thank you, Father. You bring up a good point." Darcy nodded once and took a breath to settle his thoughts, not noticing Bennet's wink directed at Richard whose astounded expression matched exactly that of his father and brother, hiding his smirk in a drink when Richard had to hide his laugh in a cough.

"The truth is my late father left the living at Kympton to Wickham once he had passed a seminary and took orders. Wickham refused this living saying he had no intent to take orders, requesting and receiving instead the value of it totalling three thousand pounds where upon he resigned all claim to the living in writing. In addition, he received a thousand pounds as bequeathed from my father, all of it combined Wickham wasted in a very short amount of time. I know this because less than a year later the dastard came back to Pemberley and tried to claim the living he had less than twelve months previously roundly refused in writing."

"You must be joking!" Forster exclaimed, frowning as he looked from Darcy to his friend and then scanned the faces of the rest of the men in the room. "I mean I can see that you are not, but this is worse than anything I could have imagined," he declared.

"And that is not all." Bennet intervened, again locking eyes with Darcy for a second before turning to Richard. "I believe we can keep the exact name of the young girl secret, but I think the facts excepting that will give Forster the reason why there is so much animosity exists in the room.

"A girl we all consider part of our family and is closely related to some person or persons in this room was very nearly taken advantage of. He attempted to manipulate a genteel young lady of tender age to elope with him for her sizable dowry," Bennet relayed.

Lord Matlock chuckled at his friend's masterful handling of the situation while not revealing Georgie's name. He nodded at his oldest friend, vowing to himself he would send three bottles of this very brandy to him when he got to town.

"I will have this debaucher, this lying scoundrel who dared think he could wear a uniform flogged and in stocks as soon as I return to the camp," Forster seethed, "I do not accept men with such character or no honour in my militia unit! They are asked questions about their persons and deeds, and are only received into my unit after they affirm in writing that they are in fact men of honour."

"Please." Bennet held up a hand. "That is not what we want, at least not just yet. We have a plan, as all good military men should. As I am sure you have surmised, the last word that could ever be associated with George Wickham is honour." Colonel Fitzwilliam smirked a wink at his good friend, this was the part he was truly looking forward to. It was a long overdue comeuppance that would rival even Caroline Bingley's.

"I hold close to four thousand pounds worth of vowels he has signed for debts I have covered which he left in many places without conscience or worry about the impact on the honest tradesmen he was in essence intending to steal from," Darcy reported. "I sent for them today as they are held by my solicitor, and the messenger should arrive with them in hand tomorrow or the next day at the latest."

"In the meantime," the Earl interjected, "we hope you will let him be, but make sure he is well watched at all times. He has a predilection for young, tender-aged girls. In addition, we have warned the estate owners and non-Meryton residents of the area to protect their daughters and wives.

"We have taken the steps to warn the shopkeepers in town and asked them to covertly inform the residents of Meryton to protect the womenfolk. Also we pointed out the tradesmen should not offer credit to any of your officers." At Forster's affronted look, the Earl nodded and held up a hand to prove he was not yet done. "We do not want him to run. If he sees he is being treated differently than the rest of his brother officers, he will suspect something. You, as commander of the Derbyshire Militia, are excepted from this so you will be able to procure what you need. If any of your officers have need to buy on credit, they can get their needs met through you as an intermediary until this bane is packed off for a lifelong visit to Marshalsea." He nodded when the Colonel settled, assessing the plan as a whole.

Understanding the need not to raise Wickham's suspicion placated Forster, agreeing the measures were only intended to curb Wickham, hoping to contain the one very bad apple, and not meant as a slight against his honourable officers. At Richard's quirked brow, he nodded he had been too hasty in his initial affrontery and agreed it was a good plan.

"Knowing the wastrel as we do, we are sure he will not be able to resist causing some sort of mischief, and that along with his debts I am about to call in will put him in gaol for the rest of his miserable life," Darcy stated firmly.

Once the men had agreed on their course of action, they joined the ladies in the blue drawing room, hearing the sound of a very accomplished pianoforte playing and the voice of an angel that swelled in song emanating from within. They entered to the picture of Kitty and Georgie playing a delightful duet, while Lizzy accompanied them with her incredible voice.

Upon their entry and the expectant looks from the assembled ladies and the twins, Bennet confirmed Forster was in agreement and Wickham would not be allowed to cause his usual mischief before he received his long overdue, well-deserved comeuppance.

Everything that could be done, was either already being done or would be to protect the merchants and all of the residents of the area from the profligate, dissolute scoundrel.

CHAPTER 12

The following morning, Wickham set out with a plan to procure some items of comfort. He was denied credit at the first three merchant's shops he tried, even after applying his considerable charm. They would not relent, informing him the town had a policy to deny credit to any who were not permanent residents of the area.

Wickham was denied credit by the fourth tradesman with the same reasoning before he stopped asking. Although he was bothered that his normally unfailing manipulation skills were not working, he was not concerned because his fellow officers had confirmed the shopkeepers in this town would not extend credit to any of them.

This at least made Wickham feel a modicum of relief, believing his impunity to convince unsuspecting persons to give him anything he asked for was intact and he just needed to find a way to reach the merchants or tradesmen outside of town.

As he walked toward the tavern at the Running Bull Inn, he ruminated on the fact unless he charmed someone into buying his drinks, he would have to use his own dwindling supply of coin.

He had lost a good amount of his blunt at cards the night before; though the truth was luck had not been on his side for his gambling endeavours in a long time. Not only that, but he had also had the misfortune to join a unit where the Colonel had banned playing unless you had the blunt to pay upfront, and on top of that, even worse the prig did not allow any debts of honour among his officers.

But to make matters worse, his fellow officers he pegged as easy marks were instead very vigilant, so there was no way to cheat without being caught in the act. He had no choice, he had to remain with the infernal militia for the time being to hide from the men from London he had cheated and owed much more than he could ever pay, who were seeking him. Not to mention the dogged pursuit of a brother desiring satisfaction for one of the girls he had bedded and left behind with child. Ruined was such a nasty word, he had just introduced them to the arts they would soon need.

He looked along the High Street of Meryton as he sauntered toward the tavern, noticing there was a distinct lack of targets for him to start priming with the intent to seduce when the opportunity was right. If he could not find a willing participant, Wickham had no issue with forcing his attentions on a young maiden, so long as it got him what he wanted.

As he always did when down on his luck, he turned his anger on the source of all his woes. *'If only Darcy had not arrived in Ramsgate unexpectedly to spoil my perfect plan. He is always costing me money!'* Wickham thought bitterly. *'Even if I had not been able to get that mouse's thirty thousand, though it was but what was my due after all, I should have ruined her so I would have achieved my vengeance upon that prig Darcy. By spoiling her, I would have ruined their good name at last!'*

Wickham knew had he done so, there is nothing that would have stopped Colonel Fitzwilliam from hunting him down and killing him without even a chance to say a final prayer to get him into heaven. That caused him to shudder involuntarily, and he refocused on the entryway now before him.

He swaggered into the tavern and in seeing no possible mark to sponge off, he laid a coin on the counter and ordered an ale. No, this paying for himself and being forced to be honest was no fun. He was George Darcy's godson, he was meant to get what he wanted, and he should have been left Pemberley, not a paltry thousand pounds after all the time he spent sucking up to old Darcy.

He conveniently ignored the fact he had been given three thousand in lieu of the living he had refused. Him, a pastor, making sermons and taking orders and working to earn his blunt!? No, that was way too much effort for the likes of George Wickham who was destined to be a gentleman.

As was his wont, he assigned his failings to others as the list reran in his head. He did not have the character or honour to see his only enemy was himself so here he was again, scheming out the best way to get money without earning it. What did he care how many people he hurt, or how many maidens he ruined so long as he got what he wanted with minimum effort?

~~~~~~~/~~~~~~~

An extremely displeased, fuming, certainly very angry Lady Catherine de Bourgh was stewing in her discontent as she was wending her way into Hertfordshire to order her wayward nephew to do his duty to her daughter Anne. She had schemed about this for too many years to allow some nobody to snatch the prize of Pemberley away when it was so close to being hers.

'I will get what is my due, I will gain control of Pemberley and all of the vast wealth that goes with it.' she vowed to herself again.

That she was the only one in the world who forwarded the union did not deter her, she believed it would happen just because she wished it. That she had been told by all in her family that Anne and George Darcy had made it known her claim of an agreement was patently false was not something Lady Catherine acknowledged.

She discarded this inconvenient truth as she did all facts not fitting the narrative she spun for herself. Those who knew her were well aware her desires and actions were driven by the lies she told herself and everyone else. In her mind, she was always right, knew everything about everything, and always got what she desired.

That none of that was true never entered her stream of consciousness, but like her ex-parson who had had a date with the hangman's noose, she never allowed facts or inconveniences such as truth to sway her.

At least her useless, snivelling parson, who had dared beg her to intercede on his behalf, had performed her one last service, she had the directions to the Bennet's insignificant estate because of the missive he had sent her.

As her carriage rolled through Meryton she sniffed with disdain, as if there was a bad smell in the air while her barouche box traversed through the already forgotten country market town on the way to her destination.

Based on what her now late, former parson had imparted about them before she sent him on his fateful and doomed mission, she believed the Bennets were of the lowest circle of gentry with no fortune and an insignificant, irrelevant estate. The distinction of rank had to be maintained, so she was sure these inconsequential persons would wilt before her grandness even before she made her sentiments known.

Her first clue her parson had not imparted the truth to her came as the carriage made its way down a long drive, which was greater than a mile in length, and the manor house came into view.

Lady Catherine was shocked to discover the structure rivalled Rosings Park in size and were she someone that was willing to be honest with herself, she would have acknowledged that it was, in fact, larger. But as this did not fit the expectations, she expected all to abide by, she dismissed the visual evidence before her, presuming it was but a trick she would get to the bottom of before she departed.

After the coach came to a halt the step was lowered, and the footman stood aside before he opened the door just in case the mistress repeated her actions from when they had arrived at Matlock House. She marched up to the front door and, in her imperious manner, rapped on it with her now cracked walking stick.

The door was opened by Hill, bodily blocking her attempt to storm into the house unannounced and uninvited. The assembled party now included Anne de Bourgh, cringed as they heard the familiar refrain echoing in the entryway.

"I am most seriously displeased! Move out of my way! Do you know who I am?" Lady Catherine looked at the butler with disgust, while anyone else would have taken a moment to recognise he was dressed in the most impeccable of butler's suits. Bennet watched Reggie, waiting for the request that was, as ever, unnecessary.

"You know my house is your house, Reggie. I give you leave to act as the host to your sister in any way you see fit. I have two sons that also need a firmer hand and three daughters that had the nerve to grow up on me and are intending to make their own lives. Please order time to cease advancing as soon as you have handled your *dear* sister," Bennet ribbed.

His jest won the laugh he had hoped for from Anne, and as a bonus, the rest in the drawing room. He winked at her, nodding when Fanny went to her side and took her hand, murmuring something perfect, he was sure, and was proven right when Anne settled and relaxed.

"Thank you, Bennet. I have long since had enough of her behaviour. Now that Anne is claiming what is hers by rights, it is time to handle this harpy." He winked at Anne, who had never imagined this side of her family and giggled, which was so rare for her Richard and Darcy grinned at the hearing of it.

Richard stood behind Anne in a show of support, allowing Darcy to stay away so their Aunt would have no fuel for her delusion as his father stepped toward the hall. What swelled his heart with pride was Mary's sitting on the other side of Anne and her too whispering something that made Anne smile as she took Mary's proffered hand.

"What are you doing here, Catherine?" the Earl asked drolly as soon as she saw him.

"R-R-Reginald?" she spluttered, "how is it that you are here? I have it on most excellent authority that these people are insignificant and have no breeding or fortune to speak of but can boast a tart of a daughter that has the gall to try and steal my Anne's fiancé!" Lady Catherine demanded, presuming her own opinion comprised excellent authority to all she chose to grant it to.

"Follow me, Catherine," the Earl ordered.

Hearing this, Hill moved aside to allow the aptly called termagant into the house. Now that she was inside, even though she tried to deny it, Lady Catherine could not but notice that this family held the fortune the house initially hinted at.

She followed her brother into a drawing room with a better pianoforte than she had at Rosings Park, and her knees almost buckled under the shock of all who were assembled in the room. She blinked twice then repeated her survey of all present, a growing trepidation cemented when she saw the Countess of Matlock, Lord and Lady Hilldale, the Colonel, Darcy and Georgiana, and others she assumed were the Bennet offspring.

"To what do we owe the displeasure of your company,

and why do you intrude on us without invitation?" Thomas Bennet enquired almost jovially, anticipating her reply. She did not disappoint.

"Who are you to address your betters in such a manner and tone?" Lady Catherine replied haughtily as she started to recover from the shock of seeing so many of her family in the room.

"That, mother *dearest*," Anne stated with pent-up anger and a false smile she had been wearing for too many years, satisfaction welling in her chest when her mother slowly turned to see her own daughter behind her, "is the master of this estate and has every right to ask why you have intruded on his party uninvited and unwelcomed." Anne smiled at the fishlike workings of her mother's mouth as she tried to understand what was happening, which was so very far from her expectations of how this interview would go.

"Anne!" Lady Catherine gasped when she could again speak. "Why are you here? How did you get here? I did not give you permission to leave Rosings!" she demanded; certain her biddable daughter would apologise.

"Firstly, mother, I am of age, and I do not need your permission to do anything." Anne could not help but smile at the taken aback look on her mother's mien. "I, unlike you, was invited here. And of course, I got here in a carriage, no one here has wings though I suspect Jane, in fact, just might." she smiled sweetly at Jane, winning an answering giggle from the eldest Bennet daughter and some of the others, once they had recovered from their own shock at the display of wit.

The laughter had the added bonus of incensing her mother, which she had to admit she was not sad about, smiling even more sardonically at the woman who had run her life for far too long. "I repeat, why are you here, Mother?" she pressed her advantage, earning respect from all in the room who were then forced to admit their dislike of

Catherine had caused them to miss too much time with the pillar of strength who was Anne de Bourgh.

"To separate a fortune-hunting whore from your fiancé..." she hissed, but was not allowed to finish due to howls of indignation in the room and an enormous, oak tree-sized footman was then advancing on her with a very menacing look in his eye.

"Catherine, you will apologise to William's fiancée at once," her brother commanded his wayward sister and Bennet held up his hand to stay Biggs's progress.

"He cannot be engaged to a hussy with no fortune or connections. He has been betrothed to Anne since they were in their cradles, as was the desire of his mother and hers." Catherine stated with resolve, her nose up and the expectation of all to fall in line clear.

"One more word about my Lizzy and I will ruin you, madam," Bennet spat. Lizzy, who was now holding tightly onto William's hand and arm, thankfully looked more amused than hurt by the ridiculous woman and her pronouncements. And to help, she had whispered something to William that had him holding his tongue, for the moment, at least.

"That is more than enough about that tired old lie of yours, Catherine," the Earl corrected her. "We have asked and asked you to cease, and now it is past time you did. Besides Anne and George telling William before they left the mortal coil no such agreement existed other than in your greed-driven mind, we told you Anne wrote to Elaine and me after one of the times you tried to browbeat her with the notion of a youthful betrothal?

"She was most explicit in her statement that no such agreement was ever made, and she wanted her children to marry only for the deepest love. William knows about this letter, but he does not know his dear departed father wrote a similar letter to us with similar sentiments, nor that both of his beloved parents codified their wills so that you could never do anything to force William and Anne to marry.

"Not even a compromise would have required either of them to walk down the aisle. To be sure, Anne, even were you forced into one, there was an estate waiting for you to recover and be cared for should it have been necessary." He looked at Anne, who showed much surprise.

"I would have liked to spend my youth there," Anne sighed, wishing she had known she had someplace safe she could have run to, even to visit.

"That was my failure, Anne. I am sorry," her uncle sighed, glancing at his wife in apology for not listening to her every time she tried to tell him Anne needed time away from her mother. All turned back to Catherine when she demanded that Anne return to her side.

"You come into my house, impugning the honour and integrity of one of my daughters!" Bennet spat at the virago as all colour drained from her face. "There is only one fortune hunter in this house, and it is *you*, madam. Do you think there is anyone here who does not know your true motivation is long-held jealousy?"

Lady Catherine started to see that maybe things were not going to go the way she had ordained they should. Acknowledging her bluster was not effective, she tried what for her was a softer tack.

"Come now, Reggie, you know what a brilliant match Fitzwilliam and Anne would be. It would make us one of the wealthiest families in the country. Just think of the prestige and wealth we could have. Are the shades of Pemberley to be thus polluted by this upstart of no rank, no fortune, and no connections?" she challenged.

"You are delusional, Catherine. They have the same connections as I and more than you. Are you so blind that you do not see us all here in front of you? As to fortune? The Bennets have many times more wealth than you could imagine having, and this is but one of three estates they own. Each of his four daughters has over fifty thousand for her dowry.

"Given how you have run Rosings Park into the ground, each of the young ladies here have more wealth in their own rights than you would if you were allowed to sell Rosings Park, which we all know you are not allowed to do as it does not belong to you." The Earl's tone held some derision but was otherwise even.

As Lady Catherine tried to absorb what her brother was telling her, she was addressed by Bennet, who decided to press the advantage he could clearly see.

"Not only did you send that snivelling, sycophantic, turned criminal parson into my house, but you have the temerity to arrive uninvited and slander my daughter? You do realise I could have you arrested for conspiracy to commit murder, do you not?" Bennet's voice was rising as his anger started to vent.

"Your idiot informed us he had *your* permission to dispatch the so-called *interlopers*, who are, in fact, my sons born of my wife's body. Did he ever inform you that he was in the courtroom with his father when the judge saw the irrefutable proof of my son's birth by their mother, my wife?" he demanded, but he was not done.

"Your daughter provided us with the copy of the missive he sent you where he repeats this claim in writing. If you, madam, were a man, I would call you out! Not that anyone here cares what you think, but as my friend just informed you, my daughters have massive dowries! My combined estates alone bring in almost five times what Rosings Park should, not what it does now under your gross mismanagement. Longbourn is but one of my three estates and a fraction of my total income which earns more than

Rosings park on its own.

"As to her connections, if you had ever listened to anyone but the sound of your own voice you would have heard your brother inform you, on any number of occasions, about his dearest friends in Hertfordshire.

"But worse, far worse, is imposing your will without care on those you are supposed to protect! You come into my house uninvited, thinking something as unearned as your rank would gain you respect? In our house, our deeds, character, and care of others earn one another's respect. Your disregard for the wishes of those lives you expect to bend to your will proves you are a lady in name only. Anne, you are welcome to stay forever if you wish it. Fanny and Elaine have long since had a room for you ready in all our houses for your visits," Bennet stated, his eyes boring into Lady Catherine's as he waited for whatever she might dare say next.

"Thank you, Mr. Bennet, I too have thought of you as family for many years. See, Mother, I knew about the Bennets since I actually listen when others talk," Anne replied before her mother could form one, no one missing the disdain for the woman that had given her life but had never been a mother to her except in name.

"Not that it matters to me as they have already proven their character is far superior to most you expect me to interact with, but they do have many connections in the upper echelons of the first circles, besides our relations you see here. And it is also true they have many times more wealth than we do."

Anne paused, ordered her thoughts, and held her hand out for no one to intervene as she meant to continue. "As you well know, although you refuse to acknowledge the fact, I have been the true mistress of Rosings Park since I turned five and twenty over six months ago. I have allowed you the illusion that my estate was yours, though it never was. From this day on, I am reclaiming what is mine and I hope my family will advise me and help me find ways to reverse the damage you have done to my inheritance." Anne did not need to look around, the vocal yeses were from every quarter and repeated in some that were not yet her actual family, but soon would be.

"You cannot do that Anne, Rosings Park is mine," Lady Catherine denied with a rising sense of panic she could not hide.

"I can and I have!" Anne said with such firm resolve it again silenced any reply that might have been given by her mother. "My solicitor, who was retained to worry about my interests, not yours, is here and I have already signed all of the documents that make it a fact just before you arrived.

"Uncle Reggie, as father's appointed executor, witnessed and approved all. You are now cut off from any estate accounts and management needs. You have wasted far too much of my money on needless, truly gaudy items to try to impress no one but yourself. The first thing I will do is have all of those sold," Anne announced, feeling liberated but on some level also sad it had come to this. This was her mother, after all.

"On the subject of my betrothal. I have never desired to be married to William, and similarly, he did not desire to be married to me. I, like everyone in the family, knew it was a fabricated lie you spun in an attempt to get your fortune-hunting hands on William's money and drain it away as you drained Rosings Park's funds."

Lady Catherine looked around for support she did not find in any quarter, not even those youngest in the room whom she was sure were under her thumb, as Georgiana stared her straight in the eye and did not hide as she usually did. Seeing no one intervene with Anne's intentions, she again looked at her daughter.

"How can you treat your mother thusly?" Lady

Catherine demanded.

"You brought me into this world, but you were never a mother to me. I was another possession for you to use and abuse as you saw fit. You paraded me about as sickly to control me, and I know the quack you tried to pass of as a physician was giving me medicine to make me ill by your command!" she announced.

Her Aunt Elaine gasped at this, her eyes filling with tears and Uncle Reggie's shoulders fell. This was a scenario he had not allowed himself to believe despite Richard's and Darcy's attempts to get him to look into Anne's supposed sickness and demand real physicians from town.

"Mrs. Jenkinson helped me years ago to stop taking the poison you were forcing on me, and ever since then I have felt normal and healthy, but we hid the fact from you because we knew as long as you thought your little scheme was succeeding you would not try anything else," Anne continued. "If I had kept taking it, I would have been dead by now! Was that your aim mother? To have me die so you could claim Papa's estate as your own?" Anne pushed, not looking around despite the gasps of horror from every quarter.

"Anne, I am so, so sorry," the Earl choked out. "Had I but known, I would have removed you from her custody. I did not want to believe my sister was such a vile person when Richard and William shared their suspicions with me, it shames me that I did not investigate to learn the truth of the matter. You knew I am the executor of your father's will, and as such I could have removed you from your mother's *so called* care and offered you the protection that you deserved." Lord Matlock desperately wanted to know why Anne had not contacted him with the information directly.

"I wish I had known sooner Uncle Reggie. It is only recently that I saw a copy of my father's real will, not the fiction my birth mother tried to feed me. She had hidden the real will and tried to pass a forgery off as genuine. I only found the one my father actually signed four months ago," Anne stated, the anger she was trying to swallow tasted of bitterness.

As Anne was speaking, Lady Catherine eyed a knife with the refreshments near her. With a mad look in her eye, she grabbed the knife and held it pointed at her daughter. "You ungrateful wench, you will not have what is mine! Do you think I dispatched your miserable father so you could steal what is mine?"

Lady Catherine lunged toward her daughter with a demented, murderous look in her eyes. Before she could get close to Anne or anyone else, Biggs had her in a steel trap-like hold and the knife dropped harmlessly from her hands.

Lady Catherine's avarice, jealousy, and greed, coupled with the realisation she had no power to order the world as she saw fit, had finally made her snap. The last vestiges of the bonds between reason and madness were irrevocably severed. As she descended further and further into her mania, Biggs held her so she could not move at all, merely spout vitriol no one wanted to hear.

"Unhand me, you brute! Do you know who I am?" she demanded, the madness becoming more evident as she tried to break free.

"Lock that murderess, who tried to harm one of her own blood while my guest, in the coal cellar, Biggs. Make sure you keep the door locked and well-guarded in pairs, if you do not mind." Fanny Bennet stood as she issued her instructions, having had enough and aghast at what she had seen and heard.

"Yes, Mistress," Biggs replied calmly then carried the clearly deranged Lady Catherine away as if she weighed nothing, her rants and screams ignored by all within the sound of her voice.

"Fanny, you are of course, correct," Lord Reggie

sighed sadly. "We have always tolerated my sister's insane pronouncements, thinking she was no danger to anyone. On seeing the demonic and murderous look in her eyes, I now know my sister has crossed the line from our reality into insanity. We had suspected she had a hand in hurrying Lewis's death, but there was no proof. She had no idea he had a heart ailment that would have taken him by natural causes without her intervention.

"She should, by rights under the law, receive the same punishment, as her late parson received, for trying to murder her daughter her part in Collins' crime, and the death of her husband," the Earl stated sadly, waylaying the protests of all. "But besides it being abhorrent to me that a lady swing from the gallows, she is no longer sane and needs to be in Bedlam. At least that way, there will not be the scandal of a trial and she will be where she can never hurt anyone again. Anne, I am so very, very sorry I did not step in to protect you sooner." He went to her and took her hand in his, holding it tightly.

"I wrongly chose to keep the reality of my situation from the family, Uncle Reggie," She reminded him.

"Your aunt knew," her uncle sighed, again glancing at his wife who was struggling to maintain her countenance.

"And I could have confided in my cousins when they had their obligatory visit each Easter, but I did not. Therefore, there is nothing for you to apologise to me for. I am saddened to find out she murdered Papa, but not all that surprised," Anne admitted.

"I agree with you, Reggie," Bennet offered sadly. "However, I think whatever we decide to do with your sister, we need to get Anne's approval. She is, after all, her daughter and the true mistress of Rosings Park."

"Whatever you decide is acceptable to me, Uncle Reggie, Mr. Bennet," Anne stated, then she turned to her soon to be cousin, Elizabeth. "Miss Elizabeth, I beg your forgiveness above all. What Lady Catherine said to and about you and your family was beyond the pale and I am equally embarrassed and sorry." Anne looked Elizabeth in the eyes as she rendered the apology for her mother, shame staining her cheeks.

"We are to be cousins, so please call me Elizabeth or Lizzy like most here do." Lizzy smiled, the encouraging look from William appreciated. She reached out and squeezed Anne's hand, shaking her head slightly. "Not only did you warn us so we would be prepared for the storm heading toward us, but, someone who shall remain nameless," she looked pointedly at William with a smile, "has been told we judge each person by their own actions, not those of others including those who intend murder or even those bent on theft, be they relation or a long acquaintance. Please do not try to take the blame for that which is not yours. It took William a while to accept the truth of that, I pray it will not take you as long." She squeezed Anne's hand to support her words.

"Thank you, Lizzy. And I want to wish both you and William joy as I can see you two are perfect for each other. Please do call me Anne." She squeezed Lizzy's hand in return.

"Welcome to the family, Anne," Elizabeth said warmly.

The sentiment was echoed by all the Bennets in the room, as all present, except for the two companions, would soon be family in truth not just by choice. As Anne sat and wondered at being so easily accepted by all, she thought about how things would have been different for her had she spoken sooner.

'Is it not enough she was trying to steal Rosings Park from me, to harm me physically is one thing. However, I fear she has cost me the man that I love! Ian Ashby. We loved each other for so long and she chased him away; I hope now that I am free you are still free as well. I pray it is not too late for us and she has not irrevocably broken my heart as well. You are the love of my *life my Ian!'* Anne was brought out of her reverie as she heard Mrs. Bennet speak.

"Can we please return to the celebration for Edward, Maddie, and the children who will be leaving for Portman Square after they break their fast on the morrow? That is far more pleasant than thinking about what we just witnessed," Fanny opined.

Luckily for all, the coal cellar was so far distant none of the occupants of the drawing room were required to endure the invective and expletives emanating from the temporary resident within. The goodbye celebration for the Gardiners carried on with no further interruptions.

The Earl, as the titular head of the Fitzwilliam family, decided that on the morrow he would go to Town to meet with the solicitors and make the arrangements for Lady Catherine's transport to her new home at Bedlam.

He would make sure she would be placed in a private room, not one of the cells where the public used to be able to view and abuse the inmates. Even though she had never shown any kindness to anyone, this small but long-lasting kindness was shown to her.

~~~~~~~/~~~~~~~

A very much in his cups Wickham stumbled out of the tavern at the Running Bull Inn of Meryton, supported on either side by an officer. Lieutenant Denny held one arm and Captain Carter the other.

Things were not going as Wickham expected for a town so insulated from London. Normally his charm would get him anything he desired, but for some reason in this little nowhere town of Meryton, nothing he tried was working. He had to pay for what he wanted with his own money, something that he had never done before. And his funds were about to run out until he received his pittance of an excuse for pay from the militia in another sennight.

"Dennish," he slurred, "in town whenth you recruitmentedas me, you told me there was funsh to be hadded in the malisha! There is nonsh funsh here! No young maidensh, no nymphsss for me to hash. This is no funsh," Wickham complained as profusely as he could manage in his current state.

Denny and Carter were disgusted by the sorry excuse of a man they half carried half dragged back to barracks. Denny was mortified and embarrassed he had recruited this wastrel with his dissolute ways and fake charm.

He and seven other officers were tasked to keep Wickham under observation four and twenty hours a day or risk the considerable wrath of Colonel Jackson Forster. One did not want to face his wrath. Ever!

With disgust, they unceremoniously dumped Wickham on his cot as the libertine urinated on himself, and with a glance at one another decided not to deal with that as they took themselves off to bed.

CHAPTER 13

Lady Catherine did not sleep very well on the dark, dirty floor of the coal cellar. No amount of yelling her displeasure, demanding release, or banging on the door produced any results other than hurting her own hand. How dare they so ignore one such as she?

She was the great Lady Catherine de Bourgh! She had the power to arrange things as, and whenever she desired. In her deepening mania, she imagined how she would revenge herself on all for this affront. With glee and cackling like a witch, she planned how she would dispatch the baggage that had the temerity to interfere in her plans for her nephew and daughter.

And no one could or would ever dare take her out of her domain! Rosings Park was hers and she had the will she changed to prove it. As she descended further and further into her own reality, which others knew as insanity, she believed all of her schemes were succeeding and she was an all-powerful ruler of her desires, one that could have all her wishes granted.

There was a chamber pot in one corner, and she determined it must be morning as there was light that was coming in from a crack in the door where the coal was loaded, and a very high slit of a window. Other than the chamber pot, there was nothing else in this cellar but coal and herself.

Unable to accept the truth of her situation, she built the delusion around her that she was in the master suite at Pemberley, finally ruling over it as was her right and about to go determine what jewels she would choose for the day. She had seen a sapphire necklace she often wanted to rip off her sister's neck and claim as her own, and that was the first thing she would wear this day.

If she had not been insane, or at least observant of her reality even as she daydreamed, she would have seen further proof of the Bennet's wealth. There were very few who could afford the reserves of coal that surrounded her in the cellar.

At some point, the door opened, and a tray of food and a carafe of water were unceremoniously deposited on the floor. It confused her the new mistress of Pemberley was not served at the grand table downstairs, but she would make do for the moment, then would make changes to the staff.

In an unpleasant moment of lucidity that came as she was drinking the water, she remembered where she was and she saw even if she had attempted to escape, there were two massive footmen standing just beyond the servant that deposited the tray. There was of course no knife on the tray, not even a butter knife, because there was no butter.

'How has it come to this?' she asked herself in her thoughts. 'If only I had never heard the name Bennet,' she wished silently to herself. She ignored the inconvenience of her daughter's determination to claim her inheritance and would have even had she not met the Bennets.

It was always easier to blame someone else rather than accept she alone was responsible for her predicament. Her mind unwilling to comprehend the truth of her situation, she slipped back into her make-believe world.

~~~~~~~/~~~~~~~

The Gardiners, after wishing their family and soon-to-be family goodbye, set off in two carriages for their home at Portman Square once they had broken their fasts.

Gardiner's meeting with Sir William Lucas, Mr. Spencer Goulding, and Mr. Jonathan Long had gone as

Thomas intimated, and all three had asked to be allowed to invest with Gardiner and Associates. Edward Gardiner no longer took on investors with so little to initially offer, but they were his brother's good friends and they had looked out for and cared for his nieces and nephews since they had been born. Also, Bennet had started with a small or even smaller investment all those years ago and look at what he had accomplished.

In his inside coat pocket was a bank draft from each of the three men, and what he knew was the maximum amount each had available. As Bennet had before them, they would send all their profits to Gardiner each year.

The Earl of Matlock too had set out for town after he broke his fast, in fact shortly after the Gardiners departed. He was accompanied by his heir, Andrew, and the solicitor that had brought the documents for Anne to sign now she was finally taking control of her birthright.

The Earl was appreciative of the fact that his late friend and Anne's father, Sir Lewis de Bourgh, had secured Anne's dowry of fifty thousand pounds as well as an additional twenty thousand pounds in a way Catherine neither knew about, though even if she had she never could have touched either, no matter how many demands she may have made.

He had invested all of the seventy thousand pounds with Fanny's brother, *Midas* Edward Gardiner, some years ago. The investments had turned that twenty thousand into now well over a hundred thousand pounds so Anne would be able to return Rosings to its former glory. In addition, her dowry had more than tripled in value.

He smiled when he thought of Anne's promise of selling all of the ostentatious baubles Lady Catherine had obsessively collected because she had believed it demonstrated her wealth and superiority to all her visitors. All her décor had really done was show just how she was lacking in class and how bad her taste was.

The occupants of the carriage dozed for the four-hour trip to Town, and after thoroughly considering everything once again, the Earl was able to fall asleep with a clear conscience.

Lord Matlock was doing the right thing by helping his niece gain control of what rightfully was hers, with the added benefit of knowing all at Rosings Park would benefit under her care, and that consigning his sister to Bedlam was the safest for all, especially herself.

~~~~~~~/~~~~~~~

Wickham woke up a little worse for wear after spending most of the previous day deep in his cups and with no coin remaining. He hated that he smelled like urine, so he asked for water for a bath to try and purge the stench from his person.

After he bathed and dressed, he thought about doing what he had done so many times before, slipping away as he often was able to do as soon as things got too hard, or he was going to be called to account for his actions.

This time, maybe for the first time, it would not be to avoid unhappy relatives and debts, but because he thus far had been unable to act as he pleased due to the lack of credit and the fact there was nary a young maiden with whom he could please himself.

Once his head was a little clearer, he remembered two things. The men hunting him and the Bennet daughters and their forty thousand pounds each. He decided to stay to remain hidden and secure a fortune that he felt was his due.

He was very certain he could get it, either through marriage after the anticipation of vows or as hush money to make him go away. Who needed that little mousey Darcy's thirty thousand when he could have so much more? It was past time to start planning.

Around eleven that morning, Wickham saw a sight for sore eyes. He beheld the three most beautiful, striking young ladies he had ever seen. He was both drooling and gawking at the vision. They were somewhat older than he preferred, but beggars could not be choosers, and if begging was involved, any of them begging for his attention was a welcome thought.

Before he could approach them, he heard one of them say they would be back to make some more purchases on the morrow as they climbed into a grand carriage, assisted by one of the biggest footmen he had ever seen.

After some *discreet* enquiries, he learnt he had just glimpsed the three eldest Bennet heiresses, a blond and two raven-haired beauties. He had to have one or even all of them, then after he had his fill, he would decide which one's dowry he would claim.

Drooling over his planned conquest, he had not noticed his shadows that were ever observant and were ready to spring into action not if, but when, his predilections caused him to cross the line.

Wickham was far too preoccupied with his dreams of the great fortune he would have and had no reason to suspect he was being closely watched. These were not homely looking heiresses, they were the most beautiful girls he had ever set his eyes on, and he was more determined than ever to carry his point. After all, no one could ever resist his charms.

Without any remaining coin, the tavern was not an option unless he was able to dupe someone into buying his grog for him. If not, he would have to stay sober until he received that first pitiful excuse for pay in another five days.

He stuck out his chin and puffed out his chest as he admired himself in a store window, deciding that he looked very well in regimentals. His ego would not allow himself to notice he was being avoided by the townspeople, both because of the warnings they had received about him and the remaining smell of urine wafting from his person. He had not bathed as well as he believed he had.

~~~~~~~/~~~~~~~

"The officer practically drooling when he saw us, was that the awful Wickham the Darcys have long dealt with?" Lizzy asked Biggs who was in the carriage with them for added safety. Anger at Wickham's actions against her soon-to-be family was burning just below the surface.

Biggs just nodded, knowing he would need to add someone else to watch Miss Lizzy now, She had the look of an avenging angel in her eyes, a look they all knew well when she knew someone had hurt someone she loved. Mary and Jane shuddered as they too noticed how the man had leered at them, which could only be described as despicable.

The Bennet girls had hoped he would see them, in fact, knew their brief exposure to the dissolute scoundrel was needed as bait on the hook in order to spring the trap. They knew they would never be in such close proximity to the profligate again and even if he did manage to get close to one of them, they were never without more than adequate protection.

"I am so happy Sir William and Lady Lucas have ordered Maria to stay home unless they accompany her or at least go out with two of her older siblings at all times." Mary exhaled in relief as her older sisters nodded in agreement. What was left unsaid was the sisters all knew how easily Maria's head could be turned by a man in scarlet regimentals.

She had come very close to eloping with an officer two years previously when she was only fifteen, and only Charlotte finding out about the plan and reporting it to her parents had saved Maria and the honour of the Lucas family.

As the sisters exited the carriage, they alighted to

three very relieved young men who had been anxiously waiting for their return from the baiting mission. Even though the men knew their ladies were well protected, if not overprotected at all times, they were still deeply relieved to see their ladies arrive safely back at Longbourn with smiles on their faces and no hint of worry or concern.

All three men burned with anger, and Mary's Colonel had to be physically restrained from calling for a horse to go run the wastrel through when they were told about the way Wickham had in turn gawked, leered, and drooled at their ladies. This could not be over soon enough for their liking. Wickham had bedevilled the Darcy and Fitzwilliam families for the last time; he just did not know it yet.

They were about to enter the house when a courier pulled his horse to a stop in a cloud of dust. The man on the horse asked whether one of the gentlemen was Mr. Fitzwilliam Darcy of Pemberley in Derbyshire. Once Darcy identified himself, the courier handed the identified gent a package of papers.

Darcy smiled when he realised he now held the solution to the Wickham problem in his hands. The package contained proof of the nearly four thousand pounds of debts Darcy had bought up in the various places Wickham had slithered into then slunk away from while leaving his debts behind.

Lizzy had a groom lead the courier to the stables so his horse could rest, and be watered and fed. She also asked a groom to show the man to the kitchen so the courier could get food and drink in order to revive himself before his return trip to town.

When the six acknowledged lovers entered the yellow drawing room, Darcy, after making sure Lizzy was comfortably seated, excused himself to look for Bennet. He was informed by the butler that his master was reading in the library.

Darcy entered, and after apologising for disturbing Bennet's reverie as he sat reading flanked by his sons, Darcy told Bennet that the awaited for proof of Wickham's debts had arrived.

The two men excused themselves and walked to the study. Once inside they reviewed the vowels. As Darcy had estimated, the amount was far closer to four than three thousand pounds, which would definitely consign Wickham to Marshalsea for the rest of his miserable life, the waste of which Darcy now firmly knew was Wickham's choice alone.

The proof was locked in the very strong safe hidden behind a portrait of the Bennets from some two years ago when Sir Thomas Lawrence had been commissioned to paint the family as a whole, as well as one of each individual. The individual portraits all hung in the gallery on the second floor, along with portraits of Bennet's ancestors with a large and valuable collection of art.

"We will spring the trap tomorrow. There is no need to wait for Reggie and Andrew to return," stated Bennet. "Before they departed for Town, we discussed it and Reggie agreed if the proof arrived, we would proceed, regardless of whether or not they were present as the sooner we rid Meryton of the scourge, the better for all." Bennet nodded at Darcy's relief. "And honestly, I do not think we will be able to restrain Richard again should the blackguard come near Mary."

Bennet chuckled, appreciative of the love for his daughter, but was more interested in making sure that Richard was not tried for murder so he could, in fact, make it to the altar. He was far more scared of Mary's wrath should he not be able to than he was of Richard's anger.

Darcy nodded his head in full agreement. He considered he should feel bad for Wickham; after all, he was his father's godson. But at this point, he could not, and his conscience was clear.

No matter who he blamed, Wickham, like Caroline Bingley, was the author of his story all the way to the ending. All the decisions had been his own, so it was just and correct he alone should suffer the consequences.

Darcy knew he had done everything in his power to help Wickham in the past, and rather than learn, the more he was helped the more George Wickham expected it was his due. Fitzwilliam Darcy would not repeat that mistake of enabling him again. Ever.

CHAPTER 14

The rest of the day passed very pleasantly for all, and especially for one particular ensign in the Derbyshire Militia as he sat and dreamed about the ways he would soon spend his fortune.

He was planning the ways he would either have the Bennet chits falling for his charms, or if that failed, he would do as he had done in the past and force himself on them. In a way it excited him more when he forced them to give into the inevitable, it was more thrilling for him, a sweeter victory, in fact. The rush he felt when he exercised his power over his unwilling victims was one of the most powerful aphrodisiacs to the wastrel.

~~~~~~~/~~~~~~~

The next morning, a large Bennet coach arrived in Meryton at about the same time as the previous day, and the three Bennet daughters alighted. As expected, two footmen were on the rear platform, just as had been the case when Wickham first saw them the day before.

Wickham, already anticipating the pleasure he would have, watched as the three entered the millinery shop accompanied by a large footman, while the other man, equally as large, stayed with the conveyance.

After a while, they exited with the footman carrying packages. They then went to the haberdashery, and after a period that seemed longer than what they had taken at the millinery's they exited with more packages loaded onto the thick arms of the footman.

Wickham was starting to despair that with the two ape-sized footmen close by that he would never be able to approach his intended victims when he heard one of the sisters tell the enormous footman he should take the carriage and the packages home as they had decided a walk was in order.

While Wickham could not believe his luck, he also could not help but think that they were perfectly rich, but *stupid girls*. Wickham salivated because this was his favourite combination. *'They are going to make it almost too easy for me,'* he smirked.

This was what he was waiting for, exactly what he hoped for; and the stupid chits were going to fall into his plans like kittens desperate for a ball of string. Not only were they headed away from the watchful citizens of Meryton, but they were walking toward the woods with no protection.

It was one of the best things about small towns, people were always less on their guard and did not believe danger was around any corner unlike those in London who knew it could be waiting around every one of them.

Wickham followed the girls at a discreet distance, or what he considered discreet anyway. The three Bennet ladies headed out of town in the direction that he now knew Longbourn lay, and he heard one say that they should pick some wildflowers to take home with them.

Hearing this suggestion, Wickham almost exclaimed his added approval, watching the three girls leave the road and head to a stand of trees. Wickham could not believe they were going to put themselves in a position to be completely out of sight and in his power, and now very soon he would have his chance. He increased his pace and followed the sisters into the tree line.

He saw that the three were seemingly oblivious to all else as they were bent or crouched picking the wildflowers that grew between the grass growing around the strand of trees. Feeling very confident, he acted as if it was a moment of happenstance and stopped before them.

"Well, hello and good day to you. I have inquired into the stunning examples of beauty that graced the streets of Meryton yesterday and know you are three of the Misses Bennets. I have waited a long time to meet lovely ladies such as yourself, such beauty, and such magnificent fortunes." He bowed with a flourish.

The three giggled but still had stayed turned away from him so he started to walk toward them, expecting they were desiring him to be closer. "I am going to take so much pleasure taking all three of you here this afternoon. It was very silly of you to send your footmen away. Now, tell me, are you all still maidens, or would one of you prefer to be first? Who shall I choose? Eni-mini-miney-moe..." There was no need to bother with false charm, he could take what he wanted, and no one would hear them even were they to scream.

It was to his great shock that when he asked who wanted to be his first pleasure the girls took off into the trees. He started to run toward the point where he had seen them disappear, but instead was soon in a clearing with no Bennet girl in sight.

Wickham frowned and scratched his head, wondering where they had disappeared to, and sure he would make his irritation known to them when he claimed his prizes. As he was looking around for his prey, he heard a voice that sent a chill down his spine and made his knees go weak.

"Hello, George, I have been waiting to have some time with you," Richard Fitzwilliam spoke quietly but clearly, and Wickham felt the tip of a sword prick the back of his neck.

"Richard, not so fast. You cannot have all the fun!" Fitzwilliam Darcy said as he approached from the front and he raised a sword, the tip of which was pressed against Wickham's throat, and while he knew it was sinful, the look of terror pleased him more than a little as he knew his sister would have been terrified, and in his power, had Wickham had his way.

Wickham soiled his pants for the second time that week and heard laughter now from all sides. As he surveyed the scene around him, as much as he could with the swords held by the cousins, he saw Colonel Forster, Lieutenant Denny, and Captains Carter and Saunderson, an older man flanked by two young lads who were already the man's height or taller, and a number of very large footmen on all sides so even of his legs were able to work, he had nowhere to run to.

All Wickham could say was, "How?"

~~~~~~~/~~~~~~~

That morning, three daughters of tenants who were similar in height and colouring to the three Bennet girls were dressed in clothing belonging to each of the respective daughter that she was to imitate.

Given Wickham would never be allowed to get close enough to have contact with the girls, the three Bennet daughters had been willing to lead him into the trap themselves, but everyone from their mother and father on down, and most especially their three gentlemen, resolutely refused to allow the Bennet daughters to be the ones to lead Wickham into the well-planned ambush.

The three girls who would imitate the Bennet's—Selina Blackmore, Karen Black, and Alice Bromley—were daughters of tenants that had been at Longbourn for generations.

The tenants leasing farms from the Bennets were extremely loyal and protective of the family as all tenants were treated with the utmost respect by the Bennet family with more than fair rent, as well as timely upkeep and repairs.

If there was ever genuine need, Mr. Bennet did whatever

was required to help his tenants. He had, in fact, often kept so close in contact that genuine need was never reached, small needs were met quickly so none worried in ways most tenants had to suffer.

The Bennets had established and paid all of the costs for them to attend a school so all tenant children would learn to read, write, and do sums, enabling them to get better jobs than they otherwise would have received, and therefore higher pay so their lives continued to improve depending on their own efforts. They had also created a fund, that was very well endowed, for any children of tenants that wanted additional education beyond the basics.

While the plan was being put into place, Bennet had told the Blackmores, Blacks, and Bromleys that he would richly compensate them for what their daughters were doing for his. All three had flatly refused, only too happy to help and Bennet thanked them for their loyalty, but let them know each girl would receive five pounds from him personally not only for their time, but for helping them rid their society of a person who never should be encountered or allowed to roam freely among decent people.

The three substitute Bennet daughters *were each provided a little money to purchase a new bonnet as a thank you by each real Bennet daughter.*

When they started to refuse, it was Jane who intervened. "You are our long-time tenants and friends we have played with for many years. You are protecting us without expectation of reward, purely from the goodness of your hearts.

"With your assistance this day, you are protecting my family, my sisters, and my soon-to-be family from a vile tormenter. You will allow us to thank you for that from us to you. Goodness is allowed to be rewarded." Jane warned no refusal was to be accepted. "And besides, we said we were making purchases, it would be awkward if none were made," she reminded all three.

"Yes, Miss Bennet," was chorused.

While the carriage was departing Longbourn, the Wickham welcoming party mounted their horses to meet the members of the militia at the designated spot. The fact that Wickham had always overestimated his abilities, made certain he would believe the ladies were playing right into his hands rather than he being led into a trap.

Little did he know that he had shadows, four of the officers that were part of the group of seven tasked to watch him were out of uniform and following him far more expertly than he followed his prey.

~~~~~~~~/~~~~~~~~

As Fitzwilliam and Darcy gleefully told him how he had been duped, Wickham was furious, but knew there was naught he could do about it. He felt someone relieve him of his sword and the pistol he had shoved into his belt to use as *encouragement* if one of his intended prey tried to run or resist him. The length of rope he had slung over his shoulder with the intent to secure the girls he was not enjoying was removed as well.

Wickham had never been so petrified, or mortified, in his life. Not only was he being humiliated, but it was in front of Fitzwilliam Darcy no less. By the look in Darcy's eyes and from Colonel Fitzwilliam's tone, he suspected there was no chance of talking his way out of this one and he was about to pay the piper. Just as he thought things could not get worse, his stomach sank when he heard the very voice he least expected.

"Where is your silver tongue now, George? Have you lost your ability to offer insincere words of love, or do you need your paramour, Mrs. Younge, to help you?" Wickham rotated his head to the left as much as he could without the swords drawing blood and saw that his ears had not deceived him.

Georgiana Darcy, who he knew to be a timid little mouse, was now looking at him with pure disdain and anger in her eyes, her hands on her hips as she let lose all the pent-up emotion his actions had caused her and her brother.

"What is wrong, George," she demanded, the cutting way she said his name verified he was in his worst nightmare, "has the cat got your tongue, or are you too much a coward to speak when faced by those who can defend themselves? You will find none of your defenceless preferred prey hereabouts!" As she spoke the last, she walked up to him, so she was standing at her brother's side. It was to the astonishment of all that she slapped his cheek with all the force that she could muster, and the power of which had reeled him back so much he had been cut by Richard's sword.

In the next second cheers filled the clearing, but she was most satisfied to see when his head reset to its proper alignment, the force of the movement opened a small cut on his neck from Darcy's sword as well. At that moment he was well and truly aware she held his life in her hands, and when she raised her hand Wickham flinched, the satisfaction of which filled her so much she smiled, glancing at the blood running down his neck from two small wounds.

Darcy was never prouder of his little sister. He knew this was an important final step for her to complete the healing from the way Wickham and Mrs. Younge had manipulated her in Ramsgate.

It was certainly a dramatic way to take her power back from the blackguard, but oh the pleasure of watching Georgiana making him flinch filled him with absolute satisfaction, more so than had he done it himself. Wickham's whole right cheek was now hot, the handprint forming and as bright as the blood dribbling down his neck. It would be clear for all to see for some days to come.

"What did you think you were going to do when you

found the young ladies Wickham? Force your attentions on them like you have so many before? From the weapons you carried your intent is clear. A real man does not need to lie and manipulate young girls, and never forces himself on them.

"You are a nothing but a want-to-be rapist, Wickham, and I fully intend to announce to all gaming hells and taverns where you can be found, so that all who are looking for you to repay you for the kindnesses you showed their daughters and sisters will be able to find you! Not to mention the many you owe money to," Darcy snarled at him.

Wickham had now turned white and could no longer support his own weight. His arms were firmly grasped by the two mountainous footmen he had seen in Meryton, and Darcy and the Colonel stepped back and sheathed their swords in their scabbards. With the aid of the two less than gentle helpers; at least he was able to still stand.

Before he could contrive any answer, Colonel Forster stood before him and ripped the epaulets denoting his rank from his shoulders. "You are a disgrace to not only the uniform, but all men, and decent and honourable people should never have had to suffer your existence as you lived it.

"At the time you purchased your commission you were given a document to sign wherein you attested that you were an upstanding and honourable man who had never committed a crime. Since you blatantly lied, your commission is forfeit and so are the funds you used to purchase it."

As he turned his back and returned to stand with his officers Colonel Forster continued. "Earlier today I had your quarters searched. A number of items were found in your quarters that your fellow officers have reported stolen since your arrival." Forster growled with a murderous look in his eye. "You are the type of dissolute profligate that blackens the name of the militia around the country making us unwelcome in some towns, and you are about to feel the consequences of your actions."

"W-w-what is going to happen to me?" Wickham squeaked, then tried to muster some of his former bravado as he turned toward Darcy. "Remember Darcy, if you do not assist me, I will be very vocal about Ramsgate and ruin that mousey sister of yours. Knowing that, you should pay for my silence, and I will leave the country." Wickham was sure he had played a winning hand forgetting he was always a bad gambler.

Darcy could see Wickham's cowardice shining through his attempted bravado. He thought back to when he had started to notice a change in George Wickham, who he had thought of as a friend.

The problems started when George had become aware of the difference in their stations and wealth. George's father, Peter Wickham, had been old Mr. Darcy's steward and a more honourable man you could not find. Mrs. Wickham was a different story. She spent money faster than it was earned and was very envious of that she did not have. Unfortunately, George took after her and not his father.

George had been thirteen and Darcy fourteen and home from Harrow at the end of the school year. George had always like having fun, sometimes playing pranks, but now what Darcy saw was the so called pranks aimed to hurt others and get them into trouble for things George Wickham had done.

Darcy's eyes were at last opened to the manipulator and liar that George had become. What saddened Darcy even more was his father was taken in by George's lies. The one time he had tried to tell his father the truth, he had felt rebuked when his father had instead taken him to task.

"Gentlemen do not tattle tale, and it is but youthful exuberance..." Darcy never could understand why his father had had such a blind spot when it came to George Wickham.

Just before he entered Cambridge, he caught Wickham, no longer his friend George, trying to force himself on one of Pemberley's maids. He knew that he made an error in judgement not reporting the incident to his father, but he believed his father would have found a way to excuse it as a misunderstanding, *so he mistakenly paid the maid to not say anything and covered it up.*

A year later Wickham was sent to Cambridge to get a gentleman's education at the expense of his godfather. It was here that Darcy saw him sink into dissolution and depravity. George passed his classes by the skin of his teeth, and even at that Darcy suspected he had routinely cheated, the honour code they all signed was meaningless to the man who had no honour.

Darcy covered his debts with the merchants as well as any gambling debts, which were not insignificant. This is how Wickham had started his life of continual debauchery. In hindsight, Darcy knew covering up for him had led his erstwhile friend to the belief he could get away with things with little or no consequence. Darcy recognised he too had erred, but what was done was done.

Even though Darcy had ample and irrefutable proof, he had made the mistake of not telling his father. The rebuke he had received when he was a lad of fourteen still stung. He had allowed that memory to overrule his good sense.

As he snapped out of his reverie, Darcy admitted to himself it was part of the reason he had blamed himself for George Wickham's actions. The days of his protecting Wickham from the consequences of his own misdeeds was passed. Wickham would finally pay for all of the misery and hardship he had caused others.

"Same old George, always looking for the easy way out. If you would have paid attention to your studies rather than filling your nights with debauchery and dissipation at Cambridge, you would know when someone calls in your debts as I am, there is no trial. Tell me, George, do you have almost four thousand pounds to pay me what you owe?" Darcy received his answer as the remaining fight drained out of Wickham's countenance.

"Georgiana, anything else to say?" Darcy looked over at his sister to make sure Wickham's threat had not had a negative effect as he feared.

"Me? Talk to him? He is not worth any words I might have." Georgiana carelessly waved off Wickham's last hope, and that made all the men around her yet even more proud.

"And with that, Wickham, you are about to get a holiday in Marshalsea for the rest of your days," Darcy spat as he closed the distance between them, so he was now almost nose to nose with his long-time tormentor. "I hold all your debts from all the places that you have run from.

"After today, the merchants of Meryton will happily extend credit to the militia officers now that you will not be a problem anymore and unable to rob the honest people here. Or if you prefer, we could hand you over to the men looking for you in London and the brother of one of your victims, if you would prefer that then we will hold you until your *friends* arrive. Up to you Wickham." Seeing his former friend was deadly serious, Wickham shook his head with vigour, Marshalsea was better than what those men would do to him.

"That is only *after* the forty lashes you will receive for dishonourable conduct, conduct unbecoming an officer, deserting your post, and theft from your fellow officers," spat out Colonel Forster, whose sported a look of pure anger.

"I know it is most unladylike, Colonel Forster, but that I would almost love to see." Georgiana smiled up at him. "Would you add one for each of my sisters he intended to compromise today, one for myself, and one for my dear father whose hopes he failed with his every action?" she asked sweetly, and even Darcy could not hold in his chuckle.

"It will be my pleasure, Miss Darcy, and for your gracious considerations of his intended victims, I will add two for yourself as his intentions toward you were pure malice I cannot abide." He bowed his head in her direction then looked at Wickham with such hard eyes as he had never seen before.

Wickham had intended to try to talk down his sentence, but he could read that anything he said would but increase his punishment more than Georgiana had. Georgiana! He had never before been proven so wrong in his assessment of a woman as he was now.

Wickham was trying to swallow his blubbering, but fear made it loud enough to be heard by all as he was stripped of his shirt and bound with his hands above his head and a leg to a tree each. Colonel Forster administered the six and forty lashes. Wickham passed out after five.

Georgiana Darcy, who had been given the option to leave before the punishment was meted out chose to stay and did not look away until after the first was administered when she buried her head into her brother's chest as he held her tightly.

Although her tender heart did not like anyone suffering, she had no such compunction when it came to George Wickham. He deserved everything that was coming to him and far more, and now she knew the truth of this man and how many he had harmed.

After this first wave of punishment, his back a purpling red with thin streaks of blood and when he came to, openly begging and crying Wickham was clapped in irons, both hands and legs in case he decided to try to flee before he arrived at his new home. He was bundled into a wagon with no thought or care for his raw back. But before the cart left, Darcy walked up to it and looked at Wickham one last time.

"My dear, departed father gave you every chance in life but you decided to squander them and lead a life of real sin and debauchery. After my honoured father passed, I gave you four thousand pounds, and instead of studying the law as you claimed that you would, you wasted it on women and gaming.

"As much as you have always tried to blame everyone else, but most especially me, all of this, everything that has happened and will happen to you, is by your own hand. You let jealousy and envy of things you were never owed, which were never your due, rule your life. You became the worst form of man who not only enjoys taking a woman's innocence, but that of a young girl's which is abhorrent in and of itself, but you also were only concerned with what you could get out of honest people without working for it.

"If you had applied half of the effort you applied to lying and manipulation to hard work, you would have had a very, very good life. I am glad to finally say the time has come for you to feel the consequences of your actions," Darcy stated evenly.

Darcy handed the wagon driver a copy of the warrant and a listing of Wickham's debts, a full and complete copy was waiting for him at Marshalsea, but the originals were safely in Bennet's safe.

With that, the wagon gave a lurch forward as the two cart horses strained against the yoke, gathering speed as they pulled. This was the start of the journey to Marshalsea and his new home for the rest of his life, unless there was some miracle. Flanked by four armed outriders and one guard in the wagon, George Wickham started what was expected to be the last journey he would take in his wasted life.

As Darcy watched the cart roll off, he was relieved the Earl had arranged for Wickham to be placed in the most secure part of the gaol so there would be no chance of his escape. He thought about his father, and he was certain he would have been disappointed, even disgusted by what his godson had become.

Although he should not have withheld the truth about Wickham, he was not unhappy he had spared his grieving father suffering such a disillusionment before he departed this mortal coil to join his beloved wife, Anne.

CHAPTER 15

In London, the Earl of Matlock and Viscount Hilldale had just completed marathon sessions with solicitors, Bedlam's governor, and their family physician. The new, and more importantly, competent physician who had been engaged to look after the health of the residents of Rosings Park had been invited to join them but had been unavailable to travel to Town.

Despite that, the Fitzwilliams had achieved all of their aims. Rosings Park and all its assets were now irrevocably in Anne's name. As there was no entailment, Anne could do as she wished with the estate and will it to whoever she chose, whether she married or not.

The funds Lewis de Bourgh had hidden from Lady Catherine, with the Earl's help, were transferred back into the estate's regular accounts and were freed of any restrictions. Anne would be able to decide for herself if she wanted to continue to invest, and if so, how much.

Anne's dowry was always protected, so only with the living Earl of Matlock's approval of the groom would the funds ever be released. The additional funds earned at Gardiner and Associates on the investment of her dowry were released to her bank for her to use as needed leaving her original dowry intact still earning dividends with the company. As his father was hale and healthy, Andrew prayed it would be a very long time before he inherited the Earldom and had to make such decisions for all their family.

While the taking care of Anne was for him straight forward, Reginald Fitzwilliam was torn with regards to his sister. He loved Catherine, or at least who she had been before jealousy, avarice, and an absolute need to control everything and everyone took over her life.

There was never enough wealth for Catherine, so even while wasting and fritting away the wealth she controlled, she always expected there would be more. At the same time, she unfortunately thought she was a very capable manager of the estate, when the truth was the opposite. This was one of her biggest failings, the belief that she was infallible, that she knew all. Among other certainties about herself, she suffered from many delusions of grandeur.

The Earl and his heir were sitting in the study at Matlock house, alone now after the last meeting had been concluded and each was nursing a snifter of brandy. Lord Matlock thought back to when his brother-in-law, who even before he married Cathy had been a very good friend, Lewis de Bourgh, had asked him to be his executor and Anne's guardian.

It had been about a year before Lewis finally succumbed to the disease of his heart that he had lived with for over three years knowing it was consistently getting weaker and weaker. His condition had been hidden from his wife, so the irony was she had needlessly murdered her husband.

Unbeknownst to his wife, Sir Lewis de Bourgh had come to London and he and the Earl had sat in Matlock House's study as Lewis had asked him if he knew what had changed Cathy so much.

He used to call his wife Cathy even though she hated it, proclaiming it was undignified and suited to the lower classes, not to the daughter of an Earl. The men thought it may be that other than Anne, she was never able to bring another living child into the world, so she decided she had to control everything else around her. They had acknowledged it was pure speculation, but also opined mayhap she had always been like that but hid behind a mask until after she was securely married.

Together they had come up with a plan to protect Anne's dowry and lock away as much money as they could so if Cathy spent to excess, drove tenants away, or made bad decisions for the estate, there would be money to set things to rights once Anne turned five and twenty and took possession of her inheritance.

Anne had an illness as a child, scarlet fever, and had recovered fully. It was possible she was a little weaker than some, but not nearly as bad off as Cathy postulated she was.

De Bourgh had expressed a worry Cathy would do something to physically hurt Anne to stop her from claiming her inheritance if she felt she would lose control of Rosings Park, which at the time she imagined she controlled even while he lived.

With the help of Sir Lewis's solicitor they had drawn up an airtight last will and testament. The solicitor's son would represent Anne's interests once she came of age.

They had drawn it up in a way that even if Lady Catherine de Bourgh had attempted to challenge it, she would have failed. Copies of Sir Lewis's genuine last will and testament were held by both solicitors and the Earl.

As the Earl snapped out of his reverie, he remembered at the time de Bourgh had not put it past Lady Catherine to try and forge a will to suit her purposes, as she in fact ended up doing.

Reginald Fitzwilliam was happy to finally discharge the duty he had promised to do in his brother's stead those many years past. He thought about how he could have done more to intercede with Cathy, temper her excesses, or even council her.

He berated himself because he knew he should have done more to protect Anne, even if the abuse she suffered had only come to light now. Others had suspected and asked him to intervene, but he had been loath to interfere in the way his sister raised her daughter.

Was it his fault that things had got to this point? He thought about the advice he and Thomas gave to William and realised he too should heed it and not assume blame for that which was not his. Anne had not reached out to any of them, and he promised himself he would never again ignore a situation that caused concern in the future.

In front of him were the papers signed by the physicians committing his sister to Bedlam; to the secure, non-public wing of the facility. As much as he believed his sister needed to be locked away, he was unwilling to leave her at the mercy of those that came to gawk at the insane, who often would yell insults and throw rotten fruit at them.

Catherine would be locked away to protect others from her machinations, as well as to protect her from herself. Before leaving Longbourn for town three days ago, they had all discussed the options they had to deal with Lady Catherine. It came down to two viable choices only. A public trial resulting in his sister, the daughter of an Earl and widow of a Baronet, being led to the gallows, or the one they chose, Bedlam, where at least she would be looked after with compassion.

Far more consideration would be given to her than the lady had ever shown anyone. Luckily for her, her actions did not guide those of her relations. On the morrow they would return to Longbourn accompanied by the carriage and attendants that would convey his sister to her new home.

~~~~~~~/~~~~~~~

The carriages and outriders arrived at Longbourn in the early afternoon the following day. Both emotionally and physically tired, the two Fitzwilliams were glad to be back at Longbourn and were even more happy to be enthusiastically met by their respective wives.

As her husband was changing, Marie Fitzwilliam entered his dressing room, dismissing his valet and closing the door. On seeing his wife, Andrew enfolded her in his arms and gave her a lingering, passionate kiss. He loved her and while not as publicly obvious as Richard was with his Mary, he was just as grateful when he was able to hold his wife.

"Andrew, it is kisses like this that led to the state I am in now," Marie teased.

"What do you mean kisses lead to...oh my, are you with child again?" He stared at his wife in awe.

"Yes, you silly man, I am. I have not felt the quickening yet, but all of the other signs are there. I'm very grateful that so far, I haven't been sick in the mornings, although there are some smells, such as fish, that are starting to make me feel like I would like to cast up my accounts," she admitted.

"This is the very best possible news, Marie," Andrew stated as he hugged and showered kisses on his beaming wife. "David will love to be a big brother. Have you told anyone yet?" He looked down on her, his eyes alight with contented pleasure.

"I would never tell anyone before you, my dear husband. We told people prematurely the first time I was with child, and I had a miscarriage, so until I feel the quickening and have seen a physician, my personal preference is this should stay between the two of us, my love." She looked up at him earnestly.

"You will hear no argument from me, love, but you know my mother and Aunt Fanny can detect a lady that is with child from miles away. Have they asked you pointed questions yet?" he arched a brow.

"Nothing so far. If one of them suspect, or say something, I will not lie, but I will not volunteer the information otherwise." Marie promised.

"You have made me so happy, my Marie. But please send Finch back in so I can make myself presentable for company. He will suspect something when he sees me grinning like a fool; but luckily his sense of decorum and propriety will not allow him to broach a subject I do not open first." He winked down at his blushing wife and again fell in love with her all over again as all men do when they hear such news.

After another series of hugs and kisses, Lady Hilldale called the valet back in and departed her husband's dressing room, descending the stairs to the drawing room with a most contented look on her countenance.

Once both the Earl and the Viscount had returned to the drawing room, the drama of Wickham's capture was shared. The story of how Wickham was drawn out of Meryton by the brave tenant daughters that imitated the Bennet sisters was told.

They were informed of Wickham's intent and his plan had been most unceremoniously interrupted at the point of Richard and William's swords. Father and son were exceptionally proud of the courage Georgie had displayed when facing him and expressed their true regrets for having missed the now infamous slap, and more importantly the look on his face after, which was reported as shocked beyond belief.

The wastrel who had attempted to leech off Darcy for years was now safely ensconced at Marshalsea, and he would never be able to hurt anyone again. Both men were relieved. A blight on all levels of society had been at last excised.

~~~~~~~/~~~~~~~

The men from Bedlam, accompanied by Biggs and some of his fellow footman, were tasked with the unpleasant chore of retrieving Lady Catherine from her temporary housing in the coal cellar so they could transfer her to the conveyance that would take her to her new home.

When they opened the door, the expected stream

of expletives and vitriol burst from the lady's mouth. A moment of lucidity occurred when she saw the men in the white suits, and she suddenly realised Bedlam was not an idol threat; it was to be her reality.

She struck out with all she had, but her rebellion was quickly quelled and the great Lady Catherine, in a filthy gown, was gagged and trussed up like a chicken being made ready for roasting.

She watched helplessly as she was picked up by two of the orderlies and was taken out the servant's entry at the rear of the manor to the waiting equipage. She, Lady Catherine de Bourgh, daughter of an Earl and widow of a Baronet, was taken out of the servant's portal! This was the final humiliation she would endure, and she intended to make sure everyone knew she was most seriously displeased.

On the road, the orderlies were relieved she sank back into her fantasy world. In Lady Catherine's mind, she was sitting in her grand carriage on her way to give the monarch an audience she had but the day before condescended to grant.

Her realisation she was being taken to Bedlam was, unfortunately for those that loved her but possibly most fortunate for herself, her last lucid moment. This truth may have, in fact, been what had broken her last tenuous ties with reality.

She sat in the carriage, not grasping why she was restrained so she could not move or order any of her subjects to do what she desired. It was the last trip she would ever take in a carriage while still on the mortal coil.

As the carriage passed by the front of the house on its way up the drive, the occupants of the house watched it sadly but without remorse. This was the only way to save her life, and she had quite demonstrated she was completely insane when she attacked her own daughter with a knife.

~~~~~~~/~~~~~~~

The next day it was decided that by the end of the week, the whole party would decamp to London so Lizzy could start acquiring her trousseau. Bennet was well pleased he had not leased out their townhouse he had purchased from the down on his luck Lord who had more in common with Wickham's gambling habits than he would have liked to know.

Bennet sent an express to let the Gardiners know they were coming to London, and another to Mrs. Kerry O'Grady, and Mr. Humphrey Thatcher, the housekeeper and butler at the house on Grosvenor Square, to inform them of their plans and with the instructions to employ whatever staff was needed for their upcoming stay.

In the same express, Bennet instructed his butler that the house would be henceforth named Bennet House, thereby removing the last vestiges of the previous owner who had lost his way.

The Bennets would bring some servants with them, to include the head cook, maids, and some footmen to supplement the staff until the new servants and staff were added and the house was fully staffed.

Also travelling with the party, as always when the Bennets journeyed away from Longbourn, was Biggs and his group of very large footmen that doubled as bodyguards, as well as a good number of well-armed outriders. The Bennets personal mounts were being led by some of the outriders so they would have them available in town.

Both Darcy and the Earl sent similar expresses to their housekeepers and butlers to open their townhouses. In his express, Darcy instructed Mrs. Killion, his housekeeper, to make sure the house sparkled and to air out and clean the mistress's suite.

He stated with no improper pride he would be

bringing the future Mrs. Darcy to tour the house and he wanted her to inspect the suite and have her request whatever changes she desired made.

His mother, Lady Anne Darcy, had decorated that set of rooms over thirty years prior not long after she had married George Darcy. The rooms had been closed by his father right after his mother passed almost fourteen years ago and had not been used since.

Members of the *Ton* who were still in town would see the obvious signs of the wealth of the Bennets when the convoy of carriages arrived as the family moved into their grand townhouse, now proclaimed as *Bennet House* thanks to the new brass plaque which replaced the previous one.

Even before they arrived, the close association with the houses of Matlock and Darcy was noted, and *the Ton* would soon understand the Bennets were a family with the best of connections and they looked to be wealthy in the extreme.

Once word of the massive dowries for each daughter and the extent of the Bennet land holdings began to be whispered about, the matchmaking mamas who were still in Town salivated with the news the family would arrive any day now.

These fortune hunting mothers thought that they would have an advantage over those already in the country, only to find out two daughters were being formally courted, and another was the Elizabeth Bennet mentioned in the betrothal announcement to Fitzwilliam Darcy.

The Bennets were only known by a select few close friends of the Fitzwilliams, mostly members of the peerage, so members of polite society had been abuzz trying to find out who would have the gall to take Mr. Darcy away from their daughters.

As information about the Bennets filtered through the

gossips of the *Ton* and was passed onto those in the country, it was realised that to disparage any Bennet was to disparage some very powerful members of the peerage and a number of extremely influential members in the first circles.

The example of what had befallen Caroline Bingley had a chilling effect on anyone who considered doing so. Much to Thomas Bennet's chagrin, the anonymity he had once revelled in was no more and it was clear the *Ton* expected the Bennets to be seen as they were members of the top tier of the first circles.

~~~~~~~/~~~~~~~

Before requesting a courtship with Jane Bennet, Bingley had not considered the need to purchase a townhouse. After he received permission to court his angel, he sent word to his solicitor to keep his eyes and ears open for eligible properties that came up for sale. He had given up the lease on the rented home just a month previously.

There were enough irresolute members of the *Ton* who gambled too much, so his solicitor was sure Bingley would not have to wait too long before something became available. Darcy invited Bingley and the Hursts to stay with him, Georgiana, and his cousin Anne de Bourgh at Darcy house, and the invitation was gratefully accepted.

More than ever, Louisa thanked her lucky stars she had broken with Caroline. Had she made the monumental mistake of not doing so, she would have committed social suicide, just as her sister had.

She had no doubt if she had not, her husband would have consigned her to his family's country estate and left her there alone if he had not left her altogether. She loved her sister, she always would, and was sorry for the straights Caroline was in, however she would not reach out to her because it was clear the happiness of many would be sacrificed for the happiness of one, to include her own.

Louisa was truly enjoying the changes that her decisions had wrought on her marriage. Even though hers was arranged and was at the time considered a marriage of convenience, she had never felt closer to her husband.

Mrs. Hurst had been far too oblivious regarding him in the past but now knew her husband had never over imbibed. As he had stated that fateful day, he only feigned sleep to avoid any trouble his social climbing sister-in-law wrought.

There was genuine felicity in her marriage now, and for the first time she felt like she may be on her way to falling in love, that it was with her husband was a blessing beyond measure.

To her humiliation, she admitted she had before dreaded the marriage bed, but now she craved it. Not only for all the obvious reasons, but the time they shared there was just for her and her husband, and she was learning she not only was falling in love with the man she had agreed to marry, but she liked him, and if they were so blessed, then maybe God would soon grant them a child.

The invitation to be guests at Darcy house, coupled with the fact Louisa was invited to join all of the Bennet, Fitzwilliam, Darcy, and Gardiner ladies, who also included Anne de Bourgh, when they went on their shopping expeditions had even more positive effects than her decision to not let her sister continue to rule her life.

Seeing the genuine affection between the sisters and soon to be sisters, and the fact that she was shown as much affection as she was willing to give, proved what joy having true sisters of the heart could be.

Bingley and Hurst would often accompany the men to White's or Boodle's which was a clear signal to the members of the *Ton* still in Town that very influential members of the first circles fully accepted and supported Bingley and the Hursts.

As vowed weeks previously, it was made quite clear by Ladies Matlock and Hilldale that Caroline Bingley was persona non grata. While there were not a great number of members of the *Ton* in Town, there were always more than enough gossips and the writers of the society pages to provide the news so that all members of society, no matter their class, would know not only that Bingley and the Hursts were accepted and welcome, but that Miss Bingley was not.

Louisa knew her sister still tortured herself with the society pages and did not have to stretch her imagination to know when she read about all of them, she would be mortified and green with jealousy.

~~~~~~~/~~~~~~~

On reading about the betrothal of Fitzwilliam Darcy of Pemberley to Elizabeth Bennet of Longbourn, Miss Caroline Bingley had very nearly had an apoplexy. The woman had used some of her limited on-hand funds to travel to Town, believing her brother would soon see the error of his ways and recall her to his side with an apology and as much money as she wanted.

With such an expectation, Caroline had not drawn from what was left of her dowry. She was still certain she would be the next mistress of Pemberley and so had suffered the degradation of riding post to Town to make sure she was available for her summons to Charles's side.

Her plan was to tell her friends all about that chit Eliza Bennet and her grasping family. She was most confused when none of her friends had responded to her many letters but convinced herself they must be too busy for correspondence as they were preparing for travel.

The truth was very far from Caroline's current understanding of things. Ladies Matlock and Hilldale even before they returned to Town, had let it be known that they would not know anyone who was associated with

Miss Caroline Bingley, so every single one of her letters had been unceremoniously consigned to the fire without being opened.

When she at last arrived in town without any funds needed to stay at a hotel or return to Scarborough, it was not a concern for her. Miss Bingley was sure her friends would receive her and expected invitations to stay at a townhouse within a few scant hours after it was known she had come.

To her horror, she received a very different response and a most rude awakening. At every townhouse she attempted to gain admittance to, so she could call on one of those *friends* she had informed she would be arriving; she was told no one was at home to her and she was not welcome to return.

Already in shock over this treatment, her folly was highlighted for her in the starkest of terms when she came across two of her erstwhile friends walking and talking together in Hyde Park.

When she approached them, she saw on them the same pinched, disgusted look she often employed, and she was very publicly given the cut direct. It was indisputable, witnessed proof of her error in her treatment of the Bennets, and that the Ladies Matlock and Hilldale had not made empty threats.

Caroline Bingley was beyond humiliated, she was mortified, and knew without a doubt she could never show her face in Town again or for that matter, anywhere in society. She went to the bank where her dowry was kept and withdrew all of her funds.

She then made her way to Gracechurch Street where she hoped no one would recognise her. It had been years since she had walked the streets there with her family to and from her father's businesses. She began to purchase what she thought she would need for a long voyage.

Next, she rented a coach to take her to Liverpool and when she arrived, she purchased a ticket on the first ship to America. And so, Caroline Bingley left England's shores in absolute shame, dejection, mortification, and worst of all for her, obscurity. She finally was forced to face the truth of her own insignificance.

CHAPTER 16

Elizabeth Bennet was extremely excited. Not only would she see Darcy House for the first time, but also the newly named Bennet House as well. Excitement was palpable for all of the Bennet siblings as they got closer and closer to Town.

An added bonus was the Gardiners lived less than a mile away by carriage in Portman Square. Uncle Edward, Aunt Maddie and their children were dearly loved by all, and during the week the Gardiners had been at Longbourn friendships that had been based on business with the Darcys and the Fitzwilliams had deepened to become familial relationships.

Lizzy was equally envious and pleased that Aunt Maddie had seen Pemberley on a number of occasions as she had grown up in Lambton, which was less than five miles from the grand estate.

To Bennet's great relief, summer was not the best time to be in Town if one wanted society. Most of the *Ton* had vacated London for their country estates with the onset of the summer heat, so there would be little or no social pressure. With wedding planning in full swing, everyone who had been at Longbourn looked forward to the change of scenery and a break from the drama they had been forced to face of late.

The Bennet coaches bringing the family, their valets and personal maids, and the attendant outriders were followed by the wagon bringing the bulk of the trunks, all pulled to a halt in front of Bennet House.

The arrival was keenly observed by residents of the square who were still in Town, and information would soon reach far that the rumours of the Bennet's wealth had not been overstated but was quite probably understated.

The housekeeper and the butler were waiting for them at the front entrance to the house and the rest of the servants already employed were lined up neatly in the entrance hall. Mr. Thatcher eagerly watched for his master's reaction to the shiny brass name plate that proclaimed this as *Bennet House* which was mounted on the iron entrance gate.

Fanny instructed the senior staff to dismiss the lined-up servants, saying she would meet with everyone once the family had moved into their rooms and changed to get rid of the dust from the road.

She was impressed so many had been employed already and would decide which of the accompanying servants from Longbourn would be released to return home after she met with the housekeeper to discuss the needs of the house.

The Bennets were amused to see the Darcys exiting their conveyance across the square at Darcy house, and the same effort repeated at Matlock house but a few doors down. No one had exaggerated when they had said all three townhouses were close, and by agreement made before leaving Longbourn, the three families would meet at Darcy House for dinner that night.

Fanny Bennet was very happy as she quickly surveyed Bennet House and the quality of the staff that had been thus far employed. After she met with the housekeeper and butler, she was able to send most of the extra servants back to Longbourn.

The cook they had brought with them from home, was treated like she was as precious as any gemstone and asked to provide her list of immediate needs while the London cook had not been employed as that was one of the key positions that the housekeeper, O'Grady, would not fill without input from the mistress.

Lucy, Longbourn's cook, fully intended to make sure that whoever was brought in, that he or she would know all the likes and dislikes of her full Bennet, Darcy, Fitzwilliam, Gardiner and now de Bourgh family. Whoever Mrs. Bennet employed would need mettle, and she knew that was one of the qualities the mistress had loved about her. It was a good thing that Lucy would help the mistress make her decision.

The townhouse consisted of seven floors. On the first floor, the ground level, there were two studies, one for the master and one for the mistress, a library, a ball room, the large and small dining rooms, a music room, three parlours, and two large drawing rooms.

The kitchen with the housekeeper's office and work areas were at the rear of the house on a lower level, and there was access from the kitchen to a cellar with a cold room, pantry, wine cellar and storage.

The marble staircase in the entrance hall led up to the second floor which held the family suites. Fanny assigned rooms to all of her offspring and Tom and James were happy to have a suite with a shared sitting room between their individual bedchambers.

The master suite was a much larger version of what the twins had. Each side of the suites had a bed chamber, a dressing room and a room to bathe in. Jane and Lizzy shared a suite similar to the twins, and Mary and Kitty had another they shared. That left two more suites and four single bedchambers unoccupied, and there was a family sitting room on the family floor for meetings and shared time.

The third, fourth, and fifth floors had twelve guest chambers each, some grander than others, but all more than adequate for the needs of any who they might allow to stay.

Six of the twelve were two room suites for couples, and six were single chambers with a small but comfortable sitting room on each guest floor.

The sixth floor had a nursery, school rooms and rooms for nursemaids, as well as six nicely appointed chambers for companions and a small sitting room.

The seventh floor was where the abundant servant chambers were. The main staircase did not reach the final floor but there were two sets of stairs for servants that did, one to the female side and one for the males. Above the top floor was a large attic space for storage.

~~~~~~~/~~~~~~~

The family all changed from their travelling attire and when Fanny was done, she and her Thomas descended the stairs to meet with the newly employed servants while their children enjoyed their new rooms and made them their own, exactly as their parents hoped that they would.

The servants were impressed that the master and mistress did not just have their names stated with the expectation of being known and dismiss them; they greeted each one upon an introduction, taking care to use the servant's Christian name as they were introduced and said a few words to each, thanking them for being there and accepting the post.

Besides being paid more than most other servants in similar positions for the townhouses across London, the servants were most impressed that the master and mistress, and what they had seen of the family so far, treated them with respect and as human beings, unlike most in the *Ton*.

It was these seemingly little things that built a deep loyalty. Those that were now employed knew they were privileged to work in this house and for this family. As a collective they decided their best efforts would be their expectation of one another to help the family be a cut above in all ways, as they were being treated far better than what they too had expected. Word would soon spread that like Darcy or Matlock Houses, Bennet House was a preferred and coveted place to work.

Once introductions were complete, the Bennet siblings joined their parents and Mrs O'Grady conducted a full tour of the house for the family. Bennet still could not believe what a good deal he had received due to the urgent nature of the sale.

Thomas Bennet resigned himself to the fact that after resisting for many years, they were now full-fledged members of the *Ton* with expectations that went with the status. No matter how much time had passed, he was always amazed anew at the changes of fortune his family had gone through.

At five in the evening, the Bennets accepted their outerwear from Thatcher and made the short walk across Grosvenor Square to Darcy House. Even though it was less than fifty paces, they were under the watchful eye of two of the intimidating footmen.

The Bennets were pleased to see the Fitzwilliams walking up to join them, and as if on cue the Gardiners' carriage arrived at the same time. Darcy stepped forward to claim his Lizzy's arm with a smile which displayed a hint of his dimples.

"Welcome to Darcy House." They knew Darcy had meant the greeting for all, but he was lost in the depths of his fiancée's fine eyes, just as he always was in her company.

The large group filed into the house, walking around Lizzy and William who were caught up in the moment not moving. That was until the Earl's loud "Ahem!" snapped the couple out of their trance.

The now furiously blushing couple were the last in, and even Killion, who never allowed emotion to show, had a slight upturn to the corners of his mouth as he closed the door. As it was a large party, Killion was assisted by two liveried Darcy House footmen to relieve everyone present of their outerwear.

As agreed earlier, Georgie as the mistress of Darcy House, until her brother William gave her sisters by marrying Lizzy in about four weeks, led the rest of the party into the music room where Anne de Bourgh, Bingley, and the Hursts were waiting for them to have a before dinner aperitif.

Lizzy and Darcy hung back so Lizzy could be introduced to Mr. and Mrs. Killion, the butler and housekeeper at Darcy House. Her tour was scheduled for the morrow at ten o'clock in the morning.

Both senior staff members were relieved at the genuine affection they noted between their Master and the, until recently, unknown Miss Elizabeth Bennet, and were impressed by the way the soon to be new mistress addressed them with warmth and interest.

They both said silent prayers of thanks the once dreaded Miss Bingley or one of her ilk had not succeeded in trapping the master into matrimony by way of a compromise or some other underhanded means.

Once the introductions were complete, the couple joined the rest of the party in the music room. At the appointed time, Killion announced dinner was served. Everyone filed into the large dining parlour and other than the master and mistress's seats, the rest of the seating was informal.

Elizabeth, who had entered on his arm, was sat to the right of her beloved. The Bennets and the Gardiners were most impressed at the quality of the meal, grateful it was not unnecessarily rich or overdone.

The two elder Gardiner children, Lilly who was twelve

and George who was ten, dined with the adults and displayed the good manners and class their parents and governess had imbued in them, the expectation of many similar dinners making Georgiana possibly the happiest of all.

Only two months previously, sitting in this room looking at the anger and despair on her brother's face and trying to come to terms with her own humiliation and faults had made dining one of the quietest, loneliest times of the day.

Now looking at their expanded family, made so much richer with Anne's presence and the woman Mrs. Hurst was becoming, Georgiana was practically overcome with too much happiness.

Before a tear fell, she felt the now familiar hand of Fanny's reach over and take hers, the gentle squeeze reminding her she was as loved as she loved those with her tonight. When she glanced around, she saw only Darcy and Lizzy had noticed her almost overdone display of affection and saw her happiness was reflected in theirs.

Sometime later, after musical entertainment was enjoyed by all, the party broke up at a reasonable hour, given they had travelled that day, and all would need to be rested for the many activities which were packed into the immediate days to come.

~~~~~~~/~~~~~~~

Lizzy's eyes fluttered open, the last vestiges of the sleep state slowly leaving her body. As she stretched, she looked around the unfamiliar chamber and it slowly dawned on her where she was, and that the sun was streaming in through the cracks in the curtains.

She had slept longer than was her wont, most days awake and already starting her day at the crack at dawn at Longbourn so she could take a walk as the sun started its journey across the sky.

They had arrived home before eleven last night, but she had got to bed after one in the morning following a long, in-depth sisterly talk with Jane, neither of them noticing or caring how late it was. She allowed it was a better excuse than many for why she had slept, what was for her, so late that morning.

Elizabeth pulled the bell for her French abigail, Jacqueline Arseneault, who she called Jacqui. Being fluent in French, Lizzy was comfortable speaking to her in either language, though her Abigail spoke fluent English with a heavy French accent. The maid opened the curtains to let the sun lighten and warm the room.

"*Oui mademoiselle,* Lizzy, good morning to you. I trust that you slept well?" A cheerful Jacqui said as she entered from the servant's passage.

"Good morning, Jacqui. It took me a moment to recognise I was not in my chamber at Longbourn. I hope you are comfortable in your quarters here?" Lizzy smiled at the excited nodding from her maid.

"What a glorious morning. I am so very much looking forward to my tour of Darcy House. If only it was my wedding day already." She sighed with a dreamy far off look she always seemed to get when she thought about being married to her William. "I so love him, he is the best man I know," Elizabeth stated aloud as she hugged a pillow.

"Up with you, *mademoiselle* Lizzy. I will have water brought up for your bath so that *mademoiselle* may be ready for her tour at her new home," Arseneault informed her mistress.

"Thank you. After my tour all of us ladies are going shopping. As you well know, shopping is not my favourite activity, but it is for my trousseau, so it has a better chance at being fun than most of our excursions." Lizzy's face scrunched up playfully.

After her bath and her lady's maid had helped her to dress into an elegant day dress, the maid gave her mistress a simple up do with some curls cascading down her long neck.

Once she was deemed ready, Lizzy knocked on the door connecting to Jane's chambers, where her abigail, Antoinette de Chambé, informed Lizzy her lady had just gone down to break her fast.

Elizabeth entered the smaller of the two dining parlours which the family had chosen to use in the mornings as a breakfast parlour where she was greeted by her mother and her three sisters.

Her mother informed them their father had gone riding with Tom and James along the Serpentine in Hyde Park, and after that he was taking them to the museum of natural sciences, then to Hatchard's where Darcy and the Earl would join them to peruse books while the ladies shopped. Their menfolk planned to meet them at Gunter's for tea and treats later that afternoon.

At about five minutes before the hour, the ladies set out across the square to Darcy House. Fanny had agreed to join Lizzy on the tour and Georgie would wait with the three Bennet girls in the drawing room for Elaine and Marie Fitzwilliam, Madeline Gardner, Anne de Bourgh, and Louisa Hurst.

The Earl, the Viscount, the Colonel, Bingley, and Hurst would join Darcy at Whites until two of them would go to Hatchard's and later they too would all meet the females of the party at Gunter's. The whole party meeting at such a well-known place that members of the *Ton* frequented would send another clear message to any still in Town that they were a united, strong family unit just in case anyone still had doubts.

One of the many ironies was that had Miss Bingley behaved as she should have, she would have attained her goal of entering into the highest circles that she had always coveted.

~~~~~~~/~~~~~~~

The tour of Darcy House was everything Lizzy had hoped for. The furnishings in the house were exactly as she imagined they would be from what she had seen when they had gathered for dinner. Everything was tasteful and comfortable, nothing opulent or gaudy.

Lizzy and her mother made a list of the minor changes she would suggest to the housekeeper separate from the mistress's suite, which would be the last stop on the tour.

Elizabeth had only suggested some minor updating to a small number of the guest chambers which she had verified had not been updated since the previous Mrs. Darcy had been mistress of the house. Mrs. Killion was again very impressed and was grateful that their future mistress, unlike most, was not making changes for the sake of change, just those needed.

The mistress's side of the master suite had been decorated over thirty years previously and the housekeeper was excited to see what her new mistress, actually the first of the house in too many years, was going to pick.

As they were taking the tour, Fanny was being introspective just like she had been the day the twins were born. She imagined that the woman she had been then would have made vulgar effusions about the quality of the rooms and the cost of the furniture. And she had no doubt that she would have made exclamations about the amount of pin money Lizzy would have, and the jewels and carriages in her future.

She was again grateful she had made the changes she had, and that she was just genuinely happy to see the excitement and love in her daughter's eyes the same as she once had when she had first married her Thomas. Fanny

Bennet was forever changed, and it would have filled her heart to near bursting to know her family was convinced there was not a better or more loving mother that anyone would, or could, wish for.

She watched Lizzy be amazed at the collections of art on display in the house and tomes in the library, and how her daughter's whole face lit up when she heard from the housekeeper the library at Pemberley was many times larger than the one at Darcy house and that even more artwork was housed there.

'Papa will never leave our libraries when he visits!' Lizzy thought, her smile growing bigger even though she knew that father would not closet himself away like he was wont to do before the twins were born.

Like Bennet House, Darcy House was a house of seven stories with a very similar layout. Darcy explained to them the Grosvenor family who had owned the land and built the townhouses that created what was now known as Grosvenor Square about a hundred and fifty years ago had only built two basic models for the townhouses.

The houses that were built in the same dimensions were very similar in layout unless the owners had undertaken major renovations, and neither the Darcy nor the Bennet townhouses had been renovated besides some small and unique modifications. Matlock house was the same size as the latter two.

As planned, the last set of rooms that were toured was the master suite. Lizzy expected and was prepared to find the furniture and decoration in what would soon be her chambers and their shared sitting room was old and more worn than she would prefer. Her William informed her that he never bothered to use the shared sitting room while he was a single man.

For her new bedchambers Lizzy chose colours in

various shades of green and complimentary blues with just a touch of gold for the walls. She chose a similar palette of colours for the shared sitting room with more tones of green.

She agreed that two days hence when not otherwise engaged she and her mother would accompany Darcy to famous furniture maker Chippendale to order a complete new set of furniture for her bed chamber and the joint sitting room.

The very last rooms they saw were those used by the master of the house. Lizzy loved how the room exuded masculinity and had the biggest four-poster bed she had ever seen. She blushed as she thought that soon it would be their suite and if his hopes matched hers, she would sleep in the bed before her every night they were in residence at this house.

In his bathing room she saw an enormous brass tub. When informed that it was the twin of one at Pemberley and could easily fit two people, she blushed from head to toe in colours she had not believed herself capable of before. It was not lost on Lizzy that Darcy too was blushing furiously.

On completion of the tour, and once she was certain she had returned to a normal colour, Lizzy and her mother were escorted to the drawing room by her fiancé. As soon as they entered, she was accosted by her very enthusiastic future sister.

"What did you think Lizzy? Do you like Darcy House? Are there a lot of changes to be made?" Miss Darcy practically bounced on her toes.

"Slow down, Georgie," Lizzy laughed as she took the girl's hand and led her to a settee. Once seated, she was happy to answer all of her soon-to-be sister's questions. "The house is all that is lovely. I am sure I will love living here when we are in town. There are but few changes to make outside of what will be my personal chambers and the shared sitting room. But before the renovations start in my future chambers, and only if you would like to, please go take anything you want that would remind you of your mother, dearest." Lizzy squeezed her hands.

"Thank you from the bottom of my heart," Georgie smiled as a single tear rolled down her cheek. "I was only three when mama passed, but I would love some of the things that used to belong to her."

Lizzy nodded in understanding and hugged her sister, and Fanny and Elaine looked on with motherly pride. Elaine knew as a certainty that Lady Anne would have loved and approved of Lizzy without reservation.

When it was mentioned that there would be an outing to Chippendales in two days, Anne asked if she could join the party going as she needed to start to order liveable furniture so she could begin to sell the gaudy, uncomfortable furniture from both Rosings and de Bourgh House.

"To be honest, I have no idea how to remove all of the unwanted baubles and uncomfortable furniture Lady Catherine crammed into my houses," stated Anne, it was not lost on anyone she refused to refer to Lady Catherine as her mother any longer.

"We have the perfect solution for you, Anne." Fanny took her hand.

"I would be very appreciative of any suggestions you have for me, Mrs. Bennet," Anne agreed, looking hopefully at the woman she was fast coming to think of as Aunt Fanny and Aunt Elaine as more the mother she was grateful to have in her life.

"Anne, how many times have I told you that you must call me Fanny, or if you are more comfortable, Aunt Fanny. I told you when you came to our home that you were with family that has long loved you. And to carry my point, soon with the upcoming weddings we will in fact, be family.

"My brother Edward will be able to sell whatever you want to get rid of. He will send some of his men to your estate and townhouse and they will catalogue everything you want sold. As you are about to be family indeed as you are already in our hearts, I am sure Edward will not take his normal commission, only what he needs to cover his costs of employees and the details I could not list but we all understand are the costs of such a business as his." Fanny smiled at Anne's surprise.

"Thank you, Aunt Fanny. I will insist he take his regular commission, so long as I get all of that horrid stuff out of my houses," Anne declared. The Fitzwilliams and Darcys, who had been to the houses, nodded their agreement and understanding.

The ladies collected their outerwear and readied themselves to leave. As they were a party numbering ten, they needed to take two coaches, and in this instance, they were taking a Bennet and a Darcy conveyance.

The butler let them know the carriages were waiting in the front of the house. Each conveyance had its driver, a postilion, two footmen who rode at the rear of the carriage, and two outriders. Even though they were in town, none of the men were willing to take a chance with the security of their womenfolk.

~~~~~~~/~~~~~~~

The first visit on Bond Street was to an extremely sought after modiste, Madame Yvette Chambourg. Madame only saw clients who were referred by her existing and very exclusive client list that besides Lady Matlock, her daughter, and niece Georgiana Darcy, included some royal princesses and the patronesses of Almack's.

There were a few exemplary duchesses and countesses and besides them, few others. She was the rare kind of modiste that accepted her clients based on the character they showed and the goodness of their works. Her style reflected their personalities, so all eyes would be on them in any room they entered.

Elizabeth Bennet hated being measured, poked, and prodded, but she bore it all with good humour, constantly reminding herself that this was occurring because she was getting married to the man of her dreams in less than four weeks.

She questioned the need for so many evening, day, morning, and ball gowns, until it was pointed out to her by Georgie that Derbyshire was far colder than Hertfordshire in the winter so she would need everything being ordered and more.

Once the group of ladies had helped her pick patterns and colours, they were off with Lizzy in good humour. She could not help but be so when surrounded by women who were ready to tease her in return.

The next visits were to a haberdashery and a cobbler. As the ladies were shopping, there were a few of members of the *Ton* on Bond Street who took note of the group as they moved from shop to shop.

It was the first opportunity for members of polite society to see the Bennet ladies up close. Those who bore witness were amazed at the poise, grace, and beauty from the Bennet matriarch on down.

As jealous as some were of the beauty and the wealth on display, they made mental notes to pass onto all of their friends and acquaintances that this was a formidable group that included the Ladies Matlock and Hilldale, women one would cross at their own peril. None in the *Ton* wanted to end up ostracised as Caroline Bingley had been.

Once they were done shopping, the ladies were ready to head toward Gunter's. When the ladies arrived at the famous sweet shop, they were most pleased to see some of their men had left Whites to arrive before them and had reserved tables with sufficient chairs for the whole party.

Bennet, Darcy, the Earl, and the twins had not yet arrived. The men's last stop before Gunter's had been Hatchard's where the group of bibliophiles had lost themselves among the books. It was not long before the twins came marching in, followed at a more sedate pace by the three men.

"You know how hard it is to extract Papa from Hatchard's, do you not?" Tom offered by way of explanation for their tardy arrival, "William and Uncle Reggie are no better!" he added.

"You will not believe how many books Papa and William purchased." James smirked as he kissed his mother's cheek.

"With my Thomas, yes, I most certainly can," Fanny laughed as she playfully swatted her son's arm as she smiled at her husband.

"I am sure William's purchases rivalled Uncle Thomas's. If I know Uncle Reggie, he was not far behind them," Georgiana informed the family with a big smile.

The five sat down with Darcy making a beeline for the chair that his fiancée had reserved next to herself for him, and then the party ordered. Bennet sighed sadly because the rumours of their wealth and the girl's dowries had reached, and been disseminated around, London.

There was some relief that it was obvious the three eldest Bennet daughters were very much off the marriage market, which left no room for doubt for those that watched and were prone to gossip and were present that day. It was also obvious this was a very close-knit group with genuine affection for one another.

No one could remember ever seeing the stoic Fitzwilliam Darcy smile before, never mind the occasional guffaw that emanated from him. There was no question he had made a love match with his very stunningly beautiful fiancée.

Many a mother would be jealous so much poise and beauty had been granted to one family. The oldest, Jane, might just be thought the most beautiful due to her willowy classic look, but the other three were just as beautiful in their own right.

There would be many in the *Ton* who would lament as word that three of the most eligible bachelors were irrevocably off the market tied to three of the most desirable heiresses with magnificent dowries. Even though Bingley's fortune was from trade and he was considered *nouveau riche*, he was still looked at as a catch, thanks to his connections with the Fitzwilliams, Darcys, and the Bennets.

It was clear for all to see that none of his younger sister's downfall touched him or the Hursts. For most of the *Ton*, fortune and connection were paramount, even trumping birth at times. If they knew the truth about this particular group of friends and family, they would have found it foreign and peculiar that fortune and connection were not what was important to any within it, the content of one's character mattered far more than any other consideration.

Once everyone had had their fill and the statement they had intended to make about their solidarity had been received loud and clear by all present, the party alighted the various coaches and headed home to change so they could meet back at Bennet House for dinner at five.

~~~~~~~/~~~~~~~

At dinner, both Darcy and Lord Matlock remarked they had been away from their estates quite a bit longer than they had planned and felt they needed to return for some weeks before the wedding. Neither man was an absentee landlord and wanted to make sure all was well with their ancestral homes. Andrew Fitzwilliam added the same sentiment about his estate, Hilldale, and he wanted to see to it as well.

Fanny had left the plans for the wedding, with the engaged couple's input and approval, with Hill, so there was no immediate reason to return to Longbourn more than a week before the wedding.

It was decided they would all leave for Derbyshire in three days after the final fitting for Lizzy's gowns and the visit to Chippendales. With the over two-day trip each way, they would have a little under a fortnight in Derbyshire.

The Earl, Viscount and Darcy agreed that would be enough time for them to make sure that all was well with their estates. After dinner Darcy sent expresses ahead to the inns they would stay at to expect their party, which in each case would require just about the entirety of the inn to accommodate a party as large as theirs. He had also requested horses for the changes along the way.

For propriety's sake, it was decided the single men would all stay at Pemberley, and to their great pleasure the Bennet twins were included in that group. The Hursts and Anne de Bourgh would also be resident at Pemberley. The rest of the party would stay at Snowhaven, only an hour or so south of Pemberley.

Thinking about her upcoming nuptials to her beloved, Lizzy was not concerned with the arrangements that would have her staying in a home that was not William's as it was now a little more than three weeks until she would never be parted from her William again.

Following a request from his sister, Edward Gardiner met with Miss de Bourgh at Darcy House. Anne explained the extent and details of Lady Catherine's gaudy and excessive tastes, and Gardiner agreed to help her and sell anything she wanted to get rid of, which was practically everything in both locations.

When Anne expressed concern about being able to sell the useless and not tastefully decorative pieces, Gardiner reminded her that many in the *Ton*, and not a few tradesmen, had the same predilection as Lady Catherine and used these same kinds of items to try and impress others.

Anne refused to accept Gardiner's offer of no commission and expenses only, so the two settled on half of his normal commission plus expenses. While it was true he would receive more than he planned to, she was paying less than she preferred so everyone won.

The plans were finalised, resulting in Anne de Bourgh giving Chippendales one of the largest single orders in their history to date. The meeting at Chippendales about the needs for Darcy House was also very productive and Mrs. Bennet, her daughter, and her future son-in-law were very satisfied with the pieces that were ordered and promised to be delivered before the wedding was to occur.

The same day of Lizzy's final fittings, seven coaches, two wagons, and many footmen and outriders made their way on the Great north Road in a convoy headed for Derbyshire.

CHAPTER 17

Any highwayman with enough gumption to try ply their trade with the convoy travelling from London to Derbyshire would have made a very fatal error. Each driver, postilion, footmen, and the multitude of outriders were all heavily armed. In fact, most of the outriders were ex-soldiers. And in addition, there was a brace of pistols inside each carriage that all in the families had knowledge of how to use.

Bennet and the Earl were adamant that their ladies understand not only the safety required for guns as they were on the grounds and would be seen, but many had enjoyed hours of target practice through the years with the understanding nothing was too much to protect their sisters and family. In this rare instance, it was luckier for highwaymen and knaves that they were disinclined to interfere with this particular convoy than it was for those in it.

Even though the arrangements as to who would reside at which estate had been decided prior to departure, they would all travel to Pemberley first, and after a rest and refreshments, the group staying at Snowhaven would travel thither once Lizzy had received an abbreviated tour of her home to be. The journey was both pleasant and lively, which for Anne and the Darcys was a completely new experience as most of their travel had been lonely.

They sat in wonder at how much their lives had changed for the better in such a short time. Darcy was happy, happier than he could remember he was even before his dear mother passed away.

His taciturn and brooding nature and the famous Darcy mask, which had begun to be developed after Lady Anne's death, which he used to use to discourage being approached, was gone.

Georgiana Darcy had flourished into a happy and confident young lady approaching her sixteenth year. Instead of crying spontaneously, she was now far more likely to laugh or giggle with her sisters. She was more confident and outgoing than she had ever been, and Darcy knew the vast improvement in both their happiness and joy was thanks to the Bennets and their inclusive love.

As Darcy had planned, the travelling party stayed at two inns along the way in order to break up their journey north. Both inns had been very comfortable, and the owners welcoming the Darcys and Fitzwilliams back with deference owed to elite clientele.

These same inns were routinely used by both families on their journeys to and from London. This way the innkeepers anticipated their needs without any trouble. The only difference on this journey was the number of travellers and attendant servants.

Based on the letters requesting chambers, neither innkeeper had accepted other guests while the Bennet, Darcy, Fitzwilliam, de Bourgh, Bingley, and Hurst party stayed, and were more than well compensated for their trouble.

Not long after lunch on the third day, the convoy rolled through Lambton with many inquisitive stares by the townspeople who were not used to seeing quite so many fine-looking coaches in a row, most sporting crests of noble houses.

The town owed much of its prosperity to Pemberley and the Darcy family, so they were able to pick out that some conveyances in the convoy belonged to that family. The name of the town was well known to the Bennets as it was a favourite of their aunt Gardiner.

Aunt Maddie often opined *there was no finer shire than Derbyshire*. Lizzy would never allow any shire could be better than her home shire of Hertfordshire, but she was captivated as she became engrossed by the wildness of Derbyshire and was fascinated at her first look at the distant peaks of the Peak District.

'Yes,' she thought to herself, '*I will be very happy here and I can see that soon I will have two favourite shires.*'

Not five miles after the convoy left Lambton, the coaches and the Darcy wagon entered Pemberley. The Fitzwilliam's wagon had gone directly to Snowhaven from the last inn that morning.

The gates were attached to ten-foot high stone pillars on either side of the drive with a stone gatehouse on the right. Running above the gate was a metal arch, *Pemberley* proudly displayed in big brass letters.

The gatehouse keeper had opened the gates wide as soon as he spied the master's and his guests' equipages come into view. He had a weather eye out for the master as he had been advised the previous afternoon by the housekeeper that very important guests were expected to accompany the master to Pemberley, one being his fiancée and soon to be mistress of the estate. Burris bowed and doffed his cap as each carriage passed him by, and as soon as the wagon had followed, he closed the gates.

The gatehouse keeper fired two pistol shots in the air to send the lad waiting halfway to the house galloping toward the manor house to notify Mrs. Reynolds, the housekeeper, and Mr. Douglas, the butler, of the master and his guests' imminent arrival.

Lizzy, with permission from her father, was riding in

the Darcy carriage at the head of the convoy, accompanied by her William, Georgie, Mrs. Annesley, and Anne de Bourgh. Lizzy could barely contain her building excitement as she saw more and more of what would soon be her home.

On either side of the drive which led to the manor house was the most magnificent forest. Elizabeth could imagine endless rambles and rides on Mercury through these majestic trees. After thirty to forty minutes of rolling through the woods, the coach negotiated a turn toward the right, then started to ascend an incline.

The carriage was just short of the crest of the small hill when Darcy rapped on the roof with his cane and the coach came to a stop. Darcy was in anticipation as he assisted all but Lizzy to alight, and then he turned to Lizzy, and she took his hand as he led her from the carriage. As they started to walk the little distance left to the crest before she could see beyond it, William stopped, and Lizzy stopped with him.

"Do you trust me?" he asked quietly as he looked down into her eyes.

"With my life William!" was her emphatic answer.

"Then close your eyes and keep them closed until I request that you open them. Do you agree?" As he asked and she nodded her agreement, the twins, feeling the relief of stretching their legs, came running up the incline followed more sedately by the rest of the party. William stopped and waited for everyone to reach the crest before he led Lizzy to the front of the party where she would have a clear view of the valley below.

When he had her standing in the perfect spot he turned to her alone and leaned down, "Open your eyes, my Lizzy," Darcy murmured close to her ear, then pulled back so she could have the view he'd been wanting to show her for a long, long time.

She blinked a little as her eyes adjusted to the

sunshine, then she saw the most magnificent sight: "Oh my, of all of this I am to be mistress?" she gasped as she tried to absorb what she was seeing.

As Elizabeth surveyed the sight that greeted her, she couldn't help but continuously return to the very large, handsome stone manor situated perfectly on rising ground. The stonework, the same used on most houses in the area, quarried and formed in the Peak District, seemed almost to glow with a golden hue as the sun light shone on the facade of the huge manor house.

Behind the house was a gently rising hill with trees dotted about, to the left Lizzy could see a vast vegetable and herb garden, a conservatory, and beyond that very extensive and well-maintained stables. In the centre and to the right of the manor house at its rear was an area with benches with various flower beds full of colour and a fountain in the middle of it all.

In front of the manor she saw verdant gardens that, although well maintained, still retained the look of not being overly manicured or ordered as some were wont to do. There was a stream that wound its way lazily until it spilled into the lake in the front of the house beyond the formal gardens.

Beyond the stream was the very inviting forest calling out to Elizabeth to explore its paths and secrets. In the centre of the formal gardens Lizzy could see a divine rose garden that sported more benches strategically placed at random intervals for one to sit and enjoy the sights and aroma from the magnificent roses.

There was a gazebo in the garden where she could imagine many relaxing hours spent out of doors reading or enjoying the company of her very soon to be husband, when the weather permitted.

In her mind's eye she could imagine them sitting in the gazebo with their future children, sipping chilled lemonade and enjoying the natural bounty that she saw before her. On the other side of the stream, nature was allowed its head and there was no attempt to improve what nature and God had designed.

"Do you approve my love?" asked her fiancé.

"William your estate is spectacular; I understand now why you and Georgie light up whenever you talk about Pemberley. I have never seen a place nature has done more for and where the natural beauty has been so little counteracted by the awkward tastes of man."

"I just knew you would love your new home." Georgie gushed with a glow of happiness.

"William," James looked at his soon to be brother, "promise us we will ride and explore a lot of Pemberley while we are here."

As William looked at his eager brothers to be he smiled indulgently, "I will have a lot of estate business to catch up on," he bit back a smile as their shoulders fell, "however, Richard and Charles know the estate well and while I may be busy, they will be available to go with you so you will not be bored. That is a solemn promise. In addition, I promise to join you whenever I am able." He winked at James, who couldn't contain his excitement at the prospect.

Colonel Richard Fitzwilliam stood behind his beloved Mary. '*I need to talk to Uncle Thomas, I will beg if need be, but I, we, do not want to wait almost a year to find the bliss William will have in a short time when he marries his beloved Lizzy,*' he thought as he looked longingly at the Bennet that he was courting.

As William looked at the glow on his fiancée's face, he smiled, "I am very pleased you approve Elizabeth, especially as your approval is the most important one to me."

After absorbing the Bennets' approbation for Pemberley, a very happy and proud Fitzwilliam Darcy suggested that everyone return to the carriages so they could make the short journey to the house.

Lizzy could see her beloved had no improper pride, anyone would be proud of such a home, she was already.

~~~~~~~/~~~~~~~

The coaches came to a halt in front of the manor house in an internal courtyard. Standing at the base of the wide half dozen stairs leading to the house's massive doors in anticipation of their first look at the new mistress were the butler and housekeeper.

They had both received glowing reports from the Killions at Darcy House and wanted to see if there really could be such a wondrous lady as had been described to them.

Before they arrived, Darcy had explained Douglas had been promoted to butler fifteen years before while Mrs. Reynolds had been the housekeeper since he was six. He further explained all retainers who did not have family to go to after retirement were given one of a good number of pensioner cottages that the Darcys had built for their loyal staff over the years.

As soon as the conveyances drew to a halt, footmen all wearing the distinctive green and gold Darcy livery materialised and opened the doors and placed the steps for the occupants to descend and others started to unload the trunks of those staying at the estate.

From up close the house looked even more impressive. Once everyone had alighted, the Bennets who were the only ones in the party previously unknown to the two head staff members were introduced and received polite bows and curtsies.

Darcy took special pleasure introducing his fiancée as the soon to be mistress of Pemberley to the two senior members of staff. Both Reynolds and Douglas were already impressed by the gentility and amiability they could see in the Bennets.

The lady who would soon be the mistress after the master married her in a little more than a fortnight seemed, at first blush, to be completely without artifice. Mrs. Reynolds smiled as she watched her *dear boy* as the happiness radiated from him. He was the best landlord and best master that could be and there was not a single servant or tenant who would contradict that fact.

Based on the longing and loving looks that passed between the couple, the senior staff members were very happy to see that this exquisite young woman loved the master, seemingly not his possessions.

When Mrs. Reynolds spied Bingley and the Hursts, she scanned the rest of the party then let out an audible sigh of relief when she noted Miss Caroline Bingley was not a guest.

As they all entered the house, Lizzy could see right away, that like Darcy House, Pemberley exuded wealth and comfort with only the best of everything, but also was in no way ostentatious or gaudy. The furniture was acquired for comfort, not to impress.

Darcy had told her the house had four more stories above the first floor and an extensive cellar and cold room below. There was an extremely impressive marble grand staircase that rose up from the rear of the entrance hall with various doors that lead off on both sides. The vaulted ceiling went all the way up to the second floor and was tastefully painted with a fresco. Georgiana, as she was still hostess until she gained Lizzy as a sister in about three weeks, led everyone to the larger orange drawing room for refreshments.

As they entered, Lizzy turned to William and gained his immediate focus, "When we return here from our wedding trip William, am I to be given a map so I do not get lost and cannot be found for days on end? How am I to learn to be mistress of all of this?" she asked playfully with a subtle hint of impertinence.

This caused a round of good-natured laughter from the whole party. "My dearest, departed sister Anne was intimidated when she first married George, and she grew up at Snowhaven which as you well know is quite large, but it only lasted some few days. And you, Lizzy, have always stated your courage rises at every attempt to intimidate you," the Earl countered.

"That is true, Uncle Reggie." Jane laughed gently then looked at Lizzy. "This house will be another challenge for you; however, we all know how you enjoy, and rise to, a challenge." Jane supported her sister in the best way possible, reminding her that she was happier when she was faced with new things than when things were the same.

"Yes, my Lizzy," Fanny said affectionately as she squeezed one of Lizzy's hands, "remember this is only a house. You and all of my girls have been well educated in the running of a house. However, like ours, I can already see this is a home, not just a house for show. That, my dear, you know very well how to maintain. It only takes love and a plan for dinner," Fanny teased her Lizzy, winning a laugh from many in the room.

"You my dearest loveliest Elizabeth," Darcy said in a teasing manner, "have always told us how you do not allow anything, or anyone to scare you so I have no doubt you will soon know your way around like a native. Besides, I would never allow you to stay lost for more than a few minutes. Where would I be without my beloved?"

Elizabeth relaxed as the momentary self-doubt, which had been disguised as humour, passed. The last thing she wanted to do was disappoint William. As she looked into his eyes and saw the most ardent love shining back at her, she knew he would never allow her to fail, and he had already promised her they would have a true partnership.

When one faltered, the other would provide the support to move on together. Looking into her fiancé's eyes, she was sure all would we well as long as she was with him.

The party enjoyed refreshments consisting of tea, water, and lemonade, served with finger sandwiches, and the most delightful selection of biscuits, cakes, and fresh fruits from Pemberley's conservatory, which included the very hard to acquire and rare pineapple. Once all were sated, Lizzy, accompanied by all of the Bennets and Darcy, followed Mrs. Reynolds as she gave them a tour of the first floor of the house.

There were two public drawing rooms, the music room, a welcoming receiving room, a study for the master and another next to it for the mistress, a breakfast parlour, and a large and small dining parlour. The large dining parlour could seat up to seventy people.

They also saw the magnificent ballroom and were informed that the last time Pemberley had hosted a ball was before the death of Lady Anne Darcy. Mrs. Reynolds pointed out the entrance to the kitchen and the rest of the service area, expecting the soon to be mistress would just note where the kitchen and servant areas were, and they would proceed with the tour.

To her joy, Miss Elizabeth wanted to see the kitchen, the pantry, storerooms, and the housekeeper's office. This boded well to Mrs. Reynolds because she could see Miss Elizabeth wanted to be in their spaces with them, not expect to always be met somewhere outside the busiest areas of the house. This indicated the lady respected the time of those that worked in these areas.

In the kitchen she was introduced to their cook who had been born in Scotland, Gertrude McInnis, and had been raised in England, and the French chef, Claude-Michel Henri who she charmed as she employed her impeccable French to greet him.

Miss Elizabeth impressed all the servants by giving a cordial greeting to those present from the scullery maids on up. She was happy her French lady's maid would be in a house with a French Chef to talk her native language to as she was leaving the company of the other French lady's maids employed by the Bennets.

Once the tour was concluded, the Bennets minus, Tom and James who would remain at Pemberley, and the Fitzwilliams minus the Colonel, were assisted into four of the coaches to make the short fifteen mile trip to Snowhaven.

After so long with so many women, Georgiana was relieved Anne and Louisa would stay at Pemberley with her so she would not be devoid of female companionship, and they were all gladdened by knowing the two parties would be in each other's company almost daily at either Snowhaven or Pemberley.

As they departed Elizabeth Bennet was lamenting the separation from her beloved, as he was from her, but both were consoled that all too soon they would never have to part again.

~~~~~~~/~~~~~~~

Snowhaven's manor house consisted of the old Matlock Castle which looked like it had welcoming arms reaching out on either side of the drive. Over the more recent generations, and finished by the current Earl of Matlock, two wings had been added for additional living space and chambers.

Unlike many others, the Fitzwilliams had not allowed their castle to fall into disrepair and ruin over the years. The Castle and lands had been presented to the first Earl of Matlock in December of 1485 when Sir Fredrick Fitzwilliam; a knight at the time, had supported and significantly helped the winning side in the Wars of the Roses.

As his reward, he had been elevated to the title of Earl of Matlock and presented with the Castle, renamed Matlock Castle at the time, and the vast Snowhaven estate.

Reggie and Elaine Fitzwilliam as well as the rest of the family loved and were justifiably very proud of their home. The land was slightly more level at Snowhaven than at Pemberley as they were further from the peak district than the Darcy's estate.

The Derwent River ran through Snowhaven as the water flowed from the split with the Trent River in Derby. One of the Fitzwilliam ancestors had had a canal dug that fed into a manmade lake to the right-hand side of the manor that was a boon to anglers as it was a fisherman's paradise.

In the front of the manor was the formal garden with a complex maze the Bennet siblings had long loved playing and hiding from each other in on their previous stays at Snowhaven.

'If it would not mortify him, I would remind James of his first time in the maze when he had got so lost,' Elizabeth thought as they approached the end of their short trip.

The estate had more extensive formal gardens than Pemberley, but nature was still given free rein in the surrounding woodlands. As the coaches pulled up in the circular drive in front of the castle, the travellers were met by the butler and the housekeeper. Both had been in their positions for over twenty years and kept Snowhaven running like a well maintained clock. As it was only an hour to dinner, everyone retired to their chambers.

~~~~~~~/~~~~~~~

Andrew and Marie Fitzwilliam along with their son had chambers in the east wing that was their home whenever they were in residence at Snowhaven. Their apartments gave them the privacy that a young family craved while still being near to family and friends. Their estate of Hilldale was less than twenty miles to the east of Snowhaven, just over the border in Staffordshire.

The family wing was in the castle and the guest chambers were situated in the west wing. There were additional chambers for guests in the east wing, but those were only used when all others were filled.

Jane and Lizzy were in their regular suite directly across the hall from the suite Mary and Kitty shared in the family wing. Their parent's suite was a few doors down from the girls, next to the suite Tom and James used when they were with the family.

After washing off the dust from the road and changing for dinner, everyone met in the warm and large family sitting room. Elizabeth could not but think about how much she missed the man she loved above all others. She was now in his home shire, less than two hours from his beloved Pemberley, so near, but yet so far. On the morrow, they would depart after luncheon, and she would see her beloved fiancé and enjoy the promised full tour of her soon to be home. Tomorrow could not come fast enough for her.

'The more I know him, the more I fall in love with him. I wish that we were married already.' As Elizabeth thought about him, she had a beatific smile that spread to her eyes and beyond as she felt warm all over and especially *down there*, 'Oh my, what thinking about this man does to me, I hope no one notices. It will not be much longer my beloved William before we are married, and we will never have to be apart.'

"What was your first impression of Pemberley?" The Earl asked Lizzy and snapped her out of her reverie. She blushed a deep scarlet, sure everyone in the drawing room could sense her wanton thoughts about her William. She noticed that Uncle Reggie was looking at her with a big smile on his face waiting for her answer.

"I-it is magnificent Uncle Reggie, I am chagrined to say this with you, Andrew, and Papa here that I have never seen an estate its equal."

"You have nothing to be ashamed about Lizzy," her father reassured her, "it is only natural and right that you should feel such about your new home. Your love for William would not allow anything else. That being said, I cannot but agree with you, I too have never seen its equal. Sorry Reggie."

"Better looking than Snowhaven?" the master of the estate asked with mock effrontery, "I know, in all seriousness, Pemberley is one of the finest looking estates in the country, with the backdrop of the peaks, there are few that can rival it."

There was general agreement as the butler announced dinner. After dinner they eschewed separation of the sexes and a convivial evening in the company of the best of friends, that would soon all be family indeed, was had by all.

~~~~~~~/~~~~~~~

At Pemberley, Darcy was meeting with his steward, Mr. Edwin Chalmers, who had taken over on the passing of Mr. Lincoln Wickham. As he waited for Chalmers to join him, Darcy thought back to the former steward.

The late Mr. Wickham was nothing like his son, he was an honourable and honest man. The actions of his son would have caused him much grief. Unfortunately, his wife, who died when George was ten years old, had passed all of her bad habits onto her son. She was an envious spendthrift who always thought whatever she wanted was her due and to the chagrin of mankind, George Wickham had learnt from his mother and not his father.

Subsequent to his wife passing Lincoln Wickham had tried to teach his son right from wrong, but unfortunately young Wickham's godfather, Darcy's own honourable father, had a soft spot for young George, and he felt bad for the boy losing his mother.

Lady Anne had attempted to council her husband that he was not doing the boy any favours, she saw the true Wickham as his character started to reveal itself. After his wife's passing old Mr. Darcy got even closer to George Wickham as the boy was outgoing and entertaining where his own son was more serious and stoic.

What his revered father never knew was what everyone else saw in his godson. Darcy decided rather than hurt his father he would pay Wickham's debts and cover up his profligate and dissolute ways.

As he thought back, he admitted to himself that covering for George Wickham was neither good for his late father nor for George himself.

Darcy was snapped out of his reverie by a knock on his study door; so he called out "Enter."

Chalmers seated himself in front of the large, highly polished oak desk. Darcy's aim was to cover as much ground with his steward as possible so he would have time on the morrow to take the twins on a tour of the park on horseback and be ready and available when his fiancée was scheduled to arrive for a tour of the rest of the house after luncheon. There was nothing too serious in all that the two covered.

When they had completed the planned business, the steward asked, "Is there anything else that we need to cover, Mr. Darcy?"

"No, thank you Chalmers. I believe that is all for now. If I need you again, I will have one of the grooms let you know. If not before, we will have our scheduled meeting on Thursday afternoon," Darcy stated in closing.

With that, Chalmers left his study and Darcy looked through his correspondence. He had two letters of business he knew could not be delayed, so he answered them as needed. When he was complete, he repaired to the drawing room just as the dinner gong was rung. He was happy he had managed his time well so that he would be free on the morrow for some sport with Bingley, his cousin, and the twins.

The party from Snowhaven was scheduled to stay until after dinner on the morrow. He was impatient waiting for the pleasure of his beloved Lizzy again being at Pemberley for a more extensive tour of the house.

Whenever he had not an occupation, his thoughts were of his beloved fiancée. Darcy ruminated again about what a change these last months had made. He had gone from thinking dark, pessimistic thoughts to optimistic, dare he say happy ones. He had believed he would never find the kind of love his beloved parents had shared, and now he had found it in his beloved Lizzy and oh so much more. Before he had seen a bleak, lonely future. And now he saw a long, wonderful future full of companionship and love.

When his eyes had locked onto Lizzy's that first time, he had been both lost and found. '*I cannot wait for my Elizabeth to be my wife. She has invaded every corner of my heart and I belong to her mind, body and soul and will do so until I breathe my last breath. How I love her,*' he thought with a dreamy look on his countenance all thoughts of dinner forgotten.

CHAPTER 18

Andrew Fitzwilliam was leaving for his estate at dawn. The Viscount's estate was about half the size of his father's, but it was very profitable and well taken care of. He hated to be away from his family for any length of time so he would make sure he finished his business at Hilldale as quickly as possible before returning to Snowhaven.

By the time the Earl and Countess joined Marie, Bennet, and Fanny who were breaking their fasts, they noticed Andrew had already departed, and their daughter Marie appeared deeply saddened as she already missed her husband who she loved beyond all reason.

"He will return as soon as he can," the Countess stated, as she took Marie's hand in her own in a display of motherly understanding. "By the way, where are your daughters?" she asked the Bennet parents.

"For old times' sake, they decided to negotiate the maze," said Fanny, "on the condition they all return and leave none lost, we saw no harm in allowing them to go."

All who had been present remembered the first time the Bennet children had attempted the maze and returned not noticing that four-year-old James was not with them. He had been found quite quickly but the young boy had been wailing at being left behind, lost in the maze.

"Your daughters have known their way around the maze for some years and will not get lost," the Earl reported with a chuckle.

After the *James incident*, all of the Bennets had been taught how to find their way out of the maze. No one reminded James of the occurrence any more so as to not embarrass him.

After her reminiscence in the maze, Elizabeth took a morning constitutional before joining the rest of the residents of Snowhaven to break her fast. As she walked, she was again lost in thoughts of her William.

She had felt she would be his, almost from the first time she got lost in those intense, cerulean orbs that were his eyes. They were so expressive, and though he was sometimes reserved and stoic, even what she considered as occasionally dour, she could see a man who was trying to hide his pain from the world.

If you knew what to look for, his eyes conveyed the real William, what he was truly feeling. From that first instant connection in the drawing room at Longbourn, Lizzy had recognised the possibility of the deepest love because he was one who allowed himself to feel things as deeply as she did. It was with a dreamy look on her countenance when Lizzy seemed to float as if on the wings of the wind into the breakfast room to join the others.

"I thought it was only birds that could fly," teased Marie Fitzwilliam feeling much better herself, "but look at Lizzy, love has enabled her to float."

"I would have never suspected our most intelligent daughter would be walking around with that dreamy expression all the time." Fanny teased her second daughter with an indulgent smile.

"Two of our four daughters show all the signs of being in love," Bennet agreed as he looked toward Mary and Lizzy.

"Enough teasing! I am sorry I was preoccupied," Lizzy re-joined playfully, "you old married people must remember what it was to be in love I am sure. If I am correct in my supposition, Papa it is three of your four daughters as my older and prettier sister will be in that state very soon, if she is not already so."

"No, no I will not be." Jane corrected Lizzy with calmness that did not fit the words of one declaring she was going to terminate her courtship with Charles Bingley. "I will not be, because I already am." She continued eating calmly with a sly smile that grew as those around the table reacted to her declaration.

At her pronouncement Lizzy who was closest to Jane swatted her on the shoulder. "That is for making us all worry for poor Charles. Are you going to indicate the change in your feelings to him, Jane?"

"You know I am not as open with my feelings as you are Lizzy." Jane smiled benevolently at her sister.

"True," agreed the Countess. "Men are usually not open until they have some sign their feelings are returned. I think your Charles will hold back until he thinks you are in love with him. If you are waiting for him to declare himself to protect your heart, you could be in for a very long wait. Remember he was unsure of his reception in the beginning."

"I agree with Elaine." Fanny nodded once at her first daughter. "No one is suggesting you breach the rules of propriety, but a signal or clue of some kind would be most appropriate. Remember, you told him you were not in love with him yet when you agreed to the courtship.

"That is all he currently knows and as you correctly stated, you do not show your feelings as readily as Lizzy or the rest of your siblings. Just a little help will be needed." She smiled lovingly at her most reserved daughter, knowing the reserve was because Jane felt pure emotions deeper than most could fathom or handle. That she admitted she was in love with Charles meant her love for him would never fade, and also, she would never be able to love another.

"I believe it was the wise and generous Charlotte Lucas that said a lady had better indicate her feelings rather than lose a man for his not knowing her heart." Lizzy offered the sage advice of her friend.

"I will think on it, and if I feel comfortable, I will give Char... Mr. Bingley a clue." Jane blushed, both from the continued observation of all at the table and the idea of what clue she might allow herself now that she knew her own heart.

~~~~~~~/~~~~~~~

At Pemberley, the same subject being canvassed at Snowhaven was being discussed. Bingley was pacing back and forth in the billiards room while the other three gentlemen watched him with amusement.

Luckily the twins were not there to see their possible future brother in such a state. They were out riding the estate with Pemberley's steward. An early morning ride with Darcy and the other two men had not been enough for them.

"What if she does not love me? What if she never comes to love me, how will I live without my angel? I do not want to be without her, but I know I am reaching too far above my station. She would be right to reject me..." he moaned in misery at the thought Jane would, in fact, reject him.

"Bingley, why are you working yourself into such a state?" Darcy refocused his friend from inward doubt.

"I have no idea whether Jane loves me, or if she ever will," Bingley replied despondently.

"Has she done or said something to indicate such to you?" the Colonel prodded.

"Well...no. She has not yet...said anything," Bingley admitted, his head down.

"Have you asked her?" The Colonel cut the younger

man off.

Bingley went silent, mimicking a fish trying to breathe out of water; he was opening and closing his mouth emitting no sound. He was a man overcome with the misery of, so far, unrequited love and nervous the object of his affections may not ever return the affections he felt so deeply. Up to this point, logic was not part of the equation.

After what seemed like an age, politeness finally forced him to respond. "No, I have not asked her. Do you think I should?" he looked at the Colonel then glanced at the others to see their opinion.

"Only if you want an answer. Currently you are worrying without reason and consequently are wearing out Darcy's rugs," his brother Hurst stated drolly.

"What if she says no?" Bingley's reply closely resembled a squeak. they would remind him of this after Jane relieved his suffering. If she did not, they would never mention it.

"Then at least you will know. Is that not better than uncertainty, my friend?" Darcy voiced the obvious truism. "Even if the answer is negative, which I personally do not think it will be, it is better to know one way or the other. Certainly, it would be better than sending yourself to Bedlam worrying about that which you cannot control. If you are lucky the cell next to Lady Catherine's may yet be available."

"As scared as I am of a negative response, I suppose you are all correct. I will find an opportunity to talk to her today. If one does not present itself, I will ask Mr. Bennet for a private interview with Jane, Miss Bennet," Bingley stated with resolve, and as soon as he had determined to talk with her, he started to recover his good spirits and relax, which was appreciated by all.

~~~~~~~/~~~~~~~

As agreed, the carriages from Snowhaven arrived a

half hour after lunch. All three single men were anxiously waiting on the front steps to see their loves, none more so than Charles Bingley.

Elizabeth and her mother joined Darcy and Mrs. Reynolds to start the tour, during which the approbation Pemberley's housekeeper had for her soon to be mistress grew even more. The young miss was not going to make changes just because she could, which matched the intelligence provided by Darcy House's housekeeper, and proved her taste matched the Master's.

The group toured the three upstairs floors, leaving the master suite and the library for last. Darcy knew his Lizzy, like her father and himself, was a bibliophile. He wanted to see her face when she beheld the library.

The house was even bigger than Elizabeth had imagined. There were twenty chambers and the nursery with chambers for nursemaids on the family floor, and more than seventy guest chambers spread about on two floors with a number of sitting rooms for the guests.

There were also several rooms on the top floor set aside for education of children, and six suites of chambers for tutors. As they toured, Lizzy's apprehension about becoming mistress of all she surveyed faded away.

She was sure she would receive whatever support she needed from William, Georgie, Mrs. Reynolds, and the rest of the servants watching her unobtrusively and with the hope to please and be pleased.

Elizabeth was amazed at the size of the mistress suite as they entered through the left-hand door of the shared sitting room between the mistress and master suites. It consisted of an oversized bedchamber, with a sitting area that led onto a balcony overlooking the grounds at the rear of the house and the woods that grew on the hill beyond.

There was a larger than she could fathom sized

dressing room with a walk-in closet. Lizzy imagined it would take her a long time to fill half such a space. In the bathing room off her dressing room was the twin of the enormous brass tub she had seen in Darcy's rooms at Darcy House.

She blushed a deep scarlet as she remembered this tub could easily fit both her and William. That was a very pleasant thought, but it made her blush even more and feel warm in places she was sure she should not be, no matter how good it felt.

Like at Darcy House, the mistress's chambers had not been updated in over thirty years, so this was the only room for which Lizzy, in consultation with her mother and Mrs. Reynolds, planned major redecorating.

The sitting room did not need any changes as William used it all the time, unlike the one he had never used at Darcy House, so it was up to date and very comfortable. Darcy listened to the conversation, loving how she was going to make the chambers her own. That way he would feel like he was surrounded by his Elizabeth when he walked in, rather than ghosts of memories past. But it occurred then that he had hardly heard her speak of changes until now.

"Is there anything you would like to change in our sitting room?" he frowned, wanting her to know she could and worried she was not requesting changes she would prefer.

"No, William. I love the furniture and colours in our sitting room, and I especially love the fact that there are bookcases so that there will always be reading material for us here." Elizabeth looked in William's eyes so he could see she was in earnest.

"In fact, William," Fanny interjected, "when we walked in, I wondered if Lizzy had already sent ahead her wishes. Bookshelves on two walls so you can place each of your favourites nearby, and a shared one for those you discover both of you always want close by. It is a perfect way to connect a shared favourite hobby. I believe I will suggest the same to Thomas. I think I could surprise him yet with some of my favourite books that I have discovered while reading with our daughters."

"I confess, if I am indoors and have a moment to spare that is not spent writing to those I miss, I prefer it is spent reading. Our sitting room is perfect as it is, William," Elizabeth agreed.

"I am well pleased you like it, and that I am assured you do. Your mother assuring me eases my worry you were not refusing to ask for changes just to placate me." He bowed his head to Mrs. Bennet and offered a private, loving smile to his Lizzy.

'I cannot wait to see the look on her face when she sees the library,' William thought to himself.

They then proceeded into the master suite, which Lizzy felt could not be more perfect for her William. Just like his rooms at the house in Town, it was very masculine. The walls were in hunter green with light browns used for highlights and the trim.

Lizzy blushed all over again when she saw the bed in his bedchamber was the twin of the giant one in London. When Darcy turned to see her expression, he caught her looking at the bed with a blush deepening the longer she looked.

Darcy looked down with heightened colour at having divined her thoughts because he could barely hold himself in check now that she was in his bedroom where he had long imagined their spending many nights and some days. His colour deepened when Mrs. Bennet cleared her throat.

"Were there any other rooms on the tour?" Fanny asked Mrs. Reynolds, giving the young couple a moment to collect themselves, the older ladies sharing a smile that agreed it boded well.

~~~~~~~/~~~~~~~

In the drawing room where all had initially assembled, a somewhat apprehensive Bingley asked Jane Bennet if she would like to take a turn in the garden. Louisa and Hurst said they would like a walk as well and would act as chaperones.

As they left, Richard shared with the rest how nervous Bingley had been that morning and he had finally decided to take the bull by the horns and ask Jane what she felt. Thinking they would be slightly amused; he could not understand why those ladies and Bennet who had come from Snowhaven for the afternoon were doing their best to hold back laughter.

Once he was informed of Jane's proclamation that morning as they were breaking their fasts, he knew Bingley would return a very happy man, and probably engaged to Jane Bennet.

Richard was happy for them, but he was also envious. He knew there was a little more than a week to go before they returned to Hertfordshire, but he steeled his resolve to talk to Thomas Bennet before the Snowhaven party returned to that estate after dinner later that evening.

~~~~~~~/~~~~~~~

Jane and Bingley were slowly walking through the very extensive rose garden in the front of the house. The Hursts had ensured they stayed behind at a distance they could see but not hear the couple.

"Jane, will you sit here with me for a while?" Bingley requested, indicating one of the benches that were placed to allow moments of quiet reflection or conversation amidst the beauty of the garden.

"Thank you, Charles." Jane sat elegantly on the indicated bench. At seeing their brother and Jane sit, the

Hursts found a bench to sit on which was out of hearing distance.

"Jane, I feel I must ask you something. If it is too forward, I will understand if you choose not to answer." Seeing Jane nod her agreement he plunged ahead, knowing his future happiness and the direction of his life was in the balance.

Regardless of how anxious he was, he knew this was what he had to do. Cowardice was not acceptable when one had a chance at winning a life with Jane Bennet. "Three weeks ago, I requested, and you granted me the honour of a formal courtship. When I asked, I admitted I loved you, and I can tell you my love has only got deeper during these weeks of our courtship. At the time, you said you were not in love with me, and you would not enter any marriage without love."

"Yes, that is correct. That is what I said then." Jane smiled, which for him seemed too serene and he almost stopped himself, dreading hearing her say that she did not love him still.

"My question, Jane, is if there has been a change which would further my suit. Or do you wish for longer to learn if you could love me, or have you determined you will never be able to love me in return?" Bingley asked, a slight tremor in his voice the only proof he was deeply afraid of her proclaiming the last.

Once his question was asked, he searched her eyes and in them found his answer, and his heart was beating so rapidly he was sure it would never again have a normal rhythm.

"I love you too, Charles. I admit it came on gradually, I was in the middle before I realised it had begun. Yes, I now love you deeply and have determined you are the only one for me." Jane spoke the words he had prayed to hear, and he was ecstatic.

"You have no idea how joyful you have made me, my angel. You have given my heart wings and it soars to the highest heavens now." He dropped onto one knee, "Jane Bennet, you are the love of my life, and like you I know you are my one and only. I could never see a future with anyone else. Please make me the happiest of men and say that you will join your life with mine, that you will be my wife."

"Yes, Charles! Yes, I will marry you. I will only marry you," Jane consented as tears of joy rolled down her cheeks.

It seemed there was no need for a clue or a push, her Charles had got to the point on his own. Her eyes were closed as she regulated her emotions, and she felt a light brush of her fiancé's lips on her own.

Discovering Jane receptive, he kissed her again, this one a much deeper kiss, and he would have kissed her sweet lips more if his brother and sister had not started talking loud enough to remind them that they were not alone. Jane and Bingley were flushed with embarrassment as they jumped apart, having forgotten others existed in the world in their extreme joy.

"Congratulations Brother! Congratulations Jane, and welcome to the family." Louisa Hurst smiled as she and her husband reached the very embarrassed couple. Louisa hugged her soon to be sister while her husband shook Charles's hand vigorously.

Jane was relieved to see Louisa was sincere in her wishes and was genuinely happy for her younger brother. She would be happy to gain such a sister.

~~~~~~~/~~~~~~~

Darcy led his fiancée and future mother down to the main floor and back into a wing he had so far mostly avoided until this moment, excitement growing for him as he guided them to the double doors that led into the library.

"Do you trust me?" he asked Lizzy just as he had before she saw Pemberley for the first time.

"With my life," she promised, using the same words she had then.

"Close your eyes and give me your hand, my dearest." He held his hand out for hers. As she placed her delicate, petite hand in his much larger one, Lizzy closed her eyes.

Darcy opened the doors, and they walked in. Even before she opened her eyes, she knew she was to behold something exceptional as she had heard her mother try to stifle a gasp of wonder and she could smell the wonderful scent of leather and parchment.

"Open your eyes, my love," Darcy murmured down to her. Lizzy was dumbstruck.

Never in her wildest imagination had she envisioned such a place. The library was the only room that went up to a height of three floors with spiral staircases on either side that allowed access to the second and third levels. There were ladders on wheels on each level of the library to get to the upper shelves. Books filled almost every available space. If she lived five lifetimes, she doubted she would be able to read half of the tomes she could see.

"Put a bed in here with a goodly supply of port when I visit you, Lizzy, as wild horses will not remove me from this magnificent library," Bennet, who had joined them for this part of the tour, teased as he broke the silence.

Elizabeth was surprised to see her father in the library with them. Then she realised William must have arranged for him to be there so she and her father could see the library for the first time together.

Fanny smiled as she thought about her Thomas. Before the twins were born, Thomas would have closeted himself in this room to the exclusion of all else. Even if she had not spied the sly, sardonic smile on her husband's face, she knew her Thomas, the one that had the epiphany after her sons were born, would certainly enjoy time here when they visited, but not at the exclusion of all else.

"The smell of the leather and the number of books is wonderful. William, you told me your library was big, but this is beyond my wildest imagination." Elizabeth again looked around in awe then her eyes finally found his and he chuckled at seeing the reaction he had hoped for and so much more.

"This collection is the work of many generations, starting with Pierre D'Arcy in the time of William the Conqueror. He was gifted the land Pemberley stands on, and soon after our name was anglified and changed to Darcy.

"He brought a large collection of tomes with him from France and started collecting books in England as soon as he had the original house built, so even then he had a sizable library in his house.

"Every subsequent master of Pemberley has added to the collection, including the current master. You see the results of my efforts and those of many generations of my forefathers surrounding us in this room," Darcy explained.

"I will never want to leave Pemberley," Lizzy stated.

"I would not complain about that," Darcy returned Lizzy's tease, but meant what he said wholeheartedly.

"You have chosen the perfect mate for you, my Lizzy," her father agreed wistfully, "as I told you at Longbourn, I could never have parted with you my Lizzy to someone less worthy."

~~~~~~~/~~~~~~~

As soon as Bennet entered the drawing room, he was approached by Bingley who requested an interview. Requesting a private location, Darcy told Bennet to use his study. Guessing the subject of the interview, Bennet asked Fanny to join him.

Bingley closed the door and turned one of the chairs in front of the massive oak desk to face the settee where the Bennet matriarch and patriarch sat. "You requested this meeting, Charles, so the floor is yours," Bennet invited.

"Thank you, Mr. Bennet, Mrs. Bennet." Bingley cleared his throat and met Mr. Bennet's eyes in that man to man way that gave respect. "I would like to request Miss Bennet's hand in marriage, so I am asking for your consent and blessing."

"You got straight to the point; I see. Has Jane agreed to marry you?" Fanny arched a brow and gained the focus of both men.

"She has, Mrs. Bennet, this afternoon while we were walking in the rose garden with my sister and her husband chaperoning us. I know I am merely a tradesman's son and was not born on an estate, but I love your daughter with all of my heart and my being, and today Jane shared with me she also loves me, is in love with me.

"I will spend every waking hour, every breath, every beat of my heart proving I am worthy of her, and it will be my life's mission to make her happy," Bingley stated.

With such sentiments avowed, neither parent could reproach him for using Jane's familiar name. They were certain she had been Jane to him for a long while now and were actually surprised he had not done so before.

"You know the true value of her dowry, is that a factor in your requesting her hand?" Bennet challenged, knowing Bingley was no fortune hunter, but posed the question as a test of sorts.

"I remember what you told us when we first met with you, that the dowry exceeds forty thousand pounds. But I have no need for Jane's funds. I intend to have the marriage settlement reflect Jane's dowry will remain in her control. I will be settling five and twenty thousand pounds on her regardless of her dowry and she will have pin money of two thousand five hundred pounds per annum.

"Although I am not as rich as Darcy, I too invest with your brother, Mr. Gardiner. Darcy introduced us after I graduated Cambridge three years ago. My true income is close to seven thousand a year, so I am very confident I can keep Jane in a style she is accustomed to.

"My father bequeathed a principal amount of one hundred thousand pounds for me to use to purchase an estate, and since I have invested with your brother, that principal has grown to over one hundred and thirty thousand pounds.

"One of the things I am doing while here, with the assistance of Darcy's steward, is to look for available estates in the area. I know how close Miss Elizabeth and Jane are, so I am sure they would love to be close to each other. They will miss you, as well as their brothers and sisters, but I hope to ease their distress by making sure they can see one another as often as they wish."

"Very impressive, Bingley. I know you to be resolute as you demonstrated in the dealings with your sister. I want you to understand we do not consider your roots in trade a factor in our decision to grant or not to grant your request." This statement by his beloved's father made Bingley nervous of a possible negative response.

"That would be very hypocritical considering Fanny's father was the local solicitor in Meryton and her brother Edward, who you know and invest with, is in trade as well. Rejecting you on those grounds would be rejecting our closest family, and that we would never do.

"The only thing that counts is the content of your character and that you have clearly captured our Jane's heart. As to the latter, both Fanny and I have seen the way she looks at you. We have no doubt you will make her happiness your daily priority and will never treat her ill. As demonstrated with your dealing with your sister, we know you will protect our precious girl with all of your being should the need arise. We are also sure you are not marrying her for her dowry of more than *fifty thousand* pounds." Bennet smirked when Bingley sat, open mouthed stunned at the true amount of Jane's dowry.

"F-F-i-fifty thousand?" Bingley stammered. It took a few breaths to recover his equanimity "That changes nothing, her dowry will remain under her control to use as she sees fit," he stated resolutely.

"Fanny is there anything you wish to add?" Bennet smiled knowingly at his Fanny.

Jane was their first and letting her go would be hardest on her. At one time he would have said Lizzy would be the most affected, but now knowing Bingley intended to help the sisters live close to one another, it was Fanny who would feel the loss of Jane most keenly.

"Always treat her like she is your greatest treasure, Charles," Fanny spoke softly as a tear rolled down her cheek. "One can become very forlorn when one's daughters start to leave the nest. On the other hand, it is a mother's dearest wish to see her daughters married to deserving young men who love them as they deserve to be loved and will treat them as the treasures their parents know they are."

After he looked at his wife for confirmation, Bennet extended his hand to Bingley. "You have our consent and our blessing. Welcome to the family, Son. When would the two of you like to get married?"

"I have not yet asked Jane, Sir. As soon as we have discussed it, we will come to you with our requested date." Bingley replied excitedly. He was gratified that both of Jane's parents felt he would do very well for their Jane.

Although Jane showed a serene, sometimes inscrutable, countenance to the world, her parents knew that behind what everyone saw hid a steely resolve and deep feelings and emotions those that feel as deeply rarely handle their emotions half so well.

Jane was also very intelligent, not to the same extent as Lizzy, but not too far off. They knew Jane, like Lizzy, did not like decisions made for her without consultation, so Bingley saying he would consult with her about the wedding date before asking them was a very good sign for their daughter's future felicity.

The three returned to the drawing room and as soon as he entered, Bingley's eyes found those of his fiancée, and he gave a slight nod of the head. Jane's face lit up like the sun rising on a fine summer day.

Thomas Bennet asked for everyone's attention, and with Fanny next to him, he announced Charles Bingley had requested and been granted Jane's hand in marriage. Much warm congratulations ensued.

The newly engaged couple was sincerely wished well by all present. Darcy whispered in Georgie's ear, and she went out to request from the butler he have some champagne brought to the drawing room. Once the glasses were distributed, a toast was offered for the felicity of the eldest Bennet daughter and her fiancé.

"We are to be brothers," Darcy grinned as he slapped Bingley on the back in a playful manor.

"Charles, I wish you and Jane happy," Louisa Hurst offered, overjoyed for both. "You could not have chosen a better helpmeet for yourself. You will do very well together. You are both so complying that the servants will cheat you and you will always exceed your income," Louisa teased her younger brother lovingly.

"Jane's dowry is over fifty thousand, so I think that we will manage," Bingley whispered in his sister's ear, more for the dramatic response than the idea it would change anything.

Louisa Hurst was speechless with shock. She knew the Bennets were wealthy, but not this wealthy. When she collected herself, the full scope of the news hit her heart.

'Caroline, what you gave up because of your inability to hold your tongue and your unyielding pride.' Mrs. Hurst shook off melancholy thoughts of her ruined sister and joined in the merriment of the rest of the party, anxious to claim so loving a sister as Jane.

CHAPTER 19

A few days after Jane and Charles's engagement, Colonel Richard Fitzwilliam, survivor of among others the battles of Roliça and Badajoz with only minor injury, was unsure how to mount the most important campaign of his life.

The residents of Pemberley all noticed the Colonel was distracted and often deep in thought. He spent a lot of his time withdrawn from the group when they were not with the party staying at Snowhaven. When the third Bennet daughter that he was courting was near him, he would be his normal, jovial, flirty, and ebullient self. When Mary Bennet was not nearby, or worse, at Snowhaven without him, he again would withdraw.

Georgie was worried about her co-guardian and decided the situation could not continue as it was. One morning before those in residence at Pemberley were about to depart for Snowhaven, Georgie knocked on the study door.

"Enter." Her brother's rich, baritone voice gave her leave. Georgie, who would never have been so bold as to approach her brother about the subject she now intended to discuss or even initiate a conversation before she had met and grown to love the Bennets, entered and closed the door with firm resolve.

She sat in one of the chairs in front of the desk, waiting patiently while Darcy finished a thought he was writing in a business missive, knowing he would not be long since he had not asked for a minute's reprieve.

"Yes sweetling, how may I be of assistance?" Darcy looked up at his sister as he put down his quill.

"I am worried about Richard." Georgie came right to the point. "Unless Mary is near him, he is not at all like himself. He seems morose, distant, and very unhappy, and I love my cousin. I am very concerned there is a serious problem he has been attempting to fix. Either that, or there something wrong with him that he is trying to hide from Mary since he is only normal when he is near her."

Darcy was very proud his younger sister had been aware of her family enough to notice a change in Richard, but even more that she was willing to raise the issue with him.

Taking her concern as seriously as she had offered it, he considered his own recent interactions with Richard. He had noticed something off with him, but given that when he wasn't with his Lizzy, he was trying to get all the estate business completed with his steward, he had possibly not paid as much attention to Richard's mood as he could have.

"What do you mean Georgie?" Darcy asked, his concern growing when he saw her relief that he wanted more information.

"When Mary is not with him, he looks to be contemplating or trying to overcome a problem. He is not only not his normal self; he seems to be withdrawn or is trying to figure out how to manage something alone when we are all here to help him. Please speak to him, Brother, and tell him whatever is going on, we love him and would be willing to help. I asked Anne and she too has noticed the difference. Both of us believe the change in him happened soon after Jane accepted Charles," Georgiana offered.

"I am very proud of your care and concern for Richard, Georgie. Even more than that, I am overjoyed you felt you could come to me unbidden. I will speak to Richard as soon as I am done with my letter. Thank you for bringing it to my attention, sweetling." Once his task was done, Darcy asked the butler to summon the Colonel to his office.

~~~~~~~/~~~~~~~

At Snowhaven, Thomas and Fanny Bennet were having a conversation with their third daughter. They had noticed Mary was not her normal, happy, contented self when she was not with her beloved Richard. And more alarming, when she played the pianoforte without Richard around, the music was a lot more sombre and pedantic.

Bennet and Fanny asked Mary to come see them in their private sitting room. "Mary my love," Fanny's voice was filled with concern, "we have noticed you have not been yourself lately. You know we do not keep secrets from each other in this family, will you not share with us what has caused your melancholy?"

Her parents concern increased as tears started to run down Mary's cheeks. "I love Richard so much, and we waited almost three years loving each other strongly and truly before he was even allowed to ask for a courtship.

"Even though you have allowed him to shorten the time before he asks for my hand, it is still weeks from now until the end of the courtship, and then another three months of engagement. It is so hard waiting to never be parted from my beloved. We have stayed true and faithful already for years, so it is hard not to feel like I am being punished when you allow Jane and Lizzy to marry weeks after meeting the men they chose..." She was cut off as a sob racked her body.

"Mary," Bennet looked at Fanny in regret, Mary's words cutting through like a knife hurt them deeply. From her perspective it was punishment and being punished for truly loving someone was abhorrent to both parents, "when we set the limits we did it was with consideration for your age, we may have not taken into account the time you and Richard have been in love. Will you wait outside so Mama and I can discuss this? We will call you back in soon, my sweet daughter?"

Mary nodded her acquiescence and exited the sitting room, softly closing the door behind her and pausing once she had to try to collect herself before she went back in.

"Thomas, have we caused our daughter heartache by trying to hold onto her a little longer than was necessary." Fanny could not even manage a sad smile; the folly was on their side alone.

"I am afraid that we may have, my love," Bennet sighed dejectedly, the hurt in Mary's expression as condemning as any proof.

"What are we to do to fix this situation?" Fanny offered him the question, hoping he would have the strength to say what in her heart she knew was the right thing.

"What do you say that we give Richard permission to propose now, and then they can get married in a double ceremony with Jane and Charles if everyone agrees to the plan?" He offered the right answer though his heart hurt at the thought of so quickly losing three daughters. "And mayhap we can get our sons to marry next month so we can have a house full before we set the Yule log," Bennet teased to help his wife smile again.

"Oh Thomas, do you think they could? One of them will surely pick Georgiana!" she teased back. He laughed; her wit never ceased to amuse him no matter the circumstance.

'I tease, but I have seen the way Tom and Georgie look at each other, mark my words, one day they will marry,' Fanny thought to herself.

"Let us correct our unintended wrong first and get our three daughters married off before we worry about Kitty and the boys. We will need to refresh the nursery for grandchildren, my dear. Then you may plan our sons' lives for them." He hugged her and kissed her soundly when he saw her excitement of the promised grandchildren.

"Mary first. If we offer this solution, it will be four weeks after Lizzy and William marry. I think that will work, Thomas. I am already planning a second wedding, so to add another couple is no hardship. The weddings are for our daughters, not me, so their preferences will decide what we do. And to be honest, Jane and Mary have more similar tastes. If I was trying to plan a double wedding with Lizzy and Mary or Jane, now that would be a hodgepodge of things for each rather than a shared vision," Fanny stated in agreement. "Let us find Kitty a husband to marry her off with Lizzy so I would have four shots at gaining a grandchild before next Christmas."

"Mayhap we will get to keep Kitty forever." Bennet grinned. "Let us offer Mary our apology and see what she thinks of the plan first before we even ask Jane and Charles. She deserves to have a day all of her own if it is what she wants." He kissed his wife's hand then Mary was called back into the sitting room.

"Mary, first we want to apologise for not considering the fairness of our allowances for your sisters and holding you back from your well-deserved, well-earned happiness." Fanny took Mary's hand. "In our defence it was only to keep you close for just a little longer, we were not aware you wanted to run from us so quickly," Fanny smiled sadly when Mary started to protest.

"To follow your mother's apology, I will add mine, Mary. Your happiness has long been determined, so we were just enjoying this time with you," Bennet sighed. "But you are correct, it was not fair and so we would like to make amends." He took her other hand in his and informed Mary of the decision.

Once she listened to their offer Mary was incandescent with the glow of happiness and she could not wait until the party from Pemberley joined them that afternoon.

~~~~~~~/~~~~~~~

At Pemberley, about ten minutes after Darcy had sent the butler to find him, the Colonel stalked into the study. He closed the door and flopped down dejectedly into one of the chairs in front of Darcy's desk. Darcy could now plainly see what had caused the worry for Georgiana. This was not the happy go lucky Richard he was used to seeing. He had dark rings under his eyes from lack of sleep and looked very forlorn.

"Richard, what is going on? I cannot remember a time when you have looked so dour and unhappy. You remind me of myself before I was snapped out of my melancholy. I have been busy, but Georgie and Anne are very worried about you and Georgie actually is so worried she brought it to my attention this morning," Darcy asked, assessing his cousin to see if he could see the issue at hand.

"It is nothing cousin, or nothing anyone can help with. Only time will fix it." Richard replied with more bitterness than he usually expressed.

Based on the response, Darcy had a good idea what was ailing his cousin, so he decided to test his supposition. "Are you regretting your courtship of Mary and thinking about the best way to break it off with your honour intact?" he asked, getting the exact response he expected.

"**BREAK IT OFF WITH HER**?!!" Richard shouted. "If you think that, William, then there is a cell next to Aunt Catherine's at Bedlam waiting for you. Why on earth would you say something so utterly ridiculous?"

"Just checking, Cousin." Darcy smirked. "You can sit down and relax."

"Checking what, William?" Richard frowned. "If it is my constancy..." he stopped when Darcy held up a hand.

"I was verifying my supposition that you do not want to wait much longer to marry your Bennet daughter, and Jane and Charles's betrothal has sent you down the rabbit hole of frustration," Darcy offered evenly.

"You know me too well, William. Wait, did you say Georgie noticed? She came and talked to you?" he enquired, much surprised.

"Affirmative on both counts. Our young charge is no longer a child. With help from the Bennets, she has become a confident, mature, and poised young lady. Being able to confront Wickham before he was led away was the final step in her transformation and recovery.

"Now back to you. You are a man of action, a survivor of multiple battles against the enemy forces. So, what are you going to do? Sitting around here moping and feeling sorry for yourself and doing nothing will not get any results other than for you to sink further into frustration and soon despair," Darcy stated, and as one who had allowed himself to sink into the depths of despair, he was anxious to help his cousin avoid it.

"I do not think there is anything to do short of an elopement..." The Colonel sighed when he saw that his cousin was about to take him to task. "Peace, William. I am not like Wickham; I would never dishonour Mary like that or put the longstanding friendship between her parents and mine in jeopardy. We have been in love for almost three years, we just do not want to wait so many more months before we say our vows before God and are never able to be parted again."

"Never be parted? Are you to sell your commission?" Darcy looked at him in surprise.

"I am. Once we knew we loved each other, I promised Mary, as well as her parents and mine, that as soon as I am engaged to her, I would sell out. I refuse to leave her the widow of a soldier or alone for long periods not knowing if I live or have died," Richard related.

"I know your parents as well as Andrew and Marie will be overjoyed when they do not have to worry about you going into battle anymore. Are you in a financial position to take a wife?" he asked with concern, chuckling at Richard's arched brow. "I suppose with Mary having fifty thousand..."

"How much did you say? I thought it was around forty thousand for each of the Miss Bennets!" Richard's eyes were so wide Darcy could not help but laugh.

"I assumed you knew, based on the closeness between your families. Yes, the amount is over fifty thousand." Darcy agreed, now truly amused.

"We will not need to touch that to live reasonably well, thanks to Edward Gardiner's help. I have saved up over sixty thousand pounds due to my investments since I entered the army," Richard answered the original question.

"I am very impressed, Cousin. With that you can purchase a small to mid-range sized estate if you want to. Now back to your situation with Mary. Why do you think there is nothing that can be done?" Darcy asked, interested in Richard's opinion.

"I had previously requested, and the Bennets agreed, to a shortened courtship period of two months rather than three. I cannot go back to him again. I get it, they do not want all three of the older daughters to leave home at the same time, but Mary and I have waited years and you and Bingley have only known...." Richard stopped himself before expressing too much bitterness.

"Richard that is nonsensical! My future father-in-law is one of the most approachable and reasonable men I know, other than Uncle Reggie. What is the worst he can say if you ask? No? He and Mrs. Bennet love their daughter too much to terminate the courtship because you want to marry her sooner," Darcy suggested, understanding the reasons and could not fault Richard for the frustration he felt, which he and Bingley were the unwitting catalyst for.

"There is some truth to what you say, William," Richard agreed. After a moment he started to visibly brighten as a plan of action formed in his mind, and the thought of even the possibility of a shorter time before he and Mary recited their vows to each other made his zest for life return.

"Now go get ready. We leave for Snowhaven in an hour but before you do, please let Georgie see you smile again," Darcy ribbed his favourite cousin.

~~~~~~~/~~~~~~~

Two hours later the two carriages from Pemberley arrived at the entrance to Snowhaven. Greetings were made and the party assembled in the drawing room, but Richard was focused on his Mary who was glowing with happiness.

"Ask my parents to join us in the study please, Richard," his beloved whispered to him as he walked over to greet her.

The Colonel did not have to be prompted twice as this request fit his own intentions perfectly. After conveying the request to Mary's parents, all four excused themselves and repaired to the Earl's study. It was a large study with a huge desk, two chairs in front of the desk, and two settees lining the walls, one below the window that looked out onto the formal gardens.

"You requested a meeting, Richard?" Bennet looked at the young man who he had watched grow and could not be prouder of the man he had become.

"Actually, Uncle Thomas, er, Mr. Bennet, I was following instructions from Mary." Richard nodded at Bennet then smiled encouragingly at Mary.

"Do not tease the boy, Thomas. Tell him." Fanny

feigned exasperation as she playfully swatted her husband's arm.

"Tell me what?" Richard regarded Mary first to ensure he had not read her mood incorrectly and that she was indeed happy. She was.

"Well, Son, this morning our Mary took us to task," Bennet began, winking at Mary when she giggled. He then told Richard about their daughter's plea to them that morning, how they had reflected on the situation and decided the reasons for the time restrictions they had placed were no longer valid. They had apologised to Mary but wanted to apologise to him as well because it had not been as fair as they initially thought.

Richard was flabbergasted and explained he was called into Darcy's study and had a similar conversation. If Richard and Mary had been happy before, they were bowled over by what Thomas and Fanny Bennet told them next.

"We know that as a second son you do not have an estate, Richard. We remember your pledge to resign from the army and sell your commission when you and Mary get engaged. We also know you have a good amount of capital saved and Mary has a very healthy dowry to ensure that you have the life you both are looking forward to." Bennet looked at his wife, and at her nod he carried on. "Our wedding present to you will be Netherfield Park." They grinned at one another as their Mary and her soon to be fiancé stared at them in shocked silence.

"We thank you for your being willing to give us Netherfield Park. That is most generous of you Mr. and Mrs. Bennet, but we cannot accept such a gift that will reduce your income and take away from Thomas and James's inheritances," Richard replied, knowing without having to ask that Mary felt the same.

"Longbourn's income rivals and even sometimes

exceeds Pemberley's. The income from Netherfield Park will not be missed, and with the land I have added to both Longbourn and Bennet Fields, neither of my sons will be adversely affected.

We always intended to gift that estate to one of our daughters. It is partially selfish, you know. This way we ensure one of our daughters will remain in the neighbourhood, and it is more important now that Lizzy, and by the looks of things Jane, will soon be resident in Derbyshire." Fanny reached out and took Mary's hand, squeezing it gently.

After looking at Mary and getting her nod of agreement, the soon to be former Colonel slowly nodded at his soon to be in-laws. "In that case Mr. and Mrs. Bennet, we would be very humbled by such a gift." He was almost overcome with gratitude and understood wanting to keep his Mary close by. He himself hated parting from her for hours, let alone for months.

"Firstly, no more of this Mr. and Mrs nonsense. We have known you for many years, Richard Fitzwilliam. I am Bennet and Fanny would enjoy being called Mother Bennet. You always used to call us uncle and aunt, but as you are to be our son, those monikers do not apply anymore. Just so you know, there will be an entailment put in place on Netherfield Park.

"Not one determining what sex of child can inherit, but the same one I have put in place on Longbourn and Bennet Fields. The irrevocable entailment stipulates that the estate, in part or whole, cannot be sold but only inherited by a direct blood descendant, so that way it will always stay in the family," Bennet explained, grateful to see Mary's smile.

"That is an entail Mary and I will accept with no issues or undue alarm. Mr., Uncle, er, I mean Bennet and Mother Bennet. May I request a private interview with Mary please?" Richard attempted, and failed, to keep his grin in check.

The request was granted and once they were alone talking was not necessary, they fell into each other's arms and their lips met. It started with some chaste kisses, but they soon became much more ardent and passionate. The couple pulled apart, not wanting to take advantage of the trust that had been placed in them and Richard got down on one knee.

"Mary, you know I have loved you for many years, even before I declared myself when you were sixteen and not out yet. At that point, waiting was the only option, but now I find I cannot live without you by my side any longer. Mary Ingrid Bennet, will you put me out of my misery and be my wife. Please will you marry me Mary?" he pleaded, begged, demanded, commanded—all encompassed in a single question—and hoped as any man in his shoes would.

"Yes, Richard, a million times and more, yes. I have loved you for just as long as you have loved me, even longer, I daresay. I cannot imagine my life without you in it. Yes, yes, yes, absolutely and definitely, yes, I will marry you Richard," Mary replied, choking on a sob of relief and happiness, startled to find it was far more intensely felt than her feelings of sadness. Happiness *was* a far more powerful emotion. She had not understood her mother's promise that it was so until this moment.

Richard stood and they hugged tightly. Richard then opened the door and asked Mary's parents to join them. Consent and blessings were bestowed with alacrity. When Mary hugged her mother, she whispered she now understood happiness was far more powerful and Fanny smiled knowingly, sorry she had caused her beloved daughter such pain but glad she was now truly happy. Her other daughters had said they understood, but they did not yet. They would, one day.

"Are you sure you do not want to wait some weeks

after Jane is married to have a day just dedicated to you, Mary?" her father asked, and Richard paused and was about to agree to it before Mary held up her hand to silence both.

"I want to be married to my Richard sooner rather than later, Father. Jane and I are so similar in tastes it will be my wedding as much as hers, and even better, I get to share the joy of my day with my beloved sister. Had you suggested I get married in a ceremony with Lizzy, I may have delayed," Mary teased, and Fanny laughed as she squeezed Mary's hand.

"That is just what your mother said," Bennet chuckled, nodding that they were now assured she was happy.

And just like that, three Bennet daughters were engaged.

~~~~~~~/~~~~~~~

During the conference in the study, Andrew Fitzwilliam returned to Snowhaven from Hilldale. He had completed everything he needed so now he could return to Marie's welcoming arms with his conscience clear. In addition to his wife, he could not wait to hug his son David.

When the four returned to the drawing room, the looks of bliss on both Mary and Richard were enough for one and all to know what had transpired and the couple was surrounded by well-wishers even before Bennet made the official announcement.

Richard's mother and father were not only overjoyed at officially claiming Mary as a daughter but were deeply relieved he would be soon selling out his commission and resigning from the army.

Without having to be prompted, the Colonel stated he had sent an express to General Atherton tendering his resignation and stating his intent to sell out his commission right away. When they all headed back to Longbourn, Richard would instead go to London for the sale of his commission, also to have the marriage settlement drawn up.

Jane and Bingley were applied to and agreed with the request for a double wedding. Their acquiescence was applauded by all. It was never thought they would say no, but they appreciated being asked beforehand, not presented with a *fait acompli*.

That evening's dinner at Snowhaven became a raucous and very happy engagement celebration. There were many toasts to the felicity of all three couples and besides being over the moon at gaining Richard as a brother, Georgiana was even more pleased to see her jovial Richard back. It was considerably later than normal when the carriages departed back to Pemberley.

~~~~~~~/~~~~~~~

Once the Pemberley party departed, the Earl, Countess, Bennet, and Fanny retired to the master suite sitting room. The gentlemen were sipping brandy while the ladies had sherry.

"Well, Thomas, we will soon share a son and daughter in addition to gaining Lizzy as a niece. It is long since we have considered all of you family, and now at long last it will be official." Reggie winked at his Elaine.

"I could not be more in agreement with you, Reggie. What you say, Fanny and I feel as well, and we could not be happier. To gain an honourable son such as Richard would make any father happy. We know he will always treat our Mary well, and there can be no doubt in the shared love and respect they have for each other." Bennet chuckled. "I will advise him when she takes one to task it is for good cause, but he will not recover quickly. She inherited that from…" he paused when Fanny cleared her throat, "my mother." Fanny's laugh filled the room with Elaine's lower one mixing in perfectly.

"Thomas, it is good that you and Fanny have decided

you will no longer hide from the *Ton*," Lady Elaine stated with a sly smile to Fanny. "Once this engagement is announced following so closely on the heels of William's marriage and Bingley's betrothal all to Bennet girls, the excitement to associate with you that you saw when we were in town will grow a hundred-fold. Your connections and wealth are no longer a secret, but we will have a larger force at work to keep the fortune hunters away from both Kitty and Georgie when they come out."

"You know what I was thinking, Elaine? As Kitty and Georgie are so close in age, what say you to our bringing them out together once they are both eighteen?" Fanny suggested, liking it even more now it was said aloud.

"That is an excellent Idea, Fanny. And I think the girls would love the scheme. Even before they were to become sisters through marriage, they were already as close as real sisters could be," Elaine agreed immediately.

"Thomas, did I understand from Richard correctly that you and Fanny are gifting Netherfield Park to him and Mary after they marry?" Reggie asked seriously.

"That you did, Reggie. Fanny and I decided to do that even before their formal courtship was requested. It will give them a home without Richard having to use his funds he has built up so well over the years, and neither will there be a need to touch Mary's dowry.

"With the close to six thousand a year from Netherfield Park, and more than four thousand from their combined fortunes, they will not want for anything. At least I hope they will be able to scrape by on ten thousand a year." Bennet smirked as all three laughed at his joke. "As we told Richard," he nodded when they settled, "selfishly we will ensure that at least one daughter will be settled close to our home as the other two will already be closer to yours."

"I will smother them enough to be mildly annoying at

times," Elaine promised, winning a laugh from the others.

For a moment, Fanny considered what she may have been like before her sons were born with a daughter settled so well close by and had to admit Mary and Richard were very lucky she was not the same person she had been prior to the birth of the twins.

That Fanny would have been at Netherfield Park every day, trying to direct their lives and giving them no space to grow as husband and wife. Fanny would now visit when invited, give advice where asked, and make sure the couple had all the space they needed to live their lives as they saw fit. She would not be a cause should they ever choose to move for their own reasons.

"I was elated when Richard informed us that he had already sent an express to General Atherton resigning from the army and asking the General to make inquiries to see if someone would like to buy his Colonel's commission," the Countess admitted with a supreme look of relief.

"You have no idea how it makes a mother's heart sing to know her baby son will not be sent into battle again. After the battles he was in, Richard was altered. He was not physically changed, but I could see he was haunted. It is only now his future is secure that I have seen my Richy return fully. Thank you, Fanny and Thomas for granting his most favourite wish, and my most ardent one as well, that he will be safe from war and for making sure he has an occupation and a purpose."

"What do you think about us all returning to London after Lizzy and William wed?" Bennet suggested as he watched Fanny share in Elaine's relief and pleasure, grateful she was his wife and as compassionate a woman as he could ever hope to find. They had long feared for Richard as well, so they were almost as relieved. Their Mary would not have recovered had he been lost to war.

"Yes, Thomas," answered his wife, "we need to shop for a trousseau for both Jane and Mary, and I am sure Elaine would like to be with us as we set up our daughters. We will let their desires guide us, and you do not have to say it, Thomas, I promise not to push for too much lace." Fanny winked lovingly at her husband.

"I am sure Anne will want to come to Town with us to purchase a new wardrobe, she hates the horrid fashions Lady Catherine used to force on her," Lady Matlock opined. "She has ordered a number of dresses and other items of clothing from Lambton, but she needs to visit Madame Chambourg as well."

"My niece Anne is always welcome, Elaine," Fanny arched a brow and Elaine laughed brightly as she nodded in concession.

"I have to get the boys to Cambridge right after Lizzy's wedding, so I will join all of you in London as soon as I return. We will bring them home for Jane and Mary's wedding. None of the family would be happy if Tom and James missed their sister's weddings, least of all the boys." Bennet chuckled, the separate warnings he had received from both were still diverting.

With many decisions of the following weeks made, two very happy sets of parents wished each other a good night and Thomas and Fanny retired to their suite.

~~~~~~~/~~~~~~~

On the short ride back to Pemberley, the soon to be former Colonel, rode in the coach with Darcy, Georgiana, and Bingley while the second carriage transported Tom and James Bennet, Anne de Bourgh and the Hursts. Seeing her cousin was not able to stop smiling, Georgiana let out a contented sigh.

All was right with their world again. Darcy and Bingley could not help smiling as they watched the soon to be *the Honourable Mr. Richard Fitzwilliam*. They were engaged to a Bennet daughter each, and understood the feelings of deep, ardent, and requited love that Richard was feeling.

"You are to become a landed gentleman like me, Richard," Darcy grinned.

"Yes William, I could not believe it when the Bennets told us what our wedding present was to be. Netherfield Park! I tried to beg off, but they were adamant. And once Bennet had explained it would not have any adverse effects on either his sons' future fortunes or his income needs, Mary and I had no choice but to accept," Richard admitted, "and I do not doubt it was also true they will be glad to have one of their daughters settled so close to Longbourn."

"So that means I will be evicted after your wedding?" Bingley frowned dramatically.

"I forgot you had a yearlong lease, Bingley. We will make other plans until you are ready to quit the place," Richard stated with the finality of his military position, showing off his decision-making skills in a way that made Georgiana grin.

"Fitzwilliam, I am jesting!" Bingley laughed, winking at her when Georgiana did as well. "You forget I have been seeking an estate in the area, and I think I have found one I would be very comfortable in, thanks to Chalmers's assistance." At the questioning looks from the other occupants of the luxurious Darcy coach, he elaborated. "The Longfield estate, Longfield Meadows, has been on the market for more than six months. The old Mr. Longfield died with no issue.

"A distant cousin, his heir, has a large and prosperous estate of his own south of London so he wants to sell Longfield Meadows as he has no interest in managing two estates so far apart from each other. He had been asking more than the estate's current worth, but I happened to see the property quite soon after he had instructed his agent to significantly lower the price. I made an offer; it was accepted, and it is in the hands of our solicitors now.

"Pending Jane's approval, I will sign the sale and conveyance documents tomorrow. I was waiting until then to announce my purchase to our whole party. As such, you and Mary will not be displacing your brother." Bingley tested the new moniker out for both of them. Never had they imagined being brothers before they met the Bennet daughters, and now they would be marrying sisters in the same ceremony.

"The Meadows is but ten miles to the west of Pemberley!" Darcy grinned at the thought of how comforting that would be for his Lizzy.

"Yes, Darce, that was one of my considerations when seeking an estate to purchase. I know Jane and Lizzy will love being so close to one another. It is under one and one half hours by carriage, and even less on horseback. The estate clears close to four thousand per annum, but I could see with some effort it could be significantly higher. The place has been neglected since Longfield took ill over two years ago, and more so since he passed. I am most fortunate, however, to know someone in the neighbourhood who will be able to advise me when I need it," Bingley ribbed Darcy.

"Bingley, you know even if you were not to be my brother that I would help you anytime. Does Jane know yet?" Darcy could imagine Jane keeping quiet and serene while they waited for the sale to complete before they shared their news.

"She knows I have been looking. Tomorrow morning, right before I sign the documents, Jane, her parents, and I will go to Longfield Meadows. After we view the house and the property, and if they approve, I will make it official and Jane and I will become members of your society here once we wed. As the name accurately describes the look and feel of the estate, I am of a mind not to change it unless Jane prefers a different name," Bingley reported.

Congratulations were liberally bestowed on Bingley, and along with those of his family around him, he could imagine his parents smiling down on him from on high in heaven as he fulfilled their dearest wishes.

The Bingleys were to become part of the landed gentry in a matter of days.

~~~~~~~/~~~~~~~

The next morning Bingley was collected at Pemberley by Mr. and Mrs. Bennet and Jane. Their carriage approached the gate that proudly proclaimed 'Longfield Meadows' in large, blackened copper letters. As the carriage passed the unmanned gatehouse, Bingley informed them that there was only a skeleton staff at the estate. They consisted primarily of the steward, the butler, and the housekeeper.

He imparted he had good reports on all three of the senior staff, so he was inclined to keep them for continuity, unless Jane objected. There were also two maids of all work, one footman that maintained the manor, and the estate's former head gardener was still working part time in an effort to keep the gardens in as reasonable a shape as possible with limited resources.

The carriage travelled for a little over a mile with open meadows on either side of the drive. The meadows had a good number of sheep grazing in them and were dotted with many kinds of wildflowers, giving a pleasing pallet of colour to the eye.

The drive turned to the right and crossed over a strong flowing stream, after which they entered the formal gardens. It was easy to see there had been far more extensive gardens than was currently displayed. It was obvious Barrow had tried his best to maintain some semblance of order, but it was an uphill struggle.

Fanny, who loved working in her gardens, could see a wide variety of flowers and told Jane she could see so much potential it was exciting. As they approached the circular drive in front of the manor, they observed overgrown rose gardens on either side of the drive.

The manor was a four-story house, built in the stone used most in Derbyshire. One wing had been added to the west of the house, and from what they could see the house looked around the same size as Netherfield Park's, perhaps a little larger.

In front of the entrance to the house stood the heir's agent waiting for them. He welcomed them to the estate, and once they had alighted from the coach Bingley introduced the agent to his fiancée and her parents.

They were then led inside the manor house where lined up to greet them were the three senior staff, all looking a little apprehensive as they had not been given any indication whether their services would be retained or not. After the introductions Bingley addressed their immediate concerns.

"If my fiancée approves of the estate and we make the purchase, and subject to the new mistress's approval, we will be retaining all current servants, including the three of you. This depends as much on you as it does on us for someone may not want to stay in service with us.

"We believe that having people working here who know the estate will be good and helpful to us as we familiarize ourselves with the estate and the running of it." Bingley related.

"Thank you, Sir. We welcome you all to Longfield Meadows," the three senior staff chorused as they visibly relaxed.

The house consisted of three levels above ground, a cellar below ground that had a cold room, a wine cellar, a general and gun storage, and the pantry. On the first floor was a large dining parlour, a large drawing room, a smaller sitting room, a nice sized ball room, and a music room.

The kitchen, scullery, and housekeeper's office were all at the rear of the house. They would be able to entertain a large party as sections of the walls which were not load bearing in the public rooms could be removed when needed to make a much larger ballroom.

In the newer west wing was a study for the master, one for the mistress, and a nice sized library with empty shelves waiting for books that would make it one in more than name only.

Upstairs on the second floor was the family wing that housed the master suites, four family suites and six individual chambers. There was a nursery in the family wing. In the guest wing located in the newer west wing, spread between the second and third floors, there were eight suites and ten single bedchambers and a nice sized guest's sitting room on each floor.

The fourth floor in the older section of the house contained the school rooms, places for nursemaids and governesses and a music room for children to learn to play various instruments.

The relatively low sleeping capacity in the manor house was not a concern for Jane and Bingley given how close they were to Pemberley, Snowhaven, and also Hilldale. That way if there were ever large gatherings in the future it would be easy to have guests stay between all four family estates without major inconvenience to any.

In the large attic that spanned both the original house and the added west wing, there were ample servant quarters, with the female and male quarters separated by a space for storage. There were separate stairs that led to each of the three sections of the attic.

After the tour, Bingley requested the agent wait in the public sitting room for them. As the door to the master suite sitting room closed Bingley turned to the Bennets, their opinion, and especially Jane's, were extremely important to him. "What did you think Janey, Mr. and Mrs. Bennet?" he walked over to Jane and took her hand, trying to contain his excitement.

"Now Charles, in six weeks you will be my son, so please call me Mother or Mother Bennet, and I am sure Thomas will be more than happy if you address him as Father Bennet or Bennet." Her proclamation was seconded by a nod from Bennet, and with that most pressing requirement covered, she then addressed his question. "I think you two can be very happy here, but make no mistake there is work to be done. The whole house needs to be painted, papered, and decorated. Almost all of the furniture is in disrepair and needs to be replaced. You will need to redo the whole kitchen with all new equipment and find a good cook and a baker. But all that being said, I think you should take the place as it has good bones."

"My Fanny has the right of it," Bennet agreed. "I have had my man of business check, and you have been asked a more than fair purchase price. I would recommend that you tell the agent you want to reduce the price by five thousand pounds to cover the cost of some of the repairs to the house and the tenant cottages.

"I am almost positive he has that flexibility from the heir. In fact, I would tell him you want to reduce by seven thousand five hundred, then let him negotiate down to no less than five thousand, that way he can feel like he did not give you as much as you wanted."

"Just the proximity to Lizzy and William and the Fitzwilliams would be enough for me Charles, but I do like the house and the estate feels like a place that we and our future children can and will be very happy. So yes, Charles.

I agree we should purchase it. If we need more space in the future, there is more than enough room to add another wing or more," Jane blushed with pleasure at the thought of having so large a family.

Once he had the recommendations, and most importantly Jane's agreement, Bingley went down to the sitting room to meet with Mr. Brown, the agent. After almost an hour of back and forth, the agent agreed to reduce the sale price by six thousand pounds toward the needed refurbishments and the sale agreement was signed.

It would take a week to be finalised after solicitor review and for the deed to be issued in Bingley's name on the transfer of the funds to the heir. In a week, Charles Bingley would be the first in his line to be a landed gentleman.

After the documents were signed and the three Bennets joined him in the sitting room, Bingley told the lone footman to summon all of the servants and to bring them into the sitting room.

The current staff and servants were all asked if they would like to work for the new master and mistress of Longfield Meadows. All of them agreed with pleasure they had not imagined they would feel that morning, and Barrow was overjoyed at being restored to full time employment as the head gardener once more.

The servants were dismissed and thereafter the senior staff members were asked to come in one by one to discuss the needs for each of their respective areas of responsibility. Jane sat with Mrs. Pattinson, a widow of five and forty years, and took an instant liking to the woman. The housekeeper told Jane what she believed the number of upper and lower maids and kitchen staff they would need.

"May I have your thoughts on those we could employ for a cook and a baker?" Jane asked the most important question for the whole house's ability to thrive.

"I am so glad you asked," Mrs. Pattinson smiled brightly. "The former cook, who is very good at her craft and very pleasant, a Mrs. Loretta McKean, and her daughter Fran who in my opinion is the best baker in the county outside the ones at Pemberley and Snowhaven, are now employed at an inn not five miles away. They would be most grateful to be considered for their former positions at the Meadows and both will be most pleased to return here and also to be away from there."

"Then let us bring them home. Today, if it can be arranged. We will have funds released so we can have all the stores replenished and you all deserve a feast of your own for taking as good a care of my future home as you have. There will be a lot of work in the days to come, so consider it a bribe." Jane smiled as Mrs. Pattinson laughed delightedly. Fanny watched with pride as her sweetest daughter won over her entire house in under five minutes even before she officially was its mistress.

Jane gave the housekeeper leave to employ four more maids and three more for the kitchens than had been requested. Jane had her own lady's maid, so the housekeeper did not need to worry about filling that position.

Bingley had a similar meeting with the butler, Mr. Haverson, a man of one and fifty years whose wife, Bingley was told, was a very good seamstress. He informed Bingley how many footmen he thought he needed in addition to the one existing man.

He was authorised to employ the nine he had asked for, plus five more. They discussed the empty wine cellar and library. Bingley informed his butler that both would be stocked before he took residence. Before Haverson was dismissed, he was told to have his wife contact the housekeeper, as the new master knew that his fiancée would be very happy with a seamstress on staff. Next Bingley met with Barrow, the head gardener.

"Mother Bennet? Would you mind verifying I am on the right path?" Bingley asked Fanny to join him. Bingley told Barrow to work with the steward to hire as many under gardeners as he needed to restore the gardens to their former glory.

The herculean task would be to affect as much repair as possible to the gardens before the Bingleys took up residence. Fanny's opinion was canvassed regarding her thoughts on how to restore the gardens.

Lastly, Bingley met with the steward, Mr. Anthony Timmons. He had been the steward at the Meadows for over ten years and was three and forty years old. He, his wife and three children lived in the steward's house a little under a half mile from the manor house.

Bingley authorised the steward to start repairs on the existing tenant houses and the six empty ones as soon as the sale was final, and the deed was in his hands. At the same time, he told Timmons to give Barrow whatever he needed in men and resources to fix the gardens.

Bingley laid out his plan to attract tenants to fill the empty tenant farms, and the improvements he intended to make on the estate. The steward agreed the scope of all equalled the aim to raise the income by two to three thousand pounds per annum and was very realistic.

Once everything Jane and Bingley needed to impart to their new household staff was completed, they left a very happy group of servants and senior staff behind who saw the new master and mistress of the Meadows were very good people who cared about their estate, and with the relief of now knowing it would be very pleasant to work for the Bingleys.

The fortnight flew by with lots of activities; soon they were all on the way to Hertfordshire to prepare for Lizzy and Darcy's wedding.

CHAPTER 20

There had been a flurry of activity of wedding preparation since they had arrived back at Longbourn and Netherfield Park. Mrs. Hill and the very competent Longbourn servants had everything well in hand, and Hill had followed the instructions from her mistress and Miss Lizzy to the letter.

For this stay, the Fitzwilliams joined Darcy, Bingley, the Hursts, and Anne de Bourgh at Netherfield Park to take some pressure off the servants and the Hills as the final preparations for the wedding were made. Only Georgiana Darcy stayed at Longbourn to be with her Bennet sisters. Three days before the wedding, the Gardiners arrived at Longbourn.

Six-year-old May Gardiner was to be the flower girl. Jane would stand up with Lizzy and the now former Colonel, the Honourable Mr. Richard Fitzwilliam, would stand up with his cousin and soon to be brother. Bingley did not begrudge Richard the position as he knew the two cousins had been as close as brothers for the whole of their lives.

With Meryton only a four-hour journey from London, friends would be coming on the day of the wedding. They were to be married by Darcy's cousin, Archibald Darcy, the Archbishop of Canterbury, who would arrive on the morrow, two days before the ceremony.

Richard Fitzwilliam had returned from town the day before. The Bennets and the Gardiners had joined the Netherfield Park party for dinner to celebrate the selling of Richard's commission and his official honourable discharge from His Majesties Own Royal Dragoons.

As sad as General Atherton had been to lose an officer of Richard Fitzwilliam's calibre, the Countess and her soon-to-be daughter Mary were ecstatic Richard would never have to go to war again. The man himself felt relief after trading the uncertainty of the army for the peace and love that would be his life from now on.

Darcy spent almost every waking hour of every day at Longbourn with his beloved Lizzy. Luckily with a mother as understanding as Lizzy's, they were only disturbed if no one else knew their preferences.

At times, when they walked in the park, up to Oakham Mount, or rode their horses, they were chaperoned by Kitty, Georgie, Tom, and James, either all four or some combination thereof.

The day before the wedding they sat with Darcy's cousin, the Archbishop of Canterbury, in a formal meeting any clergyman marrying a couple would normally have. It turned out to be rather less formal than what the couples expected.

"William, I can see you and my soon to be cousin have made a love match, just as I did with my wonderful Eugenia and your late father did with his Anne." The Archbishop smiled warmly at Lizzy before again meeting his cousin's eyes.

"We most certainly have made a love match, Cousin Archibald. I do not know what I have done to be lucky enough to have secured the love of this wonderful, caring, and compassionate woman," Darcy agreed with a dreamy look as he locked eyes with his beloved.

"I am the lucky one William. You are the best man I know, and I am blessed to become your wife on the morrow," Lizzy replied sweetly.

She marvelled at how relaxed she felt because this

was the natural next step in their journey, and she looked forward to each one. The archbishop was amused and knew without his presence the two lovers would be lost in their own world.

"No need to argue over who had the biggest share of luck in your love for one another. I would say you are equally blessed. William, I have no doubt your parents are shining their love down on you from heaven.

"I can confidently say they would whole heartedly approve of your Elizabeth. Although they are by God's side now, they are still sorely missed. My late father Gerald loved his older brother, your grandfather, Gilroy, to distraction as they were the only two Darcy sons. Although George was more than two decades younger than me, I always enjoyed spending time with my father's favourite nephew. I am sure my parents and yours are celebrating your good fortune on high," he offered soothingly to both.

Both Darcy and Elizabeth expressed their emotions in tears that ran down their cheeks in reaction to what the archbishop had said. It was something Darcy had needed to hear because the closer his wedding was, the more he missed his parents and wished they were there to witness his marriage to the love of his life. Darcy's cousin could not have said a more perfect thing, and it caused the unacknowledged sadness of his parents not being there to lift.

"Now now, you two, I understand why and appreciate that my words gave ease and relief, but there is truly no more need for tears. Tomorrow you will join your lives together for eternity, and a more suited couple I have never had the honour of conducting the holey sacraments of marriage for," he smiled benevolently.

"Thank you for what you said regarding my parents, Cousin Archie. Until you did, I had not realised how sad I had been that they were not here," Darcy replied.

"They are here; they are and always will be a part of you, my love," Lizzy said as she placed her hand over his heart.

"Your fiancée has the right of it, William. They are always with both you and Georgie," the Archbishop agreed.

In acceptance of the fact his parents were and would always be with him, Darcy lifted his countenance to the heavens and held his Lizzy's hand. "Mother, Father, this is the woman I love, Elizabeth Bennet, she is the best thing that has ever happened to me and although no one can ever replace you mother, I know she will be an excellent mistress of our estates and houses. Her family has accepted both Georgie and me without reservation and for ourselves, not what they can gain from us," he offered in reverence and a level of joy he had not yet been able to feel when talking to his parents until now.

"I would have been honoured to meet both of you, and I promise I will always love and cherish your son," Lizzy added gently, her eyes lifted to the heavens.

With a tear running down his cheek at the touching scene before him, the Archbishop waved the couple away as the emotions in the room were thick enough to cut with a knife.

~~~~~~~/~~~~~~~

That night after a pre-wedding dinner at Netherfield Park, Fanny Bennet knocked lightly on Elizabeth's bedchamber door. On hearing the invitation to enter, she sat on the bed with her second daughter and held Lizzy's hand.

"This is your last night we have sole claim on you as a daughter living under our roof. Tomorrow your William will have the honour, and I dare say pleasure, of your protection, though you must know all of us will protect and love you all of your days. He really understands you Lizzy, and your father and I are equally happy and relieved your marriage will be a true partnership, which is the only kind of marriage in which we knew you would find your own happiness. Tomorrow night will be your wedding night and I need to talk to you about what to expect in the marriage bed," Fanny offered softly. With a blush rising in her cheeks Lizzy nodded for her mother to proceed.

"The intimacies of the marriage bed are not something to be feared, especially not with someone who loves you the way your William clearly feels for you. When there is love like the two of you share, the marriage bed will be a wonderful, even pleasurable experience for both of you. Anyone that advises their daughter to *lie back and tolerate* the relations between man and woman has no idea of what they speak.

"Never be afraid to inform William of what you like, and do not like, and let him know you want to know the same from him. Just as you want your marriage to be a true partnership Lizzy, the same is true of the marriage bed. My wish for you is that you will discover it is as pleasurable to give as to receive, and never be ashamed of the relations you will have in private with your husband. A good relationship in the marriage bed enhances your marriage as a whole and gives a depth of joy you will both benefit from.

"I will not lie to you Lizzy; there will be some pain and blood the first time, but it is only the first time when this should happen. The pain will be but a moment and marks your becoming a woman in every sense of the word. William cares about you so if you need to stop for a moment at that point, I am sure he will understand. He is a man who will never force you to do that which is unacceptable to you. That is why telling each other what you enjoy, and do not enjoy, is so very important.

"If you never think of your relations with your husband as a chore, they will never be so. No matter what anyone else may say, both the husband and wife deriving pleasure from the marriage bed is a good thing and does not make you a wanton, nor is it a sin to love your husband as only a wife can.

"Both you and William are passionate people, so I believe you will both take much pleasure in your marriage, both out of and in the marriage bed. Never be afraid to be spontaneous, and regardless of what society professes, night-time is not the only acceptable time for relations with your beloved husband. Whenever the two of you have privacy and you both desire the same thing, it is never wrong.

"I am jumping ahead, but when you are with child there is no reason to stop having relations with your husband until you feel it is too hard for you as you approach your lying in.

"Remember, you will have a partnership, and like any good and equal partnership the shared experience of love, passion, and pleasure will be very fulfilling. Do you have any questions for me Lizzy? If you feel the need, I can summon your aunt Maddie to see you and talk to you as well." Fanny gently squeezed her daughter's hand.

After she calmed down at the thought of the pleasure and experiences she would start to share with her husband starting on the morrow, Elizabeth shook her head. "No Mama I have no questions. I always love to talk to Aunt Maddie, but your talk was very thorough, so there is no need for more information at this time. Thank you, Mama, you have helped me look forward to the marriage bed with pleasure and not fear." Lizzy squeezed her mother's hand in return.

Mother and daughter shared some memories, some words only they would ever be able to share from moments they had made theirs, then hugged and shared tears of joy. After kissing her second daughter on both cheeks, Fanny Bennet slipped out of her daughter's chambers.

On her way back to the master suite, she could not help feeling a little forlorn that after the service at the Longbourn church on the morrow, she would not have four daughters at home anymore, and would have the hard task of seeing her Lizzy leave with her husband to her own home.

And soon after two more daughters would follow Lizzy into marriage, but at least Mary would only be three miles away. Thankfully there was another four weeks before the double wedding.

~~~~~~~/~~~~~~~

At Netherfield Park, Darcy was experiencing some good-natured teasing from the three married men in residence as they were drinking brandy while playing some billiards.

"Do you need any pointers or advice, William?" the Earl winked at Andrew.

"No thank you, Uncle Reggie, I think I will be just fine." Darcy's colour deepened and he could think of little worse than getting advice on his relations with his Lizzy from his uncle, Andrew, or Hurst.

"Are you sure William? We do not need to give you *the talk*?" Andrew ribbed his cousin.

"Absolutely not, Andrew! I do not need to be mortified the night before Lizzy becomes my wife, thank you very much for not giving it!" Darcy proclaimed.

"Darcy, us *old married men* just want to make sure you know what to do tomorrow night," Hurst jested gleefully, glad to partake in the effort as there was so little he could find to rib Fitzwilliam Darcy about.

"I am not uneducated! I have an extensive library and have studied up on the subject a lot since my engagement," Darcy replied with all the dignity he could muster.

"Theoretical knowledge is not the same as practical,

William," the Archbishop chimed in.

"Not you as well, Cousin Archie! I would have thought at the very least you would not tease me on this subject." Darcy looked at him in horror. He corrected his previous thought, hearing advice about the marriage bed from a priest was infinitely worse than it would be from Hurst, Richard, or his uncle.

"I am but a mere man with all the weaknesses and foibles of most men, I just control them better when I am performing my pastoral duties," the Archbishop said with a wink at his cousin.

"Leave him alone. We all know he is completely besotted with his fiancée so I am sure there will be no issues tomorrow night," Richard chuckled.

"That is rich. You are no less besotted with your Mary. Is your defence of William in hope we will not start in on you and Bingley before your weddings, brother?" Andrew smirked at his younger brother.

"No!" he denied too quickly. "Well, mayhap, Andy, but leave the man alone. We all know we have never seen him so happy before, even before Ramsgate, so let him enjoy his last night in the bachelor state. You would not want to make the man worry so he is not rested for his nuptials on the morrow. You do not want Lizzy angry at you for sending a tired William to the altar. For such a slip of a woman, she can be very scary when she is not pleased," Richard reminded all present.

"Just some good clean fun, William. You know how proud we are of you, and we love you. Elaine and I have thought of you and Georgie as our children much more than niece and nephew, and we always will," his uncle told him as he rested his hand on Darcy's shoulder.

"Thank you for all you have done for us, Uncle Reggie. We could not be happier to have you, Aunt Elaine, and the rest of your family in our lives." Darcy replied for both Georgie and himself.

It was not long after that the men returned to the drawing room where Ladies Matlock and Hilldale, Anne de Bourgh, and Louisa Hurst were having pleasant conversation and enjoying each other's company. An hour later, starting with the Earl and Countess, everyone retired for the night.

Darcy, like his fiancée Lizzy did, took a while before sleep claimed him with the excitement and expectation of their wedding day on the morrow.

~~~~~~~/~~~~~~~

Miss Elizabeth Bennet woke up just after dawn and knew she would not be able to get back to sleep. She pulled the bell to summon her maid, and after dressing in a riding habit, made her way down to the stables collecting some carrots in the kitchens for her horse.

Mercury was saddled and waiting for her as she fed him the treats and rubbed his forehead. She set off with a groom following at a respectful distance toward Oakham Mount. Giving Mercury his head Elizabeth felt exhilarated as her mount galloped across the fields.

On arriving at the base of the mount, she noticed her beloved's horse, Zeus, was tethered there. She handed the accompanying groom Mercury's reigns and luckily had one carrot left that she fed to Zeus who whickered his thanks for the treat.

When she arrived at the top, she saw her beloved as he looked to the east which was ablaze with red and orange light heralding the sun which would soon rise.

Elizabeth silently approached her betrothed as he was lost in his reverie watching the changing colours as the sun was preparing to bless their wedding day with perfect weather. He made an audible gasp as she enfolded her arms around him from behind.

"I was wishing you would come this morning my love, my loveliest Elizabeth," he offered quietly.

"Even though some have the superstition we should not see each other before my father escorts me up the aisle, I am very happy you are here, William." Elizabeth pressed in closer.

"It seems like a dream, but you will be my wife and fulfil my dearest wish in a scant few hours from now, Lizzy. You have no idea how my heart is filled with all of the love I have for you." Darcy's voice had turned husky with emotion.

"I have been pinching myself from the first day I saw you in the drawing room at Longbourn, William. You are the only man in the world I could ever agree to marry. You complete me, and I could not imagine spending the rest of my life with anyone but you." Lizzy's voice hitched with the power of her words.

Their lips met, softly at first but soon their tongues were duelling as the kisses deepened to reflect their growing need for one another. Lizzy let out a moan of satisfaction as his hand grazed her breast, which almost sent them over the edge. With the evidence of ardour clear to be seen, Darcy stepped back just before they tumbled over the precipice of uncontrolled passion.

"Not here, and not now my Lizzy. As much as I want you and have since we first met, we must wait. I have waited seven and twenty years to be with a woman, and I will not dishonour you like this when we are so close to reciting our vows in God's house." Darcy regulated himself, knowing he had to, no matter how difficult it was.

"You...you have never been with a woman?" she looked at him in surprise.

"No, my love, I have never been with another woman. You will be my first and my last, my love," he vowed.

"That means this is a journey of discovery we will

embark on together as equals." She smiled brightly as her love for him washed over her in unending waves.

"Yes, my beloved, as with everything else in our marriage, in this we will be equals as well," Darcy agreed as he leaned his forehead against hers.

The soon to be wed couple stood hand in hand facing the sun as it peeked above the horizon and started its upward journey into the sky to warm the earth below. After watching for a while and feeling its warming rays, the couple descended, mounted their horses, and parted ways as they galloped into destiny.

They would soon meet and join their lives forever at the very church Fanny Bennet had once beseeched God's grace over sixteen years previously.

CHAPTER 21

O n leaving Mercury with the capable groom, Lizzy made her way to the breakfast parlour where she joined the family to break her fast.

"Why did you not wake James and me to join you on your ride, Lizzy? After today it will be a while until we can ride with you again. We leave for Cambridge on the morrow," Tom Bennet asked.

"I will miss you both as well, Tom, and everyone else. I will see you at Jane and Mary's wedding, and do not forget when Mama and Papa collect you for the Christmastide term break you will all be joining us at Pemberley for the festive season, so we will be seeing each other, Lizzy reassured her brother.

"I know that, but I will miss you ever so much, Lizzy," he sighed resignedly.

"Me also!" James chimed in.

"I will miss you and my sisters, and Mama and Papa as well, but I promise we will see each other quite often and I will write to you. Do not forget that even if I were not marrying my William today, I would only see you on your breaks from school," Elizabeth offered placatingly.

Tom and James acknowledged the truth of what Elizabeth said, but they knew there would be a major change to the family dynamic today, and another, possibly even larger one in four weeks when Jane and Mary wed.

"Before you know it, Mama and Papa will collect you from Cambridge and you two boys will be joining Georgie and me with Lizzy and William at Pemberley, and we will all have a very good time. Do not forget the Fitzwilliams, the Gardiners, the Hursts, Anne, Mary and Richard, and Jane and Charles will all be there as well," Kitty stated in sympathy, as she knew exactly how they felt.

"We know that, Kitty." James replied with a tight smile. "However, it will be different when you, Tom, and I are the only Bennet children still living at Longbourn."

"Life would be very boring if there was never change, my sons," Bennet stated gently as he walked in.

"We know Papa," answered Tom on behalf of his brother and himself. "We will just miss our sisters, that is all."

"Missing your sisters is normal and natural. Do not forget Mary will be with Richard at Netherfield Park, and we will be visiting Pemberley and Longfield Meadows during the summers. With your being at Cambridge, you will see your sisters almost as much as if they were still living here," Fanny pointed out with a genuine smile.

What better proof that she and Thomas had done well guiding them into loving, kind people than in a moment of change there was regret at the losses of those they loved from their everyday lives.

"Yes Mama," the boys chorused.

"Miss Lizzy, it is time. I instructed Arseneault to have a bath ready for you after you broke your fast." Fanny stood.

Elizabeth nodded her acquiescence to her mother, going around the table to kiss everyone on the cheek. With that, Elizabeth Bennet went up to her chambers to get ready for the biggest day of her life so far.

~~~~~~~/~~~~~~~

After her bath, she was assisted into her wedding dress by Jane, her mother, and her lady's maid. The creation by Madame Chambourg was one of a kind, and it was exquisite. Fanny Bennet strung an elegant necklace of pearls around her daughter's neck. Her maid Jacqui assisted Elizabeth to fasten the matching earrings, and her hairpins had pearl heads which stood out beautifully with Elizabeth's raven coloured hair.

A half hour before the ceremony, Elizabeth took one long look around her now packed-up bedchamber where she had slept for the last twelve years of her life. She would miss Longbourn as the home of her childhood, but she had no regrets.

In a little over a half hour, it would no longer be the home of her heart. Considering who would be waiting at the altar in the nave of the Church, Elizabeth Bennet had to admit her heart was with William, and she was at home with him, no matter what walls gave them shelter.

Fanny, Mary, Kitty, Tom, and James Bennet made the short walk with the Gardiners and Georgiana Darcy to the Longbourn Church. They entered to find it was full and greeted neighbours as they took their seats in the Bennet Pews, on the right in the front.

Across the aisle sat the Fitzwilliams, Bingley, Anne de Bourgh, and the Hursts. Darcy stood with Richard Fitzwilliam and the Archbishop in front of the altar. The Church was very tastefully decorated with white and yellow flowers and the forest green bows set them off perfectly.

Elizabeth took her father's arm, and with Jane holding the dress' train, made the short walk to the entrance to the Church where George and May Gardiner were waiting for the bride with their mother in the vestibule. Madeline Gardiner kissed her niece on the cheek and then entered the church, signalling to the archbishop that the bride was ready.

The inner vestibule doors were opened, and May Gardiner walked up the aisle, dropping white daisy petals as she did. She was followed by her brother George who had a pillow with the rings, which he handed to Richard Fitzwilliam and then joined his family in the pew. Once he sat, the ethereally beautiful Jane Bennet walked up the aisle and the doors closed behind her.

Bingley's eyes were glued to the vision that was his fiancée, praying the next four weeks would fly by. Once Jane reached the altar, the Archbishop gave a signal, the congregation stood and then the doors opened one more time.

The sun's rays were behind Elizabeth, and Darcy thought she looked like an angel with the aura of light until the doors were closed. Without the bright light behind her, he could see her dress of off-white silk with gold trim, there was a layer of a fine white meshed organza that had pearls that matched her jewellery and hair pins. Elizabeth's veil was made of the same material and also decorated with pearls.

How he loved his gorgeous Lizzy! He could not imagine a more beautiful woman anywhere in the world. A few steps from the altar, Bennet lifted the veil, kissed his daughter on the cheek, and placed her hand on Darcy's arm. The couple walked up the steps to face the Archbishop who commenced the service from the Book of Common Prayer.

"Dearly beloved, we are gathered together here in the sight of God, and in the face of this congregation, to join together this Man and this Woman in holy Matrimony…"

They soon reached the point when Darcy was asked if he took Lizzy to be his wife, his clear and loud baritone "I do" was heard by all but only those in front saw his smile.

When Lizzy was asked the same question about William, she announced "I will, most definitely!" with the pleasure of knowing she meant it with her whole heart.

The Archbishop asked who gave the bride to the husband to marry, Bennet stated "I do" with a tear in his eye as he took Lizzy's hand and offered a gentle squeeze more so to feel her squeeze his in return. The Archbishop took Lizzy's hand from her father and placed it in Darcy's hand. They then recited their vows:

"I, Fitzwilliam George Alexander Darcy, take thee Elizabeth Rose Bennet to be my wedded Wife, to have and to hold from this day forward, for better for worse, for richer or for poorer, in sickness and in health, to love and to cherish, till death us do part, according to God's holy ordinance; and thereto I pledge thee my troth." Darcy's voice deepened during the recitation, the intensity of his emotions showing.

Next, Elizabeth recited her vows and then the couple released each other's hands and Richard Fitzwilliam placed the rings on the pages of the Archbishop's open bible. The archbishop took Lizzy's ring and handed it to Darcy who placed it on the fourth finger on Lizzy's left hand and recited the words after the Archbishop read them.

Although not normally done, the process was repeated when Lizzy placed a ring on the fourth finger of Darcy's left hand and repeated the words William had just said to her.

After the giving and receiving of rings, they knelt as the Archbishop intoned a prayer of blessing. Once the prayer was complete, he joined their right hands together. *"Those whom God hath joined together let no man put asunder."*

"Forasmuch as Fitzwilliam and Elizabeth have consented together in holy wedlock, and have witnessed the same before God and this company, and thereto have given and pledged their troth either to the other, and have declared the same by giving and receiving of a ring and by joining of hands; I pronounce that they be Man and Wife. In the Name of the Father, and of the Son, and of the Holy Ghost. Amen.

"God the Father, God the Son, God the Holy Ghost, bless, preserve, and keep you; the Lord mercifully with his favour look upon you; and so fill you with all spiritual benediction and

grace, that ye may so live together in this life, that in the world to come ye may have life everlasting. Amen," the Archbishop concluded.

Once the final blessing was given, there were many shouts of congratulations from the congregation of family, friends, and neighbours. The newlyweds followed the Archbishop to the registry where the local parson and his clerk had the parish's register open to the page where first Darcy signed and then Elizabeth, signed the name Bennet for the last time. Jane and Richard signed as witnesses.

After congratulating them, the parson, who had known Elizabeth since she was five years old followed the Archbishop, the two who had stood up with them, and the clerk out to give the newlyweds some privacy.

"Mrs. Darcy." Darcy looked down at his wife, the words a benediction of their own.

"How well that sounds, Mr. Darcy," Elizabeth whispered up to him.

Anything else they may have wanted to say was lost in a series of increasingly passionate, and deepening kisses. After they put themselves to rights, they exited the registry to the waiting arms and congratulations of their family.

Once the family, which now *officially* included the Fitzwilliams, congratulated the newlywed couple, the party made the walk back to the manor house to partake in the sumptuous wedding breakfast that was being laid out.

The ballroom was set up with tables along the walls laden with many dishes of food. There were many tables and chairs for the guests to sit and eat in comfort, with a raised platform with one long table for the bride and groom, and their family.

The newlyweds did not want to be separated, so they walked together to each of the tables to thank the guests for coming to share in their day and accept the good wishes of those that had come. Each and every time somebody addressed her as Mrs. Darcy, Elizabeth felt a thrill. Oh, how she loved to hear her new appellation.

The Darcys had been circulating for about two hours when Darcy asked his new wife if she was ready to leave, to which she nodded. She went up to her former chambers where Jane's Abigail, de Chambé, was waiting to help her as Jacqui was already on the way to Darcy House in London, along with all of the new Mrs. Darcy's belongings that had been packed up at Longbourn, which was their first stop on their journey as husband and wife.

Once she had changed into her traveling clothes and her magnificent wedding dress had been hung, covered, and put in a small trunk to go with them, Elizabeth Rose Darcy took one last look around her the bedchamber of her girlhood.

She was both sad to leave, while at the same time, extremely happy to be married and leaving with her William. From this day onward she would not have to be parted from her very handsome husband again. After her indulgent look, she closed the door on that chapter of her life and descended the stairs to the new chapter that awaited her.

Her husband was waiting for her at the base of the steps, as was her family that now included Anne de Bourgh as a cousin. The Hursts and Bingley had been included in the party that was to see the newlyweds off, it was only right as they were to become part of the family in four weeks when Bingley married Jane.

Jane, who had always been very close to Lizzy, was the first to hug her. "When will you tell me what Mama told you last night?" Jane whispered in her sister's ear as they hugged.

"Mama will talk to both you and Mary before your wedding. All I will say is her advice is very reassuring and sound," Elizabeth replied in returned a whisper.

"Lizzy, I will miss you so much. I cannot wait to see you in three weeks and hear where you have been on your wedding trip." Jane looked to her newest brother. "William, I am so happy you are my brother and please look after my younger sister." Jane smiled as she looked up at her new brother.

"You know I will, Jane. I will move heaven and earth to see she is happy," Darcy vowed as he bowed his head to her to seal his promise.

"You had better!" young Tom said with a grin. "Just because I am no longer the oldest brother does not mean I will not keep an eye on you."

"I would expect no less from either you or James," Darcy chuckled.

"Do not forget in four weeks you will get two additional older brothers," Richard smirked.

"In your case Richard, a much older brother," James teased the former Colonel.

"Hey! I am only two years older than William, so I am not that old!" Richard retorted with a fake pout.

"Tom, James, do not pick on your older soon-to-be brother. Now move over and let the mother and father of the bride talk to their son and daughter," Bennet grinned, seeing a foreshadowing of many holiday encounters to come.

"Yes, Father," they replied in unison and stepped to the side.

While Fanny Bennet hugged her daughter, Bennet shook his newest son's hand. "We know you will take care of her, Son. Have an enjoyable wedding trip and we will see you back here before the wedding next month," Bennet smiled ambivalently at Darcy. He was sure his Lizzy had married a good man, but at the same time, she had left his protection forever.

"Thank you, Bennet. I look forward to seeing all of you again. Have a pleasant trip taking the twins up to Cambridge on the morrow," Darcy wished.

As mother and daughter hugged, they shed some goodbye tears. "Lizzy, while I have no doubt you have married the best possible man for you. I will miss you so. A mother is so forlorn when her daughters leave their home. Do enjoy your honeymoon, my Lizzy, and make it as pleasurable in every way as we hope for you both." As Fanny said the last, she gave her daughter a wink that had the bride blushing furiously.

"Thank you, Mama, I will miss you as well. We will see each other soon for the double wedding and then before you know it, it will be Christmastide and we will all be together at Pemberley," Lizzy promised.

After Fanny stepped back hugs, kisses, and tears were exchanged with the remaining party. Anne de Bourgh was delighted she was now part of a much larger family circle and squeezed through to be the next to kiss Lizzy and wish her cousin well, shocked into a laugh when Darcy hugged her so hard that he picked her up clear off her feet.

"That is long overdue. I love you dearly as a cousin, Anne, but have had to curtail any demonstration of my cousinly feelings due to others." He kissed the top of her head as she squealed to be let down to Richard's laughter.

"That looks like much fun!" Andrew agreed, sweeping Anne up in his arms and hugging her tight as he reiterated Darcy's sentiments.

Anne was followed by Mary and Kitty, then the Earl, Countess, the Viscount, and his lady wife hugged the bride and groom and said their goodbyes. They were followed by Bingley and the Hursts. That only left Georgiana and Richard. Georgiana looked between the two and then threw herself into her new sister's arms.

"Have a wonderful time, Lizzy, and make sure you make my brother laugh as much as possible. It is so good to see him back to how he was before our mother passed. I was very young when she passed but Mrs. Reynolds has told me many stories about how he was with Mama.

"I thank you for gifting me with three new sisters that come with you and two more brothers. Our family is so enriched by all of you becoming part of it." Georgiana hugged Elizabeth ever tighter as she listed her causes for happiness.

"Thank you, Georgie. You took very good care of my William until it was time for him to come find me. I am very happy to have you as another sister. We will see you when we get back and then after the weddings, you and Kitty will join us on the journey back to Pemberley." Elizabeth pulled back and kissed her sister's cheek.

"I cannot believe you are the same cousin I visited all those weeks ago when Bingley extended his invitation for me to join you at Netherfield. Who could have envisaged all that has happened since? Best of all, you are fully returned to us all now, William.

"The dark, brooding man has gone forever. Lizzy would never accept that sort of behaviour, which is why she is perfect for you. She is not awed by you and will never back down from telling you when you are wrong. You could have not found a better wife, Cousin." Darcy and Fitzwilliam shook hands then Darcy found himself enfolded in a bear hug by his cousin who would soon be his brother.

"Thank you, Richard. Believe me when I tell you that I am not sorry to see that version of myself banished forever. You are so right about my Lizzy. I may be far bigger than her, but I would hate to get on her bad side and have that temper turned on me," Darcy admitted.

"That is a very wise decision. I would willingly ride into battle again rather than face her wrath," Richard agreed.

Lizzy joined her husband and wrapped her hand around his arm. "Richard, I am not that scary!" she denied.

"Oh yes you are!" Was the simultaneous reply from all of the present party that had known Lizzy for a long time.

"Richard, you know how happy we are you will never have to ride into battle again." Lizzy smiled sweetly after she had glared at everyone, proving their point.

"I love you too, Lizzy." Richard hugged his new cousin.

"Have a very enjoyable trip, Brother. I will miss you, but I am so happy to be staying with Kitty and the rest of the Bennets. Thank you for giving me such a family." Georgiana looked up at him with such joy he thought she might actually be happier than he was, though he could not fully credit the thought.

"The Bennets are such a loving and accepting family, are they not? I am very happy to have my sister back. You have no idea how proud of you I am for the way you stood up to and confronted your demons and have become the very woman you were born to be. You have grown and matured so much Georgie, and it all started after the Bennets came into our lives.

"Would that we had met the Bennets years ago when they were on a visit to Snowhaven, but we cannot change the past. All we can do is look forward with optimism to the future." Darcy smiled down at his sister.

"Ha! If you had, Lizzy would have beaten you with wooden swords and you would have run away every time she was near so this event could not have occurred," Andrew ribbed.

"She certainly made you run, Son," the Earl guffawed as he clapped Andrew on the shoulder when he protested that no one needed to be reminded of that.

Brother and sister hugged and kissed each other on the cheek. The new Mrs. Darcy hugged each one of the party again while her husband did the same. Once the second round of hugs was complete, Mr. and Mrs. Darcy boarded the coach, the largest of the current Darcy equipages, drawn by a matched set of six, started to move up the drive leaving a waving party behind it with not a few tears shed.

Once the coach disappeared from view, those seeing the newlyweds off returned to the wedding breakfast.

CHAPTER 22

The new Mrs. Darcy was gently shaken awake by her husband. She felt disoriented and could tell the carriage was no longer in motion. "We have arrived, Mrs. Darcy. We are at Darcy House, one of your new homes." Darcy gazed lovingly at his wife.

"I am so very sorry, William. I did not realise just how tired I was. I did not manage to sleep much last night, for some unfathomable reason I was very excited." Elizabeth looked up at him playfully.

"Nothing to apologise for, my beautiful wife, my Lizzy. I too slept for the same reason as you did. I only awoke a short while ago, but you looked so peaceful I did not want to wake you." He hugged her tightly to himself.

Lizzy noticed the door was still closed, so she fixed her clothing and hair and when she was done, her husband knocked on the door and the waiting footman opened it for them to alight. The Killions were ready for the master and new mistress on the steps in front of the house.

"We wish you and Mrs. Darcy congratulations on your wedding. We are sure you will be very happy for many years. Welcome home master and mistress," the housekeeper offered as the Darcys started up the steps.

"Thank you, Mrs. Killion, Mr. Killion," Elizabeth Darcy inclined her head towards Mrs. Killion.

The Darcys followed the housekeeper and butler into the house while footmen unloaded what had come with them, which was not much as a carriage with the bulk of their things, Darcy's valet and Elizabeth's lady's maid had left for town directly after the wedding ceremony.

As Killion closed the door, Mrs. Killion started to introduce Mrs. Darcy to the Darcy House servants that were lined up in two neat rows. Some of them were known to Elizabeth from her tour and the time she had spent at the house while they were all in London before the wedding.

Once she had greeted and said a few words to each of the servants, shocking the ones she had previously met by remembering their names, the newlyweds went up to the master suite to change out of their travel attire. Darcy's valet was ready for his master with a change of clothes. The lady's maid was waiting for Mrs. Darcy in her chambers.

Lizzy remembered her chambers from her tour and was very happy with the redecorated rooms and the newly arrived furniture from Chippendale. Everything that had been removed from her chambers was being stored until Georgiana had a chance to examine it and determine if she wanted to retain any of her late mother's old furniture.

Her lady's maid had just helped her mistress change when there was a knock on the door between the shared sitting room and Lizzy's bedchamber.

"Come in, please," Elizabeth invited.

"Thank you, Arseneault. You may go," Darcy instructed.

"*Oui monsieur.*" She curtsied and quietly exited the rooms.

"Why, may I ask, did you summarily dismiss..." Elizabeth started to tease her husband but anything else that she was about to say remained unsaid as her husband silenced her with a very deep kiss.

Her arms slid around his neck as his passionate wife pulled him against her body until there was no daylight between them. When they finally broke the kiss, her husband looked down at her and they looked intently into each others' eyes.

"I think we should lock the doors," Darcy suggested, his voice husky with passion and desire for his wife.

At his wife's nodded agreement, Darcy walked over to do just that then quickly was back and urgently pulling his wife into his arms once again. *'Now I will discover if what I have studied in the books about giving my Lizzy pleasure can be put into practice,'* Darcy thought as he again kissed her, the urgency of the kisses intensifying with every sigh or moan. His hand roamed over her breasts, and she let out a moan of desire.

She managed to open his waistcoat and shirt, and for the first time, she rubbed her hands over his muscled torso with a light downy covering of hair on his chest. The feel to both of them was electric.

He undid the buttons at the back of her dress, and he marvelled at her lily-white pert breasts with the pink nipples that were already hard. His hand ran down her leg and then under her skirt toward that private place that was pulsing and already moist.

~~~~~~~/~~~~~~~

Afterward, with their naked bodies intertwined, they languidly lay on her bed. Her mother had been correct; there had been a little momentary burst of pain. Her William had stopped when she had winced and waited until she signalled him to continue.

No, she had certainly not laid there unmoving like some said should be done, she had followed her mother's advice and when they both achieved release, the ecstasy had been unimagined. Darcy thanked his lucky stars his father had left the special *educational* books for him locked in the study, and he was nothing if not a good student.

He was beyond pleased he had been able to translate

his theoretical knowledge into practice so effectively as he had worried just before their coupling whether he would be able to do so. One time had not been enough for either of them. There had been a second time which was sweeter, slower, and more deliberate but just as pleasurable if not more so.

There was some blood on the sheet, but it did not embarrass her, it was expected of a maiden. After agreeing to meet in their private sitting room once they had both refreshed themselves, they reluctantly climbed off the bed. Once her husband had returned to his chambers, Lizzy rang for her abigail.

"*Oui madmois...*I am sorry, I mean yes, Mrs. Darcy," the abigail offered in deference.

"Jacqui, please have a bath filled for me. And if you could have some maids remake my bed, I would appreciate it." Now she did blush some as she instructed her maid.

"Right away, Mrs. Darcy." Jacqui curtsied.

The new Mrs. Darcy luxuriated in her bathtub. She thought about how good it would be to share the one in her husband's bathing room with said husband. Thinking about what they would do in the bath made her feel warm in anticipation of the pleasures that could be enjoyed.

After her maid assisted her to bathe and then dry off, Lizzy got dressed in one of her new day dresses. She noticed the bed had been remade and looked like it did before she had become William's wife in every way.

Thinking about the sublime enjoyment of the act with her beloved husband caused her to blush while her lady's maid was styling her hair. Yes, loving one's husband did not have to be restricted to any certain time of the night. It was the right time when they wanted it to be, and they were assured of privacy.

When his wife sashayed into the shared sitting room,

Darcy was struck by her beauty and poise all over again. *'Thank you, oh Lord our God, for allowing me to find then fall in love with this woman. She is beauty itself both inside and out, and I still cannot believe she condescended to be my wife.'* His reverie was shattered when his wife threw her arms around his neck as she sat down on his lap and kissed him soundly.

"Husband, do you not think the time has come to share where we will be on our wedding trip for the next three weeks?" she asked coyly.

"You already know I can never deny you anything that you ask of me, my Lizzy. Tomorrow morning, we travel south toward Brighton. My honourable departed father took my mother to the area for their wedding trip. He leased a cottage that sits on a bluff and has a good view of Brighton, and my dear departed mother liked it so much he purchased the cottage for her.

"It is named Seaview Cottage. It is staffed by a housekeeper, a cook, two maids, and two footmen. We will only take Arseneault and Carstens with us. The carriage, driver, and attendant servants will be housed at the Fox and Bugle Inn close by. If we require the use of the coach one of the footmen will ride to summon it. The servants at Seaview are very discreet, and we will only see them when we need them." He watched her happiness grow.

"That sounds perfect, William. You have no idea how much I love the sea, and I adore sea bathing," Elizabeth shared excitedly.

"Then you are in luck, my love. There is a secluded cove with some beach below the house that can only be reached by a path from our property. It has been a warm summer, so I am sure we will go sea bathing and whatever else we decide to do while we are in the water." Darcy wiggled his eyebrows as he said the last to his blushing wife with a very devilish look on his countenance.

The newlyweds sat and talked until they heard the dinner gong. Due to their afternoon activities, they both had a very good appetite. Darcy House's cook was seen to beam with pride at the evidence the master and new mistress liked her cooking exceedingly, judging by the small amount of leftovers the footmen returned to the kitchens.

After dinner Darcy requested and was granted some music by his wife, she sang with her divine angel-like voice as she accompanied herself on the pianoforte. The servants privileged enough to hear the new mistress sing agreed they had never heard better. The Darcys did not dally in the music room for long, they soon ran up the stairs hand-in-hand, very keen to reach the privacy of their suite.

~~~~~~~/~~~~~~~

For most of the more than four hours of travel of the final leg, the newlyweds slept in each other's arms. They had gone to bed early the previous night but had only finally gotten to sleep in the wee hours of the morning. They were both very sated but tired, so they had fallen asleep one after the other just after the carriage departed Darcy House.

At the stop just past the halfway point, the servants, upon seeing the master and mistress fast asleep, had not disturbed them. Darcy woke about twenty minutes prior to arriving at Seaview Cottage, and he gently woke his slumbering wife.

"Lizzy my darling, my sweet love," he punctuated his words with little feathered kisses to her cheeks, "we are about to arrive. Time to open those fine eyes of yours."

"I slept so well, I even dreamed I had married and was in love with the best of men, then I woke up and saw it was just you," Elizabeth said with a saucy, impertinent, and teasing smile he loved so well.

"Just you wait, my impertinent wife; you will pay for that comment later," Darcy scowled with mock affront.

"Do not make promises unless you intend to keep them, Husband." she volleyed.

As her husband was about to respond to her very forward comment, they both felt the conveyance slow down and it soon came to a halt in front of the cottage. The footman lowered the steps and after alighting, Darcy turned around to hand his wife out of the carriage.

On seeing the house, Lizzy smacked her husband's arm playfully. "This is no cottage, Mr. Darcy, why it is almost as large as Longbourn was before Papa started to enlarge and add wings to the house. Cottage indeed!" Lizzy looked at her husband questioningly.

"In my defence, Lizzy, the name is, in fact, Seaview Cottage, and it has been referred to as *the cottage* ever since the first time I heard tell about the place," Darcy explained.

Lined up in front of the entrance was the cottage's servants, led by Mrs. Agatha Spencer, the housekeeper. She introduced the cook and the rest of the servants. The footmen that had accompanied the carriage, along with the two Seaview footmen, made quick work of getting the trunks to the master suite.

His valet and her maid unpacked their clothing and personal items with quiet efficiency. After the mistress met with the cook to go over the couple's likes and dislikes, the Darcys retired to their suite for some undisturbed personal time.

~~~~~~~/~~~~~~~

The three weeks flew by. The couple did much walking, riding, reading, and relaxing. They spent as much time learning and teaching each other what they liked, and the few things they did not enjoy, in the privacy of their chambers.

There was a lot of sea bathing on their very private beach and activities in the water that newlyweds in the deepest throes of love enjoyed. Once a week they had the carriage summoned for forays into Brighton to see the sites including promenading past the Prince Regent's Brighton Pavilion. He was not in residence, but it was interesting to see the opulent place the Regent stayed at when in Brighton.

Even though her husband claimed not to like assemblies, the couple went to one and danced only with each other, not caring how scandalised anyone was with a married couple dancing exclusively with one another.

All too soon it was the morning of departure. Darcy left a substantial amount with Mrs. Spencer to be divvied up among the cottage's servants because the Darcys were most happy with the service during their stay there. The bonus was generous enough it essentially doubled the servant's annual pay for that year.

Just before their departure, the young couple pledged they would spend at least two weeks a year at the cottage, even once they were blessed with children. As they had on the trip down to the cottage, the Darcys slept almost all the way back to London, the only difference was they woke when they stopped for a break, then promptly fell back to sleep once they were on the road again. The coach pulled up to Darcy House in the late afternoon and the Darcys were welcomed home by the Killions.

They sent a note over to the Gardiners at Portman Square and received an invitation to join them for a family dinner that evening. Given both had rested on the journey back to London, the invitation was accepted with alacrity.

~~~~~~~/~~~~~~~

The Darcys were announced by the Gardiner's butler. All four children were in the drawing room. Lilly Gardiner, who had just turned twelve, felt very grown up even if she still looked like a young girl. Before dinner, the governess collected the youngest two, May and Peter. Lilly and George were to eat with the adults. The party of six went in to dinner and sat down to enjoy an informal family meal.

"How was your wedding trip, Lizzy?" Madeline Gardiner turned to Elizabeth who was seated to her left as she happily sat between her uncle and aunt she so loved.

"Aunt Maddie, it was so very enjoyable, and our house near Brighton, which my dear husband calls a cottage, is the size Longbourn was before Papa added to it. When you have some time, you must go and relax there. It has a private beach," her aunt noticed Lizzy's blush when she mentioned the beach, "and it is close, but not too close to Brighton. The house has a good number of bedchambers and a very able staff. We had the best time there, and we have pledged to return at least once every year. The views of Brighton and the sea from the property are a sight to see."

"We are so happy for you both. When do you leave for Longbourn?" Aunt Maddie asked.

"I have some business I need to take care of on the morrow, so we will leave on Wednesday morn," Darcy replied.

"When do you depart, Aunt Maddie? If you are here on the morrow, I would love you to come shopping with me while William completes his business," Lizzy requested.

"We depart on Thursday, so if my wife has no conflicts, as far as I know, she is free on the morrow," Uncle Gardiner informed them.

"Yes, Lizzy dear, Edward is correct. I am available, so what do you say I meet you at Darcy House at ten in the morning?" Aunt Gardiner asked.

"That sounds perfect, Aunt Maddie, I look forward to spending some time with you on the morrow," Elizabeth smiled brightly.

At the end of the meal Lilly and George said their good nights and took themselves upstairs to the nursery and then there was a brief separation of the sexes. Darcy sat with his new uncle discussing mutual business interests while the ladies retired to the drawing room.

"You look so very happy, Lizzy; you are glowing with contentment," Madeline offered as soon as they were alone in the drawing room.

"Oh, Aunt Maddie, being married to William is better than my wildest imaginings. He is so solicitous of my thoughts and feelings; we truly have a partnership in every sense of the word. He is so generous with me, and I love our private time together." Although she blushed as she said the last, Elizabeth Darcy knew she could share anything with her aunt without censure or judgement.

"I am going to assume what your mother told you about the marriage bed is true?" Madeline smiled as her niece nodded emphatically. "Being in love and caring one for the other makes all of the difference. I could never imagine what things must be like in a marriage of convenience. It would be dreadfully horrid to be in a loveless marriage."

"Luckily no one in our extended family will ever be in a cold, heartless marriage," Lizzy responded "None need to marry if they do not want to and come Friday morning two more of my sisters will enter the marriage state, both very much in love with their fiancés. How was the time with Mary and Jane while they were here shopping? What was it, about ten days ago?".

"The girls had an enjoyable time shopping. I was with them as well as your mother, Anne de Bourgh, Louisa Hurst, and Ladies Matlock and Hilldale. They decided on perfect wedding dresses at Madame Chambourg's modiste shop. The wedding dresses, along with each trousseau, were delivered to them after the final fittings. Anne ordered herself a whole new wardrobe, she was so happy to get rid of the horrid fashions Lady Catherine used to choose for her," Madeline conveyed happily.

"I dare say she was. I cannot wait to see what my sisters acquired for their trousseaus and Anne's new clothing as well. As much as I have loved the time with my husband, I have missed my family and am looking forward to seeing them on Wednesday. We will leave early and be there well before luncheon." Lizzy squeezed her aunt's hand to share her excitement.

The men re-joined their ladies, and they spent a comfortable evening enjoying each other's company then the Darcys took their leave after thanking the Gardiners profusely and returned home to go to sleep, well at least to go to bed.

CHAPTER 23

Early Wednesday afternoon when the Darcy coaches came to a halt in front of Longbourn, everyone, including the Netherfield Park party, spilled out of the house to welcome the Darcys back to Hertfordshire.

As soon as her husband handed her down from the carriage, Lizzy was surrounded by four sisters all wanting to hug her. Next, her mother approached with a tear in her eye, she told her second eldest she could see the glow of happiness emanating from the couple, and she was overjoyed her beautiful Lizzy had found felicity in her marriage.

Darcy was swarmed by his four sisters after they had hugged his wife. Georgiana Darcy hugged him especially tightly and kissed his cheek. The rest of the party welcomed them more sedately, but still with enthusiasm.

Once the welcome and hugs subsided Elizabeth looked around and noticed who was missing. "Mama, where is Papa?" Lizzy frowned.

"He left on Monday to go get your brothers from Cambridge. Do not make yourself uneasy, you will see him by dinner on the morrow." Mother and daughter held onto each other as everyone preceded them into the manor house. "You are glowing; I see you are as happy in your marriage as we suspected you would be. Are *ALL* aspects of your marriage good, my Lizzy?"

"Mama, you were so correct in your advice to me

before my wedding. The marriage bed only adds to the felicity and love we both feel. He is my other half in every sense of the word; I could not imagine anyone being happier than I am with William." Lizzy blushed happily.

"It warms my heart to hear this. I knew how it would be, but to hear you confirm what your father and I suspected fills me with happiness and gratitude. I have assigned you and William to the lavender suite, unless the two of you want to fit into your old bedchamber?" she teased.

"No, Mama, the lavender suite is perfect. I am so happy to be visiting Longbourn, but it no longer feels like home, my home is whichever of our houses I am residing at with William," Lizzy admitted, hoping her mother understood.

"As it should be!" Fanny agreed. "Now, away with you, go change out of your travelling attire," Fanny said as she gave Elizabeth a playful tap on her posterior.

~~~~~~~/~~~~~~~

Her husband had just left to go down to the drawing room after changing and Elizabeth was finishing up with the help of her lady's maid when there was a knock on the door. After she called out for the person to enter, the door opened to reveal Jane and Mary Bennet, who would be resigning their last names when they wed on Friday.

"Come in, Jacqui is done." Elizabeth smiled in welcome and motioned for her sisters to sit down. "Jane and Mary, how I have missed you. To what do I owe this honour of a visit before I join everyone in the drawing room?" she teased them.

"Well..." Jane said tentatively with much embarrassment, "We were wondering if, as an *old married lady*," the statement caused Elizabeth to playfully swat her sister's arm, "if there was any wisdom you can impart to us about married life...ahem...well about the wedding night." Jane and Mary were both blushing furiously but seemed hopeful.

"Has Mama given you her pre-wedding speech yet?" she asked first.

"She has not spoken to me yet. Has she done so with you, Jane?" Mary inquired.

"No Mary, not as yet," Jane replied softly.

"Mama spoke to me the night before my wedding. What she imparted was all true and excellent advice. I will leave it to her to have that talk with the two of you, I would not usurp her pleasure at sharing the moment with you as she did with me. I promise you if you listen to her and apply what she tells you to your marriage, you will not go wrong.

"The only thing I will add is unlike we have heard matrons from the area postulate, the act is not unpleasant and something to be *endured* at all. In fact, quite the opposite is true. The act is an extension of your love for each other, and as you both love your fiancés, I am sure you will enjoy and crave your private time with your husbands as much as I do with mine." Telling her still maiden sisters thus only caused a slight blush on her own cheeks.

"Oh Lizzy, thank you. We were just a little nervous, but to see the way you glowed as you stepped down from the carriage along with what you told us dispels all of that anxiety for me," Mary sighed in relief as she reached out and took one of Elizabeth's hands.

"That is true for me as well. I am looking forward to Mama's talk, and if I look half as happy being with Charles as you do with William then I will indeed be very happy," Jane offered sincerely.

The sisters hugged each other tightly and left the chamber to join the rest of the family in the drawing room. On entering, Mrs. Darcy went to sit with her husband and by popular request the newlyweds, making sure to omit private information, told everyone about their time at Seaview

Cottage.

Elizabeth first informed all who had not been there that 'cottage' was a misnomer. The Fitzwilliams had stayed at Seaview Cottage a number of times, and when the Darcys extended the invitation to anyone who would like to, to use the house freely when it was available, the Fitzwilliams related the pleasure they had experienced when they holidayed at the house.

The newly married Darcys, Bingley, and Jane were seated together and conversing. After a few minutes, Jane requested of the Darcys if the Bingleys could stay at Seaview for four weeks following their sojourn of a sennight after their wedding in the newly acquired Bingley Town house on Portman Square.

Permission was immediately and happily granted, and Darcy retired to Bennet's study to write an express to Mrs. Spencer so she would have the house ready for the Bingley's arrival in a little more than a sennight.

Conversation then turned to Anne when someone asked what her plans were after the upcoming events. "I will be returning to Rosings Park. Thanks to Uncle Reggie and Cousin Andrew, I now have a very competent steward and any remaining servants that were loyal to Lady Catherine have been weeded out.

"I will, of course, then be joining the family at Pemberley in December as Cousin Lizzy was so generous to invite me, and I hope all of you will join me for Easter this year rather than just William and Richard. I want you to come help me make some positive memories at Rosings Park," she invited hopefully.

"I think this is a grand idea, Niece. I speak for Aunt Elaine and myself in saying we will join you with pleasure." The Earl smiled lovingly at his niece. "My suspicion is visiting Rosings Park shall no longer be a chore."

"Even though my Thomas will not be home until the morrow with the boys, I can tell you with certitude Anne, that the Bennets I can speak for remaining under my roof will be there as well." Fanny smiled sadly as she scanned the room.

The Darcys and the soon to be married couples also accepted. The Hursts, who had not been sure if the invitation included them, were invited directly by Anne so there was no doubt. Anne then asked for the Gardiner's direction so she could invite them. Anne sighed in pleasure as the first house party in over a decade was starting to come together and she was revelling in her much-expanded family circle.

"I just knew you would love Seaview Cottage, Lizzy. How many of your visits to Snowhaven did we not hear you lament our estate was so far from the coast?" the Countess teased Elizabeth.

"You are correct, Aunt Elaine. We did a lot of sea bathing so I will be satisfied until we return there next year. William and I have promised one another we would be there for at least two weeks every year." She smiled lovingly at her husband then again looked at their aunt.

"Uncle Reggie and I are so happy you are now our niece, Lizzy. It has been many years that we have counted your brothers and sisters as nieces and nephews. Now in less than two days I will be able to count a Bennet as a daughter." Elaine looked at Richard and Mary and could not help but smile.

"No happier than I will be to be your daughter, Aunt Elaine. I will soon go from having three brothers to having seven," Mary teased her.

"Seven Mary, I count six?" Richard looked at his betrothed in confusion.

"I think you forgot Mr. Hurst. Charles will be my brother, and Mr. Hurst is his brother, so therefore he will be our brother as well." She looked between them playfully.

"You must all call me Harold then. I am so very touched that you will think of me in such a way, thank you, to all of you," Hurst cleared his throat as he was overcome with gratitude.

As her husband said this, a tear rolled down Louisa Hurst's cheek at the complete acceptance given by people who would be justified to never acknowledge them. She again gave thanks to God her life had taken such a good turn. Their truest gift was sharing their Jane with them, but the love and acceptance they offered was a close second.

Andrew Fitzwilliam stood and held his wife Marie's hand, waiting until he had the attention of the room, which because it was so out of character was not long. "We have an announcement we would like to make. Marie is with child; she felt the quickening yesterday," Andrew reported joyfully.

The announcement led to a round of hearty congratulations, especially from an overjoyed Countess at the thought of her second grandchild. Soon after the congratulations died down, Hill announced dinner was served.

After dinner and entertainment, the Netherfield Park party returned thither. Bingley had ordered the packing up of his and the Hurst's belongings to be carted to their respective homes in town on Friday morning so Netherfield Park would be ready for the newly married Fitzwilliams belongings to move in as their own cart departed for London.

~~~~~~~/~~~~~~~

As expected, Bennet, Tom, and James arrived in the latter part of the afternoon on Thursday. The Darcys, joined by the Gardiners, Kitty, James, and Tom Bennet dined at Netherfield Park so the two brides would have some peaceful time with their parents before they left Longbourn behind on the morrow.

Fanny Bennet's talk with Jane and then Mary went as it had with Lizzy, and they were especially receptive after the talk they had had with Lizzy. And like Lizzy, nothing Mrs. Bennet said made her daughters nervous or apprehensive, they were, after all, very educated, intelligent, and informed young women. And they were very much looking forward to the marriage bed armed with the imparted wisdom of both their mother and their married sister.

Later that evening the four Bennets had a nice dinner, after which Mary and Jane entertained their beloved parents with some music. The party who had been dining at Netherfield Park returned before ten o'clock.

Before everyone left for their chambers to sleep, or at least try to due to the anticipation for the double wedding on the morrow, Jane asked Lizzy and Mary to join her in her bedchamber once they arrived upstairs and both stated that they would be in soon.

"Jane requested Mary and I join her in her chamber before we get into bed for a little while, William. I trust that is acceptable?" Elizabeth smiled as she admired her husband's physique while she waited for his answer.

"Of course it is, my love. I will wait up for you as I want to make sure we get in some good exercise before we sleep." With the anticipation of pleasure to come, a blushing Lizzy kissed her husband then walked to Jane's door and knocked lightly.

"Come in, Lizzy." Came the dulcet tones of her sweet sister's voice.

"Mary must already be here." Lizzy laughed as she looked at her excited sisters. "How are you? Both of you? You will be married to your beloveds in the morning. Mary, are you pleased after your wedding trip you will still be in the neighbourhood near Mama and Papa? Jane, I am ever so happy we will be neighbours." Elizabeth looked from one to the other.

"I am sad to leave Longbourn, but I am very excited to become the mistress of Longfield Meadows," Jane responded. "Thank you again, both you and William, for allowing us to stay at Seaview Cottage and then Pemberley before we move to our estate. We are very much looking forward to the wedding trip." Jane blushed.

"Jane, truly, it is a pleasure. I hope you enjoy the private beach as much as we did." Elizabeth wiggled her eyebrows to leave them in no doubt of what she meant.

"*Lizzy!*" Jane retorted blushing furiously as was her sister Mary.

"Did...did you really have relations outside, at the beach?" Mary asked, caught between shock and longing.

"Yes, Mary we did. It is a completely private beach with only one access path from Seaview. There is no view of the beach unless you are on it. As I am sure Mama told you, having pleasure with the one you love is never wrong, and should not be restricted by time or place so long as you have complete privacy.

"Jane will soon see the truth of my statement when she and Charles stay at the cottage, whether or not they choose to have relations at the beach or in the sea is up to them. Not everyone enjoys the same thing," Lizzy told her sisters.

"We will have to see just how private the beach is Lizzy. The place sounds so nice. You told us that you only saw the servants when you needed them?" Jane blushed at the thoughts now whirling around in her mind causing a frisson of pleasure.

"Yes. We were not the first, nor will be the last I daresay, honeymooning couple they have catered to. After William's father purchased the *cottage*, many friends and family have used it for their wedding trip or as one destination on it, including Marie and Andrew," Lizzy gave the history as it had been provided to her.

"I assume you did not have relations when you had your courses?" Mary asked softly.

"First to your question Mary, I would imagine relations during a woman's courses would not be pleasant. To tell you the truth, Mary and Jane, and I swear both of you to secrecy," she pressed and both nodded, "I have always been so regular and should have had them last week, but they did not come. I have also noticed that my breasts are tender." She blushed with excitement.

"Oh Lizzy, you could already be with child! Have you had any sickness in the mornings yet like some women are afflicted with in the early stages?" Jane reached for her sister's hand and squeezed it excitedly.

"No, Jane. Thankfully I have not had that particular malady yet," Lizzy blushed.

"Have you told William of your suspicions?" Mary asked softly.

"No, I have not. If the signs persist and I miss my coming courses, then I will tell him. And like many of the wise women before us, I think we will wait for the quickening to tell the rest of the family. If this is real, and there are no problems, there should be an announcement when you all join us at Pemberley in December," Elizabeth related, praying it was true.

"We will be aunts, and James and Tom will be uncles. Oh, what joy." Mary gasped.

"Please Mary, keep your voice down. And please remember no one else other than William will be informed until I feel the quickening," Lizzy reminded her sisters quietly.

"Not even to our soon to be husbands? I do not know if I would like to start my marriage with keeping secrets from him," Mary frowned.

"You may both tell your husbands after you are married and on your wedding trips Mary, but only after you are both well away from Longbourn on the morrow, if you choose to share my possible news with them," Lizzy agreed, as she would feel the same.

"It would have been ever so hard to keep this from Charles. He would want to know why I was so anxious and excited for you. If you start to increase, he will notice as we will be with you until September," Jane smiled sweetly.

"Neither of you look worried about tomorrow. Did I not tell you that Mama's talk would help?" Lizzy asked slyly.

"That you did. And what you told Mary and me yesterday only reinforced what Mama told us. After listening to you and Mama, I now feel sorry for all of the matrons we have heard describe the act as a *chore* and to be *endured*. How very sad for them." Jane offered concern for those she did not know, as was often the case with her depth of compassion.

"That is the advantage of making a love match. As Mama told you, relations in the marriage bed in a loving marriage only make the bonds stronger. You become one with the other," Lizzy promised. "But I will reiterate it is very important you are honest about what you like, and what you do not. And ask the same from your husband. That makes all the difference, that depth of honesty."

It was after midnight when the sisters bade each other good night. Two fell asleep dreaming of their wedding night, and one went to bed able to act out her dreams as her husband had stayed awake awaiting her return.

~~~~~~~/~~~~~~~

In the morning, the three Darcys and three Bennet siblings not getting married took a nice ride to ensure the focus was solely on the two brides.

Darcy was to stand up for Bingley, while the Viscount

would stand up for his brother. Jane had Lizzy as her matron of honour, and Kitty would perform the office of maid of honour for Mary. The Gardiner children would perform the same roles as they had when the Darcys wed.

The group of riders returned, broke their fasts with Bennet, and went to change into their church clothes. Once everyone was ready, Fanny led James, Tom, and Georgiana to the church with the Gardiners. Bennet, Elizabeth, and Kitty waited in the entrance hall, joined by Jane and Mary resplendent in the wedding dresses that Madame Chambourg had created for them.

Both were variations of the exquisite gown Lizzy had worn. Jane's was pale pink and Mary's ivory. Bennet took a very deep breath as two of his beautiful daughters approached him. Jane took his right arm and Mary his left as Elizabeth and Kitty held their trains, and they walked the short distance to the Church.

Longbourn church's rector was waiting to conduct the ceremony. Many of those present, who had also been at the Darcys' wedding, were heard to say the ceremony was just as well done. The ceremony was soon over, and the newly married couples were escorted to the registry to sign the register.

As with so many blushing brides, both Jane and Mary felt just a little sadness as they signed the name Bennet for the final time.

Once the two newlywed the couples emerged from the registry, their waiting family gathered around them to offer congratulations. The rest of the invited guests were waiting for them in Longbourn's ballroom.

"I have a sister again." Louisa Hurst looked up into Jane's eyes, hers filled with tears of joy and sisterly love long missed.

"No, you have a bunch of sisters and brothers now!"

Jane told her as she hugged Louisa.

"I have two daughters, at long last." The Countess wrapped Mary in a second hug.

"I am happy to share Mary with you, Elaine, especially as I finally gain Richard as a son." Fanny smiled up at Richard and he bent down and kissed her cheek as he had a hundred times before and would a thousand times more.

"Fanny, I am overjoyed you, Thomas, and all of your children are now all family in fact as well as in feeling. What fun we will have during the holidays to celebrate all of our blessings together." Elaine forced herself to let go of Mary and took Fanny's arm, holding her close as one always does their dearest friend.

"Here here. I second that thought wholeheartedly," the Earl professed. "Bennet and I have been like brothers ever since our days at Trinity College. Mary is my daughter now too, and Lizzy, Jane, and Kitty are my nieces and the twins my nephews in fact but have always been daughters and sons of my heart.

"Marie was an only child, so I am sure she likes having gained so many sisters and brothers today. William and Georgie have always been treated like they were our children, and now they are brother and sister to my boys. And Anne, our niece held from us for too long, now will have family visiting her and helping with whatever she needs. What a great day."

"No need for one of your House of Lords speeches now, Reggie," Bennet ribbed his friend, "I suggest we all go to the house so we can toast each other's happiness with champagne." At Bennet's suggestion, the party started to make its way toward the house, the newlyweds bringing up the rear.

~~~~~~~/~~~~~~~

As they walked Bingley turned to his wife and met her

eyes for a moment and once again watched where they were going as he guided her towards the manor house.

"I give thanks to God on High every day that you decided to love me and accept me as your husband. The grace and class all of you have demonstrated in the way you have treated both Louisa and me is unfathomable, and so much more than most other members of the *Ton* would have done." He raised his hand to stay Jane's protestation they had done nothing special. "That is why you and your family are so very special, each of you judge a person by who they are, by their actions rather than arbitrary and capricious societal dictates. For that, I will be forever grateful my dearest wife."

"You are my one and only. The more I got to know you, the more I fell in love with you and saw I would never be happy unless you were my husband. I love you so very dearly, my Charles," Jane promised softly, holding his arm slightly tighter to punctuate her words and Bingley in turn drew her closer to his side so they were as close as possible while they walked.

~~~~~~~/~~~~~~~

"Mary, I am so very glad your parents relented and allowed us to marry without waiting the original six months. You have been my love for many years now. You are the love of my life, my darling wife. My soul's mate," Richard spoke quietly to his wife, for while the other couple was a few paces away, the moment was hers alone.

"I feel exactly the same way about you, Richard. And I am so very excited we will be going to the Lake District for our wedding trip. I have always wanted to see it. How long will we be with Lizzy and William at Pemberley on our way home?" Mary inquired.

"As we will be returning there in December, we will rest there for but three days before we make the journey to Netherfield Park. I still cannot fathom that your parents gifted us with the estate," Richard admitted.

"It will be good to see Pemberley again. And we will see Jane and Charles on their trip from Seaview to Pemberley when they break the trip at Longbourn. When all three of us married Bennet girls are back together, we will have to compare notes to see who is the happiest," Mary replied teasingly.

"My father was so right, I am beside myself that William and I are finally brothers, and now look at all of the sisters and brothers I have gained." He gazed out over the group making their way to one of their homes, this time Longbourn.

~~~~~~~/~~~~~~~

The two newlywed couples were announced to the assembled crowd celebrating their nuptials as they entered Longbourn's ball room. Both brides glowed when they heard themselves being announced with their married title as Mrs., leaving behind the appellation of Miss forever.

About three hours into the celebration, Mr. and Mrs. Bingley and Mr. and Mrs. Fitzwilliam changed into travelling attire, and after some tears and many hugs and kisses, departed for their wedding trips.

The Bingleys made for the new Bingley House, two houses down from the Gardiners on Portman Square in Town, and the Fitzwilliams headed north to the first inn of the three and one half day journey to the house owned by the Darcys. It overlooked Lake Windermere, the largest of the lakes, and had a good view of both the small Esthwaite Water and the larger Coniston Water.

~~~~~~~/~~~~~~~

After waving goodbye until the carriages were no longer visible, the family returned to the ball room with the Bennet parents bringing up the rear. Fanny had tears in her eyes and her husband knew, as happy as she was for her girls, saying goodbye to three of them as they left home in the last month was not easy. He too felt the loss acutely and understood well what his wife was feeling.

"I know you are forlorn sending Jane and Mary to their new lives with their husbands. We can rejoice all three of our married girls have made love matches, just like we did Fanny. That is a rare thing for any parents and comes with so many joys we will share with them in the future." He gently pulled her to his side as he wrapped his arms lovingly about her. Bennet looked down at his Fanny with the same love he had since their marriage, love that had only grown deeper with time, and because of their follies had the strength that few experienced.

"I am more than happy for them Thomas, but I will still miss them. Kitty is departing with the Darcys on the morrow, and on Monday you will be taking Tom and James back to Cambridge When you return it will be just the two of us in this huge home," Fanny replied forlornly.

"Do not forget, Fanny, that subsequent to Twelfth Night when we return from Derbyshire Georgie and Kitty will be with us and remain until they start preparing for their coming out next year.

Tom and James will be with us as well until I have to return them to university, and do not forget once they return from their wedding trip that Richard and Mary will be but three miles away at Netherfield Park." Bennet reminded his wife of several of the positive events in her near future.

"I know all of that Thomas; I am just being silly," Fanny smiled sadly.

"Do not say that about yourself, Fanny. You are the least silly woman I know. It is expected to miss one's daughters when they marry and leave home, most especially when you lose three in four weeks as has just occurred for us. I have no doubt you are as happy for them as I am. Do you not think I am sad to see our girls leave Longbourn as well?" he looked down into her eyes.

"Not for one second do I believe that! As long as I have you, I will always feel safe and loved," Fanny promised.

"And while I am taking the boys to Cambridge, I think you should look at what is needed in the nursery. I do believe the sooner you renovate it with all the grandparent allowed indulgences you can fit into it, the better," Bennet suggested.

Bennet took his wife's hands and kissed them and then walked with her back into the ballroom to celebrate the weddings with their friends and ever-expanding family. At least the Darcys would still be with them until the morrow.

~~~~~~~/~~~~~~~

As they were supervising the packing of their trunks, Elizabeth Darcy turned to her husband and said, "I would like to invite Charlotte Lucas to join us at Christmastide, William."

"You are the mistress of Pemberley, my love, you are free to invite anyone your heart desires," Darcy responded as he kissed his wife on her cheek. "To tell the truth, I was going to suggest it myself."

"You were? Why? You hardly know her except as my friend," his inquisitive wife asked.

"Have you not told me many times what a good person she is? How she is of unimpeachable character? If she has your affection and respect, there is not much more I need to know about her."

"I agree, she is one of the best people and friends I know. That been said, why is it that you were going to make the suggestion?"

"Two reasons, my love," he said with one of his dimple-revealing smiles that always made his wife go weak at the knees, "Firstly, I know she is your very good friend and you have told me how seldom she has a chance to travel outside of Hertfordshire. Secondly..."

"Yes, William, secondly?" Elizabeth's curiosity was peeked now, what could her handsome husband be planning?

"You have heard me talk about our clergyman, a good friend of mine from school, who holds the livings of Kympton, Lambton and Pemberley, Mr. Patrick Elliot?"

"I have, you have given him a glowing character. He was married and his wife died five years ago, and he has a very sweet daughter of five years, Grace?"

"Yes, all correct, well I know recently, after so many years in mourning for his beloved wife, he has started to talk about the possibility of considering a new wife and mother for Gracie."

"William, you are a matchmaker at heart!" his impertinent wife teased.

"Not a matchmaker my dearest loveliest Elizabeth, all I want is to facilitate a meeting, what they do after will be entirely up to them." How he loved it when his beloved wife teased him.

"I think it a fine plan, William, I will send a note to Charlotte now inviting her for Christmastide, and as long as she would like to stay with us afterward."

Mrs. Darcy wrote her note telling her friend they would send a carriage to collect her or organise things so she could ride with one of the groups travelling from Longbourn to join them for the holidays and sent it to Lucas Lodge with one of the Longbourn grooms who was instructed to wait for an answer.

About a half an hour later he returned and handed a note to the former Miss Lizzy from Charlotte Lucas. She opened the reply and read it aloud to her husband:

My dear Eliza, I thank you and your husband for your

very welcome invitation. I would be happy to join you at Pemberley. I will be available to leave after Christmas as I want to celebrate the day with my family. If that is acceptable to you, I would love to see you in your new home. When I see you at your home there is a particular subject, I would like to address with you regarding my future. With my best regards and thanks, Charlotte

A note was sent back to Lucas Lodge informing Charlotte a Darcy equipage with an appropriate chaperone would arrive at her home the day after Christmas.

Mr. and Mrs. Bennet and the twins waved to the departing Darcys with Kitty accompanying them as their carriages headed up Longbourn's drive to eventually join the Great North Road.

In another day or two, Bennet would take his sons to Cambridge and then for the first time since before Jane was born, the Bennet parents would be alone. At least they had Frank and Hattie Philips to visit and commiserate with them as well as a very good group of friends. They would be alone, but not lonely.

CHAPTER 24

The three Darcys, accompanied by Kitty Bennet, arrived back at Pemberley the Thursday following the double wedding. As this was Mrs. Darcy's first time at Pemberley as the mistress, the housekeeper and the butler were waiting for them, and had most of the staff lined up in the entrance hall in anticipation of their arrival.

Mercury, Elizabeth's horse, had been sent directly from Seaview to Pemberley, along with her husband's stallion, Zeus. As much as she loved to ride, Elizabeth knew she would soon have to forgo the pleasure since she was now sure she was with child.

She had not yet told her husband, but she had felt sick in the coach, and she had never had an issue travelling before. In addition, the smell of fish was starting to make her feel nauseated each time she had the unfortunate opportunity to encounter it. She would have to talk to cook and their French chef to let them know for family meals and any private trays requested for her, they would need to exclude fish for the next seven to eight months. The revelation of her state to her husband could be delayed no longer due to the conversation she needed to have with Cook and Chef.

The Darcys and Miss Bennet were welcomed to Pemberley by Mr. Douglas and Mrs. Reynolds. Mrs. Darcy greeted each staff member who had lined up to meet her as mistress and thanked them all for taking time out of their busy day to greet her, again, to the delight of all, remembering names of those she had met on her prior visit while she was still Miss Elizabeth Bennet.

Both of the unmarried sister's companions were part of the party and had travelled in a second carriage with Darcy's valet and the three lady's maids. In conversation between the companions, both Mrs. Chandler and Mrs. Annesley agreed they would not have much to do besides some lessons for their charges.

The two ladies had become fast friends during all of the time they had spent together and would give the new sisters their space as it was easy to see how close Miss Darcy and Miss Bennet had become.

Mrs. Reynolds showed Kitty Bennet and Mrs. Chandler to their suite in the family wing, leaving the Darcys and Mrs. Annesley to repair to their suites. Once her abigail had helped her change into a day dress, Elizabeth walked through their private sitting room to knock on the door to her husband's chambers.

"Enter," Darcy responded in his rich baritone voice she could never get enough of hearing, and she entered to find Carstens picking lint of her husband's coat.

"Could you please leave us, Carstens. I need to talk privately with my husband," Elizabeth instructed.

"Yes, Mistress, right away." The valet left the chambers with all haste.

"Yes, my love, what is it we need to discuss?" Darcy asked, concerned because she had asked his valet to leave for the first time.

"Not a discussion, my beloved husband, I only have something to tell you." She took a deep breath and met his eyes steadily. "I believe I am with child." He seemed dumbstruck for a minute and Elizabeth became concerned. "Does this news not please you William?" she asked hesitantly.

"Yes, it most certainly does my love. I am overjoyed!" her worry shook Darcy out of his stupor. "There is nothing I want more than to have a family with you." Darcy hugged his wife, then lifted her and spun her around before he caught himself. "I am so sorry, love. I should not have been so exuberant. I did not hurt you, did I?" he looked her over for injury or upsets.

"William, I am with child not a china doll. You married a hearty country girl whose mother bore six children with no trouble, so before you think I have to spend the next months doing nothing but sitting or lying around, I do not!" Elizabeth pre-empted her husband's inclination to be overprotective.

"We are to be parents? I am going to be a father! You could not have delivered better news, my love. What a gift you have given me, my Lizzy. I would like to ask Mrs. Reynolds to call Mr. Tristan Bartholomew who has been our physician since he took over his father's practice in Lambton," Darcy asked hopefully.

"I have no objection to seeing Mr. Bartholomew, my love." Elizabeth smiled benevolently as she had expected no less.

Exuding joy, he pulled the bell cord to summon the housekeeper. "When do you want to announce our news to our sisters, if the doctor confirms your suspicions, my dearest, loveliest, Elizabeth?" he asked excitedly.

"Jane and Mary know of my suspicions. It was a shared sisterly confidence the night we talked before their weddings. I suspect they have shared the news with their husbands by now but have been sworn to not talk about it to anyone else." Seeing her husband did not look happy he was not the first to be told she sighed in understanding. "Mary had asked me a question about my monthlies, and it just came out. I did not want to say anything too soon in case it was not true and then I would have disappointed you."

"Lizzy, you can tell me anything, nothing will ever disappoint me about you," Darcy assured her. There was a knock at the door and Darcy told Mrs. Reynolds to enter.

"I suspect I may be with child, Mrs. Reynolds, could you please have someone ride to Lambton to summon Mr. Bartholomew?" Mrs. Darcy asked calmly. "I would ask for you to not share this news with anyone else. We will share the news once I feel the quickening. Also, please talk to Cook and Chef and let them know there will be no fish dishes on the menu until further notice. I had not told you yet, husband, but I get nauseated at the smell of fish now," Elizabeth smiled sweetly.

"Such glorious news Master, Mistress. The next generation of Darcys on the way! Oh my! I will do as you have requested, and I swear my lips are sealed. I will not say a word until you make the official announcement," Mrs. Reynolds promised excitedly.

"Hannah, I have known you since I was four years old and I trust you implicitly, that is why we are talking to you and no one else," Darcy told the most trusted woman.

"Thank you, Master William, your confidence in me is much appreciated. Unless there is something else, may I be excused so I can send a groom to Lambton and talk to the chef and cook?" she asked, eager to help settle the question once and for all.

"You may go, Mrs. Reynolds, and thank you for your discretion," Elizabeth agreed, amused at the excitement of both.

"Thank you, Mistress." Mrs. Reynolds curtsied and left.

No sooner was the door closed than the couple fell into each other's arms. There was a shared feeling of bliss that their love had produced a son or daughter so quickly, should all go as they hoped was God's will.

"Is there a problem with an entail on Pemberley, will there be an issue if we only have girls, William?" Elizabeth asked softly. She well remembered the stories of how her mother had worried about the entail on Longbourn after she had birthed four daughters before her sons.

"No, my love. Much like your father has done, the only entail on Pemberley is that it cannot be broken up or sold and no one that is not family by blood can inherit, regardless of gender. So even if we only have girls, Pemberley will be inherited by our oldest daughter, though there is a stipulation her husband takes the Darcy name to make sure there is always a Darcy at Pemberley," Darcy reassured his wife.

This news removed any anxiety Elizabeth had about the pressure to bear a son. Now all she needed to do was to enjoy being his pregnant wife.

~~~~~~~/~~~~~~~

The following day, the day after the physician had confirmed the wonderous news, Darcy met with his friend and rector, Patrick Elliot in his study. Once they were both seated, and refreshment offered and accepted, they discussed some parish business that Elliot felt his patron should be apprised of.

When they had completed their discussion of business, the parson who knew his friend well could see he wanted to discuss something else with him, but possibly did not know how to broach the subject.

"Out with it, Darcy, I can see you have something to tell me." The intuitive friend gave his patron an opening to breech the subject he wanted to.

"Remember how you told me that you felt you were open to seeking a new wife and a mother for Gracie?" Darcy began tentatively.

"Yes... I remember, please tell me that you are not trying to be a matchmaker, Darcy!" the rector said with amazement knowing to do so was very far out of his friend's comfort zone.

"No, that is not my, our, intent at all. My wife has a very good friend, in fact one of her best friends, from her former neighbourhood who will be joining us after Christmas as she wants to celebrate the Lord's birth with her family before she travels north.

"All we want to do is facilitate a meeting, what you two do or do not do after that will be in your own hands. We will not push or try to interfere in any way." Darcy managed to get out before he was too mortified.

"Tell me a little about the lady, the fact she has Mrs. Darcy's friendship is already a recommendation as I know your wife would not befriend anyone unworthy."

"In that you are correct Elliot. I believe she is seven and twenty, no fortune to speak of, but I know that is not an issue for you," he paused as his friend nodded in agreement, "I do not know her as my Elizabeth does, but what I have seen of her indicates she is of the highest moral character. She is not a beauty like my wife, but she is also not at all homely. She is very intelligent and has a good and quick wit from what I have seen. She helps her mother run their home so she will have no problem managing a home of her own."

"Just being your wife's particular friend would be enough for me to want to meet her, but what you have told me increases my desire to know the lady. I appreciate the chance. I thank both of you for the opportunity."

The friends stood and shook hands and Elliot returned to the parsonage at Pemberley where he resided with his daughter, Grace, who would be departing to be with his parents before Christmas as she did each year.

Darcy returned to his enceinte wife and reported the

results of the conversation that he had with the parson. Elizabeth was well pleased with the results.

CHAPTER 25

For the Darcys, it felt as though the months had flown by. The love both had thought could not deepen had done so every day.

After the Bingleys took up residence at Longfield Meadows in September, at least once a week either the Darcys visited the Bingleys at their estate, or the Bingleys visited the Darcys at Pemberley.

Letters flew back and forth between Derbyshire and Hertfordshire keeping the Bennet, Bingley, Fitzwilliam, and Darcy couriers very busy. Even Tom and James wrote letters occasionally.

A month after moving into the Meadows, Jane shared her suspicion with all her sisters at Pemberley that she was with child, and a week later Mary Fitzwilliam had shared she suspected herself and Richard were soon to be parents as well.

The morning of the twentieth of December as Mr. and Mrs. Darcy were taking a walk around the lake, Darcy marvelled at how soon in her pregnancy his Lizzy was visibly larger. With no prior warning, his wife stopped walking and grabbed his arm while her other hand covered her swelling belly, which immediately caused Darcy much alarm.

"Lizzy are you well? Is there a problem with our baby? Should I summon help?" he asked, bending so he was able to see her face clearly to determine if she was in pain or scared.

"William, calm yourself." Elizabeth captured his face in her hands to soothe him. "Look at me. Do I look like I am in pain?" she asked gently, caressing his cheeks with her thumbs as she waited for him to calm.

"I am sorry." He hung his head.

"Sorry for loving me as you do? I will pretend I did not hear that and demand you strike the thought from your memories, so it is never said again," she countered, the teasing intentionally making him laugh.

"Then I am not sorry for panicking like a boy of twelve who could not catch his breath after falling out of a tree, certain he was about to meet his maker and would get a thrashing for dying so young when he got home," he chuckled, causing his Lizzy to loose one of her tinkling laughs he loved to hear.

"What tree?" she grinned up at him and he pointed to the one only ten paces away.

"Are you well, my love?" he asked huskily, searching her eyes.

"I apologise if I gave you cause for concern. No, William, nothing is wrong. In fact, all is perfect. I just felt a fluttering matching what Pemberley's midwife told me I would feel soon. Our baby just moved. I have just felt the quickening," Elizabeth reported as she smiled up into his eyes.

"This is the best of news, Lizzy. Now we can share the news with your parents and everyone who will be arriving starting on the morrow. Our local physician who confirmed your state when we arrived home, has full confidence in the midwife. He himself has very high cleanliness standards, and she is one of the few he approves of." Darcy reminded her why he would only allowed the two of them to attend her.

"Let us return to the house so we can tell our sisters. They have suspected for a while, but have not asked me anything yet." Mrs. Darcy slid her hand into Mr. Darcy's and squeezed it gently.

The Darcys walked back into the house and asked Douglas to summon Mrs. Reynolds to join them in the music room where Georgiana and Kitty were playing music. On seeing their brother and sister enter the room, the two ceased the duet they were playing on the pianoforte and looked questioningly as the housekeeper and butler joined them.

"Sisters, Mrs. Reynolds, and Mr. Douglas, Elizabeth and I have the pleasure of informing you there will be a baby born at Pemberley and should make his or her debut in late May or early June of next year," Darcy announced with pride.

"Mr. Darcy and I would like for you, Mrs. Reynolds and Mr. Douglas, to inform the staff so there will be no speculation," Elizabeth smiled as Mrs. Reynolds was bursting with the pleasure of permission to share the news she had known for months.

"Yes, Mr. and Mrs. Darcy, and may I wish you all of the best while you increase Mrs. Darcy," Mrs. Reynolds enthused, overjoyed at the proof positive the next generation of Darcys was on the way.

Douglas echoed the housekeeper, and the two senior staff members withdrew to allow the family private time, and to start informing the servants of the impending joy.

"Oh my! William! Lizzy! I am to be an aunt! Congratulations, we suspected something but did not feel it was right to ask you." Georgiana jumped up from the seat in front of the pianoforte.

"Georgie do not forget you will not receive that distinction alone! We are to be aunts, along with the rest of the sisters, sisters-in-laws like Louisa and Marie, and sisters by heart, like Anne! And James and Tom will be uncles before they turn seventeen, but they too will have to share that privilege. I am so happy for both of you. I noticed you were getting larger Lizzy, and I was sure you were not eating too much, but as Georgie said, we did not say anything." Kitty blushed.

"I suspected before Mary and Jane's wedding. It slipped out when we talked the night before, but they were sworn to keep my secret except from their husbands. Mama and Papa do not know yet. When they arrive tomorrow, Mama will know before I say anything." Lizzy laughed. "The real challenge will be the opportunity to act like aunts with Mama and Papa, and Uncle Reggie and Aunt Elaine close by." Lizzy giggled at Darcy's frown. "Perhaps we can set up a schedule." She winked at him, and he finally smiled.

It was far better to have so many that love you than the loneliness he and Georgiana experienced for so many years. "A schedule is just the thing. I get the first ten years, you the second." He winked at his wife, making the women surrounding him laugh.

"Actually, Anne wrote and told me she should arrive earlier than planned. She is travelling to Longbourn from Rosings Park. If all went to plan, then she should arrive tomorrow along with the Bennets, Richard and Mary, and the Gardiners. When will the rest of the Fitzwilliams arrive at Pemberley brother?" Georgiana remembered the letter she was meaning to share over tea.

"The Bingleys and the Hursts will get here the day after tomorrow, and the rest of the Fitzwilliams from Snowhaven and Hilldale the following day," Darcy related.

"Lizzy," Georgiana feigned minimal interest her blush belied, "when did your father collect the twins from Cambridge?"

"In her last letter, Mama wrote she was very happy to have her boys home. She says they are so grown up now. She mentioned Papa arrived home with them on the tenth of December. They asked her to let William know they are looking forward to riding with him once they are here,"

Elizabeth reported, worried about her husband's reaction to his sister growing up.

"If there is more snow then our brothers, like anyone who wants to, will be able to ride in one of the sleighs we own," Darcy stated, either not having noticed his sister's reaction, or pretending well that he had not.

"If Mama does not notice right away, we promise we will say nothing until you tell them, Lizzy," Kitty vowed.

"Thank you, Kitty, I too believe both Mama and Aunt Maddie will know as soon as they see me, but they may not say anything until I tell them. I am sure Mama and Papa will be ecstatic at the prospect of their first grandchild," Elizabeth agreed.

"William, will Georgie still travel to Longbourn with me when Mama and Papa return?" Kitty asked, understanding this may change certain plans.

"I can see no reason why not, Kitty. You two will start preparing for your coming out when Aunt Elaine and Uncle Reggie come and collect both of you from Longbourn in February to stay with them at Matlock house. Mary and Richard's plans may change, and they may not join you.

"The only difference I can foresee is Lizzy and I will not be joining you now and will come back to London for next season, so long as our little one will be healthy, and Mr. Bartholomew has no objection to our son or daughter taking a long carriage trip," Darcy explained.

"Why would Mary and Richard maybe not join us, brother?" Just then Georgiana realised the probable reason and her lips formed a silent "O", her eyes wide with the additional surprise.

"Well, now that you have realised what William means, yes, Georgiana, and Kitty? Mary thinks she too is with child, as does Jane. They have not felt the quickening, but both have suffered from sickness in the mornings, so there is no way to hide their condition for long." Lizzy nodded as Kitty's eyes widened in excitement.

"There will be three nieces or nephews, or some combination thereof, next year. How wonderful!" Kitty exclaimed.

"Yes, Kitty, we will be able to spoil them all. How I look forward to it." Georgiana hugged herself and was almost bouncing on her toes.

"Remember Georgie and Kitty, we will have to rely on the Good Lord above to see all of us have successful births and everyone is healthy. I myself feel I and all of my sisters will follow my Mama, who birthed six children with nary a problem, so I am not worried." Looking at her husband, Lizzy smiled gently. "Your brother will do all the worrying for the both of us."

The ladies giggled and Darcy looked chagrined. He remembered the trouble his dearly departed mother had suffered aside from the births of himself and his sister. His father had once shared with him that each one of her disappointments had taken a toll on Lady Anne, both emotionally and physically.

He did know he could not smother Lizzy with his worry, and what she said about her mother was the truth. With lack of reason to worry, he decided although he would be vigilant, he would attempt to temper his need to control everything concerning her health.

His Lizzy had not reacted well the one time he had attempted officious control. And honestly, he loved her the more for it. He had tried to force her to stay abed so she told him everything he told her to do, he had to do with her.

He had thought it would be simple to remain in bed all day, but she was reading and pretending to be fine, and he was only thinking about all he should be doing. When he reminded her that he had responsibilities, she had correctly asked him if she did not? But if hers obviously did not count, so also did his not. They had gotten up directly once his apology had been rendered.

As soon as Mr. Bartholomew had confirmed her state, his Lizzy had given up one of her favourite things for the duration of her pregnancy, riding her beloved stallion Mercury. That was enough of a sacrifice.

"Now I understand why you stopped riding Mercury, Lizzy," Kitty smiled sadly for her sister. I knew you would have to have a good reason not to be galloping across hill and dale on your beast of a stallion with William. If he will let me take him out for a ride, I will exercise him for you. You know I have as good a seat as you," Kitty offered.

"You have a better seat than me." Elizabeth laughed when Darcy looked at them in surprise. "Just because she does not steal my thunder when I am on him, does not mean she could not. She is a truly beloved sister." She winked at Kitty. "He is no beast, Kitty. Now you are fully grown, I fear you would love riding him as much as I do. But I agree he is as sad as I am that I am not able to ride. In the morning, I shall take him some treats, and each day he is given exercise by one of the grooms, and on occasion William rides him and gives him his head."

"I was referring to his size, not his nature, Lizzy. He has a very good nature and has had since he was a foal, especially with you. After all, you were the one who nursed him when his mother rejected him as a foal. William is the only one other than you it seems, he will allow to ride him; he must approve of the way William loves you," Kitty surmised.

"You have the right of it, Kitty. When Lizzy and I first started to know each other, he would not even allow me to approach him, then as we fell more in love, he seemed to sense his mistress approved of me, so he allowed me to join the circle of humans he trusted. The first time I rode him he was a little tentative, but now he welcomes me almost as readily as he does Lizzy," Darcy related.

As her baby made itself known again, Lizzy rubbed her rapidly expanding belly and admitted to herself the reward of becoming a mother far outweighed any remorse she had about not being able to ride Mercury.

"We can ask him for you in the morning, Kitty. He will decide." She winked at her sisters and nestled into her husband's side.

~~~~~~~/~~~~~~~

The next day, just as the residents of Pemberley finished their luncheon, Douglas informed them four coaches and a wagon had passed the gate house and would arrive shortly.

The Darcys and Kitty descended the stairs to the drive just as the first of two carriages came to a stop. The carriage with the traveller's valets and maids and the wagon and the outriders had gone to the servant's entrance.

Once the stairs were lowered by a footman the Bennet twins alighted, followed by Mary and Richard. Mr. and Mrs. Bennet, Lilly Gardiner, and Anne de Bourgh alighted from the second conveyance. Edward and Madeline Gardiner and the three youngest Gardiner children were in the third carriage.

The arriving party, save for Mary and Richard who knew, looked at the rotund Elizabeth Darcy with surprise. "Is there something you would like to tell us Lizzy?" Fanny smiled playfully at her daughter.

"I was going to wait until we were in the drawing room, Mama, but yes. I am very obviously with child. I suppose you would have to be blind not to see it as there is nothing that Jacqui can do with my dresses to hide it anymore," Elizabeth owned.

"When will your babe arrive, Lizzy?" Mrs. Bennet asked as the party headed up the stairs into the house and then the drawing room.

"End of May or beginning of June, Mama." Lizzy smiled ruefully.

"My my, Fanny. Lizzy is as large as you were at the same stage when you were pregnant with Tom and James," Aunt Gardiner offered.

"I was about to say the same, Maddie," Fanny agreed.

"Twins!" Elizabeth and William exclaimed simultaneously.

"It does run in our family; Tom and I are living proof of that are we not," James smirked.

"Oh my," gasped Mrs. Darcy as she was aided into a comfortable chair by her husband. "When I started to get so big so soon, I just thought that maybe I was eating more than normal."

"No, my love," her husband disagreed as he held her hand, "I have not noticed you eat in excess. We will have to be extra careful; we will retain the best accoucheur in London to be in residence the last six weeks of your confinement. I do not care how much it costs me." Darcy started to settle when his wife placed a calming hand on his arm.

"William, I am sure that the possibility of twins frightens you given your dear late mother's experience, but before you stands living proof all can be well in the person of my mother. Five of her children are in this room, and as you can see by your two brothers, bearing twins did not harm mama, and I am sure I will be well," Elizabeth reminded her husband.

"I could not carry on living if I lost you," Darcy stated with a look of dread on his face.

"If it will make you feel better, I will be more vigilant and I will agree to you retaining an accoucheur," she promised.

"The best one I am aware of is Sir Fredrick Gillingham,

and he is a good friend of ours so you can mention the connection in your express, Darcy," Gardiner offered. "I will give you his card."

"Thank you, Gardiner, that is most appreciated." Darcy nodded at him with relief.

"Let us show our guests to their chambers so they can change out of their travel attire and rest. Shall we all meet back here at half after five o'clock for an aperitif before dinner?" Lizzy looked at her family happily.

Everyone nodded their agreement, and the travellers followed the housekeeper up to their chambers while a worried and harried Fitzwilliam Darcy went to his study to compose his express to Sir Fredrick.

The rest of the evening past companionably, and although the worry Darcy was feeling for his young wife was evident, he did manage to keep it in check and not vex his Lizzy too much.

Their twin brothers took their minds off the pregnancy while they regaled the assembled company with tales of their experiences at Cambridge after but one term. Like their father, Uncle Reggie, cousins Andrew and Richard, and brothers William and Charles before them, the boys were enrolled in Trinity College.

Their illustrious connections were widely known, resulting in deference from other young men, even titled ones. The message that the Fitzwilliam, Darcy, Bennet, de Bourgh, Bingley, and Hurst families were not to be trifled with and would be defended by all was a lesson that had been well learnt and passed onto all members of the *Ton*, then to the circles below the first circle.

~~~~~~~/~~~~~~~

The next morning the Bingleys and Hursts arrived just after ten. The arriving party was met at the entrance to the house by Mr. and Mrs. Darcy and Mr. and Mrs. Bennet. Fanny was in her element with all six of her children together again, and the prospect of becoming a grandmother in less than six months made for an even happier Mama Bennet.

With the distance between Pemberley and Longfield Meadows so negligible, the arriving party returned to the drawing room right after changing out of their travel attire. As soon as she kissed her mama and aunts, Jane sat comfortably and smiled.

"Lizzy, I have seen women close to confinement as large as you are now," Jane teased.

"Mama thinks that I may be having twins. She says she was about the same size as I am now when she was with child carrying Tom and James," Lizzy volleyed, laughing at the surprise on Jane's face.

"Before the end of next year, we may be aunts and uncles many times over." Kitty clapped.

"It does look that way. When does your doctor think your babe will be birthed Jane? I know from what Mrs. Richardson has told Mary after she examined her and confirmed she is with child that Mary should birth her babe in July," Fanny asked her oldest daughter.

"It seems Mary and I will be in our lying ins around the same time, Mama. It is providence we birth our children about the same time as we did get married together. It will be as if the cousins are as close as brothers and sisters like William and Richard are," Jane offered sweetly.

"I should like to announce I too am with child. I felt the quickening some four weeks ago. Harold and I are beyond happy that we are to be parents," Louisa informed the family.

Louisa and Harold Hurst received a hearty round of congratulations from all those assembled. As Kitty exclaimed the pleasure of another niece or nephew on the way. Anne de Bourgh looked at the scene wistfully. She knew she was healthy enough to bear children; all she had to do was find someone she could love the same as she saw reflected in the couples around the room.

Anne would never settle for a marriage of convenience either, she wanted to be loved as if she was the only reason the sun rose and set as William loved his Elizabeth, Bingley loved his Jane, the same as all the other couples in their beloved family. It was time to be open about her plans.

"Georgie and Kitty, I hope you do not mind if I join you for your debut season as I plan to debut as well. Aunt Elaine will sponsor me for my curtsy. Lady Catherine would never hear of my having a season, and although I am already five and twenty, I am determined to make up for lost time. I have no interest in an arranged marriage, I will only marry for the deepest mutual love and respect. I see so much happiness in all of you, and I would like to at least give myself the opportunity to find the same," Anne blushed after her uncharacteristically long speech.

"Anne I am sure I speak for Kitty as well when I say we are more than happy to have you join us. The more the merrier." Georgiana smiled happily.

"Oh yes, Anne. I second what Georgie said. We too will only settle for love matches so there is no pressure to accept the first man who shows interest in us this coming season. Not even the fifth. I would rather never marry than marry without love," Kitty agreed.

"We have taught you very well, Kitty," Bennet smiled proudly at his youngest daughter. "We are looking forward to you and Georgie joining us at Longbourn until Reggie and Elaine take you to town in February to prepare for your season."

"If I do not find a love match, I know William and Richard would never force me to marry where I do not have the inclination." Georgiana looked at her guardians with a sweet smile.

"You are correct, sweetling, neither William nor I would ever force you to accept someone against your inclinations. I pity the dastard that would try to compromise you, Anne, or Kitty with so many male relatives willing to take him to task," Richard winked at them.

"I am looking forward to seeing the rest of the Fitzwilliams on the morrow, did you and Papa break your trip at Snowhaven, Mama?" Lizzy looked over at her mother.

"We did. We spent the night with Reggie and Elaine, and they wanted us to mention they are waiting for Andrew and Marie to arrive in the morning then they will join us all at Pemberley. Elaine told me it is the last time Marie will travel as she should enter her lying in in late February or early March," Fanny revealed.

"Mama, what will you do with Jane and Mary entering the final stage of their confinements around the same time?" Lizzy enquired.

"Mama will stay with Mary. By the time I enter my lying in you, Louisa, and Marie would have birthed your children so I will have plenty of support. Aunt Maddie will also come from town to be with Mary, and I am sure Aunt Elaine will want to be at Netherfield Park for Mary's lying in, so along with Mama, Mary will have good support as well," Jane stated, having wanted to make sure that no one felt torn.

"I agree with my Jane, Mother Bennet. We have a lot of family close to the Meadows so you can be with Mary without worrying Jane will not have family to assist her." Bingley held his wife's hand gently.

"Thank you, Jane, and you Charles, for your thoughtful and unselfish solution to the problem. I believe your suggestion is a good one, and unless there is a significant change; that is what we will do," Fanny nodded in approval.

"Fanny has the right of it. We will be here for Lizzy's

time, and as long as she is close to the estimated date, we will return to Longbourn well in time for your lying in Mary. Maddie, do you plan to come to Derbyshire for Lizzy's?" Bennet looked to his sister-in-law.

"As long as there is no emergency with one of the children or Edward's business then yes, we will join you in returning to Derbyshire to be with Lizzy, Thomas," Madeline agreed as she glanced at Lizzy and couldn't help but smile.

"Richard and I thank Jane for her thoughtfulness, and it is a good solution given the distance between our homes," Mary agreed.

"There is one way we would all be close for both births." Richard looked at his Mary.

"How is that? What battle plan are you considering?" Mary teased him.

"I am sure we would be welcome at Snowhaven before your lying in and remain there for your recovery. Just think about it, no need to decide now. The grandparents would have all their grandbabies born within a thirty-mile radius. And for your sisters to see ours so soon when months would otherwise be required." He kissed her hand. "I just want you as close to your sisters as I know you want to be. And my mother would be overjoyed to have her daughter home when she gives birth," Richard drawled, Fanny's answering laugh making him grin.

"Louisa, where will you be for your lying in?" Lizzy asked.

"We plan to be at the Hurst estate, Lakeside, in Lincolnshire, Lizzy. After my churching we will return to the Meadows so we can be with Jane and Charles."

"Your parents must be happy at the prospect of a grandchild and possible heir, Hurst." Darcy nodded at Hurst.

"They are. We are now very welcome at Lakeside," Hurst stated, not willing to bring up the persona non grata that had made it difficult for them in the past.

"Well now, there will soon be a plethora of babes in this family," Bennet grinned as he glanced around the room.

"Lizzy, when does Charlotte arrive? Lady Lucas told me about her invitation and that you and William are sending a carriage with a maid and footmen to bring her into Derbyshire," Fanny enquired.

"She will arrive two days before the Twelfth Night Ball we are holding here at Pemberley, Mama," Lizzy reported.

The rest of the day was very pleasant with much talk of babes, clothing, and accoutrements needed for said babes. The men executed a tactical withdrawal and went riding after lunch, all hastily agreeing to the twin's suggestion of some exercise.

~~~~~~~/~~~~~~~

The following morning, two more coaches arrived bearing the rest of the Fitzwilliams. When they disembarked, young David Fitzwilliam, now almost three, very proudly informed one and all that his Mama had his baby brother in her tummy. When his smiling grandmother told him it could be a baby sister, he scrunched up his nose and told everyone he had decided that it was a baby brother.

Once everyone met in the drawing room, the Countess and a very pregnant Lady Marie agreed with Fanny's assessment that Lizzy could be carrying twins. When the tentative plan for Mary and Jane's lying in was laid out, the Earl and Countess agreed wholeheartedly.

Decoration of Pemberley had started the day the first group of guests had arrived, and now the inside of Pemberley was almost as green as it was on the outside in the summer. There was greenery on all of the banisters, sprigs of holly were hung all over, and strategically placed mistletoe, heavy with berries, could be found when one did not look too hard.

No one missed the blush both Tom Bennet and

Georgiana Darcy sported when they were inadvertently caught under one hanging piece of mistletoe. After retrieving a berry, a very embarrassed Tom gave an even more embarrassed Georgiana a peck on the cheek. Luckily for Darcy and Richard, more so than Georgiana and Tom, the rest of the revellers did not mortify them by insisting on a proper kiss.

The invitations for the Twelfth Night Ball had been sent out and were accepted with very few exceptions and the plans for the ball were well in hand. Mrs. Darcy acceded to her husband's request she not overdo things and use the many friends and loved ones she had at her disposal for help.

On Christmas Eve, the whole party made the short walk to the Pemberley Chapel where the young rector officiated the service. He held the Pemberley living in addition to the one at Kympton and Lambton.

The Pemberley living was a small and minor one, but as Darcy was his patron for the other two livings, he had his curates officiate at the other two while he did the Pemberley services on Christmas Eve. When the family returned to the house, with the parson in tow, they were treated to a sumptuous Christmas Eve dinner that had no fish on the menu.

It had begun to snow overnight, and it was still falling when everyone met to break their fast in the morning. Afterward, they congregated in the ballroom where there was a big fir Christmas tree in the German tradition that Queen Charlotte observed, and to the surprise of some it had lots of presents at its base.

Before opening gifts, they all sung their favourite carols. Bennet was most pleased by his gifts from his married daughters and sons in law. From Mary and Richard, he received a first edition book that was not in his collection, and Lizzy and William also gifted him a first edition, a very rare one he had long sought out with no success.

Bingley and Jane gifted him with a case each of the best French cognac and the port that he loved. Bingley refused to disclose how he was able to purchase the cognac with the kingdom still at war with France.

Everyone else was more than satisfied with their gifts, especially the four Gardiner children who announced it was the best Christmas. When the twins asked about riding, they were downcast when told that there would be no riding while the snow was falling and getting deeper. Their frowns quickly turned into happy smiles when Darcy let them know there would be sleigh rides after luncheon on the morrow for anyone who wanted to participate.

Fanny and Bennet, Madeline and Gardiner, and Elaine and Matlock begged off the sleigh rides, but everyone else enthusiastically indicated that they would like to go, especially the four young Gardiner children and one young future earl.

The days flew by as everyone enjoyed the time together as a family. Five days after sending the express to Sir Fredrick, he replied he would be willing to come to attend Mrs. Darcy and would arrive with two nurses a month prior to the expected date of Mrs. Darcy's lying in and requested his warmest regards be passed onto his friends, the Gardiners.

CHAPTER 26

Charlotte Lucas could not believe what she was seeing. Lizzy had described Pemberley as a house, but in her eyes, it was a mansion! It was easily the biggest house Charlotte had ever beheld, and she was awed that Lizzy was mistress of this great estate, the house in town, and the secondary estates.

The maid who had accompanied her had told her Pemberley was big, but she had not been ready for the sight that greeted her when the carriage crested the hill and gave her the first view of the snow-covered house and park. Her mouth dropped open from the shock of the view before her.

By the time the carriage drew to a stop in front of the manor house, Charlotte had managed to pick up her jaw and had schooled her mien. As she stepped out of the conveyance, she was hugged by a very pregnant Elizabeth Darcy.

"Welcome to our home, Charlotte. William and I are very happy you agreed to join us, I hope you are able to stay with us for a while as you are welcome for as long as you would like to be here." Lizzy was practically bouncing on her toes at having Charlotte by her side once again.

"Oh my! Eliza, I see you are with child, you are glowing, and what a beautiful home you have here." Charlotte hugged her.

"Ladies, as it is cold outside, I suggest we enter the house." Darcy stepped up and offered his arms.

"As you can see Charlotte, my William is very protective of his very pregnant wife." Elizabeth smiled brightly.

"Just as it should be." Whatever Charlotte was about to say after that died on her lips. She was awed by the magnificent two-story entrance hall that had an understated elegance about it. Everything that Charlotte saw was the best, nothing out of place, gaudy, or ostentatious.

Charlotte stood rooted to her spot as she handed her outerwear to the butler after he closed the front doors.

"It may be a big house my friend, but it is still a house, our home," Lizzy leaned over and whispered to her friend.

Once Charlotte settled, her friend turned to her housekeeper and requested she show Charlotte up to her room to rest from the road. Charlotte was led up to the second floor to one of the guest wings and shown into the biggest bedchambers she had ever seen. It was bigger than Maria's and hers combined.

She then realised she had only seen the bedchamber and was taken aback as the housekeeper showed her the private sitting room, dressing room, and bathing room. Altogether it was the combined size of her and her four siblings' spaces at home. She thought she had an idea how much wealth the Darcy's enjoyed, but she now saw she had underestimated it by a great deal.

Becky, the maid that had travelled with her, had already hung her clothing in a dressing room closet that would fit many times more clothing than Charlotte possessed, asked if she would like a bath. Charlotte, used to washing out of a basin or bowl at home, said she would like to bathe to remove all of the dust from travelling.

After Charlotte had done so and changed into one of her best day dresses, she was shown by a footman to the drawing room where everyone was assembled. She had met all in Hertfordshire except for a very nice-looking man in clerical garb, who luckily looked and smelled nothing like

Bennet's late cousin who had attempted to cause mayhem at Longbourn.

"Charlotte, allow me to introduce you to Mr. Patrick Elliot. He is the parson who holds the livings of Lambton, Kympton, and Pemberley. Mr. Elliot, may I have the pleasure of introducing you to one of my best friends, Miss Charlotte Lucas of Lucas Lodge in Hertfordshire," Elizabeth offered.

"A pleasure to meet you Miss Lucas." The parson bowed in greeting.

"And you, Mr. Elliot. How long have you held your livings in Derbyshire?" Charlotte inquired; her eyes demure but captivated as she curtsied in return.

"It has been a little under three years now, Miss Lucas. I am the third son of a baronet and was lucky enough to find the church was not only my preferred option of service but my preferred path in life," Elliot related.

"I do appreciate it when providence and life's paths are so harmonious. I wish you and your family a very happy yuletide, sir," Charlotte offered sincerely knowing men as kind and handsome as he did not stay single for long in their lives.

"I thank you on behalf of myself and my daughter, Miss Lucas," he nodded at her confusion. "I was married, but five years ago my wife passed soon after delivering me a gift from God in the form of my now five-year-old daughter Grace. I was at Trinity on a short trip with my friend and patron, Fitzwilliam Darcy. We actually met when we were thirteen and in our first year at Harrow," he revealed, still plagued by the guilt though there was nothing he could have done to save his beloved late wife even had he arrived home in time.

"You have my condolences for your loss. I do not always understand the ways that our Lord in His infinite wisdom tests us. I am sure you would have been there at her side had you the slightest inkling of what would happen," Charlotte offered sincerely. "Is your daughter with you? Will I have the honour of meeting her tonight?"

"Thank you for your kind words, Miss Lucas," Elliot responded, his eyes not leaving hers. "No, Grace is with my parents at present as it is a busy time of year for my vocation and one of the curates I share duties with will be soon going home to end the holiday season with his family. For the last three years, my darling girl has spent the season with her grandparents and my brothers and their families who all love her dearly. I am sure you will have a very pleasant stay, Miss Lucas." He blushed, saying the right things to end the conversation so she would not feel obligated to continue it and relieved she did not divert her focus.

"Do you have any particular suggestions for my stay, Mr. Elliot? I often find the Parson knows the best points of interest," Charlotte offered boldly and was relieved he was glad to continue the conversation as well.

"You are already at one of them, Miss Lucas, and if it is not too forward, may I request the first dance from you at the Twelfth Night Ball?" he asked as boldly.

"You may, sir. And I thank you," Charlotte replied softly, her heart pounding in her chest as she wondered at the sensations she was experiencing, all the while hoping it meant the same thing as it had when Lizzy had described the feeling she had when she saw Mr. Darcy for the first time.

"In that case, would you write my name on your card for the supper set as well?" he asked, this time taking the chance to be intrepid, as only age and wisdom allow. Chances and moments like this were rare, and Elliot was not willing to allow it to pass him by.

"Yes Mr. Elliot, it will be my pleasure to grant you the supper set as well," Charlotte allowed as she searched his eyes, finding he was looking back into hers with the same intensity and blushing warmly. The rest of the party had been quietly watching the interplay between the parson and Miss Lucas.

"I told you so!" a smug looking Darcy leaned over and whispered to his wife. His smiling wife slapped his arm playfully and then stepped in to join them.

"I trust your chambers meet with your approval Charlotte?" Lizzy asked playfully.

"Meet with my approval, Eliza! You well know that is an understatement. I feel like I might get lost in my own chambers, never mind the rest of your magnificent home," Charlotte teased.

"To assist you to find your way around, I will request Mrs. Reynolds give you a tour of the house on the morrow if the morning is convenient for you." Elizabeth smiled warmly, appreciating the blush that Mr. Elliot had caused to bloom on Charlotte's cheeks.

"Yes, thank you, that will be perfect," Charlotte agreed with relief.

"How is my friend Sarah doing, Charlotte?" Fanny asked as she approached her daughters' good friend.

"Mama is very well, thank you Mrs. Bennet, and she sends her regards and wishes of the season to all of you," Charlotte reported.

"Your father is well? I hope it has not been too cold as he sometimes suffers from it." Bennet smiled gently at Charlotte, reminding her that she was surrounded by people who knew and appreciated her and her family as well, the message was more for Mr. Elliot, which Charlotte surmised and her blush deepened, truly grateful for their affection for her.

"Papa is well, Mr. Bennet and no it has not been too cold, so he has been his normal, affable self," Charlotte shared, her eyes thanking him and laughing softly when he winked at her playfully.

Not long after dinner was called, and Miss Lucas very willingly found herself being escorted to the large dining room by Mr. Elliot. As she expected the meal was exceptional, and she enjoyed her conversation with the clergyman.

The more they talked, the more comfortable she felt with him. She was greatly impressed with the warmth with which he talked about his daughter whom he so obviously doted on. Charlotte had long considered herself on the shelf for unlike the Bennets, whom she considered beautiful, she thought herself plain.

In addition, she had very little in the way of a dowry, although her papa had just started increasing it with help from Edward Gardiner. She felt she could grow to respect and esteem Mr. Elliot, and more surprising, mayhap something she never thought important or would happen to her, love him.

What Charlotte was unaware of was her friend and her husband had told Mr. Elliot about her. They had been honest, not making her out to be someone she was not. It was the reason for his acceptance of the dinner invitation this particular night as he most often joined the Darcys for luncheon with his daughter after services.

Normally a lot more reserved, Patrick Elliot had surprised himself when he requested the two dances from Miss Lucas, the meaningful supper set included. He also admitted he normally did not discuss Grace with ladies much, but he felt no such reserve while discussing his daughter with Miss Lucas.

The more Elliot talked to her at dinner, the more he believed they would be very compatible. She was exactly as Mrs. Darcy promised after twenty years of knowing her friend; Miss Lucas was a caring and intelligent woman.

It was undeniably fast, though perhaps not as quick

as the Darcys had in their story as it was not exactly instantaneous, more so a full moment had passed, possibly two before he allowed himself the hope he was to find the happiness they exuded as he never believed God would gift him with a second chance.

The more they talked, the more he believed she would make a perfect mother to Grace and an exceptionally good parson's wife. He did not want to frighten her and overwhelm her with attention, so he decided to take things slowly. He certainly did not want to push harder than he sensed she would be comfortable with. After the separation of the sexes, Elliot asked Miss Lucas if he could join her on the settee, and she gestured for him to sit with a welcoming smile.

"How do you enjoy your life in Hertfordshire? I understand that you live close to Mrs. Darcy's childhood home," Elliot asked.

"I like living in that county very much, and yes, my father's estate is surrounded on three sides by Longbourn and Bennet Fields. In order not to be a burden on my parents, I help out as much as I can around the house and make most of the tenant visits." Charlotte spoke honestly. She did not want him to presume she had the same level of wealth the Darcys or the Bennets claimed.

"Surely you are not a burden on your parents?" he frowned, not believing for a second that Charlotte would allow such.

"They would never say so, but I am no longer a young girl like my sister Maria, and I feel my parents should not have to support me anymore. While I am here, I intend to ask Eliza if she knows of anyone who needs a companion," Charlotte admitted quietly.

"Miss Lucas, I had wanted to move slower so I do not run you off and it may give you an impression I am hasty, but it is normally not so. However, given the circumstances and what you just shared, I have to ask you something as I do not want to see you leave here to go into service, or leave here for any reason at all."

Elliot took a deep breath and plunged ahead, "I know we have just met, literally but a couple of hours ago so this may sound forward and crazy, but in talking to you this night, and in hearing the stories Mrs. Darcy has shared about you, telling of your kindness, and love she so obviously has for you, I was already favourably inclined toward you. I have come to believe we would be very compatible. More importantly, I believe you would be a good mother to my Gracie and help guide her through life. I could never consider a woman I felt would not be a good influence on my daughter."

"I would not think you would," Charlotte replied breathlessly.

"And though I know this is too forward for a third hour of conversation, I have not been attracted to a woman since my wife passed away five years ago...until I saw you." He offered the last quietly, relieved she was not running for the door to order her trunks packed.

Elliot held his hand out for hers and was gratified when he felt her fingers against his. He covered her hand with his other hand, the world and propriety long lost in the possibility of a future neither expected but both longed for.

"What I want to ask you is, before you take a fateful step like going into service, if we could get to know one another better in an informal courtship, and then we can decide if we would like to enter into a courtship or something more. And I have to tell you, Miss Lucas, Charlotte, I am already inclined to jump into something more if you say it is that or nothing." He held his breath as he waited for her to cogitate on an answer.

Charlotte, while unaccustomed to such haste, had explained her situation just for this reason. She wanted him to know her next step so he had the chance to intervene should he feel an attraction to her as she felt for him.

It was obvious that he did. This meant she was rather inclined to jump into something else too, but reasoned they could spend a week or two in an informal courtship. She had waited this long, mayhap now she finally had her reason for why she had had to wait so long to find a man she was compatible with.

"I find myself agreeing with you Mr. Elliot, so I will do nothing to further my aim of becoming a companion and would very much like to get to know you better. I feel the great honour of your being willing to trust me to be a good mother to your daughter. Just so you know and are not misled by who my friends are, at this point, I only have a dowry of two thousand pounds, although my father said he is working to increase our portions," Charlotte related and then held her breath.

"Thank you, Miss Lucas." Elliot kissed the back of one of her hands and she felt a warm feeling spread through her body as he did. "I do not need, nor am I looking for, a bride with a large dowry. I have a reasonable fortune of my own and I make a very good living holding the livings at Lambton, Kympton, and Pemberley.

"I am looking for a wife who will love my daughter as if she is her own and a woman to love me and be a partner to me as we journey through our trials and triumphs. I believe we will be very compatible in all ways, and with faith, honesty, and respect between us. This is what I am looking for, not an heiress.

"I laid bare my guilt before you to judge me and you said I was not at fault. You have revealed your greatest fear to me, and I want nothing more than to make it go away. Mrs.

Darcy has told me how you and she took care of your younger sister and her younger brothers at all stages in their lives, so I truly believe you will be the best of mothers to my Gracie if things get to that point. I look forward to getting to know you better." He promised quietly.

"I look forward to meeting your daughter as soon as you feel the time is right," Charlotte responded softly. The two talked for some time until they realised they needed to talk to others as well.

If things progressed, they would move into the parsonage at Kympton as it was the largest of the three parsonages in the parishes he held the livings for, in fact, he decided to be optimistic and start the move immediately!

They parted with both feeling they were on the way to the happiest of outcomes of their informal courtship. After the parson walked towards where the coffee and tea was being served, Elizabeth beckoned her friend over to where she sat with her husband, her parents, and her aunts and uncles.

"Did you forget we were here tonight as well, Charlotte?" Lizzy teased her friend.

"I did not forget, Eliza, I just enjoyed talking to Mr. Elliot very much," Charlotte admitted.

"Did Lizzy inform you that I suggested we introduce you and Elliot when we were back in Hertfordshire at the time we invited you to visit us, Miss Lucas?" William teased.

"No, Mr. Darcy, Eliza did not mention that little titbit to me in my invitation, but..." Miss Lucas started to blush, "I am not at all unhappy at the introduction."

"You seemed to be quite engrossed with each other, Charlotte. And, were you not so happy when he asked to hold your hand, Thomas would have tossed him out on his ear if he upset you." Mrs. Bennet huffed as she assessed Charlotte, her eyes dancing with mirth.

"We did have a very in-depth conversation, Mrs. Bennet, and thank you for not having him tossed out of the house," Charlotte confirmed playfully.

"When you accepted my invitation, you wrote there was a particular subject you wanted to talk to me about, Charlotte. One related to your future, I believe you said. Is it something you can talk about now, or do we require privacy?" Elizabeth took her friend's hand as she asked.

"I did want to talk to you about something, but due to a conversation I just had with Mr. Elliot, the reason for my needing to talk to you is no longer valid." Seeing the questioning looks from both her friend and her mother, Charlotte offered her reasoning. "I was going to ask you if you knew of anyone seeking a companion for their daughter or widowed relative," Charlotte sighed at the looks of disbelief on the faces of those who knew and loved her. "Do not look at me so, I am seven and twenty and am long on the shelf. I have felt for some time I have been a burden on my parents and want to relieve both them and, Franklin once he becomes master."

"Even if you feel so, I am sure neither your parents nor your brother feels that way," Elizabeth countered.

"We do not have fortunes like the Bennets, even though Papa has said he is doing something about that now, so I am happy for Maria. As I said, that was my intent, but Mr. Elliot has requested an informal courtship to see if we suit, and if we both decide we do then he will request a formal courtship or more." Charlotte laughed at the surprise of some being so greatly contrasted with the lack of surprise of others. She offered no resistance when Elizabeth drew her lifelong friend into a warm embrace.

"We had a suspicion you two would be a good fit. You were correct, William!" she offered as she hugged Charlotte tightly into her arms, grateful her best friend may have her own happy ending.

"As is usual, wife of mine." Darcy winked at Charlotte; whose deeper laugh warmed the room.

"You teasing man!" Lizzy said playfully then returned her attention to her best friend. "So, what are the plans? Did Mr. Elliot tell you about Grace and his previous wife?" As his wife finished talking, Darcy headed off to go talk to his friend Elliot.

"I just realised something, Eliza. Papa sent a note with me for your husband allowing him to act in his stead. Did you and Mr. Darcy talk to my parents about Mr. Elliot when you were in Hertfordshire?" she asked in great surprise.

"We did send them a missive. Are you upset with us for our amateur attempt at matchmaking?" Elizabeth asked hesitantly, not wanting her friend to think anything malicious was at play.

"Not in the least. I think I will owe you and Mr. Darcy a debt of gratitude if all goes as I hope. I know I have always said all I needed was a good home and it was best to learn about one's spouse after the wedding, but I may have been wrong. I think I will respect and esteem Mr. Elliot, and even come to love him.

"Yes, he told me about Grace, and I could see the love for his daughter clearly, which is one of the things I already esteem about him. He explained he was married before and his wife died after childbirth. Me, who always said love was not needed to make a good match! It seems the Bennets were correct in this as well as a lot of other things," Charlotte admitted.

"Better late than never Charlotte, and I shan't even tell you I told you so," Lizzy teased causing Charlotte to smile.

~~~~~~~/~~~~~~~

Darcy found Elliot sitting on his own, seemingly deep in thought. He took a cup of coffee and sat down next to his friend. "You will make my wife very happy if you end up marrying Miss Lucas and keep her close to Pemberley." Darcy sipped his coffee.

"Sorry, Darcy, I was wool-gathering. What did you say?" Elliot started. Darcy chuckled and repeated what he had said. "Yes, well, I think unless one of us finds something wholly objectionable in the other, Mrs. Darcy's friend will be a resident of the area and Gracie will have a mother. If I suspected for a second she would not be a good mother to my Grace, then I would not consider her, no matter my wishes."

He looked over at Charlotte, his hands tight together and Darcy recognised his friend was far more physically attracted to their Charlotte than he even yet realised. He had used the same tactics to keep himself in check when so surrounded by others and without yet permission to keep his Elizabeth close every second.

"I think the two of you would do very well together," Darcy soothed. "She would be an ideal parson's wife. I agree with you and believe she will make your little Gracie a wonderful mother. She is compassionate, intelligent, and would help you take good care of your parishioners."

"That was my thought as well, but would not be enough to get me to propose marriage, especially if I did not believe she would be a good mother to Grace. She has a lot of the attributes I would like in a wife, and I already esteem and respect her. So, unless she objects it is too fast or for some other reason, I hope she does not have, I intend to ask her to marry me once we know each other a little better.

"I will have to make the journey to Hertfordshire to ask her father for his blessing. I know she is of age, but I am sure she would prefer to have the blessing of her father," Elliot stated resolutely, knowing Darcy would never deny him the request should he get a favourable answer from Charlotte.

"You will not need to do that. I have a letter from Sir William granting me authority to act in his stead. We had an idea you and Miss Lucas would be a good fit, though that is not why my wife related memories to you which only included her. Truly they are that close and were that close growing up, so many of her childhood memories naturally include Miss Lucas. If your suit is a success, then once you decide whether to marry here or in Hertfordshire, we will plan accordingly," Darcy stated.

"Since when have you become a matchmaker?" Elliot looked him over to see if he was really talking to his friend, Fitzwilliam Darcy. "Just so you know I am moving, in anticipation of her accepting me. I will begin to move to the Kympton parsonage on the morrow as it is the largest of the three." Darcy nodded his agreement with his friend's plan.

"I do not see myself as a matchmaker, merely a facilitator of a meeting. The rest was and is entirely up to the two of you as I told you when first I mentioned Miss Lucas to you. You know what they say, you can lead a horse to water, but you cannot make him drink." Darcy chuckled. "But I will tell you this. I do not know if it was divine intervention, or if an angel whispered in my ear, or if I just was imagining the moment, but the second I was introduced to her and saw her poise and love of my Lizzy with no resentment for her wealth while she herself had little, I was aware she was exactly the kind of woman you have long described, given your chosen vocation."

A parson's wife would not have all the finery that some of her neighbours would have, nor would she be as poor as others. The women who could be equally respectful and compassionate for both sides of that line were rare indeed.

He had just been blessed to find another one after his late wife, and it just so happened to also be a woman who stole his breath away from the moment she walked in. He had not imagined she would be the expected Charlotte Lucas, but he had been most grateful to learn she was. Eliot was suddenly aware he had let the silence go on too long.

"There is truth in that. I thank you and your lovely wife. Your facilitation could very well lead to a very happy outcome. I would still travel to go see her father, even though you have permission to act in his stead," Elliot told Darcy, knowing full well his friend would do the same.

"Then go to it, Elliot," Darcy agreed.

With that, Elliot crossed the drawing room where Miss Lucas was still with Mrs. Darcy and Mrs. Bennet, asking if he could have another word with Miss Lucas who answered yes before either of her companions could respond. Charlotte excused herself.

"Did you know the Darcys arranged for us to meet?" she asked carefully.

"Darcy informed me when they returned from his wife's sisters' weddings. I am not vexed, in fact, I could not be happier, I hope you feel the same way." Eliot searched her eyes for any sign of disapprobation.

"Yes, Mr. Elliot, I do. I most certainly do," Charlotte admitted softly.

"May I be so forward as to request your final set at the Twelfth Night Ball on the morrow?" Elliot pushed his luck.

"My my, that is bold, and you will cause many tongues to wag. However, I believe our ages give us leave to do so without worry about causing a scandal. I will gladly grant you the last as well. Should you want to cause a great scandal claim me for a fourth," Charlotte teased, pleased his rich, thick laugh echoed around her as he again lifted her hand to kiss it, pleased beyond measure she blushed.

"May I call on you tomorrow morning, Miss Lucas, so we can take a walk in the Darcys' rose gardens?" he pressed his suit.

"I would like that. There are no shortages of

chaperones in residence so there will be no question of propriety," Charlotte accepted, glancing out and he followed to see all eyes were on them.

"I am glad to know they are watching out for you and look forward to the time when it will also be my privilege," he murmured, her look of pleasure causing his heart to pound in hope, her nod at the pre-emptive agreement as it was what she too wanted made it soar. "Until tomorrow morning at ten. I must take my leave now."

As he said the last, he took each of her hands and placed a kiss on the ungloved back of each, lingering over both as he deeply breathed her scent in and she, for the first time, saw herself as the object of his desires as well as his happiness.

Charlotte's heart stuttered then started to race, and she was breathless as she watched him walk away, grateful when Darcy guided her to Lizzy who handed her a glass of sherry. In such moments of discovery, sometimes tea was not enough to settle one.

~~~~~~~/~~~~~~~

The morning of the ball found Miss Charlotte Lucas excited and giddy as a schoolgirl as she waited in the drawing room for Mr. Elliot to arrive to call on her. She was apparently to have four chaperones: Tom, James, Kitty, and, to her greatest surprise, Georgiana.

Elizabeth had conspiratorially told Charlotte the four would allow them to be out of earshot but be able to see them, thus preserving all of the conventions of propriety but allowing the best chance of growth of an attachment.

At five minutes before ten, Mr. Elliot was announced by the Darcy butler. Charlotte experienced a happiness and excitement she had never before felt when meeting with a member of the opposite sex.

They walked out to the rose garden with the four

younger men and women following at a reasonable distance. Mr Elliot brushed the snow off a bench so they could sit, not yet knowing it was the very same bench on which Charles Bingley had proposed to Jane Bennet. The Bennet twins, Kitty, and Georgiana cleared the snow and sat down on a pair of benches with a line of sight to the couple, but far away enough they would not overhear what was being said.

For an hour the new couple discussed a variety of topics including their families, where they grew up, and their likes and dislikes. And as so often happens when physical attraction is in play and genuine respect and honesty are offered, the more they talked, the more both accepted they were beyond just compatible. They had realised at the previous night's gathering they were starting to develop feelings one for the other, but now they were both sure the other felt the same.

"Miss Lucas, or may I call you Charlotte, and will you call me Patrick?" She nodded her agreement. "I recently turned thirty so I want to preface what I am about to say with the reminder I am not a young man prone to flights of fancy. In these scant hours as I have had the pleasure of getting to know you, I have found a lady who I believe will suit me as well as I will suit her.

"Grace is now five years old and in need of a mother. If my application this day is successful, then you will soon meet her as she is to return anon. I am not going to lie to you and tell you that I love you, but I believe I am well on the way, and I can tell you that I respect and esteem you greatly. Is there hope? Do I have reason to hope you mayhap have similar thoughts and feelings?" Elliot held his breath in anticipation.

"Yes, Mr. Elliot, Patrick, my thoughts and feelings are exactly aligned with yours. Before I met you but yesterday, I believed I was an old maid destined to be a burden on my family which prompted my desire to enter service. That all changed when I met you and felt the...liked you." She blushed and he smiled with relief because he understood exactly what she meant. She was also attracted to him and that was a relief, because wanting one's wife more than she wants you is a misery too many men experienced.

"I admit I am relieved you like me as well, Charlotte." He offered quietly so she was in no doubt of his attraction and her blush heightened most becomingly.

"Like you, I do not believe I am in love with you yet, but I do have tender feelings which I am sure will develop into love soon enough, and I already esteem and respect you greatly by position and how you have described your preferences for your parish. I would love to meet your daughter, Grace, and I am sure I will love her as I would any children I may be blessed with in the future. I will not ask she call me mother, but I will hope to earn the title with both your approvals," Charlotte revealed, looking down to find her hand in his and not remembering if she had taken his or he hers.

"It pleases me greatly you have never asked me about my financial position, which shows me that you are not interested in me for pecuniary gain. But I want you as a partner in my life as well as the wife I will get to cherish to know my situation. I own a small estate, Riverdale, in Shropshire, that I inherited from my maternal grandmother. I lease the estate out as I have no need for it at present. It brings in a clear three thousand a year.

"If I...we have a son the estate will go to him, but if not, Grace will inherit it as there is no entailment away from the female line on the property. I have a fortune of thirty thousand that I have just invested with Mrs. Darcy's uncle, Mr. Gardiner. From what I have been told of the success he has had, there will be more than enough to provide for Grace, any future daughters we have with a decent dowry, a legacy for second sons, and beyond.

"In addition, with the three livings I hold, I earn a little more than two thousand a year. I only spend a small portion, and most of the rest goes toward my investments. I hope you can see even if you had no dowry, we would not suffer financially." He held her hand tighter as he saw her eyes continue to widen.

Charlotte Lucas was flabbergasted; she had not in her wildest dream believed she would attract a man such as this. Yes, he was wealthy, but more than that he was a good man, a man willing to entrust her with his daughter who he obviously adored.

While she was considering all that had transpired in such a short time, Elliot knelt in front of her. "Charlotte Lucas, I do not think we need a courtship." He smiled as he saw her crestfallen look and went on. "Will you please make me the happiest of men and agree to marry me, to be my wife and a mother to Grace?" he asked hopefully.

Tears pooled and spilled down her cheeks as she heard what he asked, and she nodded vigorously. "Yes, Patrick, I will marry you. Yes, yes, yes! I will, I will be the best of mothers to Grace possible, and she will always feel the love of her family."

As she gave him the answer he was hoping for, Elliot stood and drew her into an embrace. Both forgetting their four chaperones, she looked up into his eyes in an invitation he did not want to ignore and gave her a light, sweet kiss, which was her first from a man not of her family. Before he could deepen the kiss, they heard an enunciated "Ahem" as the four chaperones approached them.

"I assume this means that Mr. Elliot proposed to you, Charlotte? Please tell me he did, or my brothers are about to defend your honour and I would hate to have to root against them as the hero tries to escape with his lady love," Kitty teased.

"Yes, he did Kitty. And he has made me so very happy." Charlotte blushed as she nodded then looked at their chaperones. "Though I do appreciate the willingness to defend my honour," she smiled sweetly at the four of them.

"Brother said if this happened, we were to bring you to see him in his study." Georgiana offered.

"Lead the way please, Miss Darcy." Elliot nodded once in her direction as he held his arm out to his betrothed.

~~~~~~~/~~~~~~~

Elliot, with Miss Lucas next to him, knocked on Darcy's study door. They entered hand in hand, which told Mr. Darcy all he needed to know, though too Charlotte's look of happiness would have said it as plainly, as did Elliot's expression.

Darcy had not seen him this excited or happy since before he had lost his wife, though he would never say it to his friend. After some perfunctory questions, he granted his permission and blessing on behalf of Sir William Lucas.

He pulled a chord that would ring a bell to summon Douglas and requested he ask Mrs. Darcy to join the party in the study. As soon as is wife entered and she saw the look of joy on her friend's face, she hugged Charlotte and congratulated Mr. Elliot.

They then had a discussion about timing and the location of the wedding. The couple decided they would marry in three weeks after the banns were read, and they chose to marry from the Kympton Church, since they had found each other in Derbyshire.

Darcy sent an express to Sir William Lucas and dispatched a coach and attendants to transport the Lucas family to Pemberley when they were ready to make the trip. That saved his friend Elliot the trip to and from Hertfordshire and the dreaded departure from Charlotte's side.

Once the rest of the party were apprised of the plans, everyone agreed they would stay at Pemberley until the wedding. The Earl of Matlock sent an express to the parson at the living he bestowed in Matlock with a request he come perform the ceremony and was sure it would not be an issue because his parson was a good friend of Elliot's.

At the same time, Elliot sent an express to his father, Sir Everett Elliot, to share his glad tidings. He requested his father inform the family and join them at Pemberley five days before the wedding. He also requested his mother send the engagement ring his grandmother had bequeathed him so he could present it to his betrothed.

He was sure his father and mother, Lady Ilene, and the rest of his siblings would heartily approve of his Charlotte. He asked his mother to let Grace know she would soon have a mama and asked that someone accompany his daughter back to his house as soon as possible.

His family had started to despair he would ever marry again, yet in the space of but two days that had all changed. As he thought about his Charlotte, he acknowledged he was falling in love with her, but he would wait for her to arrive at the same point before telling her. He had no desire to put pressure on her to make a declaration she was not ready to make yet.

Charlotte Lucas was almost euphoric. Not only was she, one who had decided to go into service rather than be a burden on her family, engaged, she was going to have the joy of being a mother from her first day as Patrick's wife.

The Darcys had told her their Twelfth Night Ball would double as an engagement ball for herself and her betrothed. Her life had changed so much in the space of days, changing what she saw as a bleak future into an eternity of happiness, respect, and love.

Yes, she had fallen in love with her betrothed. She

decided to wait to tell him as she did not want to rush him if he was not yet in love with her. She had not yet met her soon to be daughter, but her heart was already expanding with love of her based on the way her father talked about her.

That night at the ball, Charlotte Lucas felt like a princess. Her maid had given her a delightful coiffure, Elizabeth and Jane's French lady's maids had worked magic with her gown, and to top it all off her best friend had lent her some of the Darcy jewels to wear. Charlotte pinched herself to make sure she was not dreaming, things like this did not happen to her, did they?

Her fiancé had warned her some of the local matchmaking mamas may resent her for usurping a position they had coveted for their own daughters ever since his year of mourning was complete, but none of that bothered Charlotte this night. She felt like she was floating among the clouds, and never had she enjoyed dancing as much as she did with her betrothed.

~~~~~~~/~~~~~~~

Some days later, back in Meryton, Lady Sarah Lucas had all but fainted when her husband had shared the news with her. Like Charlotte, Lady Lucas had believed her oldest was well and truly on the shelf.

Rather she was engaged to the son of a baronet who was a very wealthy man, a landowner, and the father of a young daughter. She had to pinch herself to make sure she was not dreaming.

She was to become an instant grandmamma; her joy was boundless. She was a little upset Charlotte would not marry out of the Meryton Church where the first banns for her wedding would be read this Sunday but was mollified when she thought about not only travelling to stay at Pemberley, but in the magnificent coach that had just arrived in front of Lucas Lodge.

Not only had the Darcys sent a conveyance, but they had arranged the family's stays along the way at no expense to the Lucases. Sir William had informed his wife that they would leave on Wednesday, which had them arriving at Pemberley on Saturday a week before the wedding.

~~~~~~~/~~~~~~~

On Wednesday, Sir William, Lady Lucas, Frank, Maria, and young John Lucas all boarded the most comfortable conveyance they had ever seen or ridden in, and started the journey north.

On Saturday morning, as the coach crested the hill and gave them their first glimpse of the snow covered valley below, the five Lucases in the carriage could not believe the view that met them. They had known the Darcys were wealthy, but nothing prepared them for the view of the manor house that lay before them, and to a person they were shocked. The house looked palatial to them, it would to anyone who had never seen it, no matter their station and wealth.

"Lizzy is mistress of all of this?" asked a very awed Maria Lucas.

"Yes Maria, and they own three other estates and a house in town as well." Sir William responded.

"I had no idea. I am so appreciative of Eliza and Mr. Darcy that they are hosting the wedding breakfast here in this magical setting for our Charlotte." Lady Lucas tried to keep herself regulated as the swells of love for her daughter and their friends created great pressure in her breast and behind her eyes. Joy like this was a rare gift and she would never forget it.

"Look at the extent of the stables, Papa. They are as big as Longbourn's. Do you think we will be able to ride?" Frank asked hopefully on his and his brother's behalf.

"Weather permitting, Son. Charlotte told me in one of

her letters the Darcys have sleighs, so mayhap you will be able to ride in one with them." At the mention of sleighs, Sir William's eleven-year-old son's eyes lit up like a thousand candles were reflected in them.

"I cannot wait to see the house where Charlotte will live. She wrote to me it is a very comfortable situation and they will have more than enough servants. Do you suppose she has met her future daughter yet, my soon-to-be niece?" Maria asked hopefully. "Oh, I get to be an aunt." She clapped happily, finally starting to believe it was all coming true.

Maria had not allowed herself to believe it so far, she had wanted it all too much, some might say. Her sister had long sacrificed for her, believing she was on the shelf, and this was a just reward.

"You know a Lieutenant in the militia would not be able to provide a fraction of what Charlotte's betrothed has do you not, Maria?" Sir William looked down at her with an arched brow and a stern frown.

"Yes Papa, I promise I have been cured of chasing men in regimentals. I have talked to Mary and her husband Richard Fitzwilliam, and he did not sugar-coat the life I would have if I was stupid enough to marry an officer with no prospects," Maria acknowledged, not enjoying reflecting on her foolishness when she had thought a man in a red coat, any man in a red coat would do.

"Then we will have to thank Richard, will we not Sarah." Sir William smiled at his wife; the relief felt by them both.

"I could not agree more, William. Thank goodness you finally woke up, Maria. Just think how you could have been ruined by the likes of that wastrel Wickham whom Mr. Darcy sent to Marshalsea. You know we were only so worried because we love you and want you happy. We are not like some parents that think any match would suffice. But to answer your question, my dear girl, I assume by now Grace has been introduced to her soon to be Mama," Lady Lucas predicted.

A little while later the carriage pulled up at one of the entrances to the mansion and a footman lowered the steps. The Lucases were met by Charlotte who showed them into a drawing room where the Darcys, Bennets, and her fiancé and his shy daughter awaited them.

Grace was a pretty-looking girl with light brown hair, not dissimilar to Charlotte's. Mr. and Mrs. Darcy welcomed the overawed Lucases as they drank in the elegance and wealth on display. They knew from the facade of the house there was a lot more to see, but what they had seen so far was beyond impressive.

Charlotte introduced her parents and siblings to her betrothed and his daughter and it was with great relief to Sarah and Sir William that they did not have to pretend to like their daughter's fiancé.

They had predetermined they would do nothing to stand in Charlotte's way as her letters offered the happiness they could only hope their daughter would one day find. They liked Patrick very well, but for Sarah, she was relieved her daughter's good nature and ability to care for others was not the only value he saw in his fiancée.

It was obvious he loved to look at her demonstrating there was genuine attraction between them. No one missed Grace was holding onto Charlotte's hand tightly, not her father's, and although a little shy at first, made her curtseys to each person she was introduced to.

After introductions and sincerely thanking the Darcys for sending the coach and the consideration of arranging the inns along the way, and greeting all of the Bennets, Mrs. Reynolds showed the Lucases to their chambers in the East guest wing of the house.

As they followed the housekeeper to their rooms, the awe among the five arriving members of the Lucas family only deepened. In their wildest dreams had they never imagined being guests in a house like the one where they were currently being accommodated. Once they arrived at their chambers, awe transformed to amazement.

Like Charlotte before them, they could not believe the size of their chambers. Sir William and Lady Lucas had a suite with a shared sitting room, as did their sons Frank and John. Maria's room was part of Charlotte's suite which also had its own sitting room, and Maria, who had never had the luxury of a lady's maid before, found a maid waiting for her who informed her that she would serve as her lady's maid while she was at Pemberley.

The Lucases were sure they would never find the drawing room again and be forever lost in the mansion, and were much relieved when they were told there were two footmen on duty that would show them how to get there when they were ready.

After changing out of their travel attire and washing off the dust of the road, they were shown to the very drawing room they had initially received to find the whole Pemberley party awaited them.

Sir William and Lady Lucas gravitated toward their good friends Mr. and Mrs. Bennet, and Maria joined the young group that included the Bennet twins, Kitty Bennet, and Georgiana Darcy.

Lady Lucas had always worried Charlotte saw marriage with too much of a clinical and cynical eye, so to see how happy her daughter was warmed her heart and that of her husband's.

~~~~~~~/~~~~~~~

The Elliot family, led by Sir Everett and Lady Ilene, arrived at Pemberley four days before the wedding. They had delayed one day as one of their grandchildren was recovering from a fever and their son and daughter-in-law did not want to leave until they knew their young daughter was well and truly on the mend.

The party included Patrick Elliot's two older brothers and their wives, and his younger still unmarried sister who was to have her come out in the upcoming season. Grace was overjoyed to see her grandparents, aunts, uncles, and cousins again so soon.

It did not take the Elliots long to understand why their son and brother had chosen Charlotte Lucas. They were very well matched and, to the surprise of all considering the speed, clearly in love one with the other.

As important to them all, they were more than gratified to see Charlotte already loved their little Gracie, and in seeing so their final concerns were washed away. Grace would have a mother who saw her as a blessing even before she was her daughter.

Elliot had long regretted his former wife had been the last living member of her family, but now Grace would also get a second pair of grandparents, two more uncles, and another aunt.

~~~~~~~/~~~~~~~

The day before the wedding, Ladies Lucas and Elliot went with Charlotte to look over the parsonage at Kympton. The house was less than eight miles from Pemberley and was almost the size of Lucas Lodge with a good-sized kitchen garden, and on the glebe lands there was an orchard and other established agricultural plantings.

Charlotte had seen the house a number of times since her fiancé had moved in and other than some minor suggestions, she had changed nothing. Her mother and soon to be mother-in-law had never seen the parsonage before.

Grace held her new mother's hand as if it was natural,

and for her it now was. She decided Charlotte was her mother, and so Charlotte was that in all ways to the pretty little girl.

Glad to have *Mama* with her, Grace happily chatted with both of her grandmothers as her initial shyness had faded with the proof Charlotte was close by as she met all these new people.

~~~~~~~/~~~~~~~

That night, Charlotte Lucas fell asleep feeling content for possibly the first time. She was marrying the best of men and becoming a wife and mother on the morrow.

Patrick Elliot fell asleep in the parsonage with similar thoughts about his fiancée, and very glad it was the last time he would sleep as a widower in his home, more importantly, was very happy it was the last time he was sleeping in this bed without his Charlotte.

The next morning, the Kympton Church was filled to capacity as Sir William Lucas walked his oldest up the aisle preceded by a playful and happy flower girl in the form of one Miss Grace Elliot.

Anyone who would be so foolish as to call the bride plain on her wedding day would have prevaricated. Charlotte was glowing with joy and looked very pretty indeed. Mr. Beckman officiated, and soon the new Mr. and Mrs. Elliot were signing the registry book.

After a few minutes of privacy, they alighted the curricle the Darcys had gifted them along with two horses, and with Grace sitting between them made their way to Pemberley for the wedding breakfast.

CHAPTER 27

Before Mr. and Mrs. Darcy knew it, they were preparing for the trip to Rosings Park for Easter with a two day stop at Longbourn.

There was no more question about Elizabeth Darcy carrying twins, the Accoucheur had made a visit to Pemberley a month earlier to examine her and confirmed he could hear two distinct heartbeats with the listening device he had acquired from a physician friend in France.

When asked about the trip south, he advised them as long as Mrs. Darcy felt comfortable enough, and they took the trip slowly, all should be well. To make sure there would be no strain on his wife, the master of Pemberley planned a five-day trip to Hertfordshire rather than the normal three days to ensure there were long periods of rest in between times of travelling.

In addition, he commissioned the coachworks in Lambton to fabricate a section to join the rear and forward-facing benches on one side of the coach so a mattress and pillows could be placed allowing his wife to recline whenever she chose to. They still had half the length of each bench to sit on when that was desired.

After checking for the tenth time that his wife felt well enough to travel, the caravan with the biggest and most comfortable Darcy coach in the lead started the journey toward Longbourn.

There were two additional carriages, one for the personal servants and one spare, and a wagon with their trunks, all of which was accompanied by eight outriders including the two giant footmen that had moved to Pemberley with Mrs. Darcy.

On the fifth day, just after the final stop and rest for lunch, the caravan lumbered through Meryton, and a mile later came to a stop at Longbourn. Mr and Mrs Bennet and the twins, who were on a term break from Cambridge, met them in front of the house. An enormous Elizabeth Darcy was assisted from the conveyance by her very solicitous husband.

"My darling girl, you are even larger than I was two months before my lying in with Tom and James. How are you, my Lizzy? Was it wise to make this long trip?" Fanny rushed over to check on her second born.

"All is good, Mama. Our accoucheur came to examine me at Pemberley four weeks ago. He confirmed we are having twins, said I was very healthy, and as long as I felt well and did not overexert myself, I could make this trip. That is the reason William planned for us to take five days to get here. We never rode for more than one or two hours without a break." Lizzy held her mother's arm for support. After being seated for some time, she was a little unsteady on her feet.

"I am happy to see you are still living up to your pledge to me to always care for her wellbeing, son," Bennet welcomed Darcy.

"That is my life's work, Bennet. She is the most precious thing in the world to me." He smiled, lost in the vision of his wife.

After greeting the twins, the party proceeded indoors where the Hills, who had known their *little Miss Lizzy* since birth, were treated to hello hugs and were amazed at the size of the normally petite second Bennet daughter.

The Darcys slowly made their way up to their suite, where their personal servants had baths ready for them. When they entered the orange drawing room, Richard and

Mary had joined the party. It was easy to see Mary was with child, but she was nowhere near the size her sister Elizabeth had been at the same stage.

"Good to see my brother and sister looking so well. Lizzy, you are almost as wide as you are tall," Richard teased as he hugged each.

"Thank you for pointing out the obvious, Richard. I am happy to see you and my sister as well. How are you doing with your pregnancy, Mary?" Lizzy shifted her focus to her beloved sister.

"It is much better now, Lizzy. For more than three weeks I have not been sick in the mornings, and I am able to eat normally again. I am sure I am carrying Richard's son as he kicks me all day and night," Mary huffed at her husband playfully.

"That is what it was like for me with Lizzy. I too thought she was a boy, but as you can see, I was wrong." Fanny smiled at Bennet.

"I remember, my dear. Lizzy hardly allowed you to rest, and we were both convinced that she was a boy." Bennet looked at his wife lovingly.

"Did we kick you a lot, Mama?" James asked, certain he needed to apologise if they did.

"No James, you and Tom were very calm and only kicked me occasionally. That is why we never suspected I was carrying twins and what above all convinced me the babe was another girl. We were so sure we had already picked out the name Lydia."

"Well, I for one am glad you did not name either of us Lydia! James or I would have been teased mercilessly with a girl's name," Tom announced, bowing in appreciation to his mother.

"As soon as we knew we had sons, it was but the work of a moment to choose your names instead. It is only just now I am glad your mother and I decided Lydia was not a name for a boy." Bennet winked at his sons, who were now quite a bit taller and larger than he was. As they approached their seventeenth year, he was looking at young men, not boys any longer.

"William, have you and Lizzy thought of names yet?" Fanny asked.

"Other than the first name for our first son, no Mother Bennet we have not. We want to wait until the babes are birthed and we know what they are, and then we will choose the names together. The tradition in the Darcy family has been to name the first-born son with the mother's former family name, so our first son's first name will be Bennet." Darcy nodded at Mrs. Bennet in deference.

"William and I have spoken about it, and we will call him Ben for short, not Benny, Ben!" Lizzy warned all present.

"Yes, I can see how Benny Darcy would not sound well; maybe that is what I will call him..." Richard mused.

"Richard! No, you will not!" Was the retort from his wife as she playfully slapped his shoulder, "Stop teasing your brother and sister!" Mary sighed with feigned exasperation.

"Yes, my liege," Richard capitulated with a big grin on his face. "We forgot to ask you Lizzy and William, on the return from Rosings we know you will break here for some days, so Mary and I would like to invite you to stay at Netherfield. I am sure Mother Bennet and Bennet will not be put out as you are being hosted here now."

After looking at her husband and getting a nod, Lizzy accepted on their behalf.

~~~~~~~/~~~~~~~

That night for dinner they were joined by Hattie and Frank Philips as well as the Lucases. At dinner, part of the discussion centred on how the newly married Mr. and Mrs. Elliot were doing, and the consensus was very well.

Not for the first time, Sir William and Lady Lucas thanked the Darcys for gifting the newlyweds a fortnight at Seaview Cottage. The family had enjoyed hosting the newlyweds for two days on the way back from Seaview.

It was agreed after all of the pregnancies were over and the new babes were able to travel, there would be a house party at Seaview. All of the families at dinner were invited, and the Bingleys, Hursts, Anne, the Derbyshire Elliots, and the rest of the Fitzwilliams would be invited.

~~~~~~~/~~~~~~~

After a restful sojourn at Longbourn, two more carriages joined the convoy for the five-hour trip to Rosings Park. On the way there, Darcy told Lizzy about the new parson Anne had gifted the Hunsford living to, Mr. Graham Allenton.

He was young, only five and twenty, and the second son of a country gentleman with a small estate. The reports about him from his curacy had been glowing, and the reaction of the Hunsford flock was very positive. While anyone would have been better than the late William Collins, it seemed Reverend Allenton was a vast improvement. His first priority was the welfare of his parishioners, not his patroness.

The carriages passed the Hunsford parsonage and church just before they turned into the gates which proclaimed *Rosings Park* on them. As they arrived under the portico Anne was waiting for them, flanked by her butler and housekeeper.

Both senior staff had been replaced after Anne had given the previous couple that filled the role the generous retirement Lady Catherine, in her avarice, had long kept from them so they had worked years beyond the point when they would have liked to retire.

With help from her Aunt Elaine, Anne had found a

very competent pair, Mr. Nigel Lipton was appointed as her new butler, and the new housekeeper was Mrs. Marjorie Barlow. In the housekeeper's case, the title of Mrs. was a courtesy title as she had never been married.

While Mr. Lipton directed his footmen to unload the trunks, the housekeeper showed the arriving party to their chambers. After changing and washing off the travel dust, the new arrivals repaired to the drawing room.

Darcy and Fitzwilliam knew the house well from annual visits past they had made out of a sense of family duty, not desire. The first thing both commented on was how much better the house looked. It was no longer a dark and dank place filled with gaudy furniture and useless, overtly ostentatious baubles. It now looked like a home.

Both had remarked to their wives how much they had liked all the new furniture Anne had ordered from Chippendale when the Darcys had ordered their new furniture for the mistress's suites at Darcy House and Pemberley.

Rosings Park now displayed a similar understated elegance to that seen in the houses on each of the estates of the family party that was present for Easter. Bedchambers were comfortable and inviting, chairs were for sitting on not for show, and the rest of the furniture was acquired for utility not to try and impress and intimidate the viewer.

The cousins, now brothers by marriage, noticed the *thrones* were gone from all rooms where Lady Catherine used to hold court. The house was vastly improved under the care of its rightful owner.

The Bennets, Darcys, and Fitzwilliams entered the largest of the drawing rooms, where in addition to Anne, the Earl and Countess of Matlock, the Bingleys, and the Hursts were present. They were informed the Gardiners would arrive on the morrow.

Lord and Lady Hilldale were at Hilldale where they would remain for the foreseeable future. Marie Fitzwilliam, had disappointed her son David, who had ordered a brother, by presenting him with a little sister named for her two grandmothers, Rosamond Elaine, who would be known as Rose Fitzwilliam.

"Lizzy, I thought Fanny was exaggerating when she said how large you are with child. Are you sure you are only between your sixth and seventh months? Your belly is enormous." The Countess rushed over and felt Elizabeth's stomach for any sign of concern.

"With *children*, Aunt Elaine. And yes, we are as sure as we can be about the timing of my pregnancy. Both the local midwife and the accoucheur have confirmed it." Lizzy smiled ruefully.

"Are you sure you are well enough to travel, Lizzy? I would hate to think my invitation for you to visit Rosings has placed you or your baby, I mean babies, in jeopardy." Anne looked at her cousin worriedly.

"Anne, I promise you if I did not feel well, and I did not have the permission of Sir Fredrick, we would not have made this trip. Besides my not wishing to do harm to myself or my babies, you know William would have bound me to a bed to stop me from coming if he was not convinced by the accoucheur that neither myself nor the babes I am carrying would be hurt by the trip.

"We took every precaution. We spread the trip to Longbourn over five days so there were many stops, making the trip was as leisurely as possible. You may not know, but we remained at Longbourn for me to rest for two days before coming here. Also, if anybody would like to go see the coach, William had it modified at the coachworks in Lambton so one half is a bed for me to use so I am not sitting all of the time. Truly, every precaution has been taken, and some invented for my comfort," Lizzy related.

"I was worried when they arrived at Longbourn and I saw how big my petite Lizzy is, but when she and William explained everything to me, both Thomas and I felt a lot better," Fanny stated in support of her second daughter.

"There is some news I would like to share." Anne blushed as she asked for the attention of her family. "With Uncle Reggie's blessing, I have entered into a courtship with Mr. Ian Ashby.

"As both of you know, William and Richard, we have known each other our whole lives as his father, the Earl of Ashbury, was very close to my father, and the countess Lady Gillian was friendly with Lady Catherine for some years until that lady managed to alienate her as she did all of us. His brother and sister, Lord and Lady Amberleigh, the Viscount, and their three children live at the Amberleigh estate, also in Surry.

"Before you think he is after my fortune, he is not. He is wealthy in his own right thanks to an inheritance he received from an uncle who died without issue. There is a nice sized estate in Surry called Sherwood Park with a clear six thousand a year. We have long had a tender regard for one another, but we both knew until I took control of my inheritance and exerted my will, we would have to wait.

"Lady Catherine is no longer an impediment, and after waiting for some years, I have a sneaking suspicion I will be betrothed around Easter. In addition, Hunsford's new pastor used to be the curate at the living bestowed by Sherwood Park, so I knew he was a good man, and I could trust him with the duties for our parish."

There was an explosion of joy for her future as Anne accepted the expressions of joy and hugs from her much expanded family. Not only was Anne looking healthier than any of the Darcys or Fitzwilliams remembered, but they could see she was glowing with happiness.

After the cacophony of all who loved her trying to express it over and again, Elizabeth Darcy asked her husband to join her on a short walk in the gardens as she felt she needed to stretch her legs a little. They were joined by the Bingleys, Tom, James, Kitty, and Georgiana.

"Not only has Anne made the house into a home, but I see a vast improvement in the gardens as well. Under Lady Catherine's reign of terror, a gardener would be discharged with no character if she thought a blade of grass was out of place. Like everything else, she thought she was able to control nature.

"I see Anne has instructed her gardeners to make the gardens less managed and more in tune with the surrounding natural flora and fauna. I know how much you like the natural Lizzy; you would have hated the gardens as they were," Darcy told his wife as they viewed the gardens they meandered through.

"That is enough walking for me William, the babies are kicking a lot now, so please help me back to the drawing room." Lizzy stopped unexpectedly.

"Are you well, Lizzy?" Jane hurried close.

"I am, but when you are as large as I am you will also notice it is hard to walk for too long," Elizabeth stated.

Seeing the look of concern on her husband's mien, she assured him all was well, reminding him that he knew she tired much faster at this stage of her pregnancy.

Bingley informed the four young people the Darcys and the Bingleys were returning inside. Darcy told them to only walk in sight of the house and to be back before teatime.

~~~~~~~/~~~~~~~

The next morning the Gardiners arrived before ten as Rosings Park was only three hours from London. Once the Gardiners had changed, the group set off for the folly, set on a hill with a nice view of the estate for a picnic lunch. A number of the group rode on horses, but the four pregnant women and the countess, Mrs. Gardiner, and Mrs. Bennet rode in carriages.

The folly was made to look like a small Greek temple, and there was a nice level area at the top of the hill where tables and chairs for those that wanted them were set up. For the more adventurous and those not older or with child, there were blankets and pillows.

The estate's kitchen staff, under the direction of the cook, had provided a spread that included cold sliced beef and mutton, meat and fruit pies, sweetmeats, cheeses, fresh bread, and an array of libations from water to ale.

Just after the party assembled again, a lone horseman arrived, and after he left his mount with one of the grooms he walked up and greeted Anne with a kiss to her proffered hand. By the becoming blush, everyone that had not yet met him assumed correctly that this was the gentleman courting her, Mr. Ian Ashby.

Once she had been greeted, Anne introduced her suitor to the assembled group. He was a good-looking man just shy of six feet tall, shorter than Darcy and the Fitzwilliam men, but a good height for the diminutive Anne de Bourgh.

On seeing him, both Darcy and Fitzwilliam remembered they had met him at Trinity, he had had a sterling reputation, and from what they knew he was a very honourable gentleman.

It dawned on Darcy his erstwhile friend George Wickham had tried to charm some funds out of Ashby when they were at Cambridge at the same time. Luckily Ashby had been intelligent enough to see right through Wickham's false façade.

This memory elevated Ashby in Darcy's opinion.

Ashby was two years ahead of Darcy, so they had not the opportunity to know each other better. It turned out that Ashby had approached Anne soon after her return to Rosings Park from Pemberley in January.

Without the interference of Anne's mother, their relationship had blossomed and progressed to the point they were now at. Seeing the looks that passed between the two, it was a relief for all those meeting Ashby as Anne's suitor to see there was genuine affection between them.

After a leisurely meal, a number of groups walked in various directions for some exercise many preferred after a good meal. The four pregnant ladies and their husbands remained relaxing at the spot where they had eaten.

Fifteen minutes later, the group that was seated saw a very happy-looking Ashby approach the Earl where he was standing and conversing with Bennet and Gardiner. He said something to the Earl and then Ashby and the Earl walked a small distance from the other two gentlemen. After a short discussion, the Earl shook Ashby's hand. As soon as this occurred, a joyful and beaming Anne joined them.

"Ashby requested Anne's hand in marriage, and she has consented. He requested my blessing, which was bestowed with pleasure. Welcome to the family, Ashby, and Anne, I wish you joy," the Earl announced to all that were not exploring.

"Thank you, Uncle Reggie. I never believed this day would come, but I am so very happy, and I know Ian will always take care of me and our family." As she mentioned a possible family, Anne blushed a deep red.

"Congratulations Anne, and soon-to-be Cousin Ashby, when will you wed?" Lizzy smiled at Anne warmly.

"We are thinking in about a month, Lizzy." Anne raised her hand to forestall what Elizabeth was about to say. "Before you say it, we know a lot of you will not be able to come as you will either have birthed your babes or will be entering or nearing your lying ins. As much as we would love to have all of my wonderful family here to celebrate with us, we would rather not wait. We delayed years because of Lady Catherine, so I do not want to waste any more time."

"Anne, I have a question." Fanny walked in close.

"Yes, Aunt Fanny?" Anne linked her arm with Fanny's as she had become more than grateful for the affectionate woman's closeness.

"Besides your betrothed's family, all of your family is here for the next eight days until after Easter, correct?" Before Anne could answer with more than a nod of her head, Fanny turned to Anne's betrothed. "I heard talk of an engagement dinner two days hence when your parents, brother, and sisters will be in attendance, is that not so?"

"You have the right of it Mrs. Bennet." He agreed with respect and deference, having heard how this woman had immediately proved her love of his Anne and helped her when he had been unable.

"What are you cooking up in that pretty head of yours, Fanny?" Bennet teased, though he already knew exactly what she was thinking for her niece—the adopted daughter of her heart.

"Why a wedding, Thomas! When of late have I not been thinking of weddings?" she replied playfully, then ignored all others and turned to Anne again. "Anne, my dear, you would prefer all of your family to witness your nuptials, would you not? Are we not all here now for the next eight days?" Fanny asked with a smile that said she was having her way but was pretending to allow the bride to think she had input.

"Y-y-yes but..." Anne looked at her in wide-eyed surprise.

"Your fiancé's family will arrive in two days, will they

not?" she asked again as she looked at Anne's betrothed who nodded dumbly. "Did the both of you not tell us how you have had to waste years and neither of you want to waste more time?" Both members of the newly engaged couple nodded again.

"You have the right of it, Fanny!" the Countess interjected. "Anne there is no need to wait for the banns to be read. Your adept and apt clergyman can issue a common license as you are of age and you can marry while we are all here, unless there is a reason we do not know of why you should wait a month?" she challenged the two, getting this time a mute shaking of their heads.

"You have Fanny and me here, two now very experienced wedding organisers, and I am sure your future mother-in-law is one too," the Countess stated in a tone of voice that brooked no opposition.

The newly engaged couple had but to look at one another to see the other was hoping each wanted this as much as they did. Anne nodded as she smiled with such joy, she could barely catch her breath. "Aunt Fanny you are a genius. Aunt Elaine, you are correct, there is no good reason to wait a month. What say you we get married the day before you are all to depart?" she asked hopefully.

"What do you think, Elaine? Should we start planning?" Fanny teased Anne.

"Yes Fanny, we have our daughters here and they can all be put to work, except you Lizzy," the Countess whirled to look at her, "so do not even think about it! I could see your mind working."

"I will behave, Aunt Elaine. William will not allow me to over-exert myself even were I to be foolish enough to try to," Elizabeth admitted.

With the wedding date resolved, the party prepared to return to the house. Ashby mounted his horse and galloped off in the direction of the Hunsford parsonage to see his friend Allenton about a common license.

Knowing the parties involved and that the Earl had blessed the union, Allenton issued the common licence without delay.

~~~~~~~/~~~~~~~

Two days later the carriages transporting the Ashbys pulled to a halt under the very large portico at Rosings Park. Lord and Lady Ashbury were in one coach with their only daughter, Lady Sarah Ashby, who was nineteen. The second conveyance conveyed Lord and Lady Amberleigh and their two sons. Their baby girl was in the third carriage with her nurse and the rest of the personal servants.

Lords Ashbury and Matlock knew and respected each other from their time in the House of Lords. Their political views did not always align, but there was a lot of common ground. Ladies Matlock and Ashbury knew each other reasonably well from their time in town while their husbands were in session, and they had attended many social events.

Once the Ashby family had time to change, Ian asked them to meet with him in the sitting room between his parent's chambers. There he informed his family he was finally engaged to his beloved Anne, which made them all extremely happy as he and they had long waited for this glorious day and the congratulations equalled the relief the news gave.

Then he added the unexpected news of having the wedding in a mere sennight. Until he explained the very practical reasons why, his family was perturbed, but once they had absorbed the news and saw the basis for an accelerated wedding was reasonable due to Anne having four pregnant cousins, it was obvious waiting would mean Anne would have almost no family present.

The more they discussed it, the more Ashby's family embraced the plan, and proportionally his mother got more excited about planning the wedding with Lady Matlock and Mrs. Bennet.

When the Ashbys entered the drawing room, there was a collective sigh of relief as those waiting for them saw the happiness on their faces.

Ashbury and Amberleigh joined the group where the Earl of Matlock was talking to Bennet and Gardiner. On being introduced, rather than be upset at being in the presence of one in trade, they were well pleased.

Both Ashbys knew much of *King Midas* by reputation and had wanted to invest with him for some time now, but had long been told he was not accepting any more investors. They correctly surmised that a family connection would change that for them.

The party was joined by Hunsford's rector for dinner as he had been friends with Ashby for many years, even before he was retained as the curate at the living attached to Sherwood Park, so he had met Ashby's family a number of times before.

He had not seen Lady Sarah Ashby for more than five years, and instead of the awkward youth of fourteen he had last seen, he saw a very pretty, intelligent, and composed young lady.

Not long after Allenton joined the assembled residents, the butler announced dinner, and the party filed into the formal dining room. It was noted by certain of those in attendance that Allenton led Lady Sarah into dinner, and she seemed not to object at all.

~~~~~~~/~~~~~~~

On Easter Sunday, the Hunsford Church was filled to overflowing. Since Mr. Allenton had become the rector, and as word of his style and substance made the rounds, each

Sunday from his first onward, the number of those who came to hear his sermons steadily increased.

Once the parishioners accepted that anything they told the vicar in confidence went no further and this clergyman always had the parishioner's best interests at heart, the community served by the Hunsford Church fully embraced and accepted the new pastor.

The unfortunate few of the Rosings party that had the displeasure of sitting through a service delivered by the late William Collins noted the two were at the opposite ends of the spectrum as clergymen.

The former had been considered a poor orator at best while Allenton was among the best. Darcy knew when, or if, Graham Allenton and Patrick Elliot met, they would be fast friends as they were cut from the same cloth. Both were very proficient at the vocation they had felt called by God to do.

After a most enjoyable service and a very well-delivered and apt sermon, the rector stood just outside his church and conversed with anyone who wanted to talk to him, greeting each of his parishioners by name.

~~~~~~~/~~~~~~~

A sumptuous Easter meal was served at Rosings Park whose guests, in addition to Allenton, included three families of parishioners, none of them landed. Thankfully, no one among the present party, including the Ashbys, held to the outdated and fading belief system regarding the distinction of rank being preserved.

After the meal, the three families thanked Miss de Bourgh sincerely and took their leave. The remaining party separated by sex so the men could stay at the table and enjoy some libations and cigars. The ladies repaired to the drawing room.

"Anne, have the two of you decided where you will live after your nuptials?" Lizzy asked Anne once she had been assisted by her sister Jane and her mother to situate herself on a comfortable settee and she put her feet up on a footstool.

"We have had that discussion, Lizzy. Ian loves his estate, and it is not more than a three-hour carriage ride from Rosings Park so it will be our primary residence. William recommended Mr. Kaleb Firth to be my new steward, and Ian agrees he is as honest as the day is long and very capable.

"Rather than just leave Rosings to Mr. Firth's excellent management, we will reside here one week out of four, and as we are close, if we are needed, we can be here without delay.

"Neither Sherwood Park nor Rosings Park are entailed, we have decided our firstborn son will have Sherwood Park and the second son will inherit this estate. If we only have one son, then our first daughter will have Rosings Park, and in the case of no sons, the eldest two girls will inherit the estates." Anne smiled brightly, excited to have, at long last, the future she dreamed of within her grasp.

"It seems as if you and your fiancé have had some serious discussions about the future, Anne," Lady Elaine smiled lovingly at her niece.

"That sounds like my Ian, Lady Matlock. He likes to plan for all contingencies," Lady Ashbury revealed.

"As we will be family in but two days, you must call me Elaine. As you get to know us, Lady Ashbury, you will see in our family group we do not stand on ceremony."

"Then Elaine you must call me Gillian," Lady Ashbury agreed.

"Lady Sarah," the pregnant Mary Fitzwilliam turned towards the lady as she rubbed her stomach, "did you know Mr. Allenton before you met him here? You two seem to have a prior acquaintance."

"We do, Mrs. Fitzwilliam, and please call me Sarah." Before she could carry on, she was cut off by Elizabeth Darcy.

"So there is no more Mrs. that or Lady this, I am Lizzy," she then pointed from lady to lady, "my mother Fanny, my Aunt Maddie, my sisters Jane, Mary, Kitty, Georgiana, and Louisa. Did I miss anyone?" The ladies all shook their heads, so Elizabeth Darcy said with an impertinent smile, "Now the floor is yours, Sarah."

"Where was I?" she drawled, laughing with the women then nodded at Lizzy with amusement. "Oh yes, we met when Mr. Allenton accompanied Ian home for a term break when I was but twelve. He was a shy young man and hardly ever paid any attention to his friend's *baby* sister." At this, both Kitty and Georgiana gave her looks of understanding, "The next time I saw him was two years later, I was fourteen, and he was the new curate for the living that belongs to Ian's estate.

"He was no longer shy and was as handsome as you see him now. I had a young girl's infatuation with him, but he still paid me no heed. I have not seen him since until we came here to see Ian and his fiancée." Lady Sarah blushed as she completed her recitation.

"I think he notices you now, Sarah," Lizzy opined.

"I am sure you are wrong, Lizzy," Lady Sarah replied as her blush deepened by many shades.

It was then the men re-joined the ladies, and mortified by her blushing, Sarah dashed to the pianoforte and started to play the first piece of music she found. Her mortification increased when Graham Allenton asked to be allowed to turn the pages for her, but she steadied herself and gave him a nod of agreement.

The ladies who had heard what Lady Sarah had said about the pastor gave each other knowing looks and were relieved Lady Ashbury was not unhappy. She knew Allenton's character and she would not be opposed if her daughter accepted him as her potential husband.

~~~~~~~/~~~~~~~

Monday morning dawned and a very excited Anne de Bourgh, who had not slept much due to anticipation and not nervousness or dread, was ready to be Mrs. Ashby already. She had to admit the conversations she had had with her aunts and married cousins the previous night still left her a little worried about the wedding night, but after the ladies all told her the act, when done between two loving partners, was nothing to be afraid of and was, in fact, a source of pleasure, any doubts and fears Anne had were eased. She was looking forward with pleasure and not trepidation to her wedding night.

She would follow their advice and not be shy to ask her husband what he liked and let him know the same about her. Lizzy reiterated this was the most important part, and her words had been echoed by Jane and Mary.

When her maid entered and told her that her water was ready, she sprang out of bed and was soon soaking in a luxuriating bath. Once she was finished, she was joined by her Aunts Elaine and Fanny, who oversaw the processes of turning Anne de Bourgh into a glowing bride.

~~~~~~~/~~~~~~~

At the extravagant wedding breakfast, the new Mr. and Mrs. Ashby flitted around accepting wishes for joy and happiness from the assembled revellers. Anne Ashby was overjoyed as she had just gained a mother, father, brother, and two sisters, along with nephews and a niece.

She was incandescent with happiness. On some level, she was sad Lady Catherine was not present to witness the true joy she had found in her life and her love match, but that was but a fleeting moment, and she determined it would also be the final moment she had any regrets about Lady Catherine. The woman had hurt her in too many ways.

After staying at their wedding breakfast for a little

more than two hours, the newlyweds departed for their wedding trip, which was to Seaview Cottage. The cottage that had had so little use each year prior to Fitzwilliam and Elizabeth Darcy's wedding was now, to the pleasure of the servants working there, in very regular use and had become the wedding trip destination of choice for members of the family.

In addition, members of the family were starting to visit as individual families and as groups for vacations not tied to weddings. There was now so much use the Darcys had determined to keep the cottage fully staffed all year round.

~~~~~~~/~~~~~~~

The following day, the now expanded family headed toward their respective estates and homes. The Darcys first headed to Hertfordshire for two days at Netherfield Park to be hosted by the Fitzwilliams.

Kitty and Georgiana, along with their companions, travelled to Town with Lord and Lady Matlock and the Gardiners. Before the Ashbys left, Graham Allenton asked to take a walk with Lady Sarah, where he requested and was granted a courtship by her and received her father's permission.

After a two-day sojourn at Netherfield Park, Mr. and Mrs. Darcy started the planned five-day trip home to Pemberley. Elizabeth was ready to get home. While at Netherfield Park she had been visited by many of the local matrons who all opined on her pregnancy and how enormous she was.

Elizabeth could see a significant difference in her belly just in the little over four weeks since they had left the sanctuary of Pemberley. As they were more than halfway through the month of April, Elizabeth Darcy knew it would not be too much longer but felt she would not be unhappy if she had birthed her babes already, so long as they were healthy.

Her husband reminded her that Sir Fredrick and his nurses would be arriving at Pemberley within a sennight of their return. Darcy did not have to tell his wife to curtail her walking any longer as she could only go a short way before needing to sit and recuperate.

Her mother and Aunts Maddie and Elaine would arrive towards the end of May, and the rest of the family was joining them in mid-June. As much as she loved having family around, she had a feeling, as she neared her lying in, she would not be too social.

~~~~~~~/~~~~~~~

After what seemed like the longest five days in her young life, Elizabeth was very relieved as they crested the hill, and she could see their magnificent home. When the carriage came to a halt at the entrance, Mrs. Reynolds and Elizabeth's lady's maid were there to help the master assist the mistress into the house.

"Welcome home master and mistress. Good Lord above mistress, your belly has got so much larger in the five weeks since you left." Mrs. Reynolds looked at her in surprise.

"I agree with you, Mrs. Reynolds. I thought twins were normally smaller than a single birthed babe, but maybe these will be large babes as their father is quite tall," Elizabeth agreed with a thin smile.

On the way up to the master suite, they had to pause four times for the normally energetic Mrs. Darcy to rest and get her wind back. Once they reached the mistress's suite, Jacqui helped her mistress change out of her travel attire and then, along with her husband, she was gently lowered into the oversized bathtub to soak and relax.

After she was dried off and dressed, her husband assisted her to their private sitting room. He helped Elizabeth lower herself onto a very comfortable settee and then lifted her legs and placed them on the settee as well.

"Lizzy, we need to talk," Darcy stated gravely.

"I love to talk to you, my dear husband." Lizzy offered a smiling reply. She had a very good idea of what he wanted to talk about but refused to make it easier on him.

"You know what I mean, my love. I think the time has come for you to no longer negotiate the stairs. Even with assistance, I do not believe it is good for you, and heaven forbid something happens and you fall, and the babes are hurt, or even worse...something happens to you.

"You know I could not live without you, my dearest, loveliest Elizabeth, so I beg you to agree with me. Before we married, I promised you a partnership and I will always keep that promise. In keeping with my oath to you, I am asking you, not demanding your obedience." Darcy asked softly.

"Under normal circumstances, I would rebel against restrictions such as the ones I have to live with until I birth our babes, but after my battle today, with the help of three people mind you, I believe you are correct William my love, it is time," Elizabeth agreed easily.

"Thank you, my Lizzy, you do not know how much it relieves me that we are in agreement about this." Saying this, Darcy rewarded his wife with a long and passionate kiss. "If you desire exercise, you can walk in the halls. The house is big enough that you can walk without ever having to go up or down stairs."

"What about our meals, William?" she asked, not wishing to cause a problem for the staff.

"That is easy, my love. We will take our meals in these chambers. You did not think I would eat in the dining room while my beloved wife dines here alone, did you?" he responded, so relieved she had agreed he would do anything to reward her.

"I knew you would not, William, I just needed to

know what you thought was the best plan for us while I am confined to this floor of the house." Elizabeth smiled sadly. She knew it was the right thing to do, but she would miss her freedom.

"If it would please you, I can have Mrs. Reynolds turn one of the unused chambers in the family wing into a dining room so when we are more than the two of us, you will be able to dine with more people at a time. Does that meet with your approval Lizzy?" he asked thoughtfully.

"Oh yes, William, that would be perfect!" She rewarded her husband with some more very deep kisses.

"Be careful," he winked at his extremely pregnant wife, "kissing me like that is what got you into the state that you are now in."

"And all the while I was under the impression it was the actions that followed the kissing that got me like this!" His impertinent wife stated saucily with a look of feigned innocence.

"You are lucky you are so heavy with child, or I would tickle you mercilessly now if you were not," Darcy replied huskily.

"Then I will thank God for small mercies like you not tickling me in this state," she teased.

He kissed his wife again then went into his room to pull the bell to summon Mrs. Reynolds. In a very short while she arrived, and Darcy informed her of the decision regarding his wife and the stairs.

He added they would be taking all of their meals in the private sitting room until after Mrs. Darcy's lying in and recovery after the birth. At the news about the stairs, both of the Darcys could see the housekeeper's obvious relief. He then proceeded to outline the plan to convert one of the large, unused suites into a dining room for when it was more than him and his wife dining.

Once he was done explaining what he wanted, Mrs. Reynolds bobbed a curtsy to the Darcys and then left the sitting room to start implementing the instructions she had been given.

CHAPTER 28

The days sped by, and the Friday after the Darcys arrived back at Pemberley the accoucheur and his two nurses arrived. Darcy was paying a small fortune to have him and his nurses in residence until his wife delivered her babes, but to a man of his wealth it was a pittance and the peace of mind it brought him was priceless.

Sir Fredrick was not a tall man; he was maybe five foot seven inches and was rotund. He was balding on his crown so the circle of baldness on the top of his head looked like that of a monk, except his baldness extended to where is forehead met his former hairline. Darcy bowed to the accoucheur which was returned, and then the men shook hands.

He requested Mrs. Reynolds take the accoucheur and his two nurses to chambers in the family wing. He wanted them very close to his wife at all times. Sir Fredrick stated after he had washed and changed he would like to examine Mrs. Darcy.

Darcy was restlessly sitting in the shared sitting room while the accoucheur, with the help of his nurses, examined his Lizzy.

After the doctor washed his hands, he called Darcy into his wife's bedchamber. "Mrs. Darcy looks very healthy, and I applaud you for making the decision to no longer use the stairs. I am not sure there are twins..." Sir Fredrick hedged.

Then why is my wife's belly so large?" Darcy tensed,

worry flooding in.

"As I was about to say, I am not sure there are twins, I suspect that there may be three babes that your wife is carrying," Sir Frederick announced.

"**THREE!!**" both Elizabeth and Darcy exclaimed simultaneously.

"Possibly. When I listened to the heartbeats, I heard two clearly, and then I thought I heard a third, fainter heartbeat. Before you start to worry, that is not an indication of the health of the babe, it is more than likely position; his or her womb mates are making it hard for me to hear the third babe," the accoucheur explained gently.

"Good Lord above, I knew you were needed here, Sir Fredrick." Darcy tried to absorb this new, and troubling information.

"I believe God does not give us more than we are able to deal with. I will leave you two now and go and rest before dinner." He nodded at them both and left their chambers.

After Sir Frederick left, a flabbergasted Mr. and Mrs. Darcy tried to absorb the news. The possibility of triplets did explain a lot. Mother Bennet had observed her daughter was a lot larger than she had been at the same point in time when she was carrying Tom and James.

"As much as I do not like being restricted, I am very grateful you had the foresight to ask me to stop using the stairs, my beloved husband. If I had been my normal obstinate self and had fallen..." she tried to collect herself.

"Lizzy, you are berating yourself for something that never did and will not happen. You did not fight me at all, so deep down you knew it was the right thing for you to do. Under normal circumstances, I would never suspend any pleasure of yours, but I have seen how hard it is for you to negotiate stairs, so there is no good reason for you to put yourself or our babes at risk.

"Your motherly instinct ruled your decision-making even before our babes are here. You will not be bored; Charlotte will visit you and bring Grace with her, and the Bingleys will come as soon as they are notified of the situation," Darcy soothed.

"Will you please bring my portable *escritoire* to the bed so I can write to Mama and the rest of our family to prepare them in case Sir Frederick is correct in his assertion?" she asked playfully, his words having the hoped-for effect. Once she was comfortably situated with some pillows behind her back Elizabeth Darcy started to write her missives, the first one to her mother.

16 May

Pemberley

My dear Mama and Papa,

I need to share some potential news with you, so you are prepared when you arrive here to join us for my lying in.

Please do not be alarmed it is not bad news, just very surprising, and William and I are still coming to terms as Sir Frederick Gillingham has this very afternoon shared his suspicions with us.

He examined me today, using his listening device to listen to the babe's heartbeats. He related that besides the two babes we have been told that I am carrying, he believes he can hear the faint heartbeat of a <u>THIRD</u> babe. Yes, Mama and Papa, I did not write in error, he thinks he heard three, not two.

Before you start to worry, the fact the third one is faint is not indicative of the health of the babe, but more than likely the positioning vis-a-vis the other two babes. He also told us it is very likely with two or more babes I will deliver earlier than the date range we were given originally after my first examination by a physician.

If you are able, please leave for Pemberley earlier than

you had planned. William and I ask you bring Kitty and Georgie from Town with you.

  Your loving daughter,

  Elizabeth Darcy

Similar letters were written and sent by express to all the extended family.

~~~~~~~/~~~~~~~

It was two days later in the evening when the Darcys' courier delivered the missive to the Bennets. On reading the missive, Fanny Bennet almost had an attack of her long-banished nerves, but as it had been for these many years, her rational mind prevailed.

She knocked once on her husband's study door and entered without waiting for his summons. Once he read the missive, he agreed they would leave at dawn on the morrow for Town to collect the girls and then for Pemberley. Bennet wrote missives he sent by his express rider to the Inns they would stay at, and to make sure there would be horses available for changes along the way.

The Bennets called the Hills and informed their long-serving butler and housekeeper they would be leaving on the morrow so the couple could issue the necessary orders for all to be ready and the Bennets could leave without unnecessary delay in the morning.

~~~~~~~/~~~~~~~

The Bennet carriages and outriders arrived at Matlock House a little after eight in the morning. To their surprise, they saw much activity and two coaches being prepared in front of the house. Once they alighted, they were shown into the house by the butler and were met by the Countess.

"Welcome Fanny and Thomas, we expected you as we assume you received Lizzy's missive yesterday as well." Elaine smiled as she hugged Fanny and accepted a kiss on the cheek from Bennet.

"That we did, Elaine. We are here to collect the girls. We noticed your carriages being prepared, are you and Reggie returning to Snowhaven early?" Fanny smiled at her dearest friend.

"No, Fanny, we are to Pemberley. She is your daughter, but she is my niece, and we want to be there to help and support William and Lizzy wherever we can." She stated airily knowing neither would do anything different if the roles were reversed.

Bennet went off in search of the Earl and within an hour the caravan of conveyances was on the road heading north. Fanny had told Elaine that Mary and Richard would not be joining them as Mary was on bed rest for the next three to four weeks.

Mary had experienced some light bleeding, and although Mr. Jones did not think there would be a problem, he suggested the bedrest as a precaution. Elaine was thankful to hear the news as the post had not been delivered yet, so she had not known about her daughter-in-law until Fanny told her.

~~~~~~~/~~~~~~~

On the third day after the travellers had left London, they pulled up to the entrance of Pemberley where a swarm of footmen started to unpack their trunks and convey them to their rooms. They were met by Darcy, who informed them Jane and Charles and Marie and Andrew Fitzwilliam had arrived the day before, and that Jane, Marie, and a newly with child Charlotte were visiting Lizzy in their shared sitting room.

When he explained on their return from the Easter trip, they had decided there would be no more using stairs, both Lizzy's parents and her aunt and uncle were very relieved, all knowing how much she loved to exercise under normal circumstances.

After hugging their brother hello, Georgiana and Kitty took off up the stairs to go see their sisters, and friend. Elizabeth was reclining on a chaise in the master suite sitting room when two very exuberant young ladies burst into the room. The two caught themselves as Mrs. Darcy looked at them with an arched brow.

"We are so sorry, Lizzy, but we have not seen you since Easter at Rosings and we have been missing you." Georgiana walked closer at a more sedate pace.

"I appreciate the sentiment, Georgie, but I am sure you did not think too much about your pregnant sisters while you were both having a grand old time in London preparing for your season," Lizzy teased them.

"Hello Jane, Marie, and Charlotte. Lizzy, do not tease us so," Kitty affected a pout, "you know we love all of you and missed you while we were away."

"Relax Kitty; you know I was teasing you and Georgie. I am very happy to see you both. Before someone else informs you, Sir Fredrick suspects that I am carrying three, not two babes," Elizabeth added nonchalantly.

"*THREE*! Oh my goodness Lizzy, no wonder you are so very big." Georgiana Darcy clapped her hand over her mouth at her exclamation but relaxed when she saw all of her older sisters and Charlotte Elliot smile.

"There you both are, you ran up the stairs so fast. What happened to the young ladies that were with me in Town these last months? I had just told Fanny how well-behaved you two had been," the Countess teased her nieces she loved as much as she did her daughters.

"Sorry, Aunt Elaine, and you too Aunt Fanny, but we could not wait to see Lizzy. We are sorry Mary was not allowed to travel, but we will see her, Richard, and hopefully a new babe when we return to town for the little season,"

Georgiana explained.

"There is no harm done, of course, it is acceptable for young ladies to relax in their homes when only family is present," Lady Elaine allowed.

"You two go change from the road and if you wish to, have a rest before dinner. Aunt and Uncle Gardiner and the cousins will arrive in two days. I will still be here after you have changed. I no longer go downstairs so we dine on this floor. You will see William had a suite of rooms made into a temporary dining parlour three doors down," Elizabeth caught them up on the largest of changes.

"I need to return to the parsonage and see to dinner for Patrick and Grace. It was good to see you again Mrs. Bennet and Lady Elaine." Charlotte curtsied.

"It was good to see you, Charlotte, and all the best for your pregnancy. Please send our best wishes to your husband and daughter," Elaine smiled at her as Fanny approached her very pregnant daughter.

After Charlotte left, the two friends left the master suite to go to their chambers to wash and change. They decided not to rest as they wanted to spend time with their sisters. Fanny Bennet commented on how well Charlotte looked and then focused on her daughter.

"How many are able to dine with you, Lizzy?" Fanny asked as she gently rubbed Elizabeth's belly.

"Eight to ten people comfortably, Mama. If more want to dine with me at any given meal, then you will all have to take turns," Lizzy replied.

"As your mother, I assume there will always be room for me to dine with my girl." Fanny Bennet said with a wink and a twinkle in her eyes, "And you Jane, my dear? How are you doing now you are about two months from your confinement?"

"I am as well as can be expected Mama, my babe is

much calmer than Lizzy's brood," Jane teased them both.

"I would love to see how you would feel if you were carrying two or three babes!" Lizzy huffed.

"Rather you than me. I am very happy to see both you and Aunt Elaine, Mama. This works out well as you and Aunt Maddie can come to the Meadows when you are ready after Lizzy has delivered her babes. No long trip this time." Jane smiled at the positive that meant the family could come to her home with little inconvenience.

"I must say, Fanny, your girls timed this rather well. Marie and I and our husbands will travel to Netherfield Park to be with Mary before she enters her lying in. Our family is expanding rapidly." Elaine winked at Fanny.

Seeing Elizabeth's energy was flagging, the attendant nurse signalled the family to let the expectant mother get some rest. After sleeping for two hours, Elizabeth was attended by her very solicitous husband and the rest of the family.

That night for dinner Mr. and Mrs. Darcy were joined by her parents, the Bingleys, aunt and uncle Fitzwilliam, and Andrew and Marie. It was decided the young ladies would be present for all three meals on the morrow, so they did not feel left out.

On the expected day, the Gardiners arrived in their three-coach convoy. They were welcomed by Darcy, and after resting visited Elizabeth in the sitting room. The children were allowed to remain for a short while then they were soon on their way to enjoy Pemberley's splendours accompanied by Georgiana, Kitty, the young ladies' companions, and the children's nursemaid.

~~~~~~~/~~~~~~~

Life at Pemberley for the residents was very pleasant until after midnight on a Wednesday just a sennight later. The first sign something was happening was when Darcy yelled for one of the footmen stationed in the hall near the master suite and instructed him to wake Sir Fredrick, his nurses, and the midwife. It was a matter of minutes before everyone was wide awake except for the Gardiner children, who were all asleep and blissfully unaware in the nursery.

Fanny Bennet entered her daughter's bedchamber where she was already being attended by the midwife and the accoucheur, with his nurses assisting as needed. She looked at her daughter and could immediately tell that she was in labour. Fanny was followed in by Elaine and Marie Fitzwilliam, and minutes after them Jane entered the room.

"Oh my, what is all this wetness?" Elizabeth demanded, holding tightly to William's hand while he looked on nervously.

"Those, my dear Mrs. Darcy, were your waters." said Sir Frederick with authority. "Mr. Darcy, it is time for you to go join the men downstairs, in the library I assume."

"Unless my Elizabeth wants me to leave, I am not going anywhere," Darcy stated emphatically.

"But sir, it is not done," the midwife frowned.

"Unless my *wife* does not want my presence, it will be done!" he countered. Anyone who knew Darcy could tell from the firmness and tone of his voice, he would brook no opposition.

"I want William to stay with me. Propriety be damned! I am giving birth to two or three babes, and *I WILL HAVE* William here!" Lizzy yelled out, hers being the final say.

"William will stay, Lizzy. No one will ask him to leave for as long as you want him here with you." Fanny soothed her daughter with a cool cloth to her face and a gentle promise.

"Thank you, Mama." Lizzy relaxed as much as she could.

For the next three hours, Darcy felt helpless, other

than allowing his wife to squeeze his hand with all of her might as each contraction hit her. When she felt the need, she yelled out in pain using words no one who knew her had any idea were in her vocabulary. It was just after the three-hour mark when the midwife said she could see a head crowning. Lizzy was instructed to push, and five minutes later there was a healthy wail of an indignant baby boy who had been expelled from his warm home.

The babe was cleaned, and a blue ribbon was tied to both his wrist and his ankle before he was swaddled. The heir to Pemberley had been born. His parents were in wonder of the babe with his scrunched-up face as he informed the world of his displeasure when Lizzy's pains began again. The babe was given over to his grandma to be admired as the first grandchild for Fanny.

Soon the room filled with the plaintive wail of the heir's brother. After he was cleaned, a green ribbon was tied to his wrist and ankle so that the order of birth would be preserved in case there was a third son. He was swaddled and passed to his Great Aunt Elaine. Just like before the pains recommenced, and within ten minutes a baby girl entered the world with a head full of dark curls. Although smaller than her brothers, she was much louder, causing Fanny Bennet to smile.

"There she is, Lizzy. You have been blessed with a babe just like you." Her mother kissed her daughter's forehead.

Everyone thought all that was to be delivered was the afterbirth, but it was soon evident there was another babe on the way. Worry for his wife peaked as Darcy was silently praying she would survive the ordeal.

The fourth babe was very much smaller than her sister who had been born ahead of her. She was born blue and was silent unlike her three siblings. Sir Fredrick attempted to help her breathe by gently breathing into her nose and mouth, but it was for naught. The young Miss Darcy passed from the mortal coil without ever making a sound or opening her eyes.

The afterbirth was finally delivered. Darcy was inconsolable when his wife lapsed into unconsciousness. "**Nooooo**, my Lizzy," he wailed, "I will not be able to live without you."

"Do not talk nonsense, William! We all pray Lizzy will recover, but do you think my daughter will want you to give up if God calls her home?" Fanny demanded hotly.

"William, you do not want to repeat the mistakes your father made withdrawing from the world after my sister Anne passed. You know how hard that was on both you and Georgie. Would you wish for your children to have to live that way?" Elaine soothed his brow as he knelt by his wife's bed.

"You are both correct, and I know that, but I cannot imagine living in a world without my Lizzy," William replied quietly, unable to take his eyes off his wife.

"I do not believe that you will have to, Mr. Darcy," Sir Frederick thought it was now finally the right time to intervene, now that the wisdom of his patient's aids on earth had helped the new father return from the brink.

"W-w-w-what d-did you say, Sir Frederick?" Darcy looked at him in hopeful fear.

"I said I do not believe you will have to. There has not been any excess of bleeding. I think your wife just needs time to recover a little from the ordeal her body just experienced. I have seen this with births of two or more before and without other factors, none of which are present in your wife, the patient normally wakes up within four and twenty hours and is no worse for wear. You employed two wet nurses as I suggested?" Sir Frederick asked calmly.

"We did, Sir Fredrick, and I will take what you said and use that as the basis for my hopes and prayers," Darcy promised.

"Do. There is a reason women bear the children, Mr. Darcy. Underneath it all, we are the weaker sex, and your wife has just birthed four. You would have passed out after the first," Sir Frederick reminded him.

"Thank you." Darcy saw the truth in Sir Frederick's eyes and took a few deep breaths before turning to face the rest of the room.

The last baby girl born had been cleaned and wrapped in a shroud and was quietly removed by Mrs. Reynolds. She would be kept in the cold room so her mother could meet her if she wished before the babe was buried.

"Come meet your children, William." Fanny beckoned him to her.

Darcy gently took his firstborn son from his mother-in-law. He had a tuft of dark hair similar to his parents and crystal-clear cerulean eyes just like his father. After passing his first son back to Mother Bennet, he took his second son from Aunt Elaine.

He immediately noticed his second son looked identical to his brother; the only difference now was the colour of the ribbons that marked their order of birth. After returning his son to Aunt Elaine, he took his daughter from his sister Jane. He was instantly lost to her. She had the potential to be a carbon copy of her mother with the same colour hair. Like all babes, her eyes were a deep blue, but those could change up to six months after her birth.

It was impossible not to be sad his second daughter had not lived, but God had given them three blessings to help balance His will, so he allowed himself at this moment to feel joy for the three babes that were living, and who by all accounts so far were strong and healthy.

Darcy would worry about his wife until she woke, but he was heartened by what Sir Frederick had told him.

While Lizzy was being cleaned and changed and her bedding replaced with a clean set, a process directed by her maid Arseneault, Darcy followed his children as they were carried into the nursery.

Present were two nursemaids and two wet nurses. Knowing he could not be present when the wet nurses fed his babes, he kissed each one gently on the forehead and withdrew from the nursery.

In the hall, he bumped into the midwife and was grateful for the chance to ask a question he had not dared to ask in company so he could deal with the answer privately if there was cause for concern. "Mrs. Mathers, all three of my beautiful babes seem to have pointy heads is there something wrong with them?" he held his breath.

"No, sir." she tried to stifle a laugh. "What you see is perfectly normal. We do not know how it all works, but the head is always like that when the babe is born. Within a sennight, you will see all of your children will have perfectly normal, round heads.

"We know from experience that the crown of the head can be soft until that process is complete, so everyone needs to be extra careful with the babe's heads. That is why whenever you are passed a newborn babe, that is the warning that comes with them to all new parents, grandparents, aunts, uncles, nieces, nephews, brothers..." she trailed off when he chuckled.

"Thank you for explaining, Mrs. Mathers. Thank you for everything that you did to assist my wife, Darcy offered quietly.

The midwife bobbed a curtsy and walked toward the servant's stairs to go and get some rest before she left for home. It was past six in the morning already and the first tendrils of light of the new day were creeping over the horizon.

~~~~~~~/~~~~~~~

When Darcy woke, his first visit after he kissed his still unconscious wife on her forehead was to the nursery. The sight that met him was one that warmed his heart. The new grandfather was sitting in a chair with one grandson in one arm and his granddaughter in the other. His uncle Reggie was sitting in another chair holding his other son, while Lord Hilldale and Bingley were looking on with pleasure. Georgie and Kitty were bouncing from foot to foot with excitement waiting for their turn to hold a niece or nephew.

As he walked in and was noticed, Kitty asked how her sister was doing. Darcy explained she was still having her much-needed rest to aid her recovery and thankfully she, thus far, had not developed a fever. Once Kitty and Georgie were seated in a chair, to their delight they were passed a baby boy each. Andrew retrieved little Miss Darcy from her grandfather.

"Did you and Lizzy decide on names before the birth William, and when will you notify people of their arrival?" Andrew asked his cousin as he held his Miss Darcy, his words for William, his eyes not leaving her.

"Other than Bennet for our first son," he nodded at Bennet, "no, we have not. We felt we would be tempting the fates to pick names before our children were with us. Once Elizabeth is awake and we choose names, we will send the notifications out.

"However, I am sending a note to the Elliots today, as Charlotte and Lizzy are so close, and to Anne and Ian, and Richard and Mary as they will be most anxious, and we do not want to cause Mary any unnecessary anxiety or Richard will call me out with pistols at dawn."

"I will write the missives to my brother and cousin. You focus on the one to the Elliots and your wife and babes," Andrew offered, "and I suppose we can call them numbers one, two, and three," the Viscount stated with a playful twinkle in his eye.

"Never!" Darcy retorted playfully with a fake look of outrage, then again grew serious. "Once we have named them after Lizzy is awake, we will inform all of you what our second son and daughters are to be named." He looked at each again. "And thank you, Andrew, I appreciate your sending those on our behalf. You have had experience in writing these, after all."

"Daughters?" Georgiana asked, confused as she looked around the room.

"I see no one has told you and Kitty yet. Lizzy delivered four babes, but the last one, a very small girl, God called home to him. Once we have spoken, Lizzy and I will name her, and she will be buried with all of her Darcy relatives in the family plot," Darcy explained, the emotion in his voice thick.

"We are so sorry, William," Kitty whispered, both she and Georgiana crying silently for the niece they would never know.

"I was very sad when she passed, and I still am, but as was pointed out to me by a very wise lady, at the same time God took her home, even before he had, He had blessed us with three healthy babes to counter the toll." William walked over and touched both of his sisters, soothing them, and letting their sadness remind him of his blessings.

The rest of the day, when the babes were not asleep or being fed, there was no shortage of visitors to the nursery, especially once Mrs. Bennet, Mrs. Bingley, the Countess, and Lady Hilldale woke up and joined the rotation.

CHAPTER 29

Just before midnight, as Darcy was sitting and holding his wife's hand, the accoucheur's prediction came to pass. He felt a weak squeeze of his hand and looked up to see his beloved's eyes fluttering. After what seemed like an interminable amount of time but was really only a minute or two, Lizzy opened her eyes.

"Water," she croaked out, her throat feeling dry as desert sand after not drinking for almost a full day. Darcy poured some water into a glass for Lizzy and helped her raise her head so she could drink a few drops. After three or four sips he helped her settle back onto her pillows. Sir Fredrick's nurse for the night shift went to wake the man himself so he could come and examine his patient.

"The babes?" asked Elizabeth as she looked at her husband to gauge his mood, and for once she had a hard time reading his expression.

"As soon as Sir Frederick examines you, my love, I will tell you all." As he said the last, he gave Lizzy's hand a gentle squeeze.

"I am very happy to see you have decided to join us, Mrs. Darcy," Sir Frederick quipped as he walked into the room dressed in his robe and slippers. "I apologise for my casual style of dress, but I felt examining Mrs. Darcy took precedence over making myself presentable."

"You have nothing to be sorry for, Sir Frederick. In fact, I laud you made my dear beloved wife your first priority," Darcy said with relief.

Realising even should he request it Mr. Darcy would not leave his wife's side, the accoucheur did not bother asking him to. After a twenty-minute examination assisted by his night nurse, the accoucheur looked at the nervous parents, his expression telling them he was pleased with what he saw.

"For a woman who delivered multiple babes less than a day ago, you are doing remarkably well, Mrs. Darcy. My nurse informs me there has been no trace of fever and no more than the expected bleeding. The longer we go without any adverse signs, the less the chance of any negative consequences. It is very serendipitous you are such a fit woman. I have no doubt your overall health made you a much better candidate to survive multiple births than most. Do either of you have any questions for me?" he enquired.

"What happened? How many babes did I birth? Are they all well?" Elizabeth was babbling, something out of character for one as intelligent as her but given the ordeal she had experienced, it was understandable, even expected.

"It was a long and hard birth. You lapsed into unconsciousness about twenty hours ago, but before you panic, that is not out of the ordinary for multiple births. The body needs to take some time to relax, rest, and recuperate. The rest is for your husband to tell you, and unless there is nothing else you need specifically from me, I will retire for the night. My nurse will wait in the hall until you have finished your discussion.

"Just call out if you need her assistance. Do not worry, Mrs. Darcy, if you feel very tired over the next week or so, it is natural and expected. Your body will crave rest, and the more you allow it, the faster you will heal. I will take my leave of you now, Mr. Darcy, Mrs. Darcy." He bowed slightly to each as he said their name then he and the nurse left Elizabeth's bedchamber, closing the door behind them.

"Please William, tell me everything, and do not feel you need to protect my sensibilities." Elizabeth looked at him in fear. Darcy took his wife's hand and looked at her lovingly, hating that he would have to deliver devastating news but glad that at least there was considerably more good news than bad news to impart. "You delivered four, not three babes my love," Darcy informed her gently.

"*FOUR!!*" exclaimed a very flabbergasted, if tired, Elizabeth Darcy. "Are they all well, William?" she asked, already feeling the answer in her heart as no one had heard even a faint fourth heartbeat.

"Three are very well, my Lizzy. The last babe was a tiny girl who took one small breath with us, but never opened her eyes before she went to be with God." He fought to maintain his equanimity, needing to be strong for her in this moment.

"One daughter passed away?" his distraught wife choked out, tears streaming down her cheeks before she could ever say the words.

Darcy passed his wife one of his handkerchiefs and soothed her as best he could without lifting her into his arms, his thumb gently caressing along the back of her hand to help her feel his love while she let go of one she had loved without even knowing she was there. It took some five minutes for her crying to ease, while they experienced their shared grief.

"You said four and our daughter passed?" Elizabeth asked once she could again speak.

"That leads us directly to the good news, my love. We were blessed with three healthy and hearty babes. Two sons and a daughter, and oh, my love, your Mama says the baby girl is an exact copy of how you were as a babe. Even arriving in the world crying louder than her brothers," he smiled. The grief would never be discounted, but the joy should also be celebrated.

"We have two sons *and* a daughter?" she gasped, then looked at him and locked their eyes. "Have you decided on names yet?"

"You wound me by asking, my love. You must know I would never make that decision without you. We have a partnership in all things so I could as soon presume to name our children without you as I could make them without you, which the doctor assured me I could not. I hope you agree, I would first like us to name our daughter that passed and have her buried with her grandparents."

"I am so sorry I said that William, I know you would not name them without my input. You have my full agreement and I have a suggestion for the name of the babe that passed. When Tom and James were born, my parents were convinced they would be daughter number five so they had the name Lydia picked out for my mama's late great aunt. Can we name her Lydia Bennet Darcy?"

"That is perfect, my love. As sad as we are about little Lydia not being alive to grow up with her brothers and sister, I am counting my blessings from God on high for the three healthy babes as we will have our hands full caring for them. We need to name the other two of them soon, my love, to stop our sisters and brothers calling them numbers two and three. The firstborn is Bennet as we agreed ahead of time.

"Also, other than the Elliots, Andrew sent announcements to Anne and Ian, and Richard and Mary, I have not sent any notifications out yet. Charlotte was here earlier today, and she will wait to hear you are awake before she comes again. Anne was not able to come but would have taken us to task and *that* none of us want to see should her anger be anything like her..." he cleared his throat, "and no one wanted to cause Mary any undue anxiety as she is on bedrest and required to keep calm."

"Thank you for caring so for my sister's wellbeing

with so much going on here." She caressed his cheek. "Now, what names should we choose William, my most beloved husband?"

"You know the Darcy tradition to name the heir with the last name of his mother before marriage, and we chose Bennet for our first son, so for our oldest son and heir's full name, I suggest Bennet Alexander Darcy," Darcy suggested the second name he had contemplated while he waited for his wife to wake up.

"I agree with one amendment; Bennet Alexander Fitzwilliam Darcy, who as we have previously decided, we will call Ben. I think the name Fitzwilliam should be in the names of each of our sons." She smiled up into his eyes.

"Well then, we now agree on the name of our first son, who is less than ten minutes older than his identical brother," Darcy chuckled.

"Identical? Oh my. With Tom and James, it was easy to tell them apart since they look as dissimilar as Jane and I do. How will we tell them apart? I am sure they both will need scolding, but I would hate to apply it to the wrong one!" she looked at him in alarm and he laughed as he nodded.

"I am sure that they will. And, I am equally sure as they grow, we will see subtle differences in them. For the time being, Ben has blue ribbons on his wrist and ankle and his brother has green." Darcy chuckled.

"How about George Thomas Fitzwilliam Darcy for our second son? As Ben honours my family with his name, our next oldest will honour your father," Lizzy suggested.

"That is perfect, my love. I agree, so George Thomas Fitzwilliam Darcy it shall be, and no more number two! Now what do you think an appropriate name for our daughter should be? I am thinking of Francine Anne Elizabeth Darcy. If all the boys are to have Fitzwilliam in their names, then it is only fair the girls have Elizabeth. I think we should leave

Lydia's name as it is, it honours both families and her as an individual."

"I love that name for our daughter, and I have no objection to Elizabeth being part of the girl's names if we have more. I think we should call her Franny or Fran. And yes, I too think we should leave Lydia's name as it is." Her husband kissed her hand and just then they heard a chorus of cries coming from the nursery as their children woke up demanding sustenance and changing.

"I want to see our children, please my love, and I want to feed one of them at least," Elizabeth pleaded.

"Hold on while I go get them to introduce them to their Mama, though without a third arm, it will not be all at once. It is suggested that you should feed Franny. She is the smallest of the three and Sir Frederick said no matter the societal norms, he believes it would be beneficial for her to be fed by her Mama." William smiled when he saw hers. Darcy stepped into the nursery, and once they were changed, he returned carrying two fussing babes, one with a green ribbon and one with a blue.

"Mrs. Elizabeth Darcy, it is my pleasure to introduce you to Master Ben and Master George Darcy. More importantly, boys, this is your most beautiful mama, who will be the best one in the world. And I will tell you a secret, she is already the best mother in the world as she is yours, but I would not boast about that around the Bingleys or Fitzwilliams so very much." He teased his wife, causing her to laugh so their sons could hear that most perfect sound first.

After holding and kissing each of her sons, Darcy returned them to the wet nurses and then came back carrying little Franny. She was most indignant at being disturbed, but soon was suckling happily at her mother's breast. Lizzy found it very fulfilling, and she agreed that she would be the primary source of nourishment for Miss

Franny, but she would nurse each of her sons at least once a day as she felt the bonding while she fed her daughter.

Once Franny was done feeding, she marvelled as William put some cloths on his shoulder then took Franny, holding her upright and gently patting her back until she had a very satisfying belch then promptly drifted off to sleep.

Once he had placed Franny in her cradle, he instructed the on-duty nursemaid to have each of their children's names written on a card and placed on the relevant cradle. He returned to find his wife fast asleep, so he called the nurse back in, gently kissed his wife's forehead, then retired to his chambers.

~~~~~~~/~~~~~~~

When Elizabeth awoke, she knew it was late due to the angle of the sun. She shook her head to banish the sleepiness and looked around. She saw Jacqui sitting and chatting with the day nurse, then she saw her beloved husband and her mother talking quietly. Darcy sensed his Lizzy was awake and was at her bedside in an instant, followed only a little more sedately by her mother.

"Oh, Lizzy, I love the names of all four of your babies. If I am not careful, I will again start crying at the thought of them." Her mother held her hand tight.

"I dare any of my sisters to do it better," Elizabeth stated, smiling as she won her mother's laugh.

"Oh dear, I will not tell them they are in competition or there will be many a late-night planning session." She kissed her daughter's forehead as Darcy chuckled, agreeing the men would be up many a night were they issued such a challenge.

After she was examined by Sir Frederick and pronounced out of danger, Elizabeth ate a light breakfast then her husband asked everyone to give them some privacy. Before she left, he whispered an instruction to Lizzy's maid who nodded and headed for the servant's stairs.

Soon there was a soft knock on the door and Mrs. Reynolds entered. Now the mistress was informed about her daughter who had gone to God, Darcy told the housekeeper to see to the arrangement for Lydia to be buried between her Darcy grandparents on the morrow in the morning.

The mood lightened as the family all took turns visiting Elizabeth when she was awake. After being notified her friend was well on the way to recovery, Charlotte Elliot visited, along with Grace and her husband.

Grace was fascinated by the three new Darcys, proclaiming she would be a good *older* friend to them. Now the three new Darcys were named, notifications were sent to friends and family as was a notification to the papers.

Invariably when awake, all three of the babes were in the mistress's chambers being admired by grandparents, great aunt and uncle, or their newly minted aunts and uncles. Tom and James after completing their first year at Trinity College, were staying at the estate of a friend from university and would travel to Derbyshire a few weeks after Jane's lying in.

News of the birth of an heir of Pemberley, as well as his brother and sister, spread like wildfire through the staff and out to the surrounding community. The news brought great joy and relief, the continuity of the Darcy line being secured, and with it the livelihood of so many that depended on Pemberley for their economic prosperity, was the news anxiously anticipated from the day a Darcy was betrothed.

The one sad note was the day their tiny Lydia was laid to rest between her paternal grandparents. The service was conducted by Mr. Elliot and attended by all of the men residing at Pemberley, along with the senior male staff.

The women and Charlotte Elliot sat with Elizabeth to give her strength during her daughter's funeral. The sadness was not allowed to overshadow the joy of three healthy babes now resident in the nursery at Pemberley.

~~~~~~~/~~~~~~~

Life settled into a comfortable pattern of time spent with the children and visits with the family and the Elliots. A sennight after the birth, Mrs. Elizabeth Darcy felt strong enough to get out of her bed and walk the halls of the floor their chambers were on.

After her walk, Sir Frederick examined Mrs. Darcy one more time and announced her perfectly healthy, and proclaimed she could return to her normal level of activity, including walking and riding, as soon as she felt able to. The accoucheur and his two nurses departed Pemberley the next morning to return to Town with many thanks from the family and a substantial amount of money for services rendered.

Now that his wife was out of bed, Darcy asked his friend Patrick Elliot to conduct the christening on the following day. Even though they could not travel, Richard and Mary Fitzwilliam were named godparents of the heir, Bennet Alexander Fitzwilliam Darcy, Jane and Charles Bingley were asked to be godparents of George Thomas Fitzwilliam Darcy, while Francine Anne Elizabeth Darcy gained Charlotte and Patrick Elliot as godparents.

After the christening, the Bennets and the Bingleys departed for Longfield Meadows to prepare for the final stages of Jane's confinement, while all of the Fitzwilliams headed south toward Netherfield Park to prepare for Mary's lying in.

The new and very proud aunts, Georgiana and Kitty, remained at Pemberley. Now that the family had departed and the house was a lot quieter, the Elliots were often in their company. Charlotte and Grace would come and visit two or three times each week, and Elliot joined them, when not too busy with pastoral duties, to spend time with his good friend and patron.

~~~~~~~/~~~~~~~

Six weeks after the Darcy three were born, Jane Bingley entered her lying in. After a six-hour labour, a daughter who was named Maureen Fanny Bennet Bingley entered the world. She had been named for her late grandmother and her living one, with the Bennet name honoured as it was with the Darcys' children.

Little Maureen was as serene as her mother, with the same colouring, tufts of blond hair, and deep blue eyes. In addition to Jane's parents and Aunt and Uncle Gardiner, from Charles's side Louisa and Harold had arrived days before the birth with their daughter Maryanne Shirley Hurst, who was then strong enough for travel. The Hursts were very honoured when they were asked to be the godparents of little Maureen Bingley and heartily accepted the honour.

At Pemberley, there was much joy expressed at Jane's safe delivery and relatively quick recovery. Pemberley's midwife had attended Jane and practised her usual standards of cleanliness, not a wide practice at the time, which she believed accounted for the fact she had never lost a mother to child bed fever. Once the name was chosen, like the Darcys before them, the Bingleys sent notification to all friends and family.

Two weeks after the birth of young Miss Bingley, Tom and James Bennet arrived at the Meadows looking very handsome. They had both shot up in their first year at Cambridge and now sported stubble in the evenings where none had been visible not six months before.

Georgiana, who had come with Kitty to see their new niece Maureen, was struck anew by how handsome the twins were. She was somewhat embarrassed to have thoughts about young men, especially Tom Bennet who were after all her sister's brothers.

She had always been close to him as a friend, but the new thoughts filling her mind were not just of friendship.

~~~~~~~/~~~~~~~

Four days after they received the express announcing Miss Bingley's joining of the world, Mary Fitzwilliam entered her lying in at Netherfield Park with her mother-in-law and sister-in-law to help her while the Earl and Viscount kept her husband calm.

After a short, less than three-hour labour, kicking and crying indignantly a very large and robust son entered the world. His paternal grandmother stated except for having his mother's colouring, he looked just like his father had as a babe. After Mary was cleaned and changed, she was joined by her loving and proud husband, who thanked her profusely for the gift that she had given him.

Once his parents had discussed names, they decided on William Reginald Bennet Fitzwilliam for the young heir to Netherfield Park. An express to Pemberley announced young Master Fitzwilliam's arrival and asked the Darcys if they would fill the office of godparents for young William Fitzwilliam, who would be called Will.

The Darcys replied immediately with hearty congratulations and acceptance of the office of godparents. Young David Fitzwilliam, now a little more than three, was ecstatic to learn his Unca Rich and Antie Mary had gifted him a boy cousin, which when added to the two Darcy sons, increased the growing number of male babes in the family.

~~~~~~~/~~~~~~~

At Rosings Park, Mrs. Anne Ashby was a little despondent at the flurry of birth notices. She did not begrudge anyone their joy. No, her discontent was with herself. It had been above four months since she had married her Ian. The first three months after they married were spent at their estate Sherwood Park in Surrey to give the former Miss de Bourgh time to learn how to be mistress of that estate.

They had returned to Rosings Park a sennight before the day the express announcing the birth of William Reginald Bennet Fitzwilliam arrived. After a fortnight stay, they would initiate their planned rotation of three weeks in Surrey and one in Kent.

Anne was worried the elixir Lady Catherine had given her over the years to try to maintain control of Rosings, if not eventually killing her own daughter to steal her estate, had affected her ability to become with child.

She had travelled to town with her husband to consult with Sir Frederick after he had returned from Pemberley, and he had told them as far as he could tell there was no impediment to Anne Ashby's ability to bear a child.

As she was worrying about her ability to become with child, she forgot to watch herself for the signs she was in the early stages of pregnancy. She used to love mutton, but in the last number of weeks she could not bear the smell, and her breasts, normally not very large, had started to grow in size and were somewhat tender.

Anne was too preoccupied with worry about not being pregnant, and the fear of never being so, it went unnoticed she had missed her last courses. She did not know it yet, but Anne Ashby was over a month into her first pregnancy.

Mornings that started with her being sick occurred within a sennight, and soon after Anne noticed she had missed her courses. She took care to consider all the weeks that had passed and realised this was the second month that her courses had been missed.

Anne invited their newly established local physician to consult and examine her. She wanted to be sure before she said anything to her beloved husband. The former local physician, after being dismissed, had been arrested by the local magistrate for conspiracy to commit grievous harm to a patient, regardless of who had given the order, and was transported to Van Diemen's Land, never to be heard of again.

After his examination, Mr. Chadwick confirmed Anne's suspicions and she was over the moon with joy when she shared the news with her husband, that in about seven to eight months they too would be parents, if all went well.

They decided not to share with anyone on either side of the family except his sister and brother who lived at the Hunsford parsonage since they recently married. Mr. Graham and Lady Sarah Allenton would divine the secret since they ate at Rosings almost every day the Ashbys were in residence. As could be predicted, the Allentons were very happy for the Ashbys and understood the need not to share the news, and promised to keep the secret until Anne felt the quickening.

At the end of the fortnight's stay at Rosings Park, they were to travel north to Derbyshire. They would first go to Netherfield Park to spend time with Mary and Richard Fitzwilliam so they could meet young Master Will.

After a five-day sojourn in Hertfordshire, they planned to travel north to Pemberley to meet the three Darcy children and stay there for about six weeks, which meant Anne would likely feel the quickening while there.

They would see the Bingleys and meet their daughter Maureen while in the area, and Anne was looking forward to furthering her friendship with the former Charlotte Lucas, now Mrs. Elliot.

Anne especially anticipated meeting Grace, the Elliot's young daughter whom she had heard so many good reports about.

~~~~~~~/~~~~~~~

After a very enjoyable five days at Netherfield Park

with Mary, Richard, and baby Will, the Ashbys set out for Pemberley. It would be Ian's first-time seeing the Darcys' primary estate. He was in great anticipation of doing so and renewing his acquaintance with the Darcys and the Bingleys, as well as meeting the newest three Darcys.

On the afternoon of the third day after they left the Fitzwilliams, the Ashby conveyance pulled to a stop at the entrance to Pemberley. They were met by Mr. and Mrs. Darcy, and after being shown to their suite where they freshened up from their travels, they entered the nursery to meet their new cousins.

Not yet three months old, the Darcy three were already quite strong, could all lift their heads, and would smile and giggle as the surfeit of adults tickled them and cooed at them. Anne remarked at how identical Ben and George were, and they agreed that little Franny was indeed a miniature Elizabeth Darcy. Her eyes had begun to change recently, and it looked like she would eventually have hazel eyes like her mother.

That evening at dinner they were joined by the Elliots and little Grace who, after polite curtseys, went to the nursery so she could *help* care for the babes. Anne Ashby shared with her family that they suspected she was with child. All present wished Anne and Ian Ashby their best wishes and hoped Anne would have an easy confinement.

Charlotte shared the news she had given Elizabeth but two days before, that she had felt the quickening of her first babe. Little Miss Grace Elliot was of course hoping for a sister, but after seeing the Darcys' sons she shared she would be happy with either a brother or a sister.

~~~~~~~/~~~~~~~

The whole family met at Longbourn for Christmastide that year. The Darcys, the Fitzwilliams, and the Bingleys travelled from Derbyshire and were joined by the Hursts and the Elliots. The Gardiners came from London, and Mary and Richard Fitzwilliam also stayed at Longbourn even though Netherfield Park was but three miles away.

The only members of the extended family who were not present were the Ashbys as Anne had been restricted from travel by Sir Fredrick. They were spending the rest of her pregnancy through her confinement at Sherwood Park.

It was a very merry party, and Mr. and Mrs. Bennet lovingly watched their family. Every new glance warmed their hearts even more. Three daughters married, five grandchildren, and a very large extended family. They proudly watched as their sons, very much men now in their own rights, were each holding a Darcy son while Kitty and Georgiana were entertaining Will and Franny.

Little Maureen was being held by her proud Papa and looked as serene and content as her mother. Reggie and Elaine Fitzwilliam were entertaining almost four-year-old David, while his sister Gillian was being entertained by her father and Uncle Richard. Lizzy, Mary, Andrew, and William were sitting and talking to the Hursts while their child slept in the nursery.

As they watched their extended family, Bennet leaned over to his Fanny. "Can you believe how our family has prospered since Tom and James were born Fanny?" He asked quietly.

"It is hard to comprehend how fully our fortunes changed that day, Thomas. We both prayed to God for a son, and we both pledged to change our ways. And most importantly, we have kept those pledges." Fanny rested her forehead against her beloved husband's.

"We have indeed, Fanny. I will never forget how convinced I was that we would have a fifth daughter, and I could not understand why you looked so serene and happy when I came to see you in the early morning of that fateful day. It took me a while to comprehend what was staring me in the face.

"I will never forget the euphoria I experienced once I saw you were well Fanny. I was so scared with your size for that last confinement that God would call you home to Him. He did not, and instead, we were blessed with our sons. Look at where we are today. God has been very good to us, Fanny," Bennet murmured to his wife.

"Yes, Thomas, He has been so very good to us. I love you as much today as I did the day that I married you, if not more so." As she said the last, she kissed her beloved husband's cheek.

EPILOGUE

The Elliots:

As much as the former Miss Charlotte Lucas had decried love as a necessary ingredient to a good marriage in the past, she was the first to admit hers was a love match. She loved her Patrick with all of her being and did until his passing many years later. Her first borne was a little girl, much to then six-year-old Grace's delight. She went on to present her husband with two sons as well.

Once Grace was seventeen, her sister, Sarah, eleven, her brother, Everett, nine, and the youngest, Paul, seven, her esteemed father decided to retire to his estate Riverdale inherited from his maternal grandmother and the estate was smaller than Longbourn before Bennet's epiphany.

At the time of his retirement, thanks to the prudence and savings of the vast majority of his earnings all invested with Edward Gardiner, Patrick Elliot had purchased a neighbouring estate and some extra land, so his estate was by then bringing in a clear profit of seven thousand per annum. He was able to settle five and twenty thousand pounds on each of his two daughters and forty thousand on his second son.

Grace, after her coming out season, was introduced to, and eventually agreed to a courtship with, the younger by two years David Fitzwilliam, who would one day be Viscount Hilldale and later, many years later, be Lord Matlock.

Sarah, Charlotte and Patrick's second daughter, ended

up marrying George Darcy, cementing the bonds that were already very strong between the Darcys and the Elliots. Their oldest boy Everett, named for his late grandfather, would eventually inherit the very prosperous estate of Riverdale and marry the second daughter of a baronet. The youngest Paul who, although with the fortune his father settled on him did not need a profession, after Cambridge decided to read the law and became one of the most sought-after barristers in the Kingdom. He married the daughter of a tradesman, a very wealthy one although that was not a consideration.

The Ashbys:

Anne, even though Sir Frederick had pointed out the danger after her first son Lewis was born of her being with child again, three years after Lewis's birth bore a second son named after his Grandfather, Rudolph Ashby, the Earl of Ashbury.

Although weakened after her second son, Anne, who was close to all of her Ashby, Darcy, Fitzwilliam, and Bennet family, insisted, much against the advice of her doctors, on becoming with child again as she wanted a daughter.

Her wish was granted four years after Rudi, but the cost was her life as she was very weak after the birth and never recovered. She succumbed some months after her daughter, named Anne Elizabeth Ashby was born.

The whole family came to Sherwood Park for her burial, as she chose to be buried at her beloved husband's estate rather than Rosings Park. Her first born son, Lewis, would eventually inherit Sherwood Park, while his brother Rudolph inherited Rosings Park when he attained the age of five and twenty.

Rudolph had lived at the estate from the time he completed his studies at Cambridge, learning all facets of managing his estate from the extremely proficient steward his Uncle William Darcy had recommended all those years ago.

He also received assistance from his uncles and aunts each year when the extended family came to Rosings Park for Easter. In what could only be viewed as irony, he married his cousin Pricilla Darcy, the seventh of eight Darcy children and the fourth and last daughter granted to the Darcys.

Lady Catherine, had she been alive, would have been seriously displeased the shades of Rosings Park would be thus polluted by her grandson marrying the daughter of the artful woman who had tricked her nephew into marriage.

Ian Ashby mourned his wife for a number of years, then when little Anne was five, he met Maria Carter née Lucas, who was visiting with her sister and brother-in-law along with the family for Easter. Her husband, Colonel Jack Carter, had died in the Canadas some three years previously and they had no children.

Less than a year later, Maria became Mrs. Ashby and little Anne finally knew a mother. She loved all three of the Ashby children as if they were her own, and they were blessed with a daughter a year after their wedding. They lived a very long and happy life together, and although Ian Ashby never forgot his Anne, he was a very contented man.

The Hursts:

Harold and Louisa Hurst lived on the estate he inherited when his father passed in Northamptonshire. They were always included in all family events of the extended family who counted them as fully fledged members. Louisa bore three children, two girls and a boy.

A month into their son's first year at Oxford, Harold Hurst passed away from complications of heart disease. He was mourned by his beloved wife and children, as well as their large extended family and friends. His oldest finished his schooling and then came home to take over the estate. His mother lived with him until her passing many years later, never marrying again.

Both Louisa and Harold Hurst enjoyed a loving relationship until the day of his passing without the toxic influence of Louisa's younger sister. Neither her children nor any of their cousins or friends knew that Caroline Bingley existed, and all were happier for their lack of knowledge.

Between their father and their Uncle Charles Bingley, the Hurst daughters had twenty thousand each and made very fine matches after second seasons. Louisa's son married the only child from an estate that bordered the Hurst's, and when her parents passed the estate devolved to her. It would eventually be passed down to Louisa's second grandson. The older daughter, Isabelle Hurst ended up marrying Will Fitzwilliam, the heir to Netherfield.

Elaine and Reggie Fitzwilliam:

It was not too many years after the events described herein that the running of Snowhaven was passed onto Andrew Fitzwilliam, Lord Hilldale. Lord Matlock still participated in the house of Lords for another ten years.

Rather than be tied to their estates, when Reggie was not needed in town, they would sojourn at one of the estates of their children or nieces and nephews to spend time with the rapidly growing number of grandchildren, grandnieces, and grandnephews.

As much as Reginald Fitzwilliam, the Earl of Matlock, loved politics, he loved spending time with his beloved wife and visiting family even more.

The Earl and Countess were counted as grandparents to the Darcy children, the Ashby children, and the Bingley children. The Earl survived to see his first great-grandson born to David and Grace Fitzwilliam before he passed on to be with God in heaven. His Countess followed him ten years later, after seeing a slew of additional greatgrandchildren born.

Andrew and Marie Fitzwilliam:

Lord and Lady Hilldale ended up having five children. Other than David and Gillian, they had one more son they named Richard, and two more daughters, Elaine and Emmaline, the latter who was called Emma named for Marie's late mother. They lived at Hilldale until Lord Matlock asked Andrew to take over Snowhaven and the other Fitzwilliam estates.

It was a very sad day for them and all of the family when Reggie Fitzwilliam passed not long after the birth of David and Grace Fitzwilliam's son. The young heir was name Reginald, to be called Reggie, after the beloved patriarch of the Fitzwilliam family.

Andrew and Marie made an excellent Lord and Lady Matlock, and the dowager Countess was never asked to go live in the dower house. Until she passed and went to join her beloved Reggie, when not at the home of one of her other family members, she lived in her suite at Snowhaven.

In addition to David marrying Grace, their other four children all made love matches as expected, given all of the examples in the family around them it really could be no other way. Gillian married the oldest son of the Duke of Bedford, not for wealth and title, but for love.

The other three children of Marie and Andrew Fitzwilliam made brilliant matches, and their son Reggie did not need a profession as he inherited an estate that was not part of the entailed Matlock estates in Shropshire which produced six thousand five hundred pounds clear a year.

Mary and Richard Fitzwilliam:

Besides Will, who would one day inherit Netherfield Park, Mary and Richard Fitzwilliam were blessed with five more children. After Will there were identical twin girls, Rachel and Amelia, who were followed by Hugh, Matthew, and lastly Rosemarie.

As Mary's fortune had never been touched and was left to grow with Gardiner and Associates, as had most of Richard's money to which he added the profits from the estate each year, the three daughters received dowries of five and forty thousand pounds each while the younger sons both received the same amount as their sister's dowries. Will would receive the substantial balance of his father's fortune that was still growing, along with the estate.

When he was six and twenty and she nine and ten, Will married the oldest daughter of Louisa and the late Harold Hurst, Isabelle. It was another love match, and at the wedding Louisa remarked to Mary Fitzwilliam about the irony that one day, hopefully far in the future, her daughter would be the mistress of Netherfield Park.

Richard and Mary Fitzwilliam loved living so close to Longbourn and the Bennets. They spent a lot of time together. Once the Earl passed the day to day running of his estates to Andrew, he and the Countess spent at least three months a year with the Netherfield Park Fitzwilliams.

After Reggie Fitzwilliam passed away, the dowager countess split her year between Derbyshire and Hertfordshire, and when she passed ten years after her beloved husband, she was mourned greatly by all of the family.

Mary and Richard loved each other with a special kind of love that grew, rather than diminished, over time. They were always surrounded by an ever increasing, loving family that eventually included grandchildren and greatgrandchildren.

Once Tom and James Bennet outgrew their habit of demanding stories of his glory days in the army, they were replaced by his own sons asking him to spin yarns for them, along with the children of all his sisters and brothers. Richard Fitzwilliam became the favourite story telling uncle in the family.

The Gardiners:

As there was more and more acknowledgement of the importance of men of business to the Kingdom, in 1828 Edward Gardiner was awarded a baronetcy in recognition of his contributions to the economy of the Kingdom, and especially the wealth of the royal family.

He was gifted the estate of Dovedale just a little south of Lambton where his beloved Maddie had grown up. In 1830 he withdrew from active participation in the daily running of Gardiner and Associates. With his advice and influence, his partners kept the business running and growing from strength to strength.

Other than his brother Bennet, his solicitor, and some trusted individuals, few knew the full extent of his wealth. When he retired, he had amassed well over a million pounds in assets and was able to give his daughters dowries of one hundred thousand pounds each.

George Gardiner would inherit his father's title, the estate, a large fortune and like his brother and sisters, five and twenty percent of Gardiner's stake in Gardiner and Associates. Peter Gardiner went into the business and followed in his father's footsteps, dubbed *Prince Midas*; Lilly Gardiner married the eldest son of Ian Ashby's brother who was now the Earl of Ashbury, so she became the new Lady Amberleigh.

Their younger daughter, May, married a member of parliament and, like her cousin Lizzy was no shrinking violet, she helped her husband become the leader of the Whigs in the commons.

Peter fell in love with, and married, the daughter of the other major partner in Gardiner and Associates, Miss Rose Riverton. The four Gardiner children produced nineteen grandchildren and eleven great-grandchildren before the Gardiner patriarch passed away many years later.

Edward and Maddie Gardiner were beloved and revered by all the extended family. They loved hosting family and friends at their estate and enjoyed being hosted by family just as much. Until he was no longer physically able to, well into his eighth decade, Edward Gardiner loved to fish. He could sometimes be found fishing in his favourite spot where he felt all of their destinies intertwined, just beyond the formal gardens at Pemberley.

The Bingleys:

Although his wife was serene, she had a backbone of steel and anyone who tried to take advantage of the Bingleys discovered this fact to their peril. Almost two years after their first daughter, Jane Bingley delivered her second daughter, Elizabeth Louisa, who would be known as Beth and who took after her aunt for whom she was named, most especially in impertinence.

Beth was followed by Johanna, and then by Rosamond. After four daughters Charles Junior made his appearance and he was the last born to Jane and Charles Bingley.

Jane's fortune was also left to grow under the expert stewardship of Uncle Gardiner, along with profits from the Meadows and the balance of Bingley's fortune after he had purchased their estate so that all four Bingley daughters had dowries of fifty thousand pounds. Charles junior would one day inherit the Meadows, and with it a fortune in excess of two hundred thousand pounds.

The four Bingley daughters all made very good love matches. Maureen married the son of Lady Sarah and Graham Allenton. Allenton was no longer parson at Hunsford, his uncle who had no children when he passed left him as his heir to a large and very prosperous estate in Wiltshire.

Her sisters all married men they loved, Beth to the son of a baronet whose family were neighbours to her Aunt Lizzy and Uncle William in Derbyshire. Jo and Rosa both married very well-off businessmen.

The Bingley heir, seven years younger than his sister Maureen, married the daughter of the late Anne Ashby. Charlie Bingley met and fell in love with Anne Ashby one year when the family met at Rosings for Easter. They were very happy together and unfortunately Charles Junior inherited the Meadows far too early.

Charles Bingley Senior had always loved to ride at great speed. One day, just before Maureen Allenton was to enter her lying in, he had taken himself for a ride on his son-in-law's family estate in Wiltshire. He did not know the land as he did at the Meadows; his stallion, Blaze, returned to the stables without him.

After an extensive search his body was found in the woods. Evidently, he had ridden through the woods at too high a speed and had not noticed a low hanging branch that had broken his neck. Jane had been beside herself with grief over the loss of her beloved Charles. It hit the whole family very hard, especially his best friend and brother William Darcy.

The only thing that kept Jane Bingley going was her family and her children. She started wearing half mourning after a full two years and would only come out of mourning after another full year.

Jane Bingley never married again, but she lived a very

long and happy life surrounded by family and friends. She helped her daughter-in-law learn how to run the Meadows while Charlie learnt how to manage it with the help of the steward and his uncles.

Once she was sure that Anne Bingley was confident in running the manor on the estate, Jane accepted her sister Lizzy's invitation and moved to Pemberley. She spent a lot of her time either visiting or being visited by family, especially her children, grandchildren, and eventually great-grandchildren.

As much as she missed her beloved Charles, she knew that he would have wanted her to carry on and be strong. And it was true her very nature would allow no less of herself because she had those in her charge that needed her care and love.

He would have wanted her to remarry, but that was one thing that she would never do, and with all the warmth of family to envelop her, she never felt the need.

Tom Bennet and Georgiana Darcy:

Once Tom completed Cambridge, he went home to Longbourn to learn how to effectively run the estate from his father, Longbourn's steward, and his brothers-in-law. He had cared for Darcy's sister above all others from the first time he met her when she had been a guest at Longbourn many years before.

Tom knew that he was irrevocably in love with her before he was halfway through his studies at Trinity College at Cambridge. He had spoken to his brother and Darcy had requested that he not declare himself until Georgie had completed her first full season.

As much as he had wanted to do so earlier himself, he accepted the logic behind Darcy's decision, and then, later on, he had spoken to his parents and found they had agreed with their son William completely.

It had killed him to watch her dance with other men that first season, and some had tried to call on her, but none were accepted. What he did not know was Georgie was as much in love with him as he was with her. She went out into society only so she would get the chance to dance with him, which would be the opening or supper set, and if he had not been able to claim both, sometimes included the last as well. She was not sure that he loved her as she loved him but was resolute that she would not settle for anyone else.

There were too many examples of love, respect, and felicity among the married couples in her family for her to ever agree to marry for anything less, as she and Kitty had declared even before their first season.

Georgiana had learnt to accept that the folly of her youth helped teach her the value of true love, but more importantly helped her learn the value of herself, which was as far as she would allow it to influence her life.

At the end of the final ball of her first season, a season she had enjoyed with her sister-in-law Kitty Bennet, Tom, at the end of the final set which had been a waltz, had requested he be granted a private interview the next day. She was then just nineteen and Tom had just turned one and twenty. She had agreed to the request with alacrity and immense pleasure.

The next day, just after ten o'clock in the morning, Tom Bennet had made the walk across Grosvenor Square from Bennet House to Darcy House opposite. Killion had opened the door and then announced him to the Darcys who were waiting for him in the family drawing room.

Lizzy and William left telling him that they would grant him ten minutes, and that the door would remain cracked open. As soon as they were alone, he dropped to one knee, told her how long he had loved her, and asked for her hand in marriage. She told him that she had loved him just as long and accepted him.

When the newly engaged couple entered Darcy's study, they were not overly surprised to see Thomas and Fanny Bennet sitting therein with Lizzy and William. No one opposed the betrothal, but both the Bennet parents and the older Darcys agreed that there would not be a wedding until one year after Tom had completed Cambridge, giving him time to learn what was needed to run Longbourn before his wedding to Georgianna. Although they would have preferred sooner, neither Tom nor Georgie argued for an earlier wedding, as they could see the sense in the decision.

After the almost two-year wait, Tom and Georgiana Bennet emerged from the Kympton Church the happiest of newlyweds. As Reggie Fitzwilliam had done with Snowhaven, Thomas Bennet turned the running of Longbourn over to Tom after he had been married to his Georgie for three years, and she had presented him with Tommy and was increasing again.

Longbourn on its own had an income well in excess of twenty thousand a year that now all went to Tom and Georgie. Georgie and Tom went on to have six children and, like his parents, had two boys and four girls, the difference being they had the boys first, followed by four girls, and no twins.

It was agreed that it was a very fair swap. William had his Lizzy and Tom had Georgie.

James Bennet:

Like his brother Tom did at Longbourn, James spent the time after Cambridge learning how to run Bennet Fields. With all of the land that Thomas Bennet had added, Bennet Fields was close to three times the size it was at purchase, and now brought in a clear twelve thousand pounds a year on its own.

There was a nice river that ran through Bennet Fields, and Bennet had built a grist mill and a textile factory that used the water to power the looms. With the income from these two operations, a further five thousand pounds was added to James Bennet's income.

On his five and twentieth birthday, his papa signed Bennet Fields over to James. Like the other Bennet properties, it had an entail that did not allow the land to be broken up or sold to anyone not a Bennet by blood, and that either male or female could inherit.

James was a lot more serene, like his oldest sister Jane, and like her, he had a backbone of steel. A month after he and Tom celebrated their six and twentieth birthday, Tom met Lady Ingrid Wilson, the oldest daughter of the Baron of Wessex. They fell deeply in love and after a short courtship, followed by a shorter betrothal, James married his Lady Ingrid. They went on to have four children, a daughter followed by three sons.

Kitty Bennet:

Kitty, although some months older than then Georgiana Darcy, came out together with her best friend and sister. Kitty knew her best friend in the world, her Georgie, loved Tom, and she was pretty sure the love was requited.

About halfway through her first season, Kitty, whose dowry had climbed to over eighty thousand pounds, met Lord Haywood Mark Rhys-Davies, the Marquess of Chatsworth, oldest son to the Duke of Derby.

At first, she thought he was the most arrogant, proud, and disagreeable man, and they argued almost every time they were in company together. Kitty could not understand why the disagreeable Lord Rhys-Davies, whose close friends and family called him by his second name Mark, kept approaching her.

After she had known him for about six weeks, he came to call on her at Bennet House. Although to most it would be considered rude, Kitty asked him why he would call on her given how much they argued and disagreed.

For the first time, Mark Rhys-Davies allowed Kitty to see the real him. He explained he was tired of all the fawning debutantes who were only interested in his title, connections, and wealth but cared not a jot for him, so he used his behaviour as a defence mechanism.

He shared with Kitty that he found her the most handsome woman he knew, and he was sure after their acquaintance to date, that if she came to like him, it would be for himself and not his title. He said he was aware she did not need to marry for wealth as her family was almost as wealthy as his.

He requested, and was granted, the chance to start again so Kitty could come to know the real person behind the mask. She agreed but warned him his second and last chance would be over if he ever treated her or her family and friends with disrespect again.

At the end of the season, he called on Kitty at Pemberley, requested, and was granted a formal courtship. The couple courted for about six months and then Lord Chatsworth requested and was granted Kitty's hand in marriage.

After his interview with Bennet, he was shocked to find out that it was very possible that the Bennets had more wealth than his family, and he almost gasped aloud when the amount of Kitty's dowry was shared with him.

Three months after Tom and Georgie married, Kitty became Lady Catherine Rhys-Davies, Marchioness of Chatsworth. Mark's father passed two months after the birth of their son, Haywood Jonathan Rhys-Davies, was born.

The Duke had passed away after a long bout of illness

due to cancer. He died happy knowing the dukedom was secure with the birth of his grandson. Kitty was now her Grace, Duchess of Derby. She went on to present her husband with four more children, twin boys and two daughters.

Though the family would sometimes tease her with deferential or irreverent *'yes your Grace,' 'no your Grace,' 'if you please, your Grace,'* Kitty and Mark were never formal with the large, extended family and loved each other very deeply. Mark kept his promise and was never rude or disrespectful to Kitty or anyone else for all their long years.

Our Villains:

Lady Catherine de Bourgh:

Lady Catherine de Bourgh slipped further and further into her mania. Toward the end, she thought herself a god that could command man and nature to do her bidding to whatever her will was at the time the command was given. Four years after her commitment she refused to be treated for a trifling cold.

That cold turned into pneumonia, and three days after contracting the disease Lady Catherine shuffled off the mortal coil. Lord Matlock was notified, and when asked what to do with the body he sent funds for burial but would not allow her to be interred at any of the family sites. And so, she was buried with others that had passed away while consigned to Bedlam.

She would have been seriously displeased had she known she was to be buried between two servants, and it could be said the thought amused the Earl as the years passed and he reflected on his family late at night and alone, wondering how many times she had rolled over in her grave between them.

Caroline Bingley:

To her detriment, Caroline Bingley did not soon enough learn that she was the author of her own downfall.

After a very long and uncomfortable sea voyage, she arrived in the Americas and eventually rented a flat in New York City. She tried to put on her airs and impress people with the same pretensions that had miserably failed to work in England but found out the people in the colonies were even less tolerant of her behaviour.

She was soon in the familiar position of the pariah no one wanted to associate with. She had a little more than ten thousand of her twenty-thousand-pound dowry left. Even though a kind soul had warned her, she was taken by a huckster who sold her shares in a non-existent gold mine believing she always knew better. She was left penniless and was forced to go into service.

It was only once she hit rock bottom she realised what her behaviour had gained her, or more truthfully lost her, and she finally accepted the fact she had caused her own fall from grace. Not long after her epiphany, on an evening in the twilight of a muggy summer day, she stepped in front of a carriage traveling at speed and ended her own misery.

George Wickham:

The most surprising was George Wickham. In his first months at Marshalsea, he tried his charms on fellow inmates and discovered the hard way there was no appetite for his lies and manipulation. He lost a tooth, suffered a broken arm, and had many cuts and bruises before he finally realised if he wanted to live, he had to change.

So in the clarity of rock-bottom, Wickham understood he had to make a real change, not the appearance of one as had been his way of portraying himself as a gentleman. For the next three years, he was a model prisoner and read the law like he had said he would when he got Darcy to pay him three thousand pounds for the living.

He was changed not just in word but also in deed. He wrote letters to each family that he could remember that he had trifled with or imposed himself on their daughters to beg their forgiveness and explain he finally saw the error in his past ways. He helped other prisoners and did his work, and sometimes the work of those not able to without complaint.

Five years after his consignment to Marshalsea he wrote Darcy a sincere letter of apology. He enumerated his faults, and took full responsibility for all, blaming only himself. Not once in his letter did he beseech Darcy to intercede on his behalf.

Darcy suspected this was another Wickham scheme, but after contacting the prison's governor was shocked, even amazed, at the report he had received. After a lengthy discussion with his wife and extended family, he decided to make Wickham an offer through the governor.

On condition he would depart England's shores forever; his debts would be conditionally forgiven. He would be given passage to the Americas and one thousand pounds. If he ever returned to England, he would be sent back to Marshalsea for the rest of his life. This result, although very welcome, was not the aim of his apology letter and Wickham accepted the terms with sincerity and gratitude.

He found his way to Boston where he rented a modest room in a boarding house and was never late with his rent. He was employed as a clerk at a prominent law firm and became one of the best clerks at the firm.

After five years he was granted his license to practice law and had a long and distinguished career defending those who needed it most. If they could not pay his fee, he helped them anyway. He eventually married and had three children who were very proud of their papa.

He did not hide the truth of his past from his wife, who was all the prouder of him for the way that he had turned his life around. He did not know it, but Darcy kept track of him for the first ten years Wickham was in Boston.

His investigator confirmed the reformation was real and some months after that, Wickham cried like a little boy when he received a letter from his childhood friend that included all his vowels cancelled and let him know he was free to travel to England without fear of arrest.

When his oldest son was twenty and studying to be a lawyer like his father, Wickham who was very well off by that time, took the whole family to visit England in order to see where he grew up. They toured the country and made a visit to Pemberley as any other visitor would when applying to tour the house.

The Darcys were home and welcomed him and his family to be guests at Pemberley for the three days they would be in the area. One day before he left, he and Darcy went to visit the graveyard where both of their fathers rested in eternal slumber. Both Wickham and Darcy agreed their fathers would have finally been proud of the man that George Wickham had become.

The Darcys:

The Darcys eventually were blessed with eight children. Next, after the triplets was a son Alexander, followed by twin girls Jane and Amanda, then came the last daughter, Pricilla, who was followed by the baby of the family, the eighth Darcy child and son, Edward. For all the happiness their children gave them, not all was smooth sailing.

Elizabeth Darcy had a miscarriage between Alex and the twin girls which caused a depression of some length. It took her mother, Jane, and Aunt Elaine assisting her husband to pull her out of the doldrums she had sunk into.

In twisted logic, much like her beloved William had after Ramsgate, she blamed herself. It took reminders of her opinion of her husband taking too much on himself to finally get through to her and she started to recover. A year later after her recovery, she birthed her twin girls.

As much as Elizabeth and William Darcy were in the deepest love imaginable, which is as would be expected with two very strong and intelligent people, they did argue from time to time. No matter how vociferous the argument, they never went to bed without reconciling, which only made the marriage that much stronger.

The servants at Pemberley very quickly learned that if a door was closed, they should walk away or knock, but never walk in unannounced. As they got older the Darcy children learned that hard lesson as well.

Ben would one day inherit Pemberley, but each of his brothers would inherit one of the additional three Darcy estates. George the largest, then Alex, and finally Edward. The smallest of the estates made more than six thousand per annum clear, so Edward had nothing about which to complain.

In addition, each of the three boys were given a fortune of one hundred thousand pounds which equalled the dowries of each of their sisters. As all the money was invested with Gardiner and Associates, each of the younger seven Darcy children had an income of more than ten thousand a year just from their investments and that was before any estate income the boys also received.

As he would inherit Pemberley and the bulk of the remaining Darcy fortune, Ben did not begrudge his siblings their fortunes. Ben, at the age of five and twenty, fell in love with the eldest daughter of the Earl of Holder, Lady Amelia Bretton, who at eighteen was having her first season.

They married a year later, and as it had for his beloved mother, the marriage settlement left Lady Amelia's dowry of fifty thousand pounds untouched, and it was invested with Gardiner and Associates for their future children.

George married Sarah Elliot, Patrick and Charlotte

Elliot's second daughter, the first born to Charlotte. George, upon his marriage, was given the largest of the other estates in Nottinghamshire, less than a day's travel from Pemberley and Kympton.

Franny Darcy would not settle for anything less than the love that she saw in her parents' and grandparents' marriages, and so it took her four seasons to fall in love with the son and heir to the Earldom of Wokingham in Berkshire.

Lord Reading, or Christopher Pierce, was the one that finally won her heart, and at the age of three and twenty she was married from the Kympton Church by her Uncle Elliot. It was the last duty he performed before he retired to his estate in Shropshire.

Jane Darcy married the second son of the Duke of York, and when the older brother died in a foolish and ill-advised curricle race, her husband became the Marquess and she the Marchioness. Some years later they became the Duke and Duchess of York.

Amanda never found anyone she felt worthy of marriage, and she became the spinster aunt that used to spend time at the homes of her siblings and cousins spoiling her nieces and nephews rotten.

Pricilla married the heir to Rosings Park, her Cousin Rudi Ashby, and they had a long and loving marriage with many children, grandchildren, and eventually great-grandchildren. They and their heirs through the ages kept up the tradition of hosting the whole extended family at Rosings Park for Easter.

In his tenth year of marriage to his beloved Pricilla, Rudi added a wing with more guest rooms to the manor house to accommodate their ever-growing family. The baby of the family, Edward Darcy, twelve years younger than the triplets, married the daughter of an associate of Edward Gardiner, his namesake, and they happily settled at his estate in the shire of Durham.

Five years after Ben's marriage, and when he and his wife had been blessed with a son and daughter already, Darcy started to intensify the training for Ben to take over the day-to-day running of Pemberley. After Ben's three and thirtieth birthday, Darcy turned the running of Pemberley over to him.

Darcy still controlled the investments and was always there for needed advice. For three months each year, Elizabeth and William Darcy were to be found at Seaview Cottage, now really a misnomer as it had been expanded three times to accommodate the ever-growing extended family and had as many servants as Longbourn.

The balance of the time they travelled to see their children, and when they came, grandchildren, and eventually great-grandchildren. Each year they took between one and three months to travel to some exciting destination like Paris, Rome, Athens, Jerusalem, or Cairo to name a few.

Through all their years, through all their triumphs and trials, neither of them ever regretted the time Darcy, out of a sense of familial obligation to his uncle, aunt, and cousins was persuaded to introduce himself to Thomas Bennet at Longbourn those many years ago.

Fanny and Thomas Bennet:

After having turned the running of Longbourn over to Tom and Bennet Fields to James some ten years previously, Fanny and Thomas Bennet were sitting on the terrace at Seaview Cottage overlooking the sea toward Brighton. They were waiting for Elaine and Reggie to join them for a three-week stay, for once just the four of them.

As he swirled the port around in his glass, Bennet looked over at his beloved wife. Yes, her hair was mostly grey now and she had some lines on her face, but she was still the beautiful and vivacious Fanny Gardiner he had married almost fifty years earlier.

After thinking for a minute, he took one of Fanny's hands. "Can you imagine what our life would have been like if God had not blessed us with Tom and James those many years ago?" he asked quietly.

"I do not even want to imagine it, Thomas," she frowned. "Look at how we were, what kind of people we had become before the boys were born. I would have let my *nerves* overtake my life and become ever sillier and more inappropriate, and you would have withdrawn even more and cared less and less for us and the estate.

"Could you imagine the horror our daughters' lives could have been had we not had sons and that criminal of a parson Collins had been your heir?" she shuddered. "I would have tried to force one of the girls to marry him to save the home, thinking only of myself and not what would have been good for the girls. No, it is too horrible to imagine, Thomas."

"You are absolutely right, my love," he agreed as he kissed her hand and took a sip of his port. "It would have been worse than we can likely now imagine. As it is, we do not have to think about it other than as a path not taken but well learned from. Look at what did in fact happen." He smiled at her, the one that was reserved only for her. "All of our children are in happy, respectful, and loving marriages. We have grandchildren aplenty and our children love to host us. We are beloved by them and all the extended family. Look at the legacy we will leave them, and I do not just mean in terms of wealth."

"I agree, Thomas. The best legacy that we have passed onto our children is the value of love, respect, and the content of one's character, not the value of the bank account. And you and me? We do not spend a day where we are not in each other's company, when before the boys we almost never spent time together even though we had made a love match.

As Lizzy says, think only of the past as its remembrance gives you pleasure. We have a lot of pleasure in our past, Thomas, and I daresay we have a lot to come." She teased him and he chuckled as he tried to swallow his port with some dignity.

"We have had a life of love, respect, and felicity," Fanny stated as she smiled at Bennet.

"We have a lot of life to live yet Fanny. Do you think our children know when we are gone they will each get an additional two hundred and fifty thousand pounds? You know what the best thing is? Even if they knew they would not care. Money and material possessions have never driven any of our children or family. Even after the bequests to his brother and sisters, Tom will still have more than enough liquid and invested money to last many lifetimes."

"I was so very happy the whole family supported us as we opened schools for not so well-off children, servants, and tenants. So far, we are in ten counties, and I know after we have gone the family will continue that legacy." Fanny sighed and then looked again at her husband. "It all started with my introspection and that waddle I made to go beseech God in the Longbourn Church. He heard us and allowed us to change our fortunes. We have done very well, Thomas, yes we have done very well indeed." She agreed quietly, smiling at him with the knowledge that only comes with age, that love is the true value of one's life.

Love was their true wealth and legacy, and with the love between them and with their extended family and dearest friends, whom they loved as deeply as family and friends could be loved, they were amongst the wealthiest people ever.

~~~The End~~~

BOOKS BY THIS AUTHOR

Much Pride, Prejudice, and Sensibility
- Without Enough Sense

Lady Catherine's Forbidden Love & Love
Unrestricted Combined Edition

A Curate's Daughter

Mary Bennet Takes Charge

Admiral Thomas Bennet

Separated at Birth

Jane Bennet Takes Charge - 6th book
in the 'Take Charge' series

Lives Begun in Obscurity

Mrs. Caroline Darcy

Lady Beth Fitzwilliam – Omnibus Edition

Anne de Bourgh Takes Charge – 5th
book of the Take Charge Series

Mr. Bingley Takes Charge – 4th book
of the Take Charge Series

The Repercussions of Extreme Pride & Prejudice

Miss Darcy Takes Charge- 3rd book of
the Take Charge Series

Banished

Lady Catherine Takes Charge – 2nd book
of the Take Charge Series

A Bennet of Royal Blood

Charlotte Lucas Takes Charge – 1st book
of the Take Charge Series

Cinder-Liza

Unknown Family Connections

Surviving Thomas Bennet

The Discarded Daughter - Combined Edition

The Duke's Daughter: Combined Edition

The Hypocrite

Coming Soon

Colonel Fitzwilliam Takes Charge
– September/October 2023